Love & other side effects

ALSO BY DEIDRA DUNCAN

Love Sick
Until I Die

Praise for *Love And Other Side Effects*

'Hilarious and deeply romantic, *Love And Other Side Effects* is the perfect friends-to-lovers romance. You can't not fall for Asher and Jocelyn!'
N.S. Perkins, author of *The Infinity Between Us*

'Devastating in its raw vulnerability and gleeful feet-kicking swoonworthiness, *Love And Other Side Effects* is a book to be devoured. Asher and Jocelyn bare their darkest feelings and highest walls on page in an honest exploration of what it means to love'
Maggie Eckersley, author of *Back In The Saddle*

'*Love And Other Side Effects* is as addictive as any drug – once you pick it up you won't want to put it down! Fair warning: side effects of this book may include the occasional uncontrollable snort-laugh, strong urges to shout "JUST KISS ALREADY!" at the main characters, and loss of sleep because you were up way too late reading this delightful gem of a love story'
Emily Krempholtz, author of *Violet Thistlewaite Is Not A Villain Anymore*

'Deidra Duncan is a specialist in rom-com and prescribes us a cinnamon roll hero who pines deliciously, and a jaded woman who falls harder and deeper than she ever dreamed. Read this one stat!'
Noreen Nanja, author of *The Summers Between Us*

'*Love And Other Side Effects* is a friends-to-lovers joyride. Packed to the brim with hilarious antics and delicious banter, Duncan brings forbidden yearning to the next level'
Christy Schillig, author of *Lessons In Falling*

Praise for *Love Sick*

'Compulsively readable, *Love Sick* is equal parts sexy and angsty. Deidra Duncan nailed all my favorite aspects from medical dramas'
Julie Soto, No. 1 *Sunday Times* bestselling author of *Rose In Chains*

'Amid a realistic portrayal of the highs and lows of medical resident life, enemies-to-lovers tension and non-stop banter fill this resonant and romantic debut. Heartfelt and smart, *Love Sick* is just what the doctor ordered'
Emily Wibberley and Austin Siegemund-Broka, authors of *The Breakup Tour*

'Bursting with laughter, the joy of found family, and spicy will-they-or-won't-they tension, Duncan's debut about the struggles of OB/GYN residency is the perfect book for *Grey's Anatomy* fans who wish they could start the Meredith-and-McDreamy journey all over again'
Ashley Winstead, author of *The Future Saints*

Love
& other
side effects

DEIDRA DUNCAN

First published in Great Britain in 2026 by Quercus

Part of John Murray Group

1

Copyright © 2026 Deidra Duncan

Published by arrangement with Canary Street Press, an imprint of Harlequin Enterprises ULC.

The moral right of Deidra Duncan to be
identified as the author of this work has been
asserted in accordance with the Copyright,
Designs and Patents Act 1988.

All rights reserved. No part of this publication
may be reproduced or transmitted in any form
or by any means, electronic or mechanical,
including photocopy, recording, or any
information storage and retrieval system,
without permission in writing from the publisher.

This book is a work of fiction. Names, characters,
businesses, organizations, places and events are
either the product of the author's imagination
or used fictitiously. Any resemblance to
actual persons, living or dead, events or
locales is entirely coincidental.

A CIP catalogue record for this book is available from the British Library

PB ISBN 978-1-52944-212-0
EBOOK ISBN 978-1-52944-213-7

Offset in 11.15/13.5pt Bembo Std by Six Red Marbles UK, Thetford, Norfolk

Printed and bound in Great Britain by Clays Ltd, Elcograf S.p.A.

Papers used by Quercus are from well-managed forests and other responsible sources.

Quercus
Carmelite House
50 Victoria Embankment
London EC4Y 0DZ

John Murray Group
Part of Hodder & Stoughton Limited
An Hachette UK company

The authorised representative in the EEA is Hachette Ireland, 8 Castlecourt Centre, Dublin 15, D15 XTP3, Ireland (email: info@hbgi.ie)

For Ali, who gets it.

Asher

> Don't think of love as the endgame.
> Think of it as the kickoff.
> **—My Therapist**

Don't laugh.

The reassuring *beep, beep, beep* of the fetal heart monitor fills the delivery room while my patient recovers from her last set of pushes, but instead of catching her breath, she's waving a hand in front of her face. "Oh, my g— Who keeps farting?"

Seriously. Don't laugh.

Carrie is a lovely woman. She really is. One of my favorite patients. But she's pushing a baby out, which often results in pushing . . . other things out. I'm 100 percent certain this woman doesn't realize the smell in the room is her.

I'm a simple man with a simple sense of humor. And this? This is hilarious.

Or maybe I'm a complex mess of a man with a child's sense of humor. Who could say?

"Doctor Foley!"

My attention snaps to Carrie's incredulous expression.

"I am *so* sorry for my family," she says. "I can't believe this."

Her mother and sister stand at the bedside. Their stoic faces are pulled into guises of concern. Meanwhile, the father of the baby tries his best not to laugh at the head of the bed. Yolanda, the nurse, wisely remains silent.

Don't laugh!

I smile behind my mask. "It's fine, Carrie. Push."

She pushes once, then glares at her sister. "Do you need to go to the bathroom?"

"I'm sorry," the sister whispers.

The baby daddy snorts then tactfully transitions to a fake cough.

"Come on, Carrie," I say. "Don't waste your contraction. Push!"

Epidural pushes are usually feeble—a fact inexplicably truer between one and four in the morning—but Carrie's a champ. A+ for effort. Pushes the baby out in less than an hour.

Thank heaven.

Wouldn't have been able to keep from laughing much longer. Not *at* her. At the situation. The irony. In obstetrics, humor must be found in the small moments. Otherwise, it's nothing but long spans of stark boredom punctuated by moments of sheer terror.

We clean her up swiftly, so she'll never know she shit all over the delivery room and blamed her supportive family for the odor.

But I know.

And the dad knows.

We share a silent moment of understanding, a nod to the unspoken brotherhood of comedy.

Him: Did you also find this comical?

Me: Yes, brother. This was priceless.

Him: Today it was spoken, ye shall triumph all funny story contests for the rest of time.

Me: Time shall wither, but this shall remain.

I leave the room, congratulating them both. My feet skid into Pod A, our dictation room, before I collapse into a chair in laughter. The counter is cluttered with travel mugs, binders sporting the Corpus Christi Medical Center logo, filled with the pervasive specter known as *Hospital Policy*—a greedy and foolish god, if we're being truthful—and four desktop computers. Above it all, the fetal monitors display squiggly lines for two other patients in labor on the floor.

Luckily, neither patient is mine.

Need sleep. Laughter is now impossible to contain. Misty eyes, aching abs—the whole bit.

"What is it?" asks Raquel, one of the nurses, peeking up from her computer.

I shake my head. Too tired to explain.

A quick badge-tap and the desktop wakes, signing me in to our electronic medical record called LEGENDARY. Aspirational thinking on the part of the people who named it, I'm sure. LEGENDARY will go down in history as nothing but an epic failure. Like Blockbuster. Or Elizabeth Holmes.

As I type, Jocelyn plonks into the rollie chair next to mine, spinning to face me. She's got her I-need-sleep-you-better-have-good-news face on.

Heh. Sleepy Joss is fantastic. Prickly. A bit cheeky. Always good for a laugh.

I grin. "Hey there, bestie, you need something?"

Small hands grip my arm and shake it, peppering my delivery note with typos. "Please tell me she delivered, so I can go home."

The harsh fluorescent lighting brings out the dark circles beneath Joss's warm brown eyes. I tug on a blond lock escaped from her bun and tickle her nose with it. "Is someone a little grumpy?"

She shoos away my hand. "It's three a.m., Asher. Only people like you are chipper at this hour."

"People like me?"

"Yeah." She gestures toward me, face scrunched. "Happy people. *Optimists*."

"Wow." I fire a bright smile at her. "How'd that word taste coming out of your mouth?"

"Like acid. So, is she delivered?"

I finish the delivery note with a relish and spin toward her. "Signed. Sealed. Delivered."

She throws her arms in the air, her chair whirling. "Hallelujah."

The anesthesiologists don't normally take their overnight calls in the hospital, but when a laboring patient has an epidural, the on-call doc is required to remain in-house until delivery. Joss isn't a fan of that rule. Or any other rules, really. She's zipped up in her white Patagonia vest—the uniform of all anesthesiologists everywhere—clearly ready to bounce. Her teal scrub cap peeks out of the breast pocket. It's patterned with little pink flowers and script letters that say *Don't Be Extra*.

Jocelyn's favorite phrase.

Once she's completed a full rotation, I grab her knees to stop her. A glance at the nearby nurses ensures they're distracted by their own conversation.

She arches one brow. "What's up?"

The mail I received this morning still burns a hole in my scrub pants pocket, and I've been waiting all day to show her. After three years of dedicated service as my best friend, Joss knows me better than anyone. She can read my expressions like words on paper. Open book. Boldface font.

Don't really want her intuiting what I'm thinking now.

Panicky feeling rises. Suppress. Suppress. Suppress.

Wouldn't bother her with this, but I just need to hear her thoughts.

With a lowered voice, I ask, "Meet me in the call room after you check on the patient?"

She fake-gasps. "Does someone have a secret? Are you the one who stole Doctor O'Malley's DIVA Cup?"

"That's a weird place for your mind to go—"

Her eyes widen comically. "Wait! Did the patient in room seven finally decide clitoral stimulation isn't adequate pain relief?"

The girl can always pull a laugh from me. "Just do it, okay?"

She sighs. "You're going to keep me awake longer, aren't you?"

I push out my lower lip, and her body goes stiff, her expression affronted. "How dare you use puppy dog face on me at three a.m., Asher? It's a sin against nature. And sleep."

"Please?"

With a sag of her petite shoulders, she submits, and ten minutes later, we're sitting side by side on a starched white bed in a tiny room with one blacked-out window, a broken lounge chair and a lamp with no bulb.

"All right." She claps once. "Lay it on me. If you're going to tell me you're pregnant, I assure you, it's not mine."

"What?" I splay my hands over my chest. "You'd abandon our love child?"

She sleepy-chuckles. "Asher. Tell me."

Welp. Must get it over with. I slap the fancy embossed invitation into her hand.

She unfolds it. "'Mister and Missus Caleb Rose joyfully request the presence of your company at the marriage of their daughter, Sapphire Grace, to Julian—' Asher, I don't know who these people are."

"She's one of the girls I told you about."

Her eyes narrow at once. "You're joking. Is this a prank?"

Fair question. Pranking her is my favorite pastime, but this is very real. Unfortunate, that. I shake my head, and the suspicion disappears from her expression. "Which one is she? The one you proposed to?"

God.

Thanks for that reminder.

Good old Katherine.

I like to shove her memory down where the unbearable things live, like the time I texted my residency class about our shitty senior resident only to realize that senior was in the group text. Or the time I took too much cold medicine and fainted in the anatomy lab.

I love you. Let's get married.

Ha! Are you serious? No way.

That was her gut reaction. *Are you serious? No way.*

Broke up with me the next day. Married a cardiologist a year later. Nice guy, though.

Memory still stings.

I laugh to cover the discomfort. "No. That was she-thought-we-were-friends-with-benefits-while-I-thought-we-were-in-love girl. Grace is the one who had no idea I was in love with her until after she fell for this guy instead." I tap the invitation in her hand.

She fiddles with the edge of the cardstock. "But you don't love her anymore, right?"

"Of course not. That was three years ago." I drag a hand down my face. "But . . . I don't know. Feels weird."

Jocelyn smacks me on the forehead with the invitation. "Why didn't you tell me about this when you got it?"

"Ow." I snatch the paper from her hand. "I was busy."

"Not too busy to tell me about the new protein powder you *have* to try, or to send me pics of the ducks outside."

"There were ducklings!" I say in defense. They were waddling behind their mom along the crosswalk. How adorable is that?

Joss throws a hand up. "I can't anymore with you and the ducks. They're just ducks."

"Your hatred of cute things is one reason I'm convinced you're part demon."

"I don't *hate* them." She yanks the invitation from my grasp, and her pretty lips curl. Is that disgust or disbelief? Not sure. Perhaps a bit of disdain, too. "Who names their daughter Sapphire?"

"What should I do, Joss?"

It would be nice to see some of my old friends again, Grace included. I'd truly like to go, but going alone, aware she knows about my unrequited crush on her . . . And did I mention the *alone* part?

Ugh.

"Obviously, you're not going." Joss continues to scowl at the invitation. "I mean, duh. Asher, the girl broke your heart. Why would she even invite you?"

"We're friends. And she didn't break my heart, really. Not on purpose." I scratch my neck. "She didn't even know. I read into something that wasn't there."

The truth? She didn't take me seriously. Same as Katherine. No one takes me seriously, it seems. I'm not even sure *I* take me seriously. That's the theme of my life—work, women, whatever. Not serious. Not important. Not good enough. Feel like a bit of a fraud if I'm honest.

Hoping the new stint in therapy will help.

But seriously. When did I get so . . . needy?

Don't like it. Not at all.

What is this . . . *squirmy* feeling that likes to linger in the dark places?

"You sure this girl wasn't just leading you on?" Joss asks.

I've considered that. Disregarded it, too. "Grace wouldn't do that. She just thought I was joking when I flirted."

Skeptical Joss emerges. "I don't buy it."

It's true, though.

Perhaps I was born with some sort of shroud over my personality, one that tells others I lack depth. Asher Foley is a running joke. Not serious boyfriend material. The funny doctor. A class clown.

A few patients recently left me for my older partner. Why's that again? I don't know. Don't know if I want to know.

Recent comments from nurses and fellow surgeons have me itchy. Implying I'm first-rate fun, but perhaps practice second-rate medicine?

Never spoken directly, of course.

But are they thinking it?

My statistics are great. Complications low. Patient satisfaction high.

But I feel like an imposter. These weights of inadequacy aren't particularly light. Who keeps putting them on me?

Oh, right.

Cue Taylor Swift: It's me. I'm the problem.

I want to laugh it off. Take the invitation from her. Trash it to avoid everything. I shrug instead. "She thought I was joking, and I thought she was shy. It's not a big deal. It's just—"

I don't want to go alone.

Can't say that.

Not even to Joss.

She doesn't know all my insecurities. Or . . . I don't think she does. And I divulge little of my love life to her, just as she does to me. She knows, however, that my awkward past with *the girl who didn't know I was in love with her* is the reason for my strict No Dating At Work policy—something that came up very early in our friendship.

"You're not going," Joss says. "It's not that complicated."

I look up and give her puppy dog face once more.

Ah. There's suspicious Joss. Not as fun, this one. "Oh, Ash. What'd you do?"

"I got the invitation this morning. Before I'd thought about it, Maxwell called me—"

"Maxwell DeBakey? That man is so fine . . ."

"You've met him *once*." Two years ago, he stayed with me when he drove down to Corpus Christi from Dallas for a weekend trip.

She shrugs. "Once was enough to know he's hot."

I pat her knee. "He's married, baby girl."

"Not in my fantasies, he's not."

"Ha. Ha. Aren't you *not into relationships*?" I say the last words with air quotes.

She gives me her crooked Joss grin, the one that promises mischief and mayhem. "There you go again, confusing sex with relationships."

Yep. She's more than *not into* relationships. She crosses herself from fear if they come anywhere near.

See? Look at us. Joss and I are burning down stereotypes left and right. She's a playboy and I'm a romance-novel heroine.

If I wasn't actively trying to strike the pairing of *pussy* with *weak man* from my psyche, I'd be chanting it in my head.

Need a better word for that.

I shake myself. "Whatever. Max is Julian's best friend. They were together when Max asked if I was coming so he could plan numbers for the bachelor party—"

"And you said yes, didn't you? Because you're incapable of saying no."

"That is . . . correct."

"Okaaay." She tilts her head. "Well, the answer's obvious, then. I'm coming with you."

I blink a few times. Didn't expect that. "What?"

She rolls her eyes and tucks some free strands of hair behind her ear. My gaze catches on the angel wing earrings her sister gave her—a tribute to their parents.

"You're nervous enough that you dragged me to this freezing-ass call room in the middle of the night instead of talking about it at a normal time of day. Like in four hours. When I'm covering your hysterectomy."

"This is the first time I saw you today—"

She sits tall. "Well, you need moral support, so I'm there."

"The wedding's in Florida."

"Ugh." She shakes her head. "That excuse for a state shouldn't even exist. Whatever. I'm still going. I'll whisper about how ugly the bride is all day and definitely won't tell her when she has toilet paper stuck to her shoe. I'll be completely head over heels in love with you and pretend like you hung the moon just for me."

A laugh crawls up my throat. Uncomfortable. Is laughter

supposed to feel barbed? "You'll come to the beach with me and pretend we're together just so I don't look pathetic?"

"Isn't it the best friend's job to prevent pathetic vibes? You'd do it for me."

"Yeah, but I love the beach."

She throws her head back and sighs at the ceiling. "I don't hate the beach."

"You won't even touch the water."

"The ocean and the beach are *not* the same thing."

Yeah, yeah. I learned early that Joss's bone-deep fear of the ocean and the danger it represents is an immutable portion of her personality—one she pretends isn't a key factor in why she lives her life like everything is tenuous and will ultimately be taken from her. Flying her to a sandbar jutting out from the ass crack of the United States, surrounded by nothing but water, just so she can shield me from gossip, is selfish. Borderline mean.

I'm being obnoxious.

Man up, Asher.

Jocelyn's fierce loyalty is her best quality. She's beautiful, don't get me wrong, but her devotion to her friends—that's the prettiest thing about her.

Someone should protect her from herself.

"I don't need a fake date," I say. "I need a real one or a way to get out of it."

She shrugs. "Then get a real date. You don't need me, you know. Anyone would go with you."

I snort. Not true. But okay. "I can't invite a stranger on a weekend getaway."

She rolls her eyes. "Right. Then do what we all do when we mess up. Fake a seizure."

Laughing again, I scrub my face, willing away the sleepy.

"Listen, Ash." Her tiny hand lands on my shoulder. "I

have to go to sleep or I will be a grumpy, hollow-eyed hag in the morning. We don't have to figure this out tonight, but if you want to go, I'll go with you. And if the ocean tries to get me, I'm counting on you to Prince Eric my ass back to safety."

I pat her cold fingers where they squeeze my shoulder. "All right. Deal. I'll tame the sea witch, and you can show up the bride."

"It's settled, then," she says. "Can I go get sleep now?"

"Sure. See you bright and early." She stands to leave, but I grab her hand. "Hey, Joss?"

"Yeah?"

"Thank you for this. Seriously."

She pinches my cheek like she's a grandma. "Anything for my little snookums."

"All right." I roll my eyes. "I see we're done with the serious portion of the evening."

"Good night," she singsongs as she flutters out the door.

Jocelyn

> Grief isn't linear. It's a circle.
> —My Therapist

Early mornings after a rough call make me want to murder things.

Well, early mornings *period* make me want to murder things, but as an anesthesiologist, I sort of brought this upon myself. Surgeries start early, and therefore, so must I. At least it's June, so it's not pitch-black outside.

My day is always better when Asher is operating. I've bullied myself into covering his cases enough times that my colleagues no longer try to assign me elsewhere. Best friends unite, yo. If Dr. Foley is operating, then Dr. Mattox is his anesthesiologist.

I sip my life-giving espresso on the OR physician lounge

couch, then begin peeling my breakfast orange when Asher enters, deep circles beneath his eyes.

"Hey, sugar duckling," he says with a yawn, falling onto the couch next to me.

"Your nicknames are getting perpetually weirder, Ash."

He sets his yellow Mountain Dew Kickstart on the side table and shoots me a crooked grin, albeit a little more languid than normal. "Not into ducks this early in the morning?"

"I'm not into anything this early in the morning." I glare at the muted TV on the wall, the channel set to—as usual—Fox News. "Who decided working the day after call was a good idea?"

He yawns again. "The people who don't want to pay for more doctors to cover."

"Cheap hospital bastards." I dig the remote from between the couch cushions to change the station to HGTV.

One of my fellow anesthesiologists, Cassie Hersl, saunters through the door and heads straight to the kitchenette. She snags a banana from the breakfast fruit pile, then pours a cup of coffee.

Asher glances at her and nudges my elbow. "You got my cases today, right?"

"Of course." I lean closer. "No one else can tolerate you."

Judging by the far livelier smile on his face, the caffeine must have hit his system. He has such an appealing smile—always bright, never forced. The man is unendingly happy.

It's gross. Sweet, but gross. How did I become best friends with a morning person? In my perfect world, I'd be a vampire.

"I'm sorry you got the short end of the stick," he says.

"Don't worry. You're buying me dinner for my troubles."

"I am?"

"Yeah," I say. "With drinks."

"Morning, Asher." Cassie approaches us with a rare smile. Her black hair isn't yet pulled into its customary bun, and it gleams like a silk negligee. Her cat-eye makeup is sharp enough to cut.

Last I heard, she was on again with her radiologist boyfriend, but it seems like her crush on Asher hasn't dimmed in the slightest. If looks could fuck, Asher would be well and truly by now.

The woman hates me. She has since my first day. I don't know why, and I no longer care. I've stopped any attempts to be friendly. The two of us subsist on snark and professional rivalry.

"Hey, Cassie." Asher's smile for her is as genuine as always. Asher loves people, and they love him. He rests an ankle on the opposite knee, showing off his crimson OU socks. "What's up, girl? Still looking at buying that condo?"

"Oh, I passed on that." She perches on the armrest next to him.

He pseudo-gasps and clutches invisible pearls. "But the view!"

"I know." She giggles—ew—and starts to say something else when her phone beeps. She checks it and waves. "Shoot. Got to go. Have a good day, Asher."

Purposely excluding me, I see. Subtle.

"Every single woman in this hospital wants you," I whisper.

He leans in and whispers back, "Then how come I'm not getting laid?"

I laugh in his face. "So full of shit." He'd be getting laid if he tried, but he rarely bothers. If he ever opened his eyes and looked, he'd find whatever mysterious woman he's searching for.

In the past, I've asked why he doesn't look, but I'm always treated to an off-kilter joke and a wink. He isn't dating, he doesn't want to talk about it and he doesn't appear to care about it. He just isn't ready, obviously.

Before I can reply, his partner, Dr. White, settles onto the couch opposite us. The wizened man holds a tumbler of coffee and smiles benignly at Asher.

"What you got today, Foley?"

Asher shrugs, his body stiffening. "A couple hysts."

The older man's chuckle is a tad derisive. "Minor leagues, son. Call me when you've got three sacrocolpopexies and a colpocleisis lined up."

Asher smiles easily, though I sense the agitation behind it. "You a prolapse specialist now?"

White waves a dismissive hand. "You'll get there. You get older, so do your patients. Lots of prolapse in your future." He laughs at his own joke. "By the way, had a few of your patients on my schedule lately. You too lazy to do Paps every year now?"

"They aren't indicated yearly—"

My pager goes off, alerting us that the patient is ready for me. I set a hand on Asher's arm. "Time to work, Doctor Foley."

He shoots off a quick goodbye to White, and we step into the hall.

"Guy's a tool sometimes, isn't he?" I say on the jaunt to the OR.

"He's just from a different generation." Asher's tone is light, but his body has remodeled itself—smile gone, shoulders a tad droopier. Hmm. What's up with that?

In the OR, he shakes it off and holds his patient's hand while I put her to sleep. He's the only surgeon in all the departments who does this. The patient has bled for two months straight, and this morning when I spoke with her, she wore a shirt with a picture of a uterus that read, *Tearing down my baby factory to build a playground*. Despite her excitement for the hysterectomy, she was shaking in her sassy shirt. But she's all smiles for him, his jokes and his compassionate hand-holding.

His patients *love* him. It's remarkable, really. He draws affection from all directions, like his personality is tinged with bunny rabbits and sugar cookies.

When the propofol kicks in, he releases her hand and lets the nurses take over, then scrubs in and claps his gloved hands. "It's a beautiful day to kill uteruses, yeah?"

As usual, the team—all female—bursts into laughter. He grabs the sterile drapes and gets to work. All's good with the patient, so I snatch my phone to rid it of the million notifications. I sigh at the repeat email from the hospital regarding optional Dragon training—a device that boasts voice-to-text for medical charts. I've suffered enough similar training sessions to last me a lifetime. Dragon is utterly useless for anesthesiologists anyway, so I don't know why they keep pushing it on us.

I delete it, watch a few TikToks, then open EverX, an exclusive hookup app for doctors and other professionals. I'm picky with my matches, but it's been several weeks since my last date, and *the itch* has returned.

Thanks to Asher, I've got more and better friends now than I ever have. He lures people like bees to nectar, and due to my near-constant presence at his side, I've gathered a thriving friend group to negate the threat of loneliness. Totally separate from that is my sex life, fulfilled by strangers because my therapist implies I'm emotionally crippled, though she uses fancier words. But it isn't my fault the concept of lasting love from anyone except my sister feels very much like a horrific lie. Trauma does that to a person.

I'm self-aware enough to know I'm broken, but not enough to fix myself. My therapist has tried innumerable times to banish these beliefs from my psyche—to no avail. Some lessons simply can't be unlearned.

Horniness, however, is a staple of the human condition, and I'm just as subject to my libido as the rest of the population.

It isn't something I advertise, though. We've come so far in society, but women are still vulnerable to censorious looks and gossip when they engage in casual sex.

Playas? Cool. Sluts? Not so much.

I don't need that in my life.

But I do need sex sans emotions.

On my phone, a guy named Sebastian—*Sebastian? Definitely not his real name*—messages me. Based on his side view profile pic, I *think* he's attractive. Brown hair. Dark eyes. Lean.

> **Hey girl**

> sup

> **so from 1 to america, how free are you tonight?**

> Syria

> **damn girl. That's cold.**

I glance up at the monitors. All's fine.

> I might have a minute. What you thinking?

> **I like it simple**

> **dtf?**

"Where you want to eat tonight, baby doll?" Asher pulls my attention to him.

His gaze is trained on the monitor, his skilled hands manipulating the instruments like the pro he is.

"Ask Geoff," I say. "He's the picky one."

Our friend Geoff, the urologist, is a very meat-and-potatoes sort of person, but we tolerate him anyway. Sometimes we indulge his ridiculousness. Other times, we make him eat shawarma.

Asher sighs. "Fine. But when we wind up at barbecue again, don't blame me."

"I'll eat my sausage without complaint," I say.

He pauses his operating to shoot a sarcastic eye roll at me. "Really?"

I give him a mock-serious stare. "Yes, Doctor Foley. I take sausage very seriously."

"That's what she said," Asher quips, and the scrub tech chuckles.

I return to my phone.

> Yeah. It'll be late though.

I'm down

EverX is the best boyfriend. Sexual satisfaction—usually—with no obligation for more. *More* is off the table. It's not worth the risk. A lesson I've learned over my thirty-four years: loving people is dangerous. It hurts like hell when they die. Sounds morbid, but it's true.

Age fifteen. Parents drown in the floods from Katrina.

Age seventeen. First love crashes his car into a dump truck.

Age eighteen. Brother overdoses on Oxy.

I could go on, but the deaths lose meaning after a while.

My sister is the sole survivor, and only she understands the pathological way in which I interact with the world.

Yes, it's wildly unhealthy. Yes, I'll die alone if I keep on this way.

But we're all alone. Most of us just don't realize it. The deaths closed me off. Locked me in a cold glass room. *Protected* me. Safe in my bubble, I may be alone, but I can't get hurt.

I don't care if I'm cold and broken so long as I'm not hurting. Besides, Asher is nothing if not warm, and spending my free time with him keeps me human. It's the perfect setup.

"Let's make him do hibachi," Asher says as he operates. "He won't complain too much."

"Perfect. We may even convince Yayoi to come for hibachi."

Geoff's wife is a homebody, but I can sometimes get her out for good food. I whip out my phone again.

> hibachi? please say yes or
> I'll kill your husband

wow. resorting straight to homicide.

can't say I'm surprised.

> pleeeeeeeeeeez

I have a bottle of pinot I was
planning to share with myself

> Yayoi

Joss

Magic Mike. Channing gonna screw
me in my dreams tonight

> Remember last weekend? Drunk
> Geoff wants a baby. I'll buy him
> all the drinks if you come.

ughhhh I want a baby so bad

fine.

> yes!

•

THE OTHERS HAVE yet to arrive at the restaurant, so I lean on the door of my Benz, waiting. Holding my phone to my ear, I chew on my nails while I count the number of rings until my sister picks up.

Pick up. Pick up.

"Joss?" comes Ali's voice through the line.

The release from the irrational fear that she won't answer comes fast and hot. "*Finally*. I hate it when you take more than five rings to answer. What if you were dead?"

"Definitely still living," she says dryly. "Though with the lack of sleep, it's more like the living dead at this point."

I fake laugh. "How's my niece?"

"She's okay," Ali says. "Finally drinking some Pedialyte."

Ali's oldest, my nephew Leo, is in third grade and thriving, but her daughter, Rosie, is only fourteen months and suffering from an unfortunate summer case of RSV. Her fevers and low appetite worried Ali enough that she contemplated taking her to the ER, but Rosie bounced back today with a little more energy.

"But seriously. Are you getting any sleep?" I ask.

"Barely." My sister's voice is drained. "And Nic's job is making him work overtime. It's a rough time in the Sanchez household right now."

Despite my short white dress, residual heat from the asphalt radiates up, breaking my skin into a sticky sweat, so I head for the restaurant entrance. "She'll get better. We're still on for you to come visit, right?"

"Yes. Twenty-seven days. Nic's mom will take the kids, and it will be glorious. I've got a countdown on my phone. So tired of Nashville right now."

I bounce in my strappy white heels while I walk. "Well, Texas can't wait to have you. It's been, like, what? Three months since I've seen you?"

"Too long," Ali agrees.

A wolf whistle catches my attention before I reach the entrance. Ready to tell off some creep, I spin in place, only to find Asher approaching, smiling like the sun.

"There's my girl." He weaves through the cars toward me.

"Hey!" I call.

Gray cotton stretches over his chest. New shirt, right? I would've remembered this one. It's . . . tight.

"Is that Asher?" Ali asks. "You're having dinner with him?"

"Of course I am. Who else would I be having dinner with?"

"I really don't understand this whole dating without screwing thing you guys do."

"We aren't dating," I whisper now that Asher is closer. "We're meeting friends."

"Your *married* friends?"

I clear my throat. "Well—"

"So you're double-dating without screwing."

"Is that your sister?" Asher asks.

"Yeah—"

Asher grabs the phone. "Ali! Did you try that cookie recipe I sent you?" Pause. "I know! You'll never go back." He laughs. "No, thank my mom. She made them when I was growing up." He swats my hand when I try to take the phone back. "Well, Karen can suck it. You'll be PTA queen."

I tickle him so he's forced to defend himself, all but climbing his much taller body to reach my phone.

His voice rises in pitch. "Shit. Your sister is attacking me. Okay. I know. Bye, honey bear."

The phone slips from his grasp, and I grab it while pushing him away. "You aren't allowed to steal my sister." Then into the phone, I say, "And you aren't allowed to steal my best friend."

"Shit! Rosie's vomiting. I have to go."

She clicks off before I can say goodbye, and I slip my phone into my dress pocket, then eye Asher. "How are you talking to my sister so much that you're exchanging cookie recipes like old biddies?"

"It's probably about the same amount you talk to my mom behind my back."

I narrow my eyes at him. "My relationship with Sue Ellen is my own business."

He smirks. "You keep at it, she'll be setting you up with my brothers."

He's not wrong. Every conversation I have with his mother involves at least one comment regarding the availability and desirability of her three single sons. I will never admit to him that at least three-quarters of these comments are actually about him.

Did you know Asher was president of his fraternity? Always such a leader . . .

Oh, I forgot to mention that Asher used to volunteer at the animal shelter, didn't I?

Such a loving man, my son. I told you about his beautiful eulogy at my mother's funeral, right?

He'll make such a good husband someday.

Sue Ellen is Asher's biggest fan, and she desperately wants grandkids. I've explained multiple times that no matter which son she chooses, those kids won't be sourced by me, but she's yet to reconcile that fact in her mind. No reproductive-aged woman is safe around her.

"One day she'll get it through her head that I'm damaged," I say with a wink.

"Oh, you're not damaged." He pulls the door to the vestibule open for me. "Just deep and dark and complicated."

I shoot him a sour face.

"Tell her I say hi when you get a chance," he says as I walk past with my nose in the air. "You know, since you talk to her more than I do."

"I already told her about our Florida wedding trip in three months. She's jelly."

He rolls his eyes. "She hates to travel."

"You should call her more. She complains you don't tell her what's going on in your life."

He opens the second door, flooding us with the scent of ginger and butter. "When there's something going on in my life worth telling her, she'll be the first to know."

"Hmm. How was your office today?"

He sighs and leans a shoulder on the wall just inside. "I got two patient reviews today, complaining they'd prefer a doctor who is more *established*."

"What does that even mean? They want an old man like White?"

He shrugs, pretending at nonchalance, but I can see straight through him. No matter how many patients gush over his greatness, Asher can't help but focus on those few who equate his raw charm to unprofessionalism or lack of expertise.

The evil empire that is Press Ganey and their "patient satisfaction" surveys has proven no doctor is universally loved, but I'm certain Asher comes close. He just can't see it. He's blinded by the idiot patients who find his care lacking, who complain he laughs too much, or in one curious instance, call him a *bro*—an offense that cut him deep.

The glory of anesthesia is that most of my patients are asleep, but OB-GYN is an intensely intimate specialty, and Asher takes those harsh patient reviews to heart.

After he checks in with the host, I pat his shoulder. "It's their loss, Ash. You know that."

He smiles. "Exactly. They can find a wrinkly geezer to shove a speculum up there."

"Hear, hear."

Once Geoff and Yayoi arrive, the four of us are seated at one end of the eight-person U-shaped hibachi table, with four girls in their twenties on the other. The girls are dressed for a night out—glitter and sequins galore—and appear to have pre-gamed prior to dining.

Oh, to be young again.

At thirty-four, I'm practically ancient to them.

To make matters more entertaining, Asher sits closest to them, and they spend a few seconds whispering behind their hands while making eyes at him.

Yayoi and I exchange interested glances. Her straight ebony hair is shining in the low light, and crystals glitter at her ears. She's dressed like she wants Geoff to drool, in a dress tight enough to flaunt every curve.

Since his arm is glued around her as he peruses his menu, I think it's working.

"Which one do you think will hit on Ash?" she asks in a low voice behind her menu.

"All four," I reply.

"Hey, y'all going out tonight?" asks the blonde at the end.

"I think we'll see where the night takes us," Asher says in that teasing tone of his, the one that reminds women he's not only handsome, but charming, too. He throws in a grin for free. "You know what I mean?"

One of the middle ones—the only brunette—makes a come-hither face. "We're going to a speakeasy."

"Ooh. How risqué." Asher's smile turns coy, and all four girls turn into starry-eyed anime characters. "Is there a password to get in?"

Smug as can be, the one beside Asher says, "Yeah, but we know a guy."

"Let me guess." Asher clasps his hands on the table. "They ask what you're doing, and you say, *Going to church*."

Their mouths drop. "How'd you know?"

"We've been there." Asher looks at me. "Remember that? You drank like seven French 75s and I had to carry you home."

"I remember," Yayoi mutters next to me. "Their Negronis put me on my ass."

I chuckle. "I *don't* remember that, but it sounds on brand for us."

"Why don't you come with?" says the blonde at the end. "Bring your . . . girlfriend?"

I pat Asher's shoulder. "Oh, I'm not his girlfriend."

"Here we go," Geoff says in a low voice, staring at his menu.

Asher's mouth tightens, and he turns back to the girls. "My girlfriend can't—"

"He doesn't have a girlfriend," I say, thoroughly enjoying this.

Blonde in the middle goes a bit feral, and I want to laugh.

I'm feeding him to a pack of wolves but watching him be lusted after is one of my favorite pastimes. The boy doesn't do hookups, much to his own detriment, and observing the many ways he finds to wriggle out of women's clutches is fascinating.

Asher has to be wined and dined. Cheap fucks are not on the menu.

We are so different.

I lean across him and mock-whisper to the girls, "Plus, he's a doctor."

"I'm going to kill you," he mutters in my ear.

"I'm trying to get you laid."

"I'm not fucking a twenty-two-year-old."

"Why not, old man? Live a little."

He turns to face me, excluding the girls from our private conversation. "If I wanted to screw strangers, I'd be on that app you use."

I bend closer to him. "Screwing strangers can be fun, Asher."

"For *you*, maybe."

Taken aback, I tilt my head. Was that a dig? "What's *that* supposed to mean?"

If he's commenting on my promiscuity, I'll—

"Just that you're not looking for a relationship. Makes sleeping around easier." He raises a hand. "No judgment."

Oh. Okay. That's fair.

Man, my hackles just flew up. This is Asher. Of course he isn't judging me.

But wait . . . Did he just imply— "And you *are* looking for a relationship?"

He stares at me with a strange expression. "Yeah, sweetheart. I thought that was obvious."

Oh.

Oh.

It wasn't obvious, actually. He's so fun-loving that I didn't think he was ready for anything serious. If he's wanting *serious*, how has some woman not locked him down? He definitely hasn't been looking long. If he had, he'd have a ring on his finger by now.

The idea of him married to some stranger stalls every other thought in my brain, like I inserted a glitch into its code. It won't compute. Doesn't consolidate. I try to picture a woman he might want long-term, but all I can come up with is Daisy Duck, and that's just—

The second the laugh bursts from me, I know it's the exact wrong reaction. His eyes shutter and he pastes on a closed-lip smile. "Didn't know I made a joke."

Uh-oh. I offended him.

Shit. How do I fix it?

"No," I start. "It's not—"

Yayoi leans toward us. "What's funny?"

I shake my head at her, giving her a panicked look and, wide-eyed, she turns back to Geoff, allowing us a measure of privacy.

I set a hand on Asher's arm. "I'm not laughing at you. It's just—"

"Just what?" His eyes cut to mine. "Hard to take me seriously?"

What? What is this?

"I'm surprised is all," I say. "You never talk about this. If you're looking for a relationship, how come you don't ever go out with anyone?"

His head gestures subtly to the girls, who are clearly attempting to eavesdrop. "Like them?"

"Sure. Maybe you'll find a relationship in—" I wiggle my fingers at the girls under the table "—all that."

He gives me a flat stare. "Which of them do you think is ready to settle down?"

I shrug, trying to play off the sudden imbalance inside. "Hey, maybe we can find you someone at the wedding? Women at those things are always thirsty."

He gives me a halfhearted laugh. "Just what I need. A girlfriend in Florida."

I nudge him with my elbow, grinning. "Long distance ain't your thing?"

"No—"

"What's your name, Doctor?" asks the brunette.

With a subtle sigh, Asher turns to the girls, thoroughly distracting them.

I exchange a brief look with Yayoi beside me. "I wasn't laughing *at* him," I whisper. "I was imagining him marrying a duck."

In the middle of a long sip, Yayoi sprays water through her nose all over Geoff. He winces and wipes his face.

"Daisy Duck, to be specific," I say.

"You are so weird," she says, still laughing and mopping at Geoff's cheeks. "But I'm glad you brought me out tonight." She nods toward Asher entertaining the girls and raises her volume a smidge. "This is going to be better than *The Bachelorette*."

Asher throws an arm across me to stick a finger in Yayoi's face. "Nothing is better than *The Bachelorette*."

Yayoi shoves his hand away.

"So how was your shoot today?" I ask her while Asher's busy. Last year, Yayoi gave up her day job with a homebuilding company to pursue her passion, and her budding photography gig has blossomed practically overnight. She's into stylistic family photos with lots of golden light and lens flares.

I *adore* her work.

She shrugs. "The lighting was great, but the daughter wouldn't behave, so I didn't get as many candids as I'd hoped."

Geoff snorts without looking at us. "The pictures are amazing. You'd never know she's been doing this less than a year."

I grin at the pride dripping through his words. He loves her so much.

"Shut up," says Yayoi. "I'm still an amateur. But what I really want is to get into engagements and weddings."

While Yayoi and I continue to chatter, Geoff looks up from his menu, observing the tableau at the other end of the table with a mild glimmer in his eye. All four of the girls are now crowded around the brunette's phone, whispering. Something scandalous is happening. Dun dun duuuun.

"Asher, look at this!" one of them says.

"Dear Lord." Geoff goes back to his menu. "This is like high school all over again."

My insides light up. "What about high school? Tell me all about high school."

"No, no!" Asher says a little sharply, turning toward us fast as lightning. "Don't—"

"Oh, you know the stories," Geoff says with a laugh. "All the girls wanted him, and he screwed them all."

I gasp, utterly in love with any talk of Asher in high school. High school Asher was a player. An irresponsible reprobate. Practically the opposite of who he is now. I adore how embarrassed he is of his past self.

"Man whore!" I say.

Asher scowls at Geoff. "Must you always bring this up? I was seventeen and hot. Was I supposed to *not*?"

Geoff shrugs. "I would have if I could."

Yayoi punches his shoulder.

"Ow! It was hard not to be jealous, okay? But I won in the end, sweetie. I got you."

Humor gleams in Yayoi's eyes.

I giggle uncontrollably as I lean closer to Asher. "Are you ashamed of your sluttiness, Ash?"

He gives me a flat stare. "No. It's just— That isn't—"

"Isn't what?"

"I . . . like women. I always have." He lowers his voice. "The only part they ever want to give me is their bodies. I take what I can get."

The amusement dies as those words stab through me. What is he even talking about? He's got some weird truths spilling out tonight. What is up with him?

He wants *serious*, but he thinks women only want a physical relationship. That can't be right. He's so . . . perfect. I mean, that's not the right word, obviously. No one's perfect. But I always imagined that when the time came for him to want to settle down, he'd have his pick of women. He oozes confidence in that sexy, effortless way. Normal women—i.e. those who are capable of earnest emotions—love that shit, right?

What am I missing here?

What other hang-ups is he hiding in there?

More importantly, how do I fix it?

"Asher—"

"Don't." He rubs his face. "I don't even know why I told you that. Forget I said it. We're just having fun tonight, right?"

Empathy is a bitch. Suddenly, I'm inundated by a need

to take care of him, to put a smile back on his face. Despite all the safeguards I've installed to keep people at arm's reach, Asher has snuck his way onto my People Who Matter list.

Nudging his arm, I shoot him a devious smile. "I like that we're both a little slutty."

His answering grin peeks through. "I'm not anymore."

"That only means you're not having as much fun as me."

The server arrives, and I order sake bombs for the entire table and a fruity drink in a keepsake mug for Geoff. I deliver on my promises. He's gettin' lit tonight, and Yayoi is getting lucky.

And then I order more water for us all.

Because responsibility.

The waitress leaves, and the girls yammer on about the coming drinks, name dropping bars where they've trashed themselves on fancy libations.

Asher eyes me, suspicious. "Sake bombs. What are you doing?"

"Alcohol is the best lube, Asher."

He lifts a finger. "As a gynecologist, I thoroughly disagree."

"Oh, you're a gynecologist?" asks the girl beside Asher, then touches his arm.

"Uh. Yeah." In a skillful maneuver, he slides his entire body away from her.

Brunette giggles and flips her perfectly curled hair. "So, you're like . . . a pussy expert?"

Oh, no. She didn't, did she?

So hard not to laugh.

Geoff chokes on nothing. Yayoi abruptly announces she has to go to the bathroom and leaves the table.

Asher merely freezes, then turns to me. "Help me," he says through his teeth.

Taking pity on the man, I throw my arms around him. "He *is* an expert. I know from personal experience."

"That's not helping," he mumbles.

"I thought you weren't his girlfriend," says the feral blonde.

"I'm not. But we fuck like bunnies. Right, sugar duckling?"

Asher coughs. I smile, set my hand over his heart and rest my head on his shoulder.

Rolling their eyes, they go back to whispering among themselves, probably about how I'm a bitch or a whore or some other equally misogynist thing.

Women really hate women sometimes. It's a damn shame.

"You're the worst," Asher says.

"I saved you." I release him, reaching for my water.

"Hmm." His lips quirk, and he puts on the Olive Oyl voice I always use. "My hero."

He has the best smile. I wish I could bottle it. Keep it in my pocket for a rainy day. It fizzles in my blood like Pop Rocks, dazzling and sunny and just so Asher.

The doubts and tension are gone. He's happy again, and I'm satisfied. Winning at life.

The chef arrives as sake bombs are placed in front of us. The free drinks perk the girls right up, and we're all best friends again. At some point, Yayoi returns to her seat beside me, still bright-eyed from the fit of laughter she likely succumbed to in the bathroom.

The chef raises his hands. "You ready?"

The eight of us nod and chant, *"Suki sake! Suki sake! Oi! Oi! Oi!"* slamming our fists on the table three times. The shots of sake fall into the beer, and we chug.

It's disgusting. It always is. But it's part of the experience, so I do it anyway.

As usual, Asher and I race to finish.

As usual, he wins.

We trade smiles, and he leans close to my ear. "Are you done making trouble tonight, angelfish?"

"I'll be making trouble for you for the rest of your life." I tap his nose. *"Pussy expert."*

"I hate you."

•

AFTER A QUICK glance in my purse to ensure my pepper spray and kitty keychain are still where they're supposed to be, I knock on the door to Sebastian's fancy apartment. He lives in the luxury apartments near the ocean, and I definitely don't hate it. Even the hallway boasts the evidence of wealth—lighted classy prints on the walls, faux colonnade lining the length of the hall. The plush blue carpet squishes beneath my feet.

Despite the grandeur, I came equipped.

EverX has a decent verification process, but even professionals can be murderers. I'm reckless, yes, but I'm a prepared sort of reckless.

My rules for these stranger hookups are few and unbreakable:

1. Do not accept food or drinks.
2. Never go inside without two weapons and two condoms.
3. Always have phone fully charged.

The door swings open seconds later to reveal a man with a kind face, a bright smile and brown eyes with the merest hint of green.

My stomach hits the floor.

He's lean. Brunette. Sexy.

This man could be Asher's brother. His twin. How did I not see it in his profile pic?

My adrenal gland hijacks my entire body, flooding it with epinephrine. This isn't good. This is very, very bad. He looks like Asher, and I'm supposed to have sex with him?

No. No. No.

I can't do that.

. . .

Can I?

He looks like Asher, but he *isn't* Asher. I could just close my eyes. And even if I did look—because who the hell wouldn't when a guy looks like that?—it's still not Asher. He merely resembles him. Uncannily. It isn't like I'm fucking Asher.

It isn't!

"Well, hello." Sebastian's bright smile turns sinfully crooked.

That isn't a smile. It's a lure, sparkling in the sun. And I'm a dumbass fish who loves pretty things.

Why is the universe doing this?

"Hey," I squeak out.

"You want to come in?" He holds the door wide for me, displaying a well-appointed open-concept apartment with what I assume would be a spectacular view of the gulf if it were daytime.

I take a single step, then pause. "I will if you tell me your real name."

He laughs and cocks his head. "It's Sebastian."

I lift a skeptical eyebrow and cross my arms.

"All right, all right." He lifts a placating hand. "I'm Ashton."

My heart stops for three full seconds, then thumps so hard it chokes me. Is he serious? Is this really happening?

Ashton scratches his head. "I don't tell people because they tend to start calling me Doctor Ashton Kutcher."

Right. That makes sense, actually. I get it. I do.

But also, this is forbidden. He looks like Asher. His name is basically the same. I would . . . undress him. Touch him. Taste him.

A strangled laugh explodes from my mouth. "I have to go."

"Uh. What?" Instead of irritated, he adopts an expression of concern, and it only increases the resemblance to Asher. "Everything okay?"

Asher would do this. Be genuinely worried when most men would become frustrated. No *what a waste of time* or *bitches always changing their minds* or *fine, bye, slut*. Seems Asher and Ashton are members of a rare species. A couple of unicorns.

"Yeah," I say. "You look like someone I know. It's . . . weird for me."

His expression clears. "Oh. Okay, I get it."

"No hard feelings?"

"Not at all." He smiles again, like Asher would.

So cute. For a few moments, I reconsider. He's handsome and obviously kind. He'd probably be good in bed. It's mere coincidence that he looks this way.

But it might seed fantasies that don't belong. Might confuse things that are currently very straight in my head.

Asher and I are friends.

Asher doesn't do casual sex.

Asher wants a wife and kids.

If I bang this lookalike and enjoy it, what will that do to my very sturdy Friend shelf where I keep all things Asher-related? Will it loosen the brackets? Bend the braces?

Tear the whole thing off the wall?

No, thanks.

With that in mind, I give Ashton a halfhearted wave. "Have a good night."

I practically flee down the hall.

Outside the building, the roar of the gulf's waves on the shore fills the air, and the warm, salty breeze carries the scent of sand and fish. Drawn to the water, I slip off my heels and carry them in one hand as I trudge through the soft sand.

The dark gulf stretches out before me, endless, somehow thunderously loud and interminably silent.

It bears a vicious sort of beauty.

At baseline, the ocean is so peaceful, but its power churns beneath the surface, unforgiving, only emerging to remind us of our insignificance when we least anticipate it.

I often wonder about the levees that broke during Hurricane Katrina. Would any levee have been strong enough to withstand that storm surge? What circumstances could have led to my parents surviving that awful storm?

The better question: Why do I still live on the coast when the fear of floods keeps me awake at night? The risk of drowning in a flood would be near zero if I moved somewhere inland, yet I stay near the beach.

But it isn't safe anywhere, really. The heat in Arizona. A tornado in Kansas. A wildfire in California. An earthquake in Alaska. A freeze in North Dakota.

Nowhere is safe, and the devil I know is preferable to the one I don't. I never swim in the ocean, but I need its proximity as a reminder of the devious power it possesses.

Friends close. Enemies closer.

I am embracing my nemesis with both arms.

To flee would be admitting defeat, and I cannot let it win.

By itself, water is a careless killer. A deceptive lover. A cunning adversary.

The ocean? It's an attestation that the most beautiful things in life are by far the most dangerous.

Jocelyn

3 YEARS AGO

The basement of the hospital is where they relegate the broken gurneys, the janky vending machines with unwanted snacks like apple fruit pie and Bugles, and the HR department. Here is where the dreams of excited new doctors go to die.

Because this is where LEGENDARY training takes place.

I spend ten minutes begging the photographer in HR to *please* take another picture. The one on my new hospital badge looks as if my blond hair spiraled through a wind tunnel prior to snapping the photo, and my chin is tucked just enough to double it. The photographer refuses, stating I'll need to pay twenty dollars to replace it.

Twenty dollars!

What new doctor can afford such extravagant prices?

Thanks to this fiasco, I'm running late, so I abandon the battle for another day. After muttering a few choice insults under my breath, I spin away from the unreasonable man and fly through the gurney graveyard toward my last stop of hospital orientation:

LEGENDARY training.

Six hours of instruction on an EMR I know better than the instructor. I've been using three different versions of LEGENDARY in three separate hospital systems since my first day as a peasant intern. Now, four years later, I've graduated from residency and I'm a pro.

The teacher has already started her spiel in the classroom when I slip in the back door. The projector at the front of the room displays a LEGENDARY login screen—complete with a UFO abducting a cow. Who comes up with their login page art?

I'm taking it as an alignment of fate that an open computer glows in the back row. I'm even more stoked that the man to my left is about my age and has a nice smile. Not to mention his physique, which is . . . distracting.

He leans close, grinning. "Well, lucky me."

Oh, great. He's a creep. Cringing internally, I turn toward him, prepared for a cheesy pickup line. Despite my misgivings, I whisper, "Lucky?" Because who can resist knowing the punch line?

"I really didn't want to be in this row alone with that guy." He subtly points to a wire-thin man at the computer on his other side. The guy is practically bouncing with excitement.

What kind of demon is excited about LEGENDARY training? It's like being jazzed to learn Excel.

My gaze drifts back to the cute man.

Not a pickup line, then.

A relieved truth.

I want to laugh, but I hold back, still unsure whether I'm being played in some way.

He smiles again. It's a *really* nice smile. "You look normal," he whispers. "And by *normal*, I mean you look properly peeved at having to spend six hours in the jaws of LEGENDARY hell."

Despite my inner giggle, I try to pay attention when the teacher instructs us to open the training folders in front of us.

The man complies, scanning over user instructions. He leans in again. "Why so late?"

"Because the HR douche wouldn't let me take a new ID photo."

At that, his attention drops to the badge clipped to the collar of my white button-up, where the unflattering picture flaunts for all to see. I fight the urge to cover it. Humor gleams in his eyes, and that nice, nice smile turns devious. "Why on earth would you want to replace that masterpiece?"

I point aggressively at the photo. "Because *this* girl looks like she's trying to hold in a fart."

The man chokes out a laugh awkward enough that the teacher asks if he's okay. He nods and clears his throat with a sip of Mountain Dew Kickstart, murmuring apologies. When the instructor turns back to the projector, he side-eyes me. "It's not that bad."

I shove the entire badge in his face. "*She* is the ugliest I have ever been."

"Have you disconnected your identity from the picture?"

"I claim no ties to her. She's exiled like the heretic she is."

"You should be nice to her. She's a friend of mine." He lifts his gaze, a half smile even prettier than the full thing gracing his stupid face. The man is disarming. Is he single? There's no ring on his left hand . . .

I fall into the bare hints of deep green in his eyes. "I doubt that."

"No, really. Best friends for life. I'm offended you're so rude to her."

Okay. So he's charming, too. Where's the catch? "She deserves it," I say.

"How dare you?" He winks. "That's my future wife you're talking about."

Definitely single, then. Or else in a very doomed relationship.

"Oh, yeah?" Begrudgingly enchanted, I point to my badge again. "This girl? This is the monster you're going to marry?"

He pastes on a playful expression. "Yeah. I'm going to marry that girl."

"Too bad for you she's not the marrying kind."

His grin doesn't abate in the slightest. "Pity."

Frustrations of the day forgotten, I can't help but laugh. This guy is uber cute. A fantastic surprise in the midst of the shit show that is this day.

But I definitely found the catch.

This pull toward another human doesn't occur often for me. Usually, I run from it, but I sense zero danger from him. A guy this fun-loving will never breach my barriers. The laugh lines around his eyes make me think he's never been serious a day in his life. He's the perfect combination of fun and safe, and I need a friend in this new city. Plus, he's far too interesting to waste on a one-night stand.

"Who are you?" I ask.

He holds up his badge. That inordinately attractive face shines out.

Asher Foley, MD. OB-GYN.

Asher points to my name on the ugly badge. "And this is Jocelyn Mattox, MD. Anesthesiology."

"It is."

"Future wife."

"Right up until I find twenty dollars to shred and replace her."

He bends closer and motions me to do the same. "You can destroy the evidence, but she'll live forever—" he taps his temple and smiles "—right here."

I narrow my eyes. "You're going to be annoying about this, aren't you?"

"Oh, yes. Very much so."

Before I can stop him, he pulls out his phone and snaps a picture of my badge.

My mouth falls open, and I subtly try to wrestle the phone from his hands without drawing the attention of the teacher.

To no avail. It's already in his pocket. He will own that picture for the rest of time.

I lower my voice. "You will suffer forever for this, Asher Foley."

He shrugs and turns back to his computer. "We'll see, sweetheart. I've got blackmail fodder now."

Asher

*It isn't a quantity of people you need
to light the shadows. It's quality.*
—My Therapist

My office in our clinic space on the second floor of the hospital is packed full of dusty books inherited from the doc who retired before I started. A single window covered with cheap vinyl blinds looks out over the parking lot, but the walls are otherwise bare.

Displayed in fancy frames, my diplomas and board certification currently lean against the wall because I've never remembered to bring a hammer and nails to work.

Pretentious pieces of paper anyway.

If I was going to hang anything, it would be my rainbow poster of a uterus being pulled out of a top hat.

I'm not a gynecologist. I'm a vagician.

Ha.

Classic.

I share the space with my medical assistant, Talia. Sassy, Southern-type woman. Bit judgy, but always funny. Our desks are catty-corner to one another, which means we are . . . quite close.

Talia is twenty-six and, if you ask her, she's a million weeks pregnant. In reality, she's almost forty weeks pregnant, and today is her last day of work. I'm inducing her Monday, much to her utter delight. She's been begging me to deliver this baby since she was thirty weeks because *it feels like someone jabbed a hunk of coral in my vagina and an evil, insane monkey is playing with a Taser attached to it.*

I love her.

Eyeing the Cardi B length nails on her hands—hot pink and bejeweled—I lean toward her. "Can I ask you a question, Tally Boo?"

She looks up from her computer, flipping long hair over her shoulder.

"How do you get anything done with those?"

She rolls her eyes. "Please, Doctor F. A real woman knows how to live life without the tips of her fingers."

"But, like, how are you going to take care of a newborn?"

Her brazenly flat stare is both insolent and hilarious. Love it. Love her. Ugh. I think I might miss her when she's gone.

"Mind your business."

"Mind *my* business? Didn't you tell me last week that I needed to settle down and have kids, too?"

She waves her hand. "I want you to share my misery. Besides, aren't you, like, forty-seven years old?"

"I'm thirty-three. You know this. You're the one who made me blow out thirty-three trick candles on my last birthday cake."

A hearty belly laugh bursts from her. "I forgot about that." She mimics blowing out candles—if the person blowing had the lung capacity of a ninety-year-old.

"Hilarious," I say, tone dry, as I push back from the desk. "Come on. We have a patient ready."

She waddles after me, and we enter a patient room to find a silver-haired woman perched on the exam table in her medical gown.

"Hello, Mrs. Mulaney," I say. "Long time, no see."

Her tremulous smile lights her whole face. "There's my Doctor Foley."

We exchange pleasantries, and she asks about *Miss Talia's* pregnancy. Mrs. Mulaney's exam is quick, and she chats the entire time, even with her legs spread. The woman treats her yearly exams like a social call.

"You know, I read on the Facebook that it's in style to go bare again," she says.

I do everything in my power to keep my eyes from widening. "Uh—"

"Should I wax down there, you think? I do want to fit in at the gym."

Talia whistles. "Go on, Mrs. Mulaney! You do you."

The older woman laughs. "You're right, Miss Talia. I *will* do me. Full bush."

I smother my laugh. "Everything looks healthy. Is there anything else I can do for you today?"

She pats my cheek like I'm a child. "It's nothing, really. I made an appointment with Doctor White. I can't quite hold my urine like I used to."

She made an appointment with my partner? With *Dr. White*, the condescending prick? For something I could help her with?

There's that feeling again. The inadequacy, all cold and heavy.

Really don't like it.

Visions swirl through my head—patients flocking to my partner, colleagues consulting better doctors, nurses telling patients to see any OB but me.

Might need a Tums.

I force my mouth into its usual smile. "Why don't you tell me about it? I'll see what I can do."

She shakes her head and waves a dismissive hand. "My appointment is next week. Doctor White has a great reputation for this sort of thing. I won't bother you with it, dear."

But I want to be bothered. This is my job. Why won't she take me seriously?

Definitely need a Tums.

The words are right there at the tip of my tongue—*I'd love to help*—but I just smile instead. "Of course. I understand."

"I'll be right back to you next year for my annual exam."

Good enough to feel up her boobs, but not good enough to fix her problems. Most patients complain their doctors don't listen, but I'm here, ready to dive into her issues, only to be told my older, humorless, more misogynistic partner will do it better than me.

But he won't do it better than me. He'll talk over her. Barely examine her. Then throw some medicine at the problem.

It's okay. It's fine. This isn't a big deal *at all*.

After the visit, Talia hums and does a jig outside the room. "That little old lady is my favorite."

I scrub my chest right above the raw ache, then search my desk drawer. I know I have Tums.

Stupid, really. Don't even like dealing with incontinence. Let's examine the silver lining here.

Aha. Tums. I shoot Talia a wink and throw some in my mouth. "I prefer the patient I'm inducing next week."

Mmm. Chalky lime. Tasty.

"Doctor Foley! You're gonna make me cry." She fans her face, then starts belly-cackling.

"Whatever. You're coming to Pool Party Saturday, right?"

We settle back at our desks to chart. "Uh. Hell, yeah. It's my last one before the baby."

"Try not to have your water break in my pool."

She gives me a sassy *mmm-hmm*, then eyes me. "Tell your skinny blonde friend she owes me a Snickers for winning volleyball last week."

That reminds me . . . Need to send Joss the latest picture of the ducklings. Rather funny, gauging her reactions. I can judge her mood based off how exasperated she is with the cuteness overload.

I pull out my phone, and oh, look. Another email from the hospital about Dragon training. They are *really* pushing that thing. Must be saving the hospital money. No other explanation for the bombardment of emails would suffice.

I hit Send on the duck pic right as Talia says, "Do you think my baby will come out with hair?"

"Ten bucks says he's covered in hair on his head *and* his back."

I'm playing the odds. Lanugo is common in newborns. Plus, Talia once showed me her baby picture to prove how cute she was. Very hairy baby she was.

She glares at me. "You think I'm having a Pomeranian or something?"

"You said it," I tease.

She stands and strides to the door, pretending to be mad.

"I'll quit, you know. You just see how you function without me, Doctor Foley."

"I *couldn't* function without you," I tell her honestly.

She huffs and marches away, but we both know she'll return in five minutes—with an empty bladder and a candy bar from the staff kitchen. In the meantime, I finish charting on Mrs. Mulaney and shove my disappointment with her visit deep beneath the surface.

Feelings of inadequacy immediately lighten.

My phone dings with a text from Joss.

> You are a strange man.
>
> I hope you only share your duck obsession with me. Other people might think you're a serial killer.
>
> Asher Foley. The duck bandit.
>
> Do you need anything from Costco?

So she's in a good mood, then. Good-mood Joss is less funny, to be honest, but still one of my top five favorite humans.

> Get me some of that protein powder I told you about.
>
> And don't worry. This level of cuteness is only for you sugar pie.

She sends a gif of a dog hiding its face like it's embarrassed. I'm smiling at my phone when Talia returns and clears her throat loud enough to snag my attention.

"What?" I ask.

With a spirited roll of her eyes, she resettles at her computer, peeling open a Twix bar. "Just so you know, Pomeranian puppies are cuter than God."

"Did you Google them while you peed?"

She ignores me. "And while my hairy baby will be cute, I prefer to think of him as a lion. He will be Simba."

"I'll anoint him with fruit juice at his birth if it will make you feel better."

She grins at her computer screen. "We'll thrust him over our heads while 'Circle of Life' plays over the hospital speakers. It'll be epic."

I laugh at her huffiness. "Whatever you want, girl. It's yours."

"Damn right, it is." She shoots me a small grin. "Thanks, Doctor Foley."

•

SATURDAYS IN THE summer have turned into an unspoken tradition of booze and swimming at my house. Pool Party Saturday. Even when I'm on call, my moocher friends find their way to my place to use my house. The Texas coast is a fifteen-minute drive, yet here they are, drinking my beer in my pool as per usual.

I collect friends like strays. Can't help it. I like people. They're all so different. So fascinating. I meet someone new, and a tickle rises in my throat until I've won them to my side.

Makes Pool Party Saturdays quite festive.

Sprawled out on a lounge chair, I wipe the pool water from my eyes and take a breather. Geoff has his wife on his shoulders, deep into a match of chicken with Jocelyn and Kevin, another anesthesiologist in her department. Several of my fellow OB-GYNs and the residents are chatting around the table on the covered porch. A couple of nurse anesthetists have taken over my outdoor kitchen, and the aroma of grilled burgers fills the air.

Talia and her crowd of nurses and MAs have commandeered all the sun-soaked places on the opposite side of the pool. A few of the ER docs have seized the TV. I crane my neck to view the screen. Is that NASCAR?

That reminds me . . .

I shoot off the customary weekly text to my NASCAR-fanatic brothers, reminding them NASCAR's weak, and they suck. The expected stream of insults regarding my physique—*"Have you ever heard of a gym, bro?"*—and my profession—*"Sad you had to become a gynecologist just to see some pussy."*—bring out a chuckle.

A playful scream draws my attention as Yayoi topples into the sparkling blue water. Joss throws her hands up in victory.

For half a second, my gaze drops to her perky chest, and something clenches in my stomach.

Don't like that.

Inappropriate.

That black bikini is a shard of kryptonite, weakening the boundary of Friend Zone.

Because . . . boobs.

Joss's boobs, though. Different than the normal kind.

Geoff swims to the edge beside me and hoists himself out. "Need a drink?"

I hold up my empty Stella. "Yeah, I'll take another."

He returns with a refill and a Natty Light for himself. Like me, Geoff is a country boy at heart. Grew up in the town next to mine, out in the boonies in Oklahoma. Small world. We wrestled each other in high school. He won State our senior year. Still holds it over me, the dick.

That we wrestled as teenagers makes Joss endlessly happy. Early on, she bullied a picture of me in my singlet from my mom. It's now my contact photo in her phone. Luckily for me, Jocelyn's hospital employee photo is the most unflattering picture she's ever taken, so naturally, it's her contact photo in *my* phone.

She once threatened me with a macabre sort of violence if I didn't delete it. As a ceasefire, I graciously allowed her to keep the wrestling photo. The conversation went something like:

"Fine. Keep it. You just want to ogle me in the spandex I wore when I was in the best shape of my life."

Blah, blah. Excuse, excuse. Childish laughter. "Little Asher leans left!"

Ridiculous woman.

"I heard you single-handedly saved a man's dick yesterday," I say to Geoff as he settles into the lounge chair beside me. The dude is rocking a sharp farmer's tan, the bright sun only accentuating the whiteness of his shoulders and chest.

Geoff cracks the tab of his beer. "It probably would have survived without me. Just . . . less aesthetically pleasing."

Not the prettiest appendage as it is. Less than ideal to make it uglier. Still, I snort at the picture in my head. "What happened?"

"Skateboarding accident. Straddled a rusty rail."

Wincing, I quell the urge to protect my groin against invisible threats. "I heard he almost severed it."

Geoff sighs. Hospital gossip annoys him. Understandable, given it's usually wrong. "It was a bad laceration, but it wasn't severed. It'll heal okay."

"Yikes. Who even skateboards anymore?"

"Teenagers." Geoff downs a quarter of his beer with a loud gulp. "We were all idiots once."

Some of us still are, I think, but I shake that off. "How'd you get up on that pedestal, G-spot? They always call you in for the tough shit." Unlike me. I'm bypassed for my more *established* partners. How do I get to Geoff level of surgical respect? It isn't enough to be a good surgeon with minimal bad outcomes—both of which I already do. There's some element I'm missing. Something that shouts *Hey! I'm who you call in a crisis!*

Would like install chip for said element, please. Will pay nicely.

Geoff shrugs. "The pedestal isn't always a great place to be. When people think you can do no wrong, it's inevitably worse when shit hits the fan."

I get that. Have made that argument to myself a million times, but . . . still would rather be on the pedestal. Respect is *earned*, however, not bought. Should I joke less? Frown more?

What's the secret?

Joss and Yayoi gather close in the pool, giggling to themselves while Talia floats by on a blow-up raft, pregnant belly shining in the sun.

I lean closer to Geoff. "Yayoi still on your case about knocking her up?"

He groans. "Frickin' biologic clock. Starts ticking and suddenly she can't stop talking about babies. You're lucky you're still keeping it casual."

Casual. Another word for *not serious*. Yeah, so, *so* lucky.

I swallow a large gulp of beer. "You've already got the dad bod, bro. Might as well earn it."

Geoff adopts the mildly panicked look married men develop when their wives talk about wanting children. "Do you think she'd notice if I gave myself a vasectomy? It'd take five minutes . . ."

"She'd castrate you, dumbass."

He chuckles. "I know."

Geoff pretends he's not ready for kids, but last week he was very drunk. Very drunk Geoff equals very truthful Geoff. He announced to us all they were trying for a miracle, and they were doing it *right now*. He then carted Yayoi off to one of my guest rooms, where they stayed until everyone left except Joss.

Yes, I made them launder every scrap of bedding in that room.

Yes, Jocelyn and I spent the entire evening making awkward jokes.

Yes, we watched *Knocked Up* later that night to poke fun at them.

"Doctor Foley!" I turn toward the table on the porch, populated mainly by OBs. Aaand they're all looking at me. What've I done?

One of the residents raises a hand in my direction. "Tell them what happened with your delivery yesterday."

Oh. Ha. This is a good one. I jog over to the table. "Right. Funny story. The dad was a little overeager, right? Every prenatal visit, he talked about skin-to-skin. Early breastfeeding. The whole thing. So, the patient starts crowning, and the dad yells, 'Is it time?' and *immediately* strips."

Evie, one of the OB hospitalists, widens her eyes. "Wait. Stripped naked? Like *naked* naked?"

"Total birthday suit," I say with a laugh. "So much dong I did *not* want to see."

Giggles and exclamations of disbelief burst from everyone at the table.

"So then what happened?" asks the only male resident, Ashesh.

"The respiratory therapist went to turn on the oxygen, not realizing the dude was exposed, and as soon as she sees it, she screeches, 'Dick! Oh, my god. It's a dick!' and the patient yells at him to put his boxers back on, but she can't stop giggling, so she basically laughs the baby out, and the nurse is so busy throwing clothes at the dad that she doesn't realize the baby was born, so we had to guess time of delivery."

Everyone at the table is laughing, and thus begins a round of OB-GYN Story Time, the classic game of one-upsmanship that can usually only be beaten by an ER doc.

Should make it into a drinking game. Everyone would win.

A poke in my side draws my attention toward Jocelyn behind me, chewing a giant bite of burger. Her platinum hair is pulled into a wild, dripping ponytail, and she's thrown a sheer cover-up over her wet bathing suit.

Good. Don't really want to be thinking about Joss boobs again. Black bikini is my least favorite. Much prefer tie-dye bikini—far less pushy-uppy-ness.

"You forgot to buy my pineapple White Claws," she mumbles around the food.

I rest my shoulder on the wooden pillar beside me. "I forgot, or *you* did? You know you could pay for your own booze every once in a while."

A look of deep affront mars her forehead, and she pokes me hard in the stomach. "Treason! Betrayal! I agreed to fly to *Florida* for you."

"Ow." I snap the bathing suit strap over her constellation-tattooed collarbone in retaliation. "I put them in the fridge in the garage, you monster. Otherwise, you'd complain when everyone else drank them."

Her eyes light from within. I sort of hate what that does to my insides. Why does making her happy give me internal hives? Always has, from the moment I met her.

She offers up a contrite smile and sidles closer, walking her fingers up my arm. "Have I mentioned you're the best?"

Her mock-flirting is masterful. I now have no desire to argue with her. "No. Feel free to gush."

"Don't be extra." Her pointy nail jabs me in the stomach again, and she grins. "Better head to the gym tomorrow, Ash. Getting a little soft there."

She skips away before I can strike back. She knows abs are my sore spot when it comes to working out. It takes so much more than exercise to keep a six-pack. The six-pack lifestyle is . . . restrictive.

I like beer. And Cheez-Its.

Come at me.

I'm in good shape. Decently shredded. With abs that are visible . . . sometimes. Mostly when I'm hungry.

Good enough.

Just like Jocelyn's tiny ass is good enough, even though she does a million squats each day to change it. When I point out the reality of genetics, she merely rolls her eyes.

"I just want a little junk back there. I don't need the whole trunk full. Only a little."

"And I want to look like The Rock. It ain't happenin', girl."

I find a seat on one of the blue cushioned chairs before the TV and take a long draw on my beer. Against my interior designer's wishes, I selected these rocking chairs for comfort. William and Larry, sitting on the matching couch nearby, are still hot for NASCAR and barely acknowledge my existence. Where are their wives?

Oh, over there in the pool.

When Joss returns with her pineapple White Claw, her bony butt perches on my armrest. "Maybe we skip the gym tomorrow. I like you a little soft."

"Oh, don't start that. You just don't want to come with."

She throws a beleaguered glance at the porch ceiling. "You always want to go so early."

"Maybe I could be persuaded to go a little later." I squeeze her knee. "You spending the night?"

"Don't I always?"

She does. Every Saturday. Even if I'm on call. Even if I have a date. Even if *she* has a date. Jocelyn spends Saturdays at my house. She claimed a bedroom for herself, and everyone knows it's hers. Joss's room.

My Saturday night roommate.

I set my empty bottle on the table beside us and steal a sip of her pineapple girl drink. "I'm not turning the air up to seventy-four for you this time. Sweated through my sheets last weekend."

Pink lips curve into a smile and her brown eyes turn mischievous. "I know where the thermostat is."

Maddening woman.

She shrieks when I scoop her into my arms and deposit her tiny frame into the chair beside mine.

"So how was your date last night?" I ask. "Was the nose ring in his picture as big as it looked?"

"Bigger, actually."

"Whoa." That thing was excessive.

"Oh, yeah," she says, eyebrows risen. "Sadly overcompensating for some things."

"Bad night, then?"

She shrugs. "I consider it a success when I don't have to finish myself off."

Behind a soft chuckle, I shove that mental image right over a cliff in my mind. "So . . . was it a success?"

She shakes her head, sighing dramatically.

"Poor girl." I pat her hand in jest. "Maybe it's time to hang up the one-night stands. You could do better."

"I know I could." She crosses her arms. "I don't want to."

Yeah, yeah. Heard that before. Jocelyn's anti-intimacy.

Sworn off love. She's not been super forthcoming about why, though. Regardless, it's so . . . sad. She deserves that movie love.

Everyone does, really.

"I feel like I'm being shamed," she says with narrowed eyes.

I blink at that. "What?" The furthest thing from my mind is that she should be ashamed, but she always goes back to this. "That's not at all— Never mind. Do whatever makes you happy, Joss."

"What about *your* love life, Honorable Judge Foley?" She pokes my shoulder.

"I wasn't judging! I'm *never* judging."

She's all skeptical with her pursed lips and her arched brow. "Mmm-hmm. When was the last time you went on a date, Asher?"

A month ago. Geoff set me up with Yayoi's cousin. I wasn't too keen, but it would've been rude to stand the woman up, silly to say no when she invited herself inside my home, and downright stupid not to fuck her when she stripped herself in my bedroom.

Didn't feel great when she left at 3:00 a.m. with a quick kiss and a "I'm free again Thursday if you want to hook up."

What else could I say except, "Yeah, sure"?

I didn't call her. Don't want a hookup. Want something real.

Is it weird to want that? All my married friends act like I'm so lucky to be alone. Like being a single man means I'm drowning in sex.

But I'm not. I could be, maybe. I'm not ugly. I'm successful. Women like me.

Sex with strangers loses its appeal after a while, though. Five years ago, sure, but in my mid-thirties, I'm kind of over it.

I stare at the cars on the screen instead of Joss. This is so boring. Why does anyone like it? "You know about all my dates," I say. "I'm not keeping secrets."

"That last girl didn't do it for you—"

"You mean *I* didn't do it for *her*."

She scowls. "Fine, but what about all the other ones throwing themselves at you?"

I roll my eyes. "No woman is throwing herself at me." The only ones I even talk to are at work.

A decorative pillow launches at my face. "They *are*. You just don't pay attention. Open your eyes next time you're at the hospital. You'll see what I mean."

I toss the pillow back. "I don't date people from work. You know this."

Her laugh is offensively incredulous. "Then just walk down the street! If you call them, they will come."

God, why did I say that thing at hibachi the other night? She'll never let this go. I glance at the guys on the couch and lower my voice. "I don't want to talk about it."

"But you said—"

"Joss." I meet her eyes, and she shrinks in her seat.

"Okay. I'll stop. But . . . what exactly are you looking for?"

For a moment, I pause to consider, sipping my beer. What *am* I looking for? My attention strays to Jocelyn's face. The pool-frizzed blond wisps at her temples. The tawny brown in her eyes. The arch of her eyebrows, a few shades darker than her hair.

My heart thumps once, twice, before I shrug. "I'll know it when I find it."

She shakes her head like I'm utterly hopeless and raises her can in another toast. "To the search, then."

Jocelyn

The nightmares are your reminder to wake up.
—My Therapist

I have this fantasy where I stand on a hill with nothing and no one visible all around me. At the top of the hill is a giant oak, and at the base of the oak is a book open for reading.

I'm utterly alone. Safe.

The fantasy appeared in the aftermath of Katrina when my sister, brother and I discovered we were orphans. Even after the immediate tragedy, the number of well-wishers barely diminished. We were bombarded—overloaded—with love.

Perhaps my siblings found solace in the company, but I was overwhelmed. I retreated into the solitude in my mind, and sometimes, I still go there for peace.

There's security in loneliness. The greatest pain in life is loss. Loss of control. Loss of self. Loss of love. At the end of my happiest days—days like today, when my friends surround me and laughter abounds—the knowledge that it's all temporary cuts deep into my chest.

Today was amazing. Pool Party Saturday is always fun, but bonding with Yayoi, teasing Geoff for his boring taste in burgers—Meat and cheese only? What even is that?—and digging deeper into Asher's wants and needs has left me . . . content. Cheerful. At peace.

I've lost so much, and I know I'll lose more. It's part of being human. But losing *this*—this happiness so bright it always temporarily blinds me—I'm not sure I could survive it.

What's worse is that I sense something changing inside me. Growing. Right at the center of all this warmth is Asher. That tiny morsel of vulnerability he showed me at the restaurant sprouted a seedling in my heart. He's so good. So comfortable. He's like the cozy blanket I use on my coldest nights.

But comfort leads to complacency, and I cannot let myself grow careless. I raised walls for a reason . . .

They keep out the floods.

These people I'm growing to love, this life I'm coming to adore—even Asher, steady as he is—it's all temporary.

Nothing lasts forever.

Every single thing I touch drowns in one way or another. I can't control death. But I can control this, and I will *not* lose myself again when this all falls apart.

This growing thing inside me can be eradicated. I can care for them and still keep myself protected. I'll just have to backpedal a bit. The others will be easy, but Asher's already too close. I thought he'd be easy to keep at a distance, so I didn't protect myself as deftly as I should have at the beginning. He snuck inside, and I need to extract him before those tendrils grow thorns. Before ripping him out grows painful. Before it makes me bleed.

I'm alone on my hill. Enclosed in a glass box that keeps me safe.

"Joss?"

My head snaps up. Asher stands in the doorway to my room at his house. I came here to change into sweats, but once dressed, I perched myself at the foot of the bed to wallow. Time must have slipped while I reburied the feelings my fear had savagely ripped open and exposed.

"Everyone's gone," he says. "You on your hill?"

A smile tugs past my ravaged insides. The man knows me . . .

He breaks out in a rendition of "The Fool on the Hill" by The Beatles, and I laugh.

"Come on, rubber duckie." He holds his hand out. "Get out of your head. I made popcorn."

"Rubber duckie?"

He shrugs. "Yeah, they're cute and small like you."

The divinely blessed scent effervescing from his clean skin ripples over me when I follow in his wake. On Movie Saturday, we enjoy a mutually agreed upon film, usually in the company of Geoff and Yayoi, who are not currently present because they're at home, banging.

Movie Saturday has rules.

Mine: 1) No sad movies. 2) No animal deaths.

His: 1) No horror flicks. 2) Never even speak of *The Ring*.

Asher's couch is cozy. His screen is big. I crawl into my usual spot while he brings in the popcorn, then stretches out in the L portion of the sofa at the other end. Here, in the serenity of his home, I stuff myself with popcorn and shove my fears down deep.

It's natural to be comfortable here.

Normal.

I'm not complacent. My walls are intact.

Sometime later, Asher wakes me with a soft touch to my shoulder. "Time for bed, sweetheart."

Without opening my eyes, I whine in protest, earning a chuckle.

"Yeah, I knew that would be your answer." His arms slide under my knees and back, and he carries me toward my bedroom. "You're the most spoiled woman I know."

"My hero," I say in my best Olive Oyl voice, keeping my eyes closed.

I'm rewarded with a not-so-gentle toss into my bed. "Sweet dreams, moocher."

I curl up at once into the pillows, and he flips off the light.

Blackness takes me.

•

I WAKE ALONE in a strange room with antique wood furnishings—a bureau, a rocking chair, a china hutch. Windows along two walls show a stormy sky, the trees bending in the wind. Rain pours like the Great Flood.

A bolt of terror locks my legs in place. Where am I?

Someone's here. I need to get them before it's too late. I spin around, but the room's empty.

"Hello?" I scream.

A door across the way won't open. I jiggle and yank on the knob, but nothing. Outside, the rain pours on, flooding the grass, creeping up the porch steps.

"Jocelyn!" screams a voice behind me.

I whirl in place. Another door has appeared. The water surges, and I'm wading through it, bumping into floating furniture. The door opens, but it's jammed.

"Hello?" I call.

"Joss, please, help!"

My lungs seize, and my heart pounds against shards of splintered fear. I recognize that voice.

Asher.

I force my arm through the crack in the door, reaching blindly for him. Fingers graze mine, and I grasp the tips before the flood rises and sweeps him away. I scream his name.

Jerking upright, I struggle to catch my breath as the dream fades. I peer into the surrounding darkness, making out the vague shapes of the dresser and chair beside it. My heart pounds like it was real, and I shove the blankets off my sweaty limbs, waiting for the rush of cortisol to subside.

Good thing the thermostat's so low, or I'd be drenched.

My shaky legs slide off the side of the bed before I've fully recovered, and I tiptoe through the hallway toward Asher's room. I just need to verify he's okay. Hands trembling, I open his door on soundless hinges and peek my head in. He's in his usual position—on his side with the pillow crushed beneath his head. His brown hair is mussed, and his chest rises and falls with the slow breaths of the deeply asleep.

Something behind my ribs that was pinched tight suddenly releases. Ridiculous, really—it was only a dream, after all—but I can't deny the relief that rushes through me at the proof he's safe. Alive.

These nightmares are insufferable.

I step back to close the door, but those soundless hinges aren't so silent anymore.

He sits up at the squeak. "What the—"

"Sorry!" I whisper.

He blinks in my direction, squinting, and his voice is rusty when he says, "Are you—watching me sleep?"

I swing the door open fully. "What? Of course not, weirdo. I had a nightmare. I was just checking on you."

"Oh." His shoulders fall. "Who was it this time?"

I hesitate, then touch my still-trembling hands to my mouth. Should I tell him the truth?

"Joss? You okay?"

"Yeah." I shake myself and decide to lie. "I can't remember who it was."

He curses under his breath. "I'm sorry." He throws the covers off his legs. "You need a nightcap?"

I force my face into a sassy expression and throw up a stop gesture. "Don't be extra. I'm fine."

And yet, I don't want to leave.

"Then get back to bed, angel duck. We have a workout tomorrow."

Three seconds of silence pass while I dillydally in the doorway, looking for any excuse not to walk away. "Did you see the protein powder I bought you for tomorrow?"

"You mean the birthday cake flavored one in the pink packaging that will help me *optimize my curvy figure*."

I smother my laugh behind my hand. I am diabolical.

"You think I won't use that? Twenty-five grams per scoop and it's probably delicious."

"I hope the powder is pink."

He hums and points at the door. "Sleep well, cupcake. No more nightmares."

I turn to leave.

"Oh, Joss?"

"Yeah?"

"There's a rubber snake in your toilet. Thought it would be funny, but you've had enough scares tonight."

•

THE OR PHYSICIAN lounge usually has snacks, the most notable being a daily basket of fruit, mainly comprised of mealy apples. The hospital supplies us with two oranges.

Two.

I'm willing to remove other people's fingers to snag one of these oranges in the morning. Especially when that morning is a Monday. A Monday following a Sunday in which Asher decided leg day needed to include four zillion crunches since his abs aren't perfectly sculpted. I reminded him a thousand times that he's hot, and I was just teasing him on Saturday about the softness. The man has zero softness unless one counts the mushy, romantic insides. Alas, he wouldn't let us leave until my entire abdomen was burning and fatigued.

My body feels like he beat it with a stick. It will only be worse tomorrow . . . because I'm in my thirties now, and for some reason, my body has learned to draw out its punishments.

All I want is a frickin' orange, and on this particular Monday, I reach the basket of fruit in time to watch Cassie Hersl take the only remaining orange for herself.

My feet skid to a stop, hackles rising.

She meets my eyes without smiling. She never smiles. "Good morning."

I eye the fruit in her hand. "Morning. Nice weekend?"

Pleasantries with this woman breach the contract I have with myself to avoid assholes, but sometimes evil attacks and I must parry.

"Mmm." She lifts one shoulder an inch. "I heard you had another get-together at Asher's."

"I didn't. Asher did. It's *his* house."

With another skeptical hum, she moves toward the couch, where two older general surgeons stare unblinkingly at the TV. It is a truth universally acknowledged that if a group of old, white doctors congregates in one place, they must turn the TV to Fox News.

As soon as they leave, I'm changing it to HGTV and hiding the remote. That'll show 'em.

Cassie settles into the couch and glances back at me. "Hope it was fun."

Anesthesiology is a male-dominated specialty. On my first day of work, I tried to make friends with Cassie and her duo of prim, straitlaced followers. She made it clear in that silent, passive-aggressive way some women use that I wasn't welcome into her group of friends. So I made other friends instead. Now she seems perpetually angry with me, like I jilted her or something.

I strongly suspect her antipathy has to do with Asher. Despite her on-again, off-again relationship with some radiologist, she still harbors an obvious crush on my best friend. The invitation to Pool Party Saturdays is open to all, but Asher has never directly invited her, likely because she's such a dick to me all the time. But hey, maybe her hatred has everything to do with me.

I choose the least mealy apple and settle into the couch across from her. "It was decent."

She peels her—*my*—orange. "Your group is a little cliquey, don't you think?"

I hide my scowl in a somewhat mushy crunch of apple. Ironic she thinks I'm cliquey given my friend group formed as a result of my exclusion from hers. "I'm . . . sorry."

"Just a piece of advice. You might start considering how your actions make other people feel."

Classic Cassie. Playing the victim.

She also complains every month that the call schedule is a personal attack against her.

She writes the fucking schedule, gives herself the worst call shifts, then bitches about it.

The girl is always *so* extra.

But maybe . . . Maybe there's some validity to her words. I don't purposely exclude her, but she's been unpleasant from day one, so I don't go out of my way to be nice. I should probably work on that.

Then the wondrous aroma of citrus fills the air, and I give exactly zero fucks about her feelings. "I'll be more cognizant of it in the future, Doctor Hersl."

Her dark eyes flick up to meet mine, smooth features cast in their typical Resting Bitch Face. She's pretty and delicate despite that. Unlike me. My RBF looks like I want to murder things.

Looks usually aren't deceiving.

My phone vibrates, Ali's name flashing on the screen. A whooshing sensation sends my stomach to the floor. Ali never calls me this early. What if she's hurt? What if she's dead? What if the kids—

"Hello?"

"Joss, hey." Ali's annoyed voice comes through the speaker. "Can you please reassure your nephew that you don't kill people for a living? He refuses to get out of the car for school otherwise."

The knot in my chest unwinds, and I laugh. "What?"

"Mommy said you put people to sleep." Leo's voice hitches, like he's trying not to cry. "Like Doctor Vannoy did with Buster."

"Oh, honey." I try not to chuckle at the pitiful tone. "I only help them take a nap. They always wake up."

Usually.

99.9 percent of the time.

"Really?" Leo asks, brightening.

"Yes, baby. I don't kill people."

Across from me, Cassie stands and leaves without further ado. Good riddance.

"Oh, okay. Bye, Mom!"

"Have a good day in school," Ali says, and a car door thunks closed. "He's been so emotional lately."

"You scared the hell out of me calling this early," I whisper. "Thought someone died."

"Crap. Sorry. I felt the same way yesterday when Nic forgot to call me on his way home from work. Why is my go-to response always absolute certainty that they're dead?"

A bitter laugh rises in my chest. "Because nine times out of ten, they *are* dead."

Eighteen people. That's how many we've lost in as many years.

Cousin. Wrapped his Jeep around a tree.

Favorite uncle. Stroke.

Ali's best friend from childhood. Leukemia.

I've attended more funerals than weddings in my life.

"If I ever lost him . . . Or you. And don't even *mention* the kids." She sighs. "I'd just throw in the towel."

"Aw! I love you, too."

She chuckles. "I have to go. Stresses me out to drive in the rain."

"Okay. Love you."

The day progresses like a typical Monday. That is, it's a shit show with a hundred add-on emergencies and epidural consults. I cover Geoff's cases and sneakily convince him to DoorDash Asian takeout for lunch since the hospital offering is meatloaf—ick.

He frowns down at the menu on my phone after his second case. "I guess I can eat fried rice."

"Wow. So adventurous."

He hands my phone back. Jeez, is that another email about Dragon training?

"You sure we can't get Chick-fil-A?" he asks.

"I'm positive. They're closed on Mondays."

"No. They're closed on Sundays."

"You sure?" I smile. "Pretty sure it's Mondays."

With a put-upon grin, he shakes his head and walks away. My phone passes to several others throughout the department, and a giant feast of Asian food soon spreads over the table in the physician lounge. I rub my hands in anticipation.

To-go containers are passed to their owners, leaving several picked-at community appetizers.

Ooh. Crab rangoon. Yes, please.

I didn't get my orange this morning, but I'll eat the hell out of some orange chicken.

And that crab rangoon, though . . .

Just one more.

Okay, three more.

I'm not ashamed there's only one left. That's what food is for. Eating.

I settle into a chair next to Geoff while we wait for the OR to be cleaned. "What's your last case again?"

"Pyeloplasty."

I hum. Long case. Good thing my phone is locked and loaded with some new novels. Romantasy is my jam. People are always coming back to life in those books. Main character died? No problem. Here comes some heretofore undiscovered magic to bring her back from the Other Side. Um . . . yes, please.

Already finished with his rice, Geoff turns toward me. "Yayoi says your sister is visiting soon."

I nod. "A couple weeks from now."

"She bringing the kids?"

I shake my head. "Just her."

His shoulders droop. "Damn. Was hoping seeing the kids would scare Yayoi off the baby train."

"Hate to break it to you, but my niece and nephew are adorable. Seeing them would only make her want a million kids."

He sighs and stirs his fork—because he would never use chopsticks—through the scant grains of rice still in his bowl.

I nudge his shoulder. "What's up, big guy?"

He leans closer, the better to secret our conversation from the two CRNAs across from us. "I'm not sure I'm ready."

"Are you ever *ready* for something like that? Even the people who think they're ready stare at the new baby in their arms and think, *What the fuck have I gotten myself into?*"

He laughs and the skin crinkles around his eyes. He's got pretty blue ones, and I can see why Yayoi hopes their kids have them. "It's just a lot of responsibility, bringing new life into the world. Half the time, I still feel like a kid myself."

"We're all pretending, Geoff. Haven't you realized that? We all just bumble through life and hope we don't fall down too many times along the way. I don't have an answer to your doubts, but I'll tell you this. You're great, and any kids you have will be lucky to call you Dad."

His cheeks burn red, and he mutters an awkward thanks before turning to face me fully. "What about you, girl? You gonna be alone forever? If I have to dive into things that scare me, why don't you?"

"I'm—I'm not scared." My spine stiffens, and I think my face contorts into an expression I want to be breezy, but must come off as psychotic because he snorts and leans away from me.

"Oooookay," he says. "You definitely just got all weird

about it, so let's talk about something else. Did Asher tell you why he never called back Yayoi's cousin?"

I choke on the bite of chicken I shoved into my mouth. "God, you're gossipy today."

"Blame Yayoi. She thought they'd be perfect together and won't stop wondering about what happened. I'm tired of talking about it, and Asher won't spill. Give me anything to tell Yayoi, and I'll owe you."

I shrug. "Asher just said she wasn't into him."

Geoff rolls his eyes. "Yes, she was. Asher's never had a problem getting ladies interested."

Oh, I'm well aware of that. He leaves swooning fangirls wherever he goes. Hot, single doctor. The holy grail.

His words from the other night replay through my head. *The only part they ever want to give me is their bodies.* Does he really believe that? If Asher wanted a woman—*really* wanted her—I can't fathom how he couldn't have her. I was *so sure* he was still playing the field. What other reason could he have for being single when he doesn't want to be? It's baffling.

For two solid seconds, the picture of him bound to some other woman, sharing his life with her, burns like an acid wash in my brain. But then I shake myself with an inward laugh. This is *Asher.*

"So do you and Yayoi just sit around and gossip like old women?" I whisper.

He shrugs. "Sometimes."

"Who ate my crab rangoon?"

My head snaps toward Cassie, holding up the single remaining puff. She's staring at the others in the room, gaze landing on each suspect. Heat saturates my face, and I turn my entire body toward Geoff, who's giggling like a little girl, tears gathering in his dumb blue eyes.

"I didn't know it was hers," I hiss. "Don't you dare say a thing."

"I won't." He leans closer and whispers, "But she's eyeing you."

My phone rings again. *Thank goodness.*

"Hello?"

"Doctor Mattox, it's Jackie in OB. We need an epidural in room seven. She's six centimeters and breathing hard."

"All right, I'm on my way." Ending the call, I glance at Geoff and grin. "Saved by OB call. Who'd have thought? Meet you in the OR."

He nods, and I head for labor and delivery. The epidural cart is already outside the room, so I log in to LEGENDARY and skim the patient's chart.

A tiny flicker of warmth lights in my chest at Asher's name in the attending spot.

Inside the room, the patient moans, but her eyes light up when I walk through the door. Well, I probably should have actually internalized it when I looked at her name because I recognize her. It's Asher's MA.

"Hey, Talia. You hurtin' a little bit?"

She reaches for me. "Yes! My frickin' savior. I'm not about to do this without an epidural."

My kind of woman.

The nurse and I help position her while the father of the baby stands behind me. Hunched over her positioning device at the edge of the bed, Talia drops her face into the headrest.

While I open the kit and prep the meds, we chat, but she pauses every three minutes to breathe through a contraction.

I have to clean her back, so I push aside the hospital gown and freeze.

Talia's lower back is inked with a large black tattoo.

Not uncommon.

But the tattoo . . .

It's a line drawing of a naked woman sitting on a man's face. His hands grasp giant fistfuls of her tits. She's headless. Footless. Back arched. Fucking his face.

"What the fuck—" The words startle out of me. Shit! Did I just say that? *At work?*

"Something wrong?" Talia asks.

I clear my throat. "No. So sorry. This will be cold."

Have I noticed a tattoo here before? She usually wears one-pieces to Pool Party Saturday. I would *definitely* remember this.

Sterile gloves donned, I scrub the tattoo with blue surgical prep and place my drape. So now they're an alien couple doing dirty, dirty things on her back. And *of course* the needle will have to go straight into Tattoo Woman's clit.

How awkward. Can I actually do that? This is uncomfortable.

Should I ask about it? I want to ask. Is it my business, though? I probably shouldn't. But here's the real question: Will I be able to stop myself?

"Um." I crack my neck. My voice is off. "This is an interesting tattoo."

"You think? I got it for my grandma."

I choke. *What?* "Oh?"

"Yeah. She always said, *Talia, when you find something you love, you embrace it. You wear it on your skin.*"

OMG.

That can't be true—

Asher loves his MA more than he loves the ducklings on the man-made pond outside, but that wouldn't stop him from telling me all about this tattoo if he knew about it. He's her doctor. How could he *not* know about it?

"This next part will sting." Because what else can I say?

"Ah!" Her shoulders bunch while I inject local anesthetic, then she chuckles. "And what do I love more than having that man over there eat a little tuna sandwich?"

A laugh bursts out of me before I can register the exact degree of inappropriateness. It's irrepressible. But come on. Tuna sandwich? Did she just say that?

"Are you laughing at me, Doctor Mattox?" Talia demands, tone full of affront.

I force myself to stop, placing the catheter. "Of course not. No. I mean . . . Yes. I was laughing, but not at you. I'm so sorry."

"That's really rude. I should write you up. I feel judged."

"No— That's not— I'm so sorry—"

She says nothing as I finish up, taping the tube to her back while apologies continued to spew from my mouth. With the aid of me and the nurse, we help her lie flat on the bed. Her lips are pinched. Arms crossed.

"Has— Has Foley seen this tattoo?" I ask.

Her demeanor breaks, and she bursts into raucous laughter. Behind me, her partner also laughs. I glance at him, and he raises his hands. "Don't ask me. This was their bet."

I set my hands on my hips. "Bet?"

"It's a fake tattoo," Talia says. "My idea, by the way, so don't let him take credit. I'm a genius, right?"

"Fake . . . tattoo?" My mind has gone mushy.

"Doctor Foley bet me you couldn't keep from laughing. He actually wanted to do a creepy clown face and see if you screamed, but I thought that was too easy."

What? Seriously? These jerks! "Christ, Talia."

"You lost me two Snickers bars. I bet him you'd stay professional."

Yeah. No way was that happening. Asher knows me well.

"I'm going to kill him. I'll buy you an entire truckload of Snickers if you deliver that message for me."

Talia roars in laughter, unaware she's in the middle of a contraction.

Epidural: 1

Labor pains: 0

Suck it.

"Clown face?" I say. "Seriously?" That wouldn't have gone over well. I might've peed my pants. "How long have you been plotting this?"

She wipes her eyes with a long-nailed finger. "I thought of it that Pool Party Saturday when you ate the last hot dog. We planned my induction for when you were on OB call."

That was *months* ago! I hide my face in my hands to laugh. Pranks are Asher's love language, but if he thinks I won't be paying him back for this one . . .

"He's lucky it wasn't the clown. I might have murdered him."

The nurse nods vigorously. "I might have, too."

"I still might do it," I mutter under my breath. "Betting on my professionalism and being right. How dare he?" My mess takes only a minute to clean, disposing of sharps and trashing the rest. "I'll be back to check on you once he's dead."

She hoots again. "You ain't mad, right?"

"Of course not, but you know I can't let him win this game." I open the door, and Asher leans against the opposite wall, arms crossed, one foot flat against the drywall.

Smirking.

The most pleased, dazzling smirk known to man.

This habit he has of leaning on walls and doors is distracting. I've suddenly forgotten to be irate.

"You ever heard of Inkbox?" he asks.

My eyes narrow.

"Really interesting company. You send in a picture. They make a semipermanent tattoo."

I stand before him, pretend-glaring up into his face. "Really? To win a bet?"

He chuckles. "I only regret not getting to see your face."

"Did she come up with the grandma story?"

His eyes gleam. "Inspired, right?"

I poke his stomach hard enough to hurt the abs that are just as sore as mine. He *oofs*. "Clown face? Seriously?"

His eyes brighten. "Yeah, it would have been way better with the clown face. Your scream would've been louder than that lady who delivered in room three just now."

"Rubber snakes in my toilet and swapping my salt for sugar are one thing, but insulting my professionalism? I'm going to pay you back so hard for this."

To my great irritation, he doesn't look appropriately terrified. "You're awful at pranks. I'm the reigning king."

"Well, don't get too comfy on that throne, Ash. I'm coming for you."

"Bring it, sugar cookie."

I raise an eyebrow, choosing to overlook his progressively more idiotic nicknames. "Drinks Friday?"

"Can't. Boys' night."

"Aw. The biweekly circle jerk?"

"You know it." He clips my chin with his knuckle. "But I hear Cassie Hersl is looking to make some new friends. You know . . . if you're searching for a place to hang."

I shoot him a sour face. "Ha. Ha. Listen to what karma did with her crab rangoon . . ."

Asher

2.5 YEARS AGO

VIP tickets to Houston's Oktoberfest include complimentary drinks. I talked Jocelyn into the pricey tickets a month ago, though it took only minor persuasion. A night of polka, German food and beer? She'd never say no.

In fact, I convinced a near legion of doctors to partake in the festivities. I'm nothing if not an expert at cajoling people to attend parties.

I'm fully aware of this superpower. I use it wisely. At opportune moments.

Like Oktoberfest.

With the night half gone, everyone is properly soused. Several call it quits and Uber home, but Joss is still in full swing. She's dressed in a dirndl that shows off her shoulders and she tosses her two blond braids while dancing with an elderly gentleman in lederhosen.

Well, *dance* is a loose term. Incredibly awkward dancer, Jocelyn is. Would be cute if it wasn't so hilarious.

I'm close to drunk. My world compresses at the edges, blackened except for the tunnel vision right down the middle—straight to her.

I'm ready to leave.

And I want to leave with her.

Perhaps it's the obscene quantities of German alcohol in my system, but that whole rule about not getting involved with women at work seems absurd, borderline moronic. Joss is perfect in all the ways that matter. She's charming. Fun. Sexy.

She doesn't want anything serious, but neither do I. Not right now.

Right now, I just really want to fuck her.

We're great together. We have fun. Sex is the natural next step for us, right? Why ignore chemistry so potent?

Solid logic all around.

Feeling quite confident about the whole thing.

When the music ends and her dance partner moves on to someone else, Jocelyn meets my eyes across the tent. The surrounding crowd continues their raucous partying, but I nod toward the exit.

She takes one step toward me. Then two. Crackling lights sizzle in my very intoxicated blood, burning through the alcohol. The band strikes up another accordion-heavy tune, but neither of us looks away. She stands before me, smiling, and something enchanting shimmers between us.

Confidence steadily grows. Warmth spreads.

"You wanna come home with me, sweetheart?" I ask.

Her hazy eyes dilate. "Yeah. Take me home."

The Uber driver is a large bald man who remains quiet on the drive. I can't stop looking at her. We don't touch. Don't speak. But my full attention is zoned in on her. Her steady breaths. The sheen of her skin. The tiny flicker of her pulse in her throat.

At my house, I open the front door, and she steps inside. She's been here before, but I'm suddenly curious how she sees my space. The style is all sharp angles and masculine textures. Leather furniture. Dark wood floors. Metal accents.

Does she like it? Why have I never thought to ask?

In a fit of nerves, I head to the kitchen. "Do you want something to drink?"

"Sure." Leaning against my large island, she sips the cabernet I pour her. Her throat works with the swallow, and my gaze follows that motion down to the notch of her collarbones.

The reservations I've always held close tumble to the floor and shatter. My hand lifts, and she allows me to draw a single finger down the line of her throat until it lands on the bare tattooed skin over her clavicle.

Her breath catches. Speeds.

My blood turns to fire in my veins, starting a slow exorcism of the alcohol. I trace my touch over the stars on her skin. "I've wondered for months what this means."

"What makes you think it means anything?" Her voice is breathy and slurred.

My attention crawls up her neck and face until it reaches her eyes once more. "Because I know you."

She smirks. "You do?"

I allow a slow smile to take over my face. "We spend a lot of time together. Or have you forgotten?"

"No," she says faintly, tipping back another sip of wine. "I haven't forgotten."

I lean farther into her space, forcing her to raise her head to look me in the eye. "Then admit it means something."

"It means something," she whispers. "Take me to your room, and I'll tell you."

My heart slams against its cage. If I take her to my room, that's it. The line is crossed.

I won't be able to uncross it.

You won't want to uncross it, whispers a small voice in my head.

But is that true? There was a reason I haven't tried this before. What was it again?

My hand drops to her elbow, and I guide her across the house to my room. It's large and cozy, decked out in forest greens and deep browns. Does she like it as much as I do?

"My bedroom." I open my arms and spin in a circle. "Welcome."

She steps into the room, takes in her surroundings and sneaks another drink of wine. "The place you sleep."

"Yep."

She runs her fingers along the bedspread. "And—" she turns to face me "—the place you fuck."

My breath stalls. "Yes. That, too."

Confidence fades to something else. No longer feeling so warm.

She sinks onto the edge of the bed and crosses her legs. The skirt of the dirndl rides up, and my focus drops to her bare legs. They look so smooth. So touchable. My dick urges me to get on my knees, run my hands up her legs, spread them.

I meet her eyes once more. Warm. Brown. Like cinnamon.

My stomach lurches. She's my *best friend*. What am I doing? Months ago, in a more sober state of mind, I promised myself I wouldn't do this, no matter the circumstances. Jocelyn is more important than this. Complicating friendship with sex *never* works, and it's unquestionably not worth losing her.

I would definitely lose her. There is no question in my mind about that.

Though it would be a magnificent way to go.

She's beautifully made—graceful curves, glowing colors. I'd be an idiot to say no, and yet . . . I think that's what I'm about to do.

I force my legs to approach until I'm close enough to touch her. But I don't. "Stand up."

She rises in one slow, smooth move, her gaze fixed on mine.

"What do the stars mean, Jocelyn?"

She clears her throat. "It's the Columba constellation. Represents the dove who informed Noah the floods were receding."

Oh. I take in the stars once more.

Receding floods.

She hasn't revealed a lot about her past, but I know enough to understand her profound fear of drowning. There's more to this tattoo than she's saying, isn't there? Something deep. Dark.

My liver must be doing a fantastic job. The alcohol has metabolized enough for me to grasp the gravity of this situation.

How did I get here?

This woman has buried secrets in me. She's taken some of mine. She's given pieces of herself and extracted parts of me. We're inside each other, and that's more important than this petty lust.

That's all it is. Lust. Sober, neither of us would consider this. She is anti-relationship and I can't do casual.

I'm horny enough to wish I didn't care, but I *do* care. Because this is Jocelyn.

"We can't do this," I whisper.

She grins like she'd reached this conclusion long ago and was only waiting for me to catch up. "I know."

Cheeky woman.

I go for casual with a shrug. "Fun thought while it lasted, though."

She laughs. "Better in theory than in practice, I'm sure."

My eyebrows fly up. "Speak for yourself."

Her laugh only grows, and in her amusement, her grasp weakens. The glass of wine slips from her fingers, and the moment officially shatters, dousing our feet and the floor with ruby regret.

"Shit!" She leaps backward and lands on the bed.

I stare at the mess on the floor. Will not be fun to clean. "Is this you trying to get away from me?"

She rolls her eyes. "Shut up, Asher."

"No means no, biscuit. Coulda just told me."

She throws my favorite pillow at me, which I dive to catch so it doesn't land in the mess, barely avoiding the glass pieces. "Christ, woman! Don't take it out on the pillows."

She holds out her arms. "Give me that back. Just because we aren't sleeping together doesn't mean we can't sleep together. This bed is hella comfy, and I'm still tipsy."

"You can't have my favorite pillow."

She lifts an eyebrow. "Then can I have a T-shirt? Or do you want to sleep next to Bavarian Beer Maiden?"

"That depends. Does the beer maiden have it out for my pillows?"

She moves to throw another one, and I fold like a Japanese fan. "All right!"

After hopping over the larger pieces of glass and puddle of red, I reach into my closet and pull out an old T-shirt, then toss it her way. "You realize I have two other bedrooms, right?"

She snuggles into my pillows. "But I'm already in this one."

I tilt my head at that non-answer. Is sleeping in the same bed the best idea? Will it be more awkward to point out that it *isn't* the best idea? While I dither, she holds up the black T-shirt I gave her and nearly suffocates from laughter. The shirt sports a print of a corgi riding a T-Rex against the backdrop of a sparkling rainbow. When she catches her breath, she turns it to face outward. "Why? Just why?"

"I dunno. Thought it was funny." I head into the bathroom to provide her ample time to change, my stomach tying itself into pretzel-like knots. What if a single flash of her body destroys what I'm trying to protect? I can't allow that.

Also can't allow myself to slip into denial.

I am *painfully* attracted to her right now. It's never been this potent before. When I'm clearheaded, I can objectively admit she's beautiful without wanting to dive deep under her clothes. It's just the alcohol, though, which is fast fading from my system. Once the judgment-altering substance is out of my blood, everything will be back to normal.

I reemerge in my pj's and throw a towel over the wine mess. I'll clean it tomorrow. She's already settled onto one side of the bed, cozied up with my favorite pillow. Little thief.

Repayment will come in the form of changing the autocorrect in her phone tomorrow. Every time she types "lol" her phone will correct to "Titty" and she's far too tech-dumb to fix it without help.

Which I will not provide.

A chuckle escapes as I imagine it, slipping under the covers on my side of the bed. The lights dim at the press of a button on my bedside table.

"Hey, Asher," she whispers into the silence.

"Mmm?"

"Everyone's going to think we slept together. They saw us leave together."

"I'll just tell them you came to your senses and shot me down. Trust me, they'll believe it."

She laughs and pinches my wrist. I jerk away with a yelp.

"Be serious," she says.

"It'll be fine, Joss. No one cares in the end."

She hums. "I don't think that's true, but I'm too tired to care right now."

"Go to sleep."

We fall asleep on opposite sides of the bed.

We wake spooning, legs entwined, as close as two humans can be without being inside each other. At first, I'm not sure why my body is so warm and relaxed. Or why the air I'm breathing carries a distinctly feminine scent. A *Jocelyn* scent.

Then something moves against me, and I become acutely aware of the slide of female skin across mine.

Wait.

Oh, god.

We jerk away from each other at the same time, darting to opposite sides of the bed. I squint at her, still trying to adjust to the morning light.

Wild-eyed, she gestures toward my lap. "You have a situation."

I glance down at myself and stare at the shameless tent beneath the blankets. Well, okay, then. I lift my knees to hide it. "Did you really think I'm some mystical man who doesn't get morning wood? This is why I pointed out we shouldn't sleep in the same bed."

She shoves the covers to the end of the bed. "Well, I wasn't expecting to get stabbed by . . . it."

This I find hard to believe. "To be fair to me, you technically came to my house with the sole purpose of getting stabbed by *it*."

"Ugh." She cringes. "*Stabbed* is such a violent word."

I take a slow breath. "You used it first."

We stare at each other. And we stare some more.

"Fine," she says. "You were right. We shouldn't have slept in the same bed. Are you happy?"

"And we won't be making that mistake again," I say, nodding my head to encourage her to agree.

"Duh. I'm not looking to get injured."

"Huh?"

She waves both hands at my *situation* again. "How do you even use that thing? It has its own zip code."

Um.

Is she serious right now?

Heat rises from my neck into my face.

"Is this where you get that big-dick energy?"

A laugh spills out of my mouth. "Shut up."

"Does it have special accessories?" She perks up. "Like Batman's utility belt. What do you call the bat boomerang things? Cock-erangs?"

I let my face drop into my hands, still laughing. "I'm sure I'm being insulted, but I'm not sure how."

"You could deep throat a girl from below."

"Oh, my god." I throw a pillow at her. "You're purposely making this more cringe, aren't you?" When I peek up at her, she's grinning madly.

"Yeah," she says. "Are you dead from embarrassment yet?"

"Yes. Dead. I really hate you sometimes."

Her grin warms, and like magic, the awkwardness clears.

"I know." She slides off the bed. A gasp rips through her chest as soon as her foot touches the floor. She falls back onto the mattress. "Fuck!"

I crawl closer. "What is it?"

"The fucking glass. Why didn't we clean it up?"

"Um. Because we were drunk idiots. We thought it would be a good idea to sleep together. Does that not tell you all you need to know about the level of bad decision-making we'd reached?" I peek over the edge of the bed. Her foot is dripping blood onto my walnut floor. "Shit, Joss."

"Fix it!" She whimpers as she fans her foot, like that will somehow stop the bleeding.

"What is that even doing? Are you going to aerate it to coagulation?"

"You're a surgeon. Don't you have . . . like . . . suture?"

I bury my face in the covers. Deep breath is scented of laundry detergent. Even that smells gross. The hangover that was drifting at the periphery of my awareness snaps into focus as I stand. Waves of dizziness and nausea roll over me. Upright, my brain expands with blood and throbs against my skull.

Don't like it.

Bad. Bad. Bad.

Alcohol is the worst. Look at the clusterfuck of fiascos it's created this morning.

Wishing I had caffeine right now.

My house shoes sit at the edge of the bed, and I slip them on before scooping Joss into my arms and carrying her to the bathroom. "You owe me, lollipop."

"Thank you!"

"Holy—" I laugh and turn my face away. "I love you, girl, but your breath is straight up trash fire."

She pats my chest. "Don't be extra. Just fix my foot, Asher."

I set her at the edge of the soaker tub I never use and hand her a bottle of mouthwash. She turns on the faucet as I leave to retrieve my kit of surgical supplies, kept neatly in a duckling-covered Easter basket. But first, a pit stop at her phone to mess with her autocorrect.

Tee-hee.

When I return, she wiggles in joy at the lidocaine in my hand. Typical anesthesiologist.

I brandish the needle in her direction. "Buck up, bunny boo. This is gonna hurt."

She twists to give me the best angle, and I numb and close the gash in her foot with a few interrupted sutures.

"There." I peck a kiss on the top of her foot. "Good as new."

"Thanks. I think we can officially label this whole episode a total fucking disaster."

At least she agrees.

I throw everything back into the basket and wash my hands. "You understand now why I don't get involved with girls at work? Same catastrophe every time."

"You've been in *this* situation before?" She motions toward herself—stitched and disheveled in my bloodstained bathtub, still wearing the corgi-riding-T-rex shirt.

Okay. Fair. Leave it to Jocelyn to take *catastrophe* to the next level.

"Not quite," I say with a smile. "Though I'd argue this is better. I thought I was in love with the last one and found out way too late that she was secretly in love with someone else. Then I was stuck seeing them every day for months, so that was fun."

Compared to that, I'd take Joss's awkward boner jokes anytime.

She sucks in a breath like *ouch* and squirms out of the tub. "Yeah, I'd probably never date at work, either."

"You don't date, period."

"True." She tests her weight on her foot and winces.

I lean against the counter and cross my arms. "Why is that again?"

She shrugs. "Life's short and everybody dies. Will you carry me to your living room?"

I sigh at her nonanswer. Always deflecting. "Such a whiny baby."

With that, I scoop her into my arms and carry her out.

Frustrating woman.

Asher

> Imposter syndrome is a saboteur. The more we learn, the more we realize how much we still don't know. Be kind to yourself. Focus on the things you've done right, and reframe your mistakes as opportunities for growth.
> **—My Therapist**

"I'm going to have to sleep her," Joss says a week after the tattoo prank.

From the other side of the OR, my head jerks up. No. No. No. No.

I've been expecting Joss to retaliate with some sort of practical joke, so surely this is it, right? She's totally faking me out right now. The spinal anesthesia went in fine. She doesn't need to sleep the patient. Not *this* patient. This very high-risk patient.

Searching her face makes my stomach curl up on itself. No silliness or mischief to be found. Just contrition.

"No spinal?" My voice is remarkably even. Light.

My insides turn to lead.

The portion of Jocelyn's face that's visible above her mask scrunches, and she shakes her head. She knows I've been dreading today's C-section for the past week. This is the patient's sixth section. She had so much scar tissue during her previous one—with a different surgeon—that she wound up with a bowel resection, a severe hemorrhage and a post-op infection.

I asked Dr. White for an assist today, and he practically laughed in my face.

Can't do it on your own, Foley? Need me to hold your hand?

Sometimes I hate that guy. Viscerally.

This C-section is not one I want to do under general anesthesia. Instead of taking my time, I'll have to go faster. Propofol crosses the placenta. Propofol makes humans stop breathing.

Broadly speaking, I like babies to breathe when they're born. It's just a thing I like. Helps them be alive and such. Especially since there are no neonatologists at this hospital to limit any potential damage. Safely digging through all that scar tissue will only increase baby's exposure to the drug.

Must go fast for baby.

Must go slow for mom.

Must balance the two and keep both alive.

Must stop being a pussy and man up.

Ack. Find replacement word for *pussy*.

Need Tums.

"I tried," Joss says. "The anatomy is difficult."

The patient, Hannah, turns toward me and grimaces, mouthing *I'm sorry*. We've talked about this exact outcome no less than seven times. She knows what she risked when she became pregnant again. She trusted me to handle any complications that arose. I will not let her down. Despite what people may or may not think—still not sure in this regard—I'm a good surgeon, and I'll get all of us safely to the other side.

Smiling with reassurance at Hannah, I remind her it's not her fault, then glance at Gabriela, the resident who planned to help me today. "Can you go get the hospitalist? Tell her it's an emergency."

While the nurses position Hannah and prepare for surgery, I lock on to Joss. We're both masked. Her *Don't Be Extra* scrub cap hides most of her blond hair. Even with only her eyes visible, the silent support and encouragement bolsters me.

The uncomfortable tightness beneath my ribs eases slightly.

She turns away and draws up the drugs, then prepares for intubation.

The harried OB hospitalist, Evie O'Hara, steps into the OR. "What've we got?"

Besides their numerous other duties, the hospitalists help the private docs with difficult C-sections. I give her a quick rundown of the current situation, and she whistles.

"Right." She slips a ring off her index finger. "Let's go scrub."

Ten minutes later, I'm standing on the right side of Hannah's OR table, a scalpel in my hand. Evie is across from me. Jocelyn's induction of anesthesia is fast, followed by a masterful intubation.

"All right, Doctor Foley," Joss says. "Go."

So I do.

I perform the surgery I've performed hundreds of times, and it's just as much of a nightmare as I imagined. The good thing about scar tissue: it doesn't bleed. But there's *so much* of it. Layers and layers of distorted anatomy and missing landmarks.

Sweat gathers beneath my scrub cap, fogging my eye mask. Evie and I work as a team, snipping, bluntly dissecting.

Guessing.

And that's when the bleeding starts.

Aberrant arteries. Oozing veins. Snipped muscle between layers of tissue that looks like—but isn't—fascia. This woman's body uses scar tissue like the US Army uses tanks—as offensive weaponry. By the time I reach the uterus—too many minutes later—there isn't enough room to extract the baby.

We do our best. Tugging. Cutting. Avoiding bowel like it's Covid.

I think there's enough room, so I open the uterus and elevate the baby's head.

There is *not* enough room.

So now we're in a deep, dark cave of an abdomen full of blood where nothing is visible. I'm operating by feel alone. Elbow-deep in a woman's body.

"I need a vacuum!" I yell.

The device is thrown into my field of vision, and I shove it into the cave. Thanks to the sheer quantity of blood, the vacuum pops off four times before the suction takes.

A head of dark, bloody hair becomes visible in the hole.

And the vacuum pops off again. Each pop sprays blood across the OR. It's on my face. Dripping down my neck. Obscuring my vision through the eye mask.

I apply it once more, and finally, *finally*, the head delivers, followed by a limp body.

The baby doesn't cry. Doesn't move.

With a clamp and a quick cut, she's detached from her cord and handed off to the nursing staff.

And I pause.

Because I *hate* this. These conceivably avoidable situations. These OB nightmares that keep me awake wondering . . . what if? Is it not enough to have one life in my hands? No, I have two. I chose OB-GYN because it's the happiest specialty.

But it can also be the saddest.

Did I fuck up? Would this have gone smoother with a different surgeon? A better surgeon? Am I a total fucking fraud?

"I need a new mask," I say, then head back into the bloody cave.

Miraculously, there are no organ injuries. About eight minutes after delivery, the baby gives her first cry. Eventually, Evie and I have Hannah closed up and ready to form new scar tissue.

Breathing is suddenly easier.

Did someone turn down the oxygen in the room just for the surgery or something? Not good form.

Evie's gloved hand touches mine, and I meet her eyes. "Good work, Doctor," she says.

"And to you."

We share a silent moment of understanding, a commiseration that only people who've suffered the same trenches can comprehend.

Yes, surgeries like this suck, but everyone is alive. Probably because of Evie's help and a dash of luck. But still.

As soon as that thought occurs, my therapist's voice rises from the depths of my brain. *Try not to attribute your successes to external factors.*

Yeah, yeah.

Behind the sterile blue drape, Jocelyn raises an eyebrow at me, then points at all the blood spatter around the room. "You went full *Dexter*."

"No judgment allowed." I snap my gloves off and slide the

soiled surgical gown off my body. "Everyone lived. You're welcome."

Blood soaked through the gown and stains my right arm nearly to my elbow. The mirror in the physician locker room is a bit of a shock. I've had a serial killer makeover. Blood on my face, my neck—anywhere that was exposed—but a quick shower erases the evidence.

Dressed in clean scrubs, I'm towel-drying my hair when someone knocks on the door. "Asher?"

I throw the towel down and lean around the lockers to see the door. "Joss?"

"Is anyone else in here?"

"Um. No—"

She launches into the room and attacks me with a bear hug.

"This is the men's locker room, sugar bee."

"I don't care. You did *awesome*, and you need a reward hug."

I laugh. "If you say so."

The door opens again, and Joss gasps. She leaps into the wet shower I've just vacated and slides the curtain closed. A laugh bursts out of me. "I feel like hiding is somehow worse than being caught in here."

"Shhhh."

"Doctor Foley." The resident, Ashesh, peeks around the corner. He's obviously confused who I'm talking to, but I don't bother explaining. "Heard that was one hell of a section."

"Yeah. Shit show galore."

He laughs. "Surprised Doctor White didn't help you."

I fight the frown, but seriously? What the hell. Even residents doubt my abilities now? "He was otherwise engaged."

A sneer I wasn't expecting pulls up Ashesh's top lip, and

he snorts. Is that . . . *derision* I detect? "Probably had a tee time he couldn't miss, right?"

And I'm off-kilter. Because that—that sounded like judgment against Dr. White. Not me.

"But you didn't need him, I guess." Ashesh raises a hand for a bro high five, which I supply with a smile.

Little boost feels quite nice. Will it last?

Focus on the positive. Reframe the negative.

"Anyway, I saw one of your patients in triage," he says. "She thinks she's in labor."

"Is she contracting?"

"No."

"Is she dilated?"

"Nope." Ashesh smirks. "Closed like Kmart."

"Sounds like she's just pregnant. Send her home."

Once he's gone, Jocelyn pokes her head out of the shower. "White really wouldn't help you? Dick move."

"You know how he is. Egomaniac. He probably would've helped if I'd sufficiently humiliated myself by begging, but I couldn't quite reach that level."

She grins. "Nothing wrong with a little shameless begging."

"I didn't need to beg, though." I throw my arms wide, faking confidence. "I am a surgical god."

Her smile falls. "There was another reason I came in here. The second instrument count was off. Missing a towel clamp. They want you to look at the X-ray."

"What?" I nearly laugh. "I don't use towel clamps."

She shrugs, and my mind goes wild. Thoughts tumble deep into chaotic disarray.

No. It can't be. Towel clamps aren't even in C-section surgical sets.

But . . .

What if . . .

I follow Joss back to the OR on numb legs. Cynthia, the nurse in the wash station outside the room, has an image pulled up on her portable rollie computer—a plain film of my patient's abdomen with a towel clamp right in the center.

No way. Is this for real?

I move closer. "I don't understand. I didn't use towel clamps."

Every inch of my skin is tingling, simultaneously cold and on fire. I can't go back into that abdomen. I just closed it. It was a nightmare. I don't even use towel clamps!

"Is the patient still on the table?" I ask, then glance at Joss, confused. "Wait. What are you doing out here if she's still asleep?"

She maintains her stoic, concerned facade for no more than three seconds before she bursts into laughter.

I turn to the now-giggling Cynthia. "What's going on?"

"Gotcha!" Jocelyn says. "Kevin is with the patient, by the way. I'm not totally negligent."

My stomach returns to its normal position, though it's unsure whether it wants to stay there. A bit wobbly.

"We pulled that picture from the internet." Joss points at the photo. "I told you I'd pay you back for the porno tattoo."

Holy hell.

This is some next-level shit. When did she get good at this?

"Cynthia!" I cross my arms, but I'm smiling now that all the tension is gone. "Cindy Loo! My main squeeze! You let her do this? You're supposed to be Team OB. She's the enemy."

Cynthia's bright eyes twinkle. "She gets her epidurals done so fast, though."

"Yeah! You hear that, Doctor Foley? I'm the fastest guns in the west."

I roll my eyes. "You can't even put in a spinal."

Her mouth drops open. "Take that back!"

"Not a chance."

Cynthia's phone rings. She logs out of her computer and heads toward L&D with a wave, leaving us alone.

Arms still crossed, I face Jocelyn. "You."

She's not even repentant. Delight glows in her expression, sparkles in her eyes. "Me?"

Aggravating, hilarious woman.

The six thousand rushes of adrenaline I've suffered today are searching for an outlet, and a perfect one stands in front of me, smirking. I step into her space, forcing her to retreat until her back meets the scrub sink and I'm towering over her. "You think this is funny? I almost had a heart attack."

She pats my chest. "Your heart is fine. I told you I was coming for your throne."

I shake my head. "You're messing with the forces of nature here, Jocelyn. You are not winning this."

The corner of her mouth quirks like she couldn't care less. "Maybe not, but what good is a throne if it isn't challenged now and again, Ash?"

Anticipation swirls, and I'm practically giddy. I'm not sure what my next move should be, but it will be epic. "This hospital may not survive us."

She laughs. "It's fared pretty well so far." A beat of silence passes before she cups my shoulder. "Seriously, though, Asher. That was great. Really, really bloody. But great."

A tiny seed of warmth sprouts deep inside. Feels nice. Comfortable.

Like Joss.

I brush my thumb over her cheek. "Thanks, angel face."

"I'm sorry I couldn't get the spinal."

"Bet Cassie could've done it."

With an offended huff, she shoves me away right as the automatic double doors around the corner open.

"Doctor Foley?" echoes a voice down the hall.

"Over here," I call.

Gabriela, the resident who was supposed to help with my C-section, rounds the corner. "Oh, hey." The woman throws a reserved glance at Jocelyn, who smiles in return. Gabriela turns toward me and places a hand on her cocked hip. "Thought you might still be back here. Heard you were a rock star."

"Uh . . . You did?" This is bewildering information. "From who exactly?"

She shrugs. "It's just the word on the street. Anyway, your patient in labor is getting close. Can I scrub with you?"

"Yeah, sure. No problem."

"Great! I'll call you when she's ready." With a kittenish smile, she wiggles her fingers, a sort of jazz-hands goodbye, before retreating through the double doors.

Joss laughs. "Oh, did you see that? She wants you *bad*."

Wait. Huh?

Got distracted by the rock-star comment. Baffling, really. Did I miss something else?

"She . . . does?" I ask.

Joss's snort echoes against the tile surrounding us. "Yeah, bruh."

Not sure what to think of this, so I just shoot her a teasing grin, hoping to brush over it. "Can you blame her?"

None of the residents have ever come on to me directly. One or two have invited me out, but it's always a group thing. I have successfully avoided all possible work entanglements for three years like a stand-up, professional citizen.

Except for that one time. After Oktoberfest. The mistake that could have had disastrous consequences. But nothing happened, so it doesn't count.

Jocelyn bites her lip. "I *can't* blame her."

Uh . . .

What?

"Oh, don't look at me like that." She waves a hand at me. "You know you're a catch."

I want to laugh. If I was a catch, I wouldn't be so easy to leave. "No, I'm not."

"Of course you are. That girl would probably faint if you asked her to come with you to Florida instead of me. Don't fish for compliments."

The mention of Florida makes my chest tighten. Do I really need the reminder Joss offered a pity date so I don't have to be alone? "I'm not *fishing*. I'm truth-telling."

An incredulous laugh bursts out of her. "What? You are absolutely a catch! You're like the catch of a lifetime. How can you not see that?"

My head tilts. "Jocelyn. There's no way you actually believe that."

"Um. Yeah, I do."

I don't even have the words to explain to her how wrong she is, nor—for the sake of my own pride—do I want to.

She flaps her hand toward my body. "If I was a normal girl, I would absolutely be all over that."

What? "A *normal* girl? You *are* a normal girl. And except for one drunken night a long time ago, you've never shown any interest in me."

Her eyes go wide, and I realize my mistake at once.

Whoa. Whoa. Whoa. I didn't mean it like that.

Sudden panicky flutters are massively unpleasant.

Must take it back.

"I mean . . . Shit. Not like I've *wanted* you to show interest. I'm just saying that *you* are the one who's a catch, and you *are* normal. You just haven't found the person you're ready to change your ways for. So no, I don't believe that you would be *all over that* because there will come a day when you are ready to change. There will be someone you trust enough to let all the way inside. That day hasn't come, and that person definitely isn't me. So don't give me fake platitudes to make me feel better. It's insulting to both of us."

Her face blanches. "That's not what I was doing." She takes a tentative step closer, her brow wrinkling with concern.

Oh, no. Is this *caring* Joss? This is the rarest Joss. And also the one that's hardest to deal with. This Joss is disarming. Confusing. Inner shields lift of their own volition. Whatever she's about to say, I must ignore. Caring Joss creeps through my defenses like smoke. Makes me feel weird things I don't understand.

"Asher, I don't think you see yourself clearly. You are such a good man. And you're *nice* and successful. And you're pretty to look at. Any girl would be lucky to have you—"

"Then why am I alone?" The words erupt from me, and I hate them the second they're out in the universe.

Ack.

This is not a good look.

So much for these useless fucking shields.

Why did I say that? These aren't things I talk about. They're safe in my head and with my therapist only. Jocelyn doesn't need to hear about my loneliness and insecurities.

But that stupid phrase.

Any girl would be lucky to have you.

Spoken by every woman who didn't think a man was good enough for her ever. None of them acknowledge the hefty yet unsaid *but* that follows.

You're great, but . . .
You're such a good guy, but . . .
You're fun to be with, but . . .

Silence follows my words. Joss blinks, brown eyes wide, and then she throws her arms around me. I stiffen at first, but finally settle into the embrace.

This is so awkward.

Why did I say that?

"I don't know why you're alone," she finally says. "But I know it isn't because you're not good enough. I'm one-hundred percent certain on that, okay?"

I settle my cheek on the top of her head. "Who deemed you the expert?"

"You did. When you made me your ride or die." She squeezes a bit tighter and lowers her voice. "I'm sorry you're alone, Asher. I'm here with you, though. I know that's not good enough, but maybe it's good enough for now?"

A trickle of warmth finds its way into my blood. The urge to chuckle at her sweetness is a hard one to suppress. Here's emotionally stunted Joss giving what she's able to give—a simple hug and a promise to sit beside me and weather the storm.

Adorable woman.

"That's always been good enough," I say.

She lifts her head to meet my eyes. "I didn't realize you believed this about yourself. I hate that you have these thoughts."

"I'm not unhappy," I say, hoping to backtrack us out of this Asher-is-pathetic vibe.

"I didn't think you were. But you're lonely. I can be lonely with you, if you want."

The smallest smile tugs at my mouth. Caring Joss is impossible to resist. I give a slight nod because that's what we've been doing for three years anyway—being lonely together. "All right. Let's be lonely."

She continues to stare. For some reason, her gaze lowers to my mouth, and she throws on her thinking face.

Not a fan of this.

Don't want her thinking about my mouth. That makes me think about *her* mouth. Spend far too much time actively avoiding thinking about her mouth. Those thoughts can only lead to bad places.

"You *are* a catch," she finally says. "I don't care if you don't believe me right now. I'll keep saying it until you do."

Stubborn woman.

"Don't you have work to do or something?" I ask.

She summons a sickly sweet smile and releases me. "Nothing's more important than you, honey dear."

My phone dings with a LEGENDARY page. I pull up the message. "I have to go."

"Fine. Go. Leave me like always. Woe is me." She presses the back of her hand to her forehead.

Great. She's going all out, isn't she? "You're going to be really dramatic about this whole thing, aren't you?"

Her eyes gleam in unholy delight.

•

IGNORING THE REPEAT—and, at this point, borderline offensive—email regarding Dragon training, I pull up the page from the ER. Possible ectopic pregnancy.

As a general rule, patients with ectopic pregnancies are either uncontrollably terrified they'll die, or pretty blasé about the whole thing.

This one is the former.

Her name is Amelia, and her partner—Boyfriend? Friend? Husband?—is at her side, dutifully talking her down from the ledge. The man looks vaguely familiar. Maybe just a generic white guy, though. As a member of the generic white guy club, I feel free to judge that this guy is particularly generic.

"It's going to be okay, baby," he says. "It'll all be fine."

Tears streak down her face, but she meets my eyes when I knock on the open door. "Are you the doctor?"

"Yeah, hi, I'm Doctor Foley."

She nods and, with the help of her boyfriend, explains that she thinks she's six weeks pregnant, but started spotting this morning and had some mild pain on her right side that's now resolved. The ultrasound I reviewed before walking into the room isn't convincing. There's no pregnancy anywhere, meaning it's either too early to see it in the uterus, she's in the middle of a miscarriage or it's an ectopic I can't see.

I explain all this, tell her we need more time for things to declare themselves, and her tears slowly dry.

The boyfriend kisses her hand. "See, baby? It's gonna be fine." He checks his phone while I explain the next steps, his brows drawn together.

"So I might have to have surgery?" she asks with a sniffle.

I lift a shoulder. "Maybe. It's hard to say at this point."

She eyes me for a moment, and I sense her hesitation.

"What is it?" I ask as gently as I can.

"It's just . . . Have you done this surgery before?"

I take a slow breath and try hard to let that roll off me, throwing on a smile and my trusty self-deprecating armor instead. "Nope. But I YouTubed it before I came in here, so I think we'll be all right."

She lets out a wet chuckle.

I force myself to laugh with her. That joke works every time. "Yes, I've done this many times, but again, you might not need any surgery at all."

"But if I do, it might be a different surgeon?"

The muscles in my neck cramp. "That's correct."

She glances at her boyfriend, then proceeds to profusely thank me even though I did nothing, and she clearly didn't trust me enough to do anything anyway.

Is it something about my face that makes people question my competence? Do I have *imposter* tattooed on my forehead?

Or maybe I'm reading into it. She doesn't know anything about me. Why do I care if she doesn't believe I could remove an ectopic pregnancy half asleep in an overheated OR with hi-def speakers blaring Nickelback?

Stranger's opinion doesn't matter.

Except it sort of does.

Reframe the negative.

As I leave, my phone dings with another page—my patient upstairs is ready to deliver. It only takes me three minutes to reach the room, but I enter a world of chaos. Gabriela stands between the screaming patient's legs, begging her not to push yet. The family is bouncing excitedly around the room while the respiratory therapist keeps reminding them to back up . . . give her space . . . "No, don't step on that!"

Cynthia, angel that she is, merely sighs as I enter the room. "Thank god."

Hey, at least Cindy Loo finds relief in my presence.

My patient is—understandably—quite agitated. "Doctor Foley! Get it out of me!"

"Gabriela, you can let her push now." I slip into my gown and gloves as quickly as possible, but the baby is out in a single push, squealing on the patient's chest before I'm fully dressed.

The family crowds around, and I sneak beside a rattled Gabriela to help.

"Here." I hand her a collection tube from the delivery table. "Get the cord blood."

She nods. The dad stands beside the patient. The patient's mom is behind him, crying. Beside her, near the patient's knees, is a woman I assume is her grandmother. She's dressed as if she's attending an upper-crust lunch with a group of old, rich ladies—a cream power jacket and matching skirt.

Gabriela tries to squeeze the chunky umbilical cord into the tube to collect the blood, but when she unclamps the cord, the remaining blood pressure within pushes the cord from the tube and it flops like an unmanned water hose, spraying blood everywhere.

A jet of it slashes across my throat before showering the grandma and her white confection of a power suit with bright scarlet.

Gabriela gasps. "Oh, my god. I'm so sorry."

The entire room pauses for two seconds. Even the baby stops crying.

Then the grandma heaves in outrage, the patient starts cry-giggling and I succumb to uncontrollable laughter.

After grabbing the cord, Gabriela freezes. She holds it in the air like a torch. I'm laughing too hard to help. My head drops behind Gabriela's back to hide it.

"Doctor Foley," she whispers over her shoulder. "Help."

"I have never—" the grandma sputters. "How dare you?"

"I'm so sorry," Gabriela says. "It was an accident."

"I'm sorry, Grandma," the patient says through a chorus of hiccup-giggle-tears.

The baby screams.

Tears blurring my vision, I exchange places with Gabriela, who scrubs out to help the grandma clean up. Behind me, she's profusely apologizing.

"At least it's just the baby's blood," she says. "It's sterile. It won't hurt you."

"This is Chanel, child. I assure you, I am hurt."

I'm dying.

And maybe *this* is why I'm not taken seriously. I am physically unable to stop laughing in hilarious situations. If that's the case, I get it. It's a character flaw I will never overcome.

The placenta plops into a basin. The rest of the process is a breeze, and Gabriela and I sneak out, leaving the family to their happiness. Or their affront, depending on which of them you ask.

"I'm so sorry," Gabriela whispers.

"It's not a problem." I squeeze her shoulder once in reassurance and head toward Pod B.

"I'm so lucky it was you," she says, following me. "If that had been Doctor White, I'd be yelled at until next week."

Hmm. Maybe I should do more yelling. But I don't even know how to yell at people. How does one get to that point of anger?

I stop in the hallway and face her. "So you're saying you should be in trouble?"

Her dark eyes widen. "It was an accident."

My head tilts. "So . . . You *don't* think you should be in trouble."

"I don't know what the right answer is."

I laugh. "There isn't a right answer. I just want to know what you think. You say the other attendings yell at you, but I don't. How would you prefer your training to progress, Gabriela? Do the strict standards for perfection help you, or do they increase your anxiety? Would you prefer that type of education, or my more laid-back style? Or do you need something in the middle?"

The panic on her face settles into thoughtfulness. "Maybe . . . the middle?"

Okay. This is feedback I can use. A teachable moment. "So the next time the cord is still that full, let some blood drain into the bucket before you try to fill the tube. The stream will be easier to control. See? You live, you learn. I'm not going to yell at you, though, especially since it was hilarious."

A grin lights her face. *"This is Chanel, child,"* she says in an affected accent.

I laugh again, picturing it. "Priceless."

Her eyes go a bit starry. "I love working with you, Doctor Foley. I hope you know that."

Aw. Well, that's another little boost, isn't it? Two residents in one day. What's happening?

"Thanks," I say. "I like working with you, too."

"You—um—may want to do something about—" She motions to my neck, where the blood she sprayed—the blood I'd forgotten about—is now drying.

With a quick thanks, I head toward the dressing room for the second time. I pass the lockers lining the walls and the benches covered in street clothes to reach the shower stalls at the opposite end, sinks across from them.

Wow. My reflection is ghastly. A strip of blood makes a perfect line across my throat, like I've had a shave with Sweeney Todd.

As I scrub it away, I consider Gabriela. Perhaps it isn't what I'm doing, but what I'm not doing, that contributes to my reputation. Joke less, advise more. I can do that. Well, the advising part anyway. That's easy, right?

But then I remember the patient in the ER, fearful of me being her surgeon just by sight alone.

I don't fuckin' know.

One step forward, two steps back.

Tired of analyzing it. Ready to get out of this place.

Luckily, my last stop of the day is to room four—my patient, Juliana, was admitted in labor half an hour ago. I enter to find her grunting through a contraction, but managing it well. Her husband rubs her back.

I freeze upon entry.

That's the same man from earlier. Generic white guy. I *knew* he looked familiar.

And this is the worst.

His gaze meets mine, and he gives his head a subtle shake before his wife grimaces in my direction.

"Doctor Foley, can I have an epidural now?"

I blink away my visceral disgust to grin at her. "Of course, Jules. Go for it."

After a quick rundown of the plan and what to expect, I bid her good-night and assure her my partner on call will take care of her if anything arises.

She's grateful, and I do my best not to look at the father of her baby. Outside the room, I head for the elevators, internally cleansing my mind.

Wife in labor. Girlfriend in the ER with possible life-threatening condition. Both of them technically his fault.

I shouldn't judge. Maybe they're in an open relationship. Maybe they're polygamists.

Or maybe he's a cheating asshole.

The elevator door catches before it closes, sliding open to reveal the man on the other side. He's wearing the most sickening smile.

"Hey, Doc. Just so you know, Jules doesn't know about Amelia, and I really plan to keep it that way. Man to man, thanks for not saying anything."

I tilt my head. "I'm not legally allowed to say anything."

"Right, well—"

"But man to man, I think you're a piece of shit."

He stiffens. Every line of his generic face hardens. "It's not really your business, is it?"

"Nope. So get your hand off the door."

He does, and after a few moments, the elevator closes, leaving me to stare at my distorted reflection in the metal.

That idiot liar has two women who want him enough to bear his children. *Two*.

My thoughts finally flitter back to Joss's claims earlier that I'm some sort of catch. I roll those words over in my mind and examine them. Joss's opinion matters more than it should, but in most ways, it doesn't matter at all.

Of all the people I know, I want her good opinion the most. But having it doesn't change anything. Joss's friendship, like her opinion, holds too much weight. It's priceless, irreplaceable even, but it's still just a friendship.

We are *only* friends. Just acknowledging she might mean slightly more than that to me has guilt tugging at my edges. Feels like a betrayal, conceptualizing something *more*, hypothetical as it may be.

She's closed up behind her walls, and if I was going to be the one to break them down, it would have happened already.

And *that* is why her opinion shouldn't matter.

But it does.

A bit irritating, that.

To distract myself, I text Geoff.

> You down for a drink tonight?

Can't tonight

Baby stuff.

IYKYK

> Ah.
>
> Have fun with that

Everything okay?

> I was hoping to talk.

Who are you and what have you done with my friend Asher?

> haha
>
> nbd
>
> We'll talk later.

So I text Joss instead.

> Want to be lonely together tonight?

Titty

Damn it!

I still don't know why it does that.

I snort loudly into the empty space of the parking lot. Glad no one's around to witness it.

I actually can't tonight. Scheduled an evening facial. FaceTime after?

> Sure thing

Everything okay?

> Just a weird day.

I shake my head at the screen. It isn't a weird day. This day sucks ass, and I decide to turn to the one guy who's been there for every mistake and misstep, and has guided me out to the other side: my big brother.

"What's doing, little bro?" Brandon says after the third ring.

"Nothing. Just had a bad day."

He laughs in his loud, boisterous way. "How come you never call me on the good days?"

"I don't need your dumbass voice on the good days."

"All right, all right. What's got you down in doctor land?"

I slip into my truck and turn on the engine, waiting for the Bluetooth to connect before speaking. "You remember Mrs. Givens in tenth grade?"

He whistles. "Yeah. The witch gave me detention for dropping a pen once."

"You remember the toilet paper prank?"

He cracks up on the other side of the line, and I chuckle as well, remembering how pissed the old crab was about having to unspool layers and layers of toilet paper from around her desk.

"That was epic," Brandon says. "Didn't you put it around her car, too?"

"I had help for that part."

"Classic." His chuckles die off. "So what about it?"

"When she found out it was me, she told me that I act like a child, I'll never amount to anything and no one will ever take me seriously because I'm an absolute screwup."

He curses under his breath. "The woman was awful, Ash. We all knew that."

"Yeah." I throw my truck into Reverse and back out of my parking space. "I think about that sometimes, though. It just . . . It kind of feels like she was right."

"Asher, you're a doctor." He says it like that's all it takes to be winning at life.

Still feel like a fraud, though. Even with that meaningless MD after my name.

Okay, maybe not *meaningless*. Took a lot of work to get, actually. Wasted my twenties on it. So why does it feel trivial?

"Being a doctor isn't enough," I say. "I want to be a *good* doctor."

"You *are* a good doctor. Do you know Mom reads us your patient reviews sometimes? She's so fucking proud of you, man. And from what I can tell, your patients think you hung the moon or some shit."

"Not all of them," I mutter.

"Well, yeah. No one can please everyone."

I sigh. He doesn't understand what it's like to work so hard at something and *still* be found wanting.

"Your whole life, people have loved you from the second they meet you, Asher. You got Dad's charm, and you're damn lucky you did. But maybe you're so used to people loving you, that the few who don't bother you more than they should."

That rings true, but it doesn't ease the ache that's taken up residence in my chest, screaming *You're not good enough and everyone knows it.*

"I'll think about it," I say. "Thanks for the advice."

"Anytime, little bro. Talk later?"

"Yeah. Later."

•

Jocelyn: I can't FaceTime you.
My face is bright red.

I don't care what your face looks like

How dare you.

Rolling my eyes, I video chat her anyway. When her face pops into view on the screen, it's indeed fire-engine red.

"Holy shit, cupcake. Did you let them douse you in acid?"

"Don't look at me," she fake screeches. "I'm hideous!"

"Does it hurt?" I perch on the armrest of my sofa.

The screen jostles, and suddenly she's in her bed, snuggled up with a million pillows. "Nah. Looks worse than it is. So hey, did you reach a sudden epiphany about your greatness after our chat today?"

"Not exactly."

She squints at the screen, probably reading my thoughts through a ticker visible only to her. Not sure how she does that.

"What's that mean?" she asks.

I slide down the armrest onto my couch while tension gnaws into my chest wall. "It's . . . nothing."

"No, it isn't. Talk to me, Foley! I'm a great listener. I gasp in all the right places." She raises her eyebrows, expectant and waiting for me to spill.

Temptation drags against my spine. What would happen if I divulged all these ridiculous thoughts? Would she laugh in my face? Invalidate my feelings? Get all awkward and push me off the phone?

Or would she listen? Understand? Make it better?

She's trustworthy. She's here. She *wants* to talk about this. Sweet, wonderful woman.

In a great rush, everything pours out of me. All the self-doubt. The unguarded vulnerability. The disgusting lack of confidence. The desire to be taken seriously. Work. Women. Life. I lay it all on the line. I tear her idealized version of me—the one that doesn't exist—to the ground and piss all over it. Because she's mistaken, right? I'm a total fraud. Or maybe I'm just hoping she'll prove me wrong, that she'll have some magical combination of words that will erase these insecurities.

I really don't mean for it to happen. Years of growing angst has finally overflowed, and she's the sieve beneath, sifting out the anxiety. Some of these thoughts I've never spoken aloud, not even to my therapist, but they gush out of me now, and she *listens*.

Wholeheartedly.

Empathetically.

Like she truly cares.

Joss is always so unapologetically herself, ugly parts and all. After so many years, it's about time I trust her with my ugly parts, too.

Though I sort of wish there weren't any ugly parts. Want to be bright and shiny all the time. Is that too much to ask?

When I finish, her eyes are glistening in her crimson face.

"Oh, god." I pull the screen closer to study her expression. "You aren't going to cry, are you?"

"No!" She sniffles. "Why w-would I do that?"

I laugh. Awkward and forced, but still a laugh to hide behind. Might die from humiliation any second. Does she *pity* me? My silly struggles have her in tears. "Why the fuck are you crying, J?"

"I'm just on my period or something. Shut up." She wipes her face. "I don't even know what to say other than that you're wrong. You're, like, so, *so* wrong. Like, wronger than those publishing houses who rejected Stephen King. Wronger than the people who believed in Y2K. Asher, you are more wrong than that guy who said the *Titanic* was unsinkable."

At this point, I'm scrunched into a corner of my couch, one hand covering my face while the other holds the phone.

"I can't believe I told you all that. Can we forget this and go to bed?"

"No. We absolutely will not do that."

I chance a glance at her face, still wet. "I made you cry."

"Shut up. I'm just a little leaky."

"Why?"

"Because this is sad, Asher! I'm so sad you don't know how special you are."

"If by *special* you mean pitiful," I say in a teasing tone, fully embracing the self-mockery—my last remaining defense mechanism.

Can a wormhole open up right now and take me back in time? How about a black hole? Can I just cease to exist?

"You know, from the outside, no one would ever guess you think like this. Do you have any idea how confident you come across? I'm just . . . I'm shocked."

"We've all got our secrets, Miss I-guard-my-emotions-like-a-gold-filled-chest."

"I'm choosing to ignore that little dig on account of you're fundamentally broken and I need to fix you." She sets the phone on something and backs away, so I can see a little more of her. She's sitting cross-legged on her bed, blanketed in an oversize T-shirt that says "I LIKE PEOPLE (under general anesthesia)." She puts her hands out, fingers splayed, all *I've got a plan!* "Okay. So here's what you're going to do. Every time a patient lets you help her through a difficult moment. Every time a resident says they love working with you. Every patient review that throws up five stars. You snapshot those moments in your mind and remind yourself that's all that matters."

That's what my therapist said. Feels more reasonable coming from Joss, though. Less silly. Still, I'm not so sure. "I don't think—"

"No! There are no *buts*. You will do this, and you will like it. Every good thing that happens to you—snapshot. Okay?"

I'm very well trained, so I know the correct answer here is a simple, "Okay."

She smiles.

See? Compliance. Pleases even the grumpiest of people.

"You are good enough just as you are," she says. "And if someone isn't taking you seriously, then you don't need them in your life anyway, so good riddance."

"Yeah. Bye, Felicia."

She sets her fists on her hips. "You aren't being serious on purpose."

"To be honest, I'm doing my very best not to end this call right now, cancel our friendship out of self-preservation and never speak to you again. This is giving me a stress ulcer."

She snorts. "Whatever. You clearly needed to get all that off your chest. Don't get awkward now. Don't you feel better?"

Yes. Sort of. Still dealing with this gnawing pain in my stomach.

Need Tums.

Should probably see a gastroenterologist.

"You have all my secrets," I say. "The balance of our friendship has shifted. You need to tell me something I don't know about you before I die of a heart attack brought on by embarrassment and the revolting sight of your blood-red face."

She sends me a flat stare that translates through the tiny screen as *If I was there, you'd be in pain right now.*

"Fine," she says. "How about this? I really don't like people thinking I'm slutty for having one-night stands."

Ah. This again.

"You've actually already told me that." Along with a lot of other confusing drunken things before she passed out at a medical conference last year.

Her eyebrows shoot up. "I have?"

"In Vegas. Remember how drunk you got? Drunk Joss is very melancholy."

She giggles, but the sound is tight, a bit uneasy. "Oh, man. I was smashed. I can't believe I told you that. That's my deepest, darkest fear."

No. She's got something far deeper and darker in there. It's always lurked between us. I wish she'd tell me what it is. Sometimes I wonder what we'd be without it. Like always, I won't press her, but I want her to confide in me more than I want to rewind time right now. "You have to tell me something that's new to me, not new to you."

She looks up, thoughtful. "All right. Here's something you'd never guess. I secretly wish Cassie was nice to me."

Ha. Not what I was expecting, but okay. "Really?"

"Yeah. Like, why does she hate me? What did I even do to her?"

"Maybe you should ask."

She jerks back. "Ew. Don't be extra. That sounds like a lot of work."

Always quick to dole out advice, never one to take it. "*You're* a lot of work."

A proud grin stretches over her scarlet face, and it strikes me somewhere deep in my chest, kicking my heart up a gear. That's weird. Probably just the anxiety. Or the embarrassment. Or the peculiar feeling that this girl is sinking into my skin like sunlight, altering my very DNA.

No, not that last one. I'm tired. That's all.

Ignore, ignore, ignore.

"But you really need to do something about your skin," I say, "because you look like Hellboy."

The grin falls. "You're dead to me. You're wonderful, but dead to me. I'm done with you."

And with that, she disconnects, leaving me to stare at my own tired face, glowing on the screen.

Jocelyn

Sex is not a replacement for real emotion.
–My Therapist

Lying beside me in his bed, eyes closed, my *date* is pretty pleased with himself, but annoyance has grappled tenterhooks into me. Why can't these men get me off? It's not that hard. All my recent hookups have been total duds.

This one is cute. Blond. Super tall. Like, freakishly tall. Looks like he should be good in bed.

He isn't.

While he catches his breath, a goofy smile on his face, my hand slips between my legs. His frisky voice rumbles near my ear. "You want some more?"

I ignore him but accept his help down below since I deserve it. My eyes fall shut, blotting out the view of him and his messy bedroom.

Behind my eyelids, a face that doesn't belong creeps up.
Why am I alone?
Argh. Not again.

This is unacceptable. Asher can't be here. Not when I'm doing *this*. But every time I've attempted an orgasm since our heart-to-heart on the phone last week, Asher's face has snuck into my mind.

I think his vulnerability flipped a switch in my genetics or something. His loneliness and uncertainties, his openness and sincerity . . . It all unlocked a secret empathy level in my heart, like an Easter egg in a video game.

He thinks no one takes him seriously.

He thinks his patients don't trust him.

He thinks women find him expendable.

I am flabbergasted, and something possessive has taken flight inside me. How can he not see how wonderful he is? Perhaps the stodgy old surgeons at the hospital don't give him a second glance, but who cares about them?

And if women don't want him, then they are fucking blind as that elderly nurse with the inch-thick glasses in the ER who refuses to retire. This is the one part I simply cannot fathom.

Just . . . how?

He is so easy to love! I'm a self-inflicted emotionless shell of a person, and he still found a way to creep inside and become my best friend. How is that not tangible proof of his lovability?

I have *seen* the way women want him with my own 20/20 eyes. Asher has surely confirmation-biased his way into a complex that doesn't exist. And now I'm fatally damaged because learning all this has messed with my mind. I don't know why I can't get him out of my head, why these strange fantasies are cropping up like weeds.

I've wondered before, yes. Idle meanderings that don't mean anything. What his lips feel like. How his hands would touch me. The places he'd linger as he undressed me. Asher is kind. Caring. I'm certain he takes care of his partners in bed.

Not like *this* guy.

But this is more than wondering. This is fantasizing. This is straight up illicit indulgence.

It's like I've opened my wrists, and I'm bleeding out control and sanity as an offering, all while reaching for Asher's strong hand.

What is wrong with me?

I don't know what brought it on or how to make it stop.

But it's thoughts of *him* that allow the ecstasy to blossom down below, and what do I do with that? I can't tell him. I can't act on it. I can't force it away.

I'm stuck in the Here And There, weirded out and uncertain, surrounded in so many shades of gray, I'm practically Anastasia Steele.

Without the . . . like . . . bondage stuff.

One thing I know for certain: If my friendship with Asher is going to survive, it has to stop.

•

HE SMELLS LIKE a sexy forest.

Can forests be sexy? Because this one is.

Even with the chlorine of the pool water obscuring the scent, it's still reaching deep inside me, yanking want to the surface like it's pulling up daisies. I try to relax on my lounger beside the pool, but every muscle is tensed, and sweat that has very little to do with the sun gathers in every crease.

"What are you doing?" Asher asks, settling on the lounger beside mine.

I jerk my attention from his abs to find him studying me, brows scrunched. It isn't the first time this Pool Party Saturday that I've caught myself staring, but it is the first time *he's* caught me staring.

It took him three weeks. Three weeks of a strict diet and focused workouts to redefine the pretty muscles that are always there but have never held me quite so captivated. Reclining on a lounge chair in the summer sun, glistening from the pool water still drying on his skin, he is a god.

It's a problem. My own personal problem, but still.

I lean closer. "You are obscene."

He looks at himself and flicks away an invisible speck near his belly button. "Why?"

"Put some clothes on."

He lifts a brow. "*You* put some clothes on."

I glance at my tie-dye bikini and shake my head. "I don't need to. No one is staring at me."

He sits up and spins so he's facing my chair. "No one is staring at me, either. No one except you."

"That entire table of residents is ogling you."

A mixture of confusion and suspicion wrinkles his brow. "Is something wrong, sunshine?"

I try to snort, but it sounds more like a painful cough. The sun's blistering rays strangle me. "No."

"You sure? Because it sounds like you're jealous, and we both know that can't be true."

An awkward laugh erupts from my chest. What is even happening right now? The residents always look at him. Always want him. That's not new, and I'm not jealous. At least . . . I don't think I am.

I'm uncomfortable. Because he is excruciatingly hot.

I've known this as fact for years. His hotness hasn't

changed, so I definitely have. Why is this weird desire rearing its head now? My blood shimmers. Simmers. Fire concentrates deep in places Asher doesn't belong.

This is *Asher*!

He sprinkles whey protein on his breakfast. He has a tiny tattoo of a stick figure jumping on a trampoline on his shoulder because *I thought it would be hilarious!*

He's my best friend.

Why have I forgotten this?

It's just empathy. It has to be. My body is urging me to give comfort to this man who so desperately needs it. Yes. Definitely. Let's go with that.

Meanwhile, something tugs in my chest. Something not altogether comfortable.

I clear my throat. "I don't like them looking at you like you're . . . an object."

A slow, lopsided smile turns his face into some sort of masterpiece that's hard to look at straight on. "Are you feeling *protective*, Jossy Poo?"

"Ugh. What do you expect after you opened up to me the other day? Don't make this a thing, Asher, or I will embarrass the shit out of you."

"I don't think you will." He grins wide and points at my chest. "I think you're growing a heart three sizes too small in there."

I narrow my eyes, hoping I shoot off danger vibes like sparks, then make my voice just a shade too loud. "You're the one who was in tears at work the other day, pouting that you're all al—"

He attacks me, half landing on my lounger to smother his hand over my mouth. "Okay, I believe you'll embarrass me. I'll stop if you stop."

I gaze up into his eyes as he leans over me. His leg presses into mine, and the hand that isn't clamped over my mouth is braced next to my head. Pool water clings to his eyelashes, making them knot together and darken like pen strokes. The green in his eyes is darker today, and that sexy forest scent lurches toward me in a forbidden miasma.

My heart thumps hard, robbing me of breath. I can't be sexually attracted to this man. Throwing sex into the mix might uproot all the sticky feelings I'm not willing to feel. I already love him too hard as a friend. Any further attachment is not allowed.

In the space of one second, I imagine the pain of losing him, of getting that call that he'd been in an accident and didn't make it. My skin goes cold. Would I survive that? It's *already* overwhelming. How would I cope if we were more?

And besides, to him, I'm just his emotionally challenged best friend, anti-relationship because I haven't discovered the healing power of love. Who says he'd even be interested in anything more?

So I nod under his hand, and he backs off, settling once again on his lounger.

"Truce," he says.

"Truce," I agree. "But real talk—the way they look at you is making me salty."

He closes his eyes. "All I'm hearing is that my abs are no longer soft. Just in time for Florida next month. Go me."

I huff. "You're not going to be shirtless at the wedding, Asher."

He smiles without opening his eyes, a dangerous edge sharpening the curve. "You don't know that."

"I hate you."

"Yo, Foley!" shouts a voice from the covered porch.

Asher turns toward Geoff, shading his eyes. "What's up?"

"Where's your remote, man? I can't get the TV to work."

Asher heads toward the porch, and Yayoi falls into the lounger he vacated. "Well, my pregnancy test this morning was negative."

I slide my sunglasses on, willing my heart to behave. "Bummer."

"Right?" She takes an obvious gulp of her White Claw—not pineapple since I hid those. "Like, what's the point of all the sex?"

"I mean . . . it's fun, right?"

She scoffs. "I guess. Yes. Yeah, okay? It's fun. But also . . . I want a frickin' baby."

"Is he a good lay? I assume so, since you married him, but I need a story to live vicariously through. My last couple dates have been . . . not great."

Yayoi gives me a commiserating smile. "What's wrong with your dates?"

"They're boring." I pseudo-shudder. "It's like a chore instead of fun. Used to be kind of exciting, you know? The stranger aspect."

She looks at me like she's trying to decode me. "And now the stranger aspect . . . isn't exciting?"

I shut my eyes beneath my sunglasses. "That's not what I mean. It's annoying having to show someone what I like every time."

"Sounds like you want a boyfriend."

Without looking, I wave a dramatic hand in her direction. "Don't be extra. I just want someone who knows his way around a clit."

"Men are like dogs. You have to train them. If you don't, they wind up jamming their face in your crotch as soon as you walk through the door, then hump your leg for a minute and fall asleep."

Imagining Geoff humping Yayoi's leg, I drop into a bucket of giggles. "Gross."

"Exactly."

I turn on my side to face her. "How's everything else? Any more annoying daughters ruining photoshoots for you?"

"The last shoot I did was senior photos. She was super cute." Yayoi runs to grab her phone, then shows me a few stills of the girl.

Her photos are agonizingly pretty. They make me want to crawl inside them. I long to walk through that meadow, bask in that sunlight and be as carefree as that girl. Yayoi's able to tug at my cold, dead heart.

"Yayoi, you are so talented."

"It's nothing." She shrugs, all humble like the beauty she can create with a camera and a little glitzy magic doesn't matter.

"Own it, girl. This is genius. Someday, I want to be photographed to look this good."

"Okay!" She bounces in her seat. "I need some updated photos for my website. Will you model for me?"

"Sure. My sister is coming soon. Maybe you could do some sister shots?"

"Yes!"

Asher returns with his sexy forest scent and perches at the end of my lounger. "Ooh. Are we getting free pictures? I want in. You make everyone look like supermodels."

Yayoi perks up even more. "Really? Could I do pretend engagement photos with you guys? I want in that game so bad. From there, it's only a stepping stone to full weddings."

Pretend *engagement* photos?

Asher and I exchange a stilted glance.

"Uh . . ." I say at the same time Asher blurts out, "Suuure?"

Yayoi throws her hands in the air. "Yes!" She turns toward the deck. "Geoff! Ash and Joss are going to pretend to be engaged for me."

He makes the touchdown sign. "One step closer to weddings! Get it, girl."

She grins at us. "I love him."

I laugh, but deep inside my protective walls, my soul writhes, certain I've agreed to something that might have disastrous consequences. That weird discomfort in my chest tugs again.

But it's just pretend. It won't take more than an hour. I can pretend to be in love with Asher for an hour. NBD. Seriously.

No.

Big.

Deal.

Jocelyn

2 YEARS AGO

When people talk about hurricanes along the Texas coast, they always say things like, *Remember Harvey?* or *I'll never forget Harvey.*

Harvey is the zenith. The benchmark against which all other hurricanes must be measured. Mostly, this is because it was the most severe storm to hit Texas in recent memory. But also—it flooded a major city.

When a tropical depression morphs into Hurricane Isaiah in mid-October, we take the same precautions we always do—gas, food, water. Those who can evacuate, do. Medical personnel, however, can't evacuate. We're assigned to Team A—in-house during the storm—or Team B—relief for Team A when the storm ends.

I'm not freaking out.

I'm *not*.

When the email confirming my team assignment comes, I immediately text Asher.

> You team b too?

Yeah. Sucks.

I call him. "Asher, I can't stay in my house for this storm. I know it says it's going to hit closer to Mexico, but—"

"Who made the schedule? Can you talk to them? Maybe they'll remove you completely, so you can evacuate."

I sigh. "It was Cassie. She's in charge of all our schedules now."

"Oh."

I can practically hear his body droop. No way will Cassie Hersl do me any favors.

"So come stay with me," he says.

Hope blossoms in my chest, the prettiest flower to ever exist. "Can I?"

"Yes. I've got impact windows, a new roof and a whole-house generator."

A growl rises in my throat. "This is why I should've bought a new build instead of renting this shanty."

"That's what I said that time your bathtub knob broke."

As soon as the words leave his mouth, I erupt into laughter. We'd been at the beach and had drunkenly stumbled into my house to eat pizza and crash. Sweaty and sandy, I went to take a shower, but when I turned the faucet, it broke in the ON position.

We tried *everything*. Wrenches. Hammers. Prayers. Eventually, Asher succumbed to scooping water out of the tub and pouring it into the toilet and sink while I begged an emergency plumber to *please* come fast.

Neither of us thought to turn off the main water valve, nor could we stop laughing as water sloshed over the ancient beige and blue four-by-four tiles in my bathroom.

Thirty minutes later, the plumber arrived and fixed the whole thing, eyeing us as if we were errant children. Now, holding the phone to my ear, I'm picturing the grumpy dude's face and cracking up all over again. "That plumber hated us."

"Yeah, and for some reason, you still live there."

I groan. "I know, but the rent is cheap, and my loans are almost paid off."

"Guess I can't blame you. You're the responsible one, while I wasted my money on the big house and truck. But now you live in a tiny cottage from the 1960s that is definitely not hurricane-proof, while I live in a fortress, so who's really the responsible one?"

"Still me, but I'll be a good hurricane roommate and bring snacks."

A couple days later, to my utter horror, Hurricane Isaiah strikes south of us as a Category 2—wind speeds up to 110 mph, storm surge around eight feet. We lose power midway through landfall, but Asher's fancy propane generator keeps us comfortable while my snacks keep us fed.

For my benefit, Asher sets up camp in his second living room—the one with fewer windows through which I might gaze out in stark fear.

I hate hurricanes.

When a particularly loud crack against the side of the house draws tears to the surface of my eyes, he touches my shoulder. I flinch—a startle reflex—then grab his hand for comfort.

"What made you so scared of storms?" he asks.

I scoot closer to him, seeking a warm body to remind me I'm not alone. "It's not storms. It's specifically hurricanes."

"Why?"

"I grew up outside of New Orleans."

Asher puts an arm around me. "What happened?"

So . . . I tell him. I take a deep, shuddering breath and unravel the whole chain of events.

In a subconscious effort to heal, I've blocked out a lot of the events of that day. Ali remembers things I don't, and vice versa. For example, Ali remembers when our parents decided to ride out the storm.

They always say it'll be bad. This won't be any different than the others.

I, however, remember the moment they realized they were wrong.

It's too late to evacuate, Lisa. The roads are flooded.

It all happened both painfully slow and far, far too fast.

The water rose, spilling into our house through cracks in the doorways and air-conditioning vents. My parents took useless brooms and buckets to the rising tide, and directed all three kids into the attic of our small home.

At the top of the stairs, my brother, Leo, a year older than me, sniffled. I touched my face, finding it wet, too. Ali, the eldest at eighteen, engulfed us both in a hug.

It'll be okay. We'll all be fine.

Outside the single attic window, rain and wind tore at the world. Shingles ripped off houses. Cars and everyday household objects floated down the streets.

The water surged higher.

Downstairs, glass shattered. My parents cursed. I rushed to the window alongside my brother and sister. Below, our minivan had shoved a tree into our front porch. Across the street, our elderly neighbors waded into the torrential street, holding bags above their heads.

They had no attic of their own. If they stayed in their flooding home, they'd drown.

We watched our parents appear below, screaming at the couple to come inside with us. The elderly pair made their way through the debris, struggling against the current.

My parents infiltrated the dangerous waters, a frantic, seemingly hopeless endeavor. The elderly couple abandoned their bags to the water and reached for my dad. Mere feet separated them. Two yards of swelling, eddying gray water.

The elderly woman lost her footing first.

Dad lunged for her. Missed. Disappeared beneath the flood.

Mom's scream was loud enough to pierce the storm.

Leo slammed his fist on the window. "Dad!"

A floating tree rode the waves, barely missing Mom, who started back toward the house despite the elderly man still fighting to stay upright.

An airborne branch whipped through the air, and all three of us leaped away from the window as it crashed through, opening the attic to the perilous world outside. Regardless of the danger, I scrambled to my feet and fell against the branch now penetrating the window.

Outside, the water continued to rise. Mom and the elderly man were nowhere in sight. No. No. No.

I spun and darted toward the stairs, now halfway drowned in water. I dove into the freezing, dirty surge, ignoring the bump and bustle of invisible objects beneath it.

Leo and Ali yelled at me to come back, but I ignored them, searching the front porch for any sign of life.

"Mom!" I screamed over and over, only to be answered by wind and rain and an ever-rising tide.

I slipped over something beneath me and submerged under the gritty, salty water. It seared my nose, stung my eyes, and I came up splashing. A hand grasped my wrist. Looking up through wet, salt-burned vision, I found my brother's brown eyes and intense stare.

I have you.

Ali stood waist-deep in water on the stairs, tear-streaked and frazzled, reaching for us both. We endured the rest of the storm braced in each other's arms, and we attended our parents' combined funeral six weeks later—after the bodies were recovered and identified. We moved into our only living grandmother's house in Tennessee.

That's where I stop the story for Asher. Because the rest hurts to talk about.

Leo resorted to an opiate addiction to numb the pain. Desperate for a home and stability, Ali married the first man she seriously dated, Nicolas Sanchez, before her twenty-first birthday.

I built glass walls.

The boyfriend I found at my new school in Tennessee—my first love—died in a car accident a year later. Grandma passed from a heart attack just after I received my first admittance to college. Leo succumbed to his addiction the year following.

With each new death, my walls grew thicker and colder. I reinforced them with diamond-hard denial and steel-coated displacement that not even years of therapy have been able to strip away. I pretended away my emotional unavailability and substituted meaningful relationships with sexual satisfaction and casual acquaintances. My therapist says I developed avoidant attachment from the trauma. I just think I'm smart to protect myself.

Regardless, pathologic lessons ingrained themselves into my head:

To love is to pierce barbs into my heart—barbs adulterated with endorphins and lidocaine, so the puncture doesn't hurt. It feels good. What hurts is the violent dislodgment, the mangled tissue left behind when the love is stolen, destroyed, killed. Echoes of the missing pieces radiate torturous pain inward. Fragments poison the bloodstream.

I no longer allow people to penetrate so deeply.

Asher is a stealth-master. He ninja-ed his way behind my walls.

His arm tightens around me. "I'm so sorry that happened to you. Definitely get why you hate storms now."

"Yep."

"Why exactly do you live on the coast?"

I shrug and look out the window, where wind whips debris through the air. "I think I like to play chicken with my fears. This time, it's definitely winning."

"Nah." He reaches forward for a handful of M&M'S. "This is just a little wind. I won't let it hurt you."

I smile up at him—the first genuine smile since this godforsaken tempest started—and give him my Olive Oyl impression. "My hero."

He throws an M&M at me.

Jocelyn

If you can imagine the worst thing, you are also capable of imagining the best thing.
—My Therapist

"Keep moving!" yells the airport security man.

I ignore him and continue hugging Ali. My Benz is blocking a lane, but I don't care. My sister flew in a death trap of steel and countless bags of pretzels and still made it to my side.

Miracles do happen.

I barely slept last night, imagining what could befall her on her trip today. When I did sleep, I dreamed her airplane crashed into the ocean.

Always the goddamn ocean. With its uncontrollability and unfathomable depths. Stupid fucking thing, truly.

My therapist will be so disappointed.

"Move it, ladies!" the guy shouts again, closer this time.

Behind me, Asher thunks my trunk closed, now full of Ali's suitcase. "All set, lovelies."

"Come on." Ali pats my back. "Let's get in the car before they arrest us. I see you picked up a stray." She quickly hugs Asher, and he pecks her cheek.

I put on a fake sigh. "You pet a dog *one time*, and he follows you forever."

Asher rolls his eyes. "Ha ha."

I let Asher drive so I can focus on Ali, allowing her to have the front seat because I'm magnanimous. Her dark hair is thrown into its *I don't care what I look like* bun, and mascara is smeared under her eyes from her plane nap.

She's perfect.

"So, what are the sister plans tonight?" Asher asks once we're on the highway.

"Takeout and Netflix," I say.

"And wine," Ali adds.

"Heaven!" Asher says in a distinctly feminine voice, earning a laugh from Ali.

"What are you doing tonight, Asher?" Ali nudges his shoulder. "Hot date?"

"Yep. With my bed."

She pulls a face. "Gross."

He glances at her. "What? Not like that, you perv. I was on call last night. I'm tired, and unlike some people, I don't have a week of vacation to look forward to."

"Oh. Well, thanks for helping Joss pick me up."

"I didn't need help." I flick Asher's ear from behind. "He tagged along because he's bored."

He throws up a single finger. "Um. Who was the one

who was all—" he shifts to a whiny voice. "—*Asheeeeer, drive me to the airport because I'm lazy and helpless and like peer pressuring you into things.*"

I grin. "I don't recall."

He doesn't stop with the whiny voice. "*Asheeeer, my car needs gas, and I want you to fill it up.*"

Ali giggles. "She really does hate pumping her own gas."

I scoff. "It's gross."

"*Asheeeeeer, the airport is so faaaar.*"

"Okay." I throw the only thing I can find at him—a wadded-up receipt. "We get it."

Asher snaps his fingers. "Oh. That reminds me. You're definitely still good to go to that wedding, right? Because I bought our plane tickets."

"Yep. We need to book the hotel."

He nods. "I keep forgetting to call them."

"I forgot y'all were doing that," Ali says.

I throw out some jazz hands. "The dynamic duo does Florida."

Ali sighs. "I want to go to the beach."

"We're going tomorrow," I remind her.

"It's no fun going with you. You won't even get in the water."

The outside scenery is dominated by billboards for lawyers and traffic signs, so I fix my unseeing gaze on the back of Ali's dark head, remembering my nightmare. "The ocean's like a casino. You play long enough, it always wins."

Without looking at me, she offers a hand. I squeeze it, and we hold hands until we reach my house. Asher dutifully helps with her suitcase, pecks us both on the cheek and bids us goodbye.

Tug, tug goes my chest.

Ali raises an eyebrow once the door shuts. "How is that guy still single?"

"I really don't know."

Why am I alone?

Ughhhhhh. My heart pulls in the absolute wrong direction as I remember his face when he said that, all strained and frowny.

It's just empathy.

"He has to have some fatal flaw," Ali says, wheeling her bag to the guest room. "Like . . . Maybe he chews his gum louder than a weed eater, or he regularly uses the word *irregardless* in conversation."

Laughter bubbles up. "Maybe he has a secret obsession with cryptocurrency."

After tossing the bag into the room, she returns, gasping loudly. "Maybe he's bad in bed."

I snort and throw myself onto my threadbare couch. "There's no way that's true."

She follows and gives me a little smirk, crossing her legs with a fair bit of sass. "Thought about it, huh?"

Heat creeps up my face, and I choose not to answer since I can't say the truth, and she'll know I'm lying.

She points at the door. "*That* was some straight-up boyfriend shit."

"It was not."

"He drove you to pick up your sister from the airport after he apparently worked all night, and he was chipper about it the whole time. The man deserves an award, or a handy or something."

I scowl. "He's always chipper. That's just Asher."

She shrugs, and we take a moment to simply smile at each other. My insides turn light and fuzzy. I missed her *so much*.

"All right, that's enough sappy eye contact." She breaks the moment by patting around on the cushions. "Where's the remote?"

I pull it from beneath me and hand it to her, content to let her binge anything she wants. "Have at it, darling sister. I'll watch whatever you want. Even if it's stupid baking shows."

She lays her head on my shoulder. "I love you, Jocelyn."

"I love you, too."

•

WITH ALI AT Pool Party Saturday, I'm like a kid showing off all my toys. My giddiness has her giggling as she greets Yayoi and Geoff.

"The sister." Geoff slaps a hand into Ali's, shaking vigorously. "Long time, no see. What's it been, like, three years?"

Ali tosses her perfect brown hair. "Three months, actually, but thanks for noticing."

After flipping her the bird, Geoff hops into the pool and Yayoi hugs her. "I finally convinced him. We're trying!"

"Really?" Ali's face breaks into a giant smile. "How'd you do it?"

"I did what you said."

"What did she say?" I ask.

Yayoi releases her. "She said when she wanted a baby and Nic wasn't sure, she told him she didn't feel complete."

"Wow." My gaze bounces between them. "That's some masterful manipulation."

Ali smacks my arm. "It's not manipulation if it's true. My babies are wanted and loved, and I am complete."

Meanwhile, I'm considering keeping my IUD until I die. Can I have two just in case?

"Anyway, did Joss tell you about the photoshoot?"

Ali nods. "Yes! I brought the best dress for it, too. We're doing it tomorrow?"

"Yeah, the weather is supposed to be perfection." Yayoi shakes her fists, finally reaching toddler-level exuberance. "I'm so excited."

"All right, calm down before you strain yourself," I say. "We have to make the rounds."

Yayoi sticks her tongue out at me, then runs after Geoff to leap into the pool, her raven hair streaming behind her.

Ali has been to Texas several times in the past three years, but she's never visited Asher's house. I tap him on the shoulder while he's grilling burgers, and his smile ignites. The red apron over his swim trunks and tank reads *Baking Queen* in scripted letters.

The man has zero shame.

"My girls. Welcome!" He kisses us each on the cheek, then calls to the partygoers. "Party can start now! Guest of honor is here."

Ali gives him a playful shove. "Shut up."

He raises a hand in surrender and turns back to the grill.

I set my chin on his shoulder. "Can I show her the house, Asher?"

"You don't have to ask, sugar bug. Just don't show her my red room." He winks. "It's private."

Snorting, I grab Ali and head inside. As usual, the A/C is cranked high, and cold, masculine-scented air coils around us.

"He doesn't really have a red room, does he?" She gazes up at the vaulted ceilings.

"No. It's green."

Ali offers a sarcastic laugh as she follows me through the modern home. I take her to the garage first so I can snag us some pineapple White Claws.

"Hallelujah." She snaps the tab. "My fave."

"Right? What is even the point of the other flavors?"

"Okay." Ali waves toward the door. "Give me the grand tour."

She oohs and aahs in all the right places, pointing out spots the decor doesn't fit Asher's happy-go-lucky, excited-puppy vibe.

"He had a designer," I whisper when she points in confusion at the trendy metal artwork on the wall in his hallway.

Ali laughs. "Did he tell the designer to make his house look like it belongs to a *GQ* cover boy?"

"I think he told the dude he has a lot of parties and to make it easy to clean."

Ali tiptoes down the hall. "Can I see his bedroom?"

"Sure." I open the correct door and let her in.

"What's this?" Ali takes three steps into the room. "He makes his bed?"

"I know, right? I thought the same thing. But he makes it every day." I sweep a hand down the green comforter, remembering that drunken night we almost ruined everything.

We can't do this.

Still true, years later. Best decision we ever made. But now, thinking about it, I'm . . . antsy? Wait, is that *regret*?

WTF is up with my emotions lately?

When I lift my gaze, Ali is staring at me, eyes narrowed. "What were you thinking about?"

I pull my hand back and clench it into a fist. "Nothing."

"You looked all . . . sad or something." She snaps her fingers. "Melancholy. That's what you looked like."

"I'm fine." I chug a gulp of my pineapple goodness.

Ali's stupidly acute gaze moves from me to Asher's bed, to the door, then back to me. "Jossy, are you suffering *feelings*?"

And there it is.

The *F* word.

My bones turn to ice, and all the organs in my body attempt to skitter away from the cold.

"You know I don't have those." Even to my own ears, the words ring false.

She sets her can down on Asher's dresser and places her hands on her hips. "You're human. I assure you, you do. Even when you ignore them."

No longer steady on my feet, I sink onto the end of the bed. "It's just—the other day, I was teasing him about a girl at work being into him, and suddenly he was hardcore insisting that girls don't think he's a catch, which is just—"

"Idiotic?"

"Yes! Thank you. So, I told him that if I was normal, I'd be all over him, and he said he didn't believe me and thinks one day I'll fall in love, and it will basically fix all my emotional wounds. Then he said he's definitely not that person."

Ali blinks a few times. "So, let me get this straight. He called out how you pretend you have the emotional depth of a teaspoon, then told you he isn't gonna be the one to fix that for you, and that makes you . . . melancholy?"

"I'm not melancholy! That's such a stupid word."

She pulls her face into an I-don't-believe-you sneer.

"It's just . . . later that night, he talked about a lot of stuff that he's never told me before. Like, insecurities I never knew he had, and I started to . . . I don't know. Things are different now."

"I think you've caught feelings."

I scowl at the floor. "Caught them? They aren't contagious. This isn't Covid."

She laughs. "You probably think it's worse than Covid, don't you?"

"It will pass." I look up, desperate for her to agree. "He's my best friend. I can't—"

"Can't what? Take a chance on something?"

"It's not that. We— We're just friends. That's all he wants to be. That's all I want to be."

"Jossy, what do I always say?" She runs her finger along Asher's dresser, then snaps up her drink.

I groan. "Ali—"

She whirls on me. "Ah, ah! What do I say?"

My shoulders fall. *"Nothing is more believable than the lie you tell yourself."*

"Exactly. If you hide your feelings behind friendship, you're lying to him *and* yourself."

I drop my voice to a whisper, suddenly afraid someone else might hear, even though the house is silent. "Maybe it doesn't matter how I feel because he straight up told me he's not my person."

Her dubious expression is on point today. "Aren't you doing engagement photos with him tomorrow?"

"*Fake* engagement photos."

"Eh. I don't know, girl. Kind of seems like there's a chance he's interested. What kind of man would agree to do engagement photos or pay for a trip to Florida with a woman he's not interested in?"

"Asher. *That* kind of man. He'd do anything for his friends. He's not interested in me. Trust me."

That idiotic tugging in my chest won't let up.

Ali shrugs. "You can't know unless you ask."

"I can't do that."

"Why not?"

"Because the last guy I loved died, Ali." The words explode from me, far too loud. "Did you forget about that?"

Her face falls. "Joss, that was sixteen years ago."

"Death is as threatening today as it was sixteen years ago."

She presses her lips together and nods, gazing around the room. "I know that fear. I look at my children's faces every night and imagine all the terrible things that could happen to them. But you have to let someone in eventually, Jocelyn. Closing yourself off doesn't make you safe. It makes you less human."

The sincerity in her expression strikes deep, and I fight the sudden burn in my throat. I look down, willing away the tears.

Ali is the only person in my life who truly understands my abnormal normality. She lived through the trauma right beside me and knows the invisible scars that grief has left. These words are hard-earned lessons she's learned from years of therapy and unconditional love from her husband.

She's further along in her journey to self-healing than I am. I'm not sure I'll ever reach her level.

My phone buzzes, and I pull it from my back pocket. A text from Sue Ellen pops up.

> **Is my son eating enough?**
> **He looks so skinny.**

> I'll feed him a cheeseburger today myself

Mwahaha. Take that, shredded abs.

> **Such a dear. He prefers cheddar.**

> I'll put on two slices

> **Did I mention he took dance classes in high school? He's quite good.**

> Ballroom?

> **Yes. And hop hop.**

> Hip hop?

> **Yes that**

I grin at my phone. Sue Ellen is pure gold. A veritable treasure trove of embarrassing Asher information.

Ali peeks over my shoulder. "Who's Sue Ellen?"

"Asher's mom."

The accusatory tone returns. "You text his *mom*?"

"I will not be judged for this." I glare at her. "Sue Ellen is the tits."

"Oh, girl. He's in there way deeper than I thought, isn't he?"

"Shut up. My walls are higher than ever." Does it matter if he might have—okay, probably has—already tunneled under them?

"Right," she says. "Keep telling yourself that."

Asher

*Sometimes, when we look too hard for something,
we fail to see the things that are right in front of us.*
—My Therapist

I arrive at the field Yayoi specified while Joss and Ali are still in the middle of their shoot. As instructed, I'm wearing light khakis and a white button-up, and I made sure my hair has enough gel to hold that purposely tousled vibe despite the breeze.

All for Yayoi.

Don't care what Joss thinks. The stern talk I had with myself earlier confirmed it. She might have gained some new power over the rhythm of my heart, but she's still just Joss.

We're besties. Nothing more.

As I walk up, Joss spots me first and waves with both

hands. "Damn, Ash! You look good!" she shouts across the distance between us.

Stupid thing in my chest responds uncomfortably to that—*thump, thump, thump.*

Hmm. Maybe care *a little* what Joss thinks. Doesn't matter, though. It will pass.

"You look better," I say and stop beside Yayoi, who has her camera risen.

"And I look better than us all," Ali says, winking.

The heat around us is tempered by a gentle wind and the scent of fresh flowers. In the distance, a family of sparrows lends us some background music.

Dark-haired Ali is clad in a knee-length black number that shows off her shoulders. Blonde Joss has on a white thing with a sheer lace overlay that teases the skin of her abdomen and back.

The effect is charming—opposite in some ways, similar in others.

"Eerie how their smiles are exactly the same, isn't it?" Yayoi says as she snaps a few with the sisters sitting side by side in the grass.

I don't know. Joss's smile seems to contain a fair bit of mischief, while Ali's is happily content. Speaks to their personalities more than anything, though. The two women share a silhouette, a general shape, but other than that, they couldn't be more different.

After a few more poses, Yayoi announces she has what she needs, and the three of them scroll through the shots on the tiny camera screen, oohing and aahing.

"These are going to be great," Ali says, and they all gush over one particular photo.

On the outskirts, I keep my hands in my pockets, the better to hide the telling clamminess going on there. I've been dreading this for days, but I can't articulate why. I'm a bit jittery, like I'm heading into a surgery without knowing the steps. Stupid feeling. Just have to take some pictures. What's so difficult about that?

"All right." Yayoi turns to me in a whirl and rubs her palms together. "Your turn."

Dread, pure and simple, washes over me.

Joss holds out her hand, grinning wickedly. Ah. I've come upon the most familiar version of Joss. Sassy Joss.

"Come on, lover," she says.

Ick.

Don't like that. She's poking at these new secret desires I refuse to give credence. Feels a bit on the nose, even for the universe. But Sassy Joss is on a rampage. I grab her hand and let her lead me into the field of flowers. Golden afternoon sun shines behind us, highlighting her in an angel silhouette. This type of sunlight must be the most romantic or something because Yayoi was *very* specific about the time.

Joss looks pretty in it. Heart-rending, yes, but pretty.

Yayoi holds up her camera, snapping a few shots while we stand side by side, two feet between us. "We'll start with some warm-ups since you guys aren't used to touching so much, okay?"

"Shouldn't be too hard," Joss murmurs.

"That's what she said," I reply out of habit.

Her laugh usually serves to loosen me up, but I can't relieve the tension in my muscles. It pulls at my bones, making my movements awkward and wooden.

"Why don't we start with some easy ones." Yayoi points a little farther down the field. "Go over there, hold hands and just walk toward me, smiling at each other."

We do as instructed. Joss's tiny hand is stiff and swallowed by my clammy one. She grins up at me, clearly trying not to laugh. Even I can tell our smiles are goofy and our body language is weird.

The gnawing starts up in my gut.

Yayoi scrolls through the shots. "Jeez. Either you're extremely un-photogenic or you guys have zero chemistry."

For unknown reasons, I take visceral offense to that. "Maybe this is why engagement photos should be taken for people who are actually engaged."

"Yeah, that!" Joss says, though it's clearly insincere because she's got her fake scowl on, aimed right at Yayoi.

"You're enjoying how awkward this is, aren't you?" I ask.

"It's a little funny, seeing you squirm." She smirks my way. "Where's all that charm now, Foley?"

"What about you? You were perfect with Ali. Now you're all—" I motion a hand up and down her tense body "—edgy."

Her eyebrows fly up. "Am not! You take that back."

"No. If I'm bad, then so are you. We'll be sharing the blame here, lollipop."

Yayoi looks between us, glances at Ali, whose eyes are wide, then clears her throat. "Let's try again."

This time, it's clear a competition has started because she gazes at me all sappily when she takes my hand. Quite hard not to roll my eyes.

Yayoi laughs. "Joss, he's your fiancé, not a basket of puppies."

"Ha!" I point at her as we walk. "Overactor."

She cackles, and so do I, and the camera snaps away. On the next take, she skips like a fool, and on the one after that, I yank her arm when she tries to do the wave with me. Laughing, she stumbles, then decides to leap on my back.

"What is happening right now?" I ask as her arms wrap around my shoulders.

"No, keep it up!" Yayoi says, motioning a big circle with one hand.

I smile at the camera, then mutter, "This is what engaged couples want pictures of?"

Joss is too busy laughing behind me to answer.

"Cute! Okay, let's do the one where you lift her up and her foot is in the air."

Try to picture that in my head. A funky splits-type image pops up and is immediately trashed. "Say what?"

Ali laughs. "Here, I'll help."

She traipses over, instructs me to widen my legs and pick Joss up so her forearms rest on my shoulders. Joss shrieklaughs when I do it, and her fingers naturally thread through the hair at the nape of my neck.

Tingles.

Ignore the tingles.

"Joss, bend one knee and point your toe," Yayoi says, snapping away.

Ah. I get it now. No splits, it seems.

I look up into her eyes as her curled hair falls about her face. "Just so we're both on the same page, I'm currently touching your ass."

She snorts. "What ass?"

Resist the urge to squeeze. "It's definitely there."

"This is incredibly awkward positioning, don't you think? How much you want to bet the picture is straight fire, though?"

Probably, but I'm too focused on the very feminine body pressed against mine to wonder about how it looks or whether it's awkward.

So soft. I always knew she'd be soft.

"Next pose!" Yayoi barks.

Thank you!

I drop Joss at once, trying not to let the slide of her body do any more damage to the *Just Friends* sign flickering inside my mind. It's getting worse, whatever's breaking it. Letting this woman in on my secrets installed something in our friendship that simply doesn't belong.

Wish I could take it back.

Suffering a sense of inevitable doom now. Maybe I'm about to have a heart attack.

Yayoi turns to Ali. "Can we borrow your engagement ring?"

With a sly smile at Joss, Ali slips off her ring and hands it over. Joss slides it on her left hand. Peculiar things happen in my chest at the sight. Did someone turn down the oxygen again?

"Aw, honey." Joss wiggles her finger at me. "You shouldn't have."

"Anything for you, dearest," I force out in a tone that is acceptably jovial.

Yayoi points at the ground. "Sit. We're doing some close-ups."

We sit side by side in a patch of flowers, allowing Yayoi to position us however she wants. My legs are stretched out while Joss's are bent and resting against mine. The skirt of her dress drapes artfully over my khakis. Yayoi sets my hand on Joss's knee, then Joss's ring-laden one over mine.

"Now," Yayoi says. "Just look at each other."

Our bodies turn slightly toward each other, and as soon as our gazes touch, they lock.

The overacting and sarcasm and laughter vanish from her expression, now slightly guarded. Her eyes always remind me of cinnamon—warm and rich. This close, in this light, little slashes of gold and jet emerge.

The effect is quite beautiful.

She is quite beautiful.

And she's wonderful, too. Trustworthy. Loyal.

Funny.

Caring.

She's sort of . . .

"Perfect!" Yayoi says, thankfully ripping through that thought. "Now put your hand on his cheek."

She does.

"No, like you're about to kiss him."

Stomach is gone now. Acid has eaten it away. Whose stupid idea was this?

Joss leans a little closer, her lips bare inches from mine. "I feel like she deserves punishment for this," she whispers, some sort of lemon candy on her breath.

My laughter combines with hers, probably making for a much better picture than the deer-in-headlights I was before.

Click, click, click.

"Now stand up and face each other."

Jeez. Yayoi has gotten really fucking bossy today. Still only inches away, Joss blinks a few times before she obeys, and I follow.

Yayoi adjusts us closer together. "I want to get that *Pride & Prejudice* shot. The sun is perfect now."

I glance at the low-hanging sun, disquiet stealing over me. Isn't *Pride & Prejudice* some powerhouse of romance or some shit? "I don't know what that means."

She stares at me like I'm an idiot. "Foreheads together. Eyes closed. Come on, you know! *Your hands are cold.*"

I look at Joss for help. "Do you know what she's talking about?"

She nods, but before she does anything, her attention strays to Ali. Something unexplainable passes between the sisters, and Ali sends her two thumbs-up. Yayoi thrusts her phone in my face, showing me the pose she wants—a sun-drenched movie scene of two characters obviously in love.

Ha.

This is just . . . torture.

Joss clears her throat and smiles at me—a pinched, artificial smile, like this might be as hard for her as it is for me. Don't know what to make of that. She erases the distance between us, standing close enough that faint traces of her sweet, girly scent snake their way inside. Straight into my bloodstream. Then she sets her ringed hand on my chest, just over my heart.

Not good.

Thump, thump, thump.

Obediently, I drop my forehead to hers like Yayoi wants and lift my hand to her chin. The backs of my fingers barely caress her throat.

Agonizingly soft, she is. Like velvet against my skin.

Urges that don't belong hammer at my nerves. I'm compelled to touch more. Tip her face up. Graze my lips across hers.

It aches, this want. And it's . . . familiar? Has it been here all this time, hiding? Like an old injury I can ignore until the weather acts up?

The camera *clicks, clicks, clicks*.

She draws in a deep breath. Does she need steadying, maybe? Because I'm really fucking unsteady. I'm hovering in a place I've never been, and I'm not sure I want to leave. Rules snap in half as I move against my will. Ever so slowly, I angle my face away from the camera, sliding to the side of hers. I push her hair away from her cheek with my nose and inhale.

Her scent is overpowering. Drugging. Have I ever been this close to it? Hints never picked up before sing across my senses. Indescribable. Sweet.

It all hits me hard. Not like a sledgehammer or freight train. No, it's more precise. An ice pick. A line drive. Striking over and over.

Want her. Want her. Want her.

Forbidden. Forbidden. Forbidden.

Thump, thump, thump.

Click, click, click.

We stand, temple to temple, barely breathing, and her hand against my chest gradually curls into a fist, clenching on the fabric of my shirt.

"This is perfect, you guys. I'm probably pushing my luck here, but how would you feel about a kiss?"

Yayoi's question wrenches me out of this terrible, inappropriate train of thought. Joss and I both turn our heads to stare at her, silent. I can't kiss her. What— Why— What the actual fuck? How could Yayoi even suggest it?

"Yikes," Yayoi says, responding to whatever incredulity must be launching off our faces like laser beams. "Never mind."

Behind her, Ali hides her silent laughter behind her hands.

Joss releases my shirt and backs away, staring hard at Yayoi. "Surely, you have enough."

Yayoi scrolls through her shots, and I do my best not to look at Joss.

Impossible endeavor. I fail utterly. Our eyes meet, dart away, then clash again. We've never been awkward. Not even in our most tricky moments. But we're awkward now.

Makes my soul itch.

"Your sister seems to think this is funny," I say, attempting to inject some levity into the situation.

Joss shoots a death glare at Ali. "My sister is a sadist who enjoys other people's pain, apparently."

That throws me. "Is this . . . painful for you?"

Fuck. I'm over here developing a full-blown crush, and she's in pain?

She does a double take when she looks at me. "No, that's not . . ."

But she trails off and doesn't finish, which leaves a bitter, stinging glaze coating the inside of my body. She stares at the ground, and her throat works with what looks like a fairly agonizing swallow.

I . . . This . . . She . . . Pain?

My previously firm foundation suffers a hairline crack, zigzagging down the middle, and I'm off-kilter. I hadn't even had time to make sense of this infatuation, but the rejection smarts like acid on my skin.

It doesn't matter. Not really. Nothing would have come of it anyway. This is Joss. We're friends.

But . . . friends don't think it's painful when you touch them.

"Just one more," Yayoi says, oblivious. "Head on chest."

Head on—what?

Yayoi motions for me to move. "Hug her, and, Joss, I want you to rest your head and ring hand on his chest."

I force my numb limbs to do as she says, ignoring how perfectly Joss fits against me. My hands land on the small of her waist, my cheek on the top of her head.

Click, click, click.

"I'm sorry," I murmur.

"Sorry for what?" Her tone is soft, if a little hesitant.

"I'm sorry it hurts."

Click, click, click.

Asher

18 MONTHS AGO

The best part of medical conferences is the location.

Jocelyn and I always search for conferences that benefit us both, and only in fun locations. This year's symposium covers OB anesthesia . . . in Vegas.

Joss nudges me as I nod off during the Friday afternoon lecture, and I jerk awake. A couple conference-goers beside me chuckle.

I wipe my face. Damn it. Is that drool?

"This is so boring," I whisper at her. "Can we skip out?"

Jocelyn jots down the lecturer's last pearl of wisdom in her provided workbook. "This could save someone's life someday."

I pull out my phone. "But it may kill me out of sheer boredom."

"Just look at porn or something. Forty-five more minutes."

"Right." I scroll through my Instagram. Must fight the droopy eyes. "Exactly what I need. A stiffy in the middle of this crowd."

Jocelyn laughs as she scribbles another note in her workbook. The lecture room is set up in one of the hotel's event halls, meaning it has excessively busy carpeting and dim, romantic lighting—not conducive to staying alert.

I'll just . . . close my eyes . . . for a second . . .

"Asher."

I startle awake.

Joss leans close to my ear. "If you can stay awake until the end of this lecture, I'll pay for your drinks tonight."

I yawn. "Joke's on you. Drinks are free if you're gambling."

"Then I'll pay for a lap dance."

Skrrrt. What? Did she just say *lap dance*? It snags in my brain, a jagged fingernail catching on satin.

She cocks a smug eyebrow at me. "Just kidding. Awake now?"

My flat stare only makes her laugh.

"Get a man's hopes up only to shoot him down," I say.

She rolls her eyes. "You are *not* a lap dance sort of man."

"I'm not?" Is there any other kind of man?

"You'd have her whole life story and make sure she was up-to-date on her Pap smear before the song was over."

"HPV is no joke, Joss."

With a snort, she returns her attention to the lecture. I continue to stare at her, narrow-eyed. She's wrong. I *am* a lap dance sort of man. The couple I've had were . . . solidly okay.

A little awkward. Expensive. Unsatisfying.

Hold up. Does Jocelyn know me better than I do? I find this annoying. Unsurprising, but annoying.

An hour later, we're exiting boredom hell, and I'm all smiles. I clap my hands together at the edge of the casino floor. "Change, eat, gamble? Eat, change, gamble?"

Joss looks down at her conference clothes and scrunches her face. "Let me change. I look like a librarian."

She kind of does. The kind who gives lap dances. Not the awkward ones, either. Definitely expensive, though.

Will never say this.

Can't even believe I thought it.

Upstairs, it takes five minutes to change into jeans and a short-sleeved button-up with tiny ducks on it. Thirty minutes later, I'm hangry and texting her relentlessly from where I'm stationed against the wall outside her hotel room.

> Are you ready?
>
> I'm near death from starvation.
>
> You are not this high maintenance.
> What's taking so long?
>
> Are you dead?

Would you chill?

I'm coming

Her door swings open, and—

Oh. The reason for the delay.

She's transformed from Tempting Librarian Caterpillar to Glitzy Vegas Butterfly. Her platinum hair is a riot of soft curls. Crystals sparkle at her ears and neck. A long-sleeved, silver-sequined minidress cinches at her waist, the tie hanging down her thigh.

"Damn, girl," I say. "You polish up nice."

She frowns. "Must you make a habit of leaning on walls like that?"

I dart a pointed glance down the empty hallway. "Where else am I supposed to lean? You took for-fucking-ever."

"Never mind." She lifts one foot. "I'm going to regret these heels."

A long expanse of visible leg is wrapped to her knee in silver crisscrosses. The effect is . . . distracting.

"So change," I say.

Deep offense creases her brow. "I can't! I look hot."

"I know." I look her up and down one more time. "People will wonder what you're doing with me."

"Obviously, they'll assume you hired me." She starts down the hall and throws a little wink back at me.

Felt a little flirty. Must be mistaken. Hunger has stolen my common sense.

The evening progresses, and with a belly full of some expensive buffet at the Wynn she just had to try, sound judgment returns. Though that quickly disintegrates when we start drinking.

Intoxicated Joss is unstoppable. She flitters from one slot machine to another, pouring in money and yelling when it gives none back. She stops at a tiny shop along the strip to buy neon-blue boozy slushies that give us both brain freeze. She tries to call the number on the naked lady fliers doled out by every street corner sleazebag.

Can't stop laughing.

Time speeds and lulls. Lights smear. Everything blurs together.

Everything but her.

The luster of her dress. The silvery-white of her hair. The mysterious smile on her lips. She's like a comet among the flashing lights and glittering casinos, leaving a sparkling silver trail everywhere she goes.

I follow blindly. The world around us is filled with people. Dopamine-inducing bells. Distracting electric displays. But she's the most distracting of them all.

Have I ever seen her this happy? Happy Joss is magnificent.

"You're different here," I say in a quieter area of the Cosmopolitan.

She throws her arms in the air, smiling wide. "I'm free."

"Free of what?"

Her smile dims to something secretive. Mysterious. "Free of everything." She clamps both hands on my shoulders, face going drunk-serious. "Because *you* . . . you're the . . . you know . . . like in that movie where the pirates are in prison, and the dog has the key. You're the dog with the key."

Hmm. Should I take offense? "I'm . . . a dog?"

"With a key!" Sounds very important, the way she says it. Must be a crucial detail.

A piece of her hair has stuck to her glossy lips, so I flick it away. "Who locked you up in the first place?"

"The angel of death," she says in a deep, dramatic voice, cracking herself up. She sashays away in a crooked line. I can do nothing but follow. Looks like no more alcohol for me. One of us has to be sober enough to find our hotel at the end of all this.

She runs out of steam earlier than I'd guessed, and we wind up at Eataly, sitting at a bistro table amidst meandering guests and other diners. She demands more wine. I demand she eat something before the alcohol shrivels her up from the inside.

We settle on a fancy cheese board and bread. She's quite

clumsy with the scooping and the bringing food to her mouth without dropping it, so I prepare individual bites for her. Must stop short of physically feeding her, though. Will if I have to. Hope it doesn't get that far.

"This will not be pleasant to throw up later," she slurs, dutifully chewing the bread.

"Don't think about that." I shove another piece of bread into her fingers.

While she eats, I distract myself with my phone, nearly spitting out a mouthful of Gorgonzola and honey when an Insta ad pops up. "Oh, my god. This is perfect."

She leans closer, tumbling slightly so most of her body weight lands on my arm. "What?"

I right her and hand over the phone. "I am so buying you this."

Her head tilts at the picture—a creepy mannequin head sporting a teal scrub cap printed with little pink flowers and the phrase *Don't Be Extra* over and over. She lets out an inelegant, intoxicated snort. "You are so extra."

Except it sounds like *You er show straw* and that's how I know it's time to leave.

"All right, baby girl. Time for bed."

"What? No! The night is young." She throws out her arms, nearly smacking a dude walking by in the process.

I haul her into a standing position. "The night is young, but *you* are wasted. Sleep it off, and we'll try again tomorrow."

I really should have thought through this drunken trek we made across the strip. Now I'm stuck with a half-conscious female a million hotels away from where I need to be. People will think I'm a date rapist with atrocious planning skills.

"Joss, I need you to walk."

She tries, bless her. She fails miserably. I catch her as she stumbles into a display of Italian bread. A couple nearby shoots her death glares.

Must not strangle strangers. Not good form.

But Joss straightens her shoulders and tries again.

Determined, inebriated woman.

"It's these damn shoes," she says when she stumbles again.

"It's not the shoes. It's your ethanol-soaked cerebellum."

She looks up at me with the most pitiful eyes. "Help."

In the end, I order a rideshare. It's that or bridal-carry her two miles over crowd-thickened sidewalks. Bad enough I have to schlep her drunk ass to her room from the car.

She leans against the wall beside her hotel door. "I think I drank too much."

I search her purse for her hotel key. "You think? What was your first clue?"

Lip gloss. Cash. Driver's license. Receipts. Wait, is that . . . a condom? Just to be sure, I pull it out, still too tipsy to understand the massive mistake that is.

She catches me eyeing it and snatches it from my hand. "That's—not yours."

I laugh. "Definitely not mine."

"Not meant for you, either."

"Wasn't thinking that." Aha. Hotel key.

She grabs her purse as soon as I've got the door open. Cold, hotel-scented air wafts toward us.

"I wasn't going to use it," she says.

"Okay." I motion her to go inside.

She trips into the room. "Just like to be prepared."

"I don't need an explanation."

It didn't even occur to me to bring condoms. Figured I'd be with her the whole time. But now I'm thinking I'm naive and shortsighted. If she was planning to hook up with someone, then so could I.

But . . . I sort of hate one-night stands. Lots of work. Reward is nice when it works out, though, even if short-lived. Who doesn't love an orgasm they didn't give themself?

Joss lets out a dramatic hiccup, derailing that thought. "I'm not a slut. Like, I know that women can do what they want, and fight the power, and blah, blah, but it's still so stigma-shtig-stigmizing, you know? To be that girl who—" her arms do this weird circular motion, like she's weaving a spell "—sleeps around."

She falls onto the center of the unmade king bed, fully clothed. Her librarian outfit from earlier is tossed across the end of it while her open suitcase has thrown up in one corner of the room.

I set her purse beside the TV. "I don't think you're a slut."

"And I don't care what the rest of them think," she slurs as if I didn't speak. "Or . . . maybe I do a little bit." She squeezes her thumb and forefinger together and squints through the tiny gap. "Teensy, wittle, tiny bit."

With a laugh, I untie the bow of one silver snake shoe. "That much, huh?"

"But you!" She flings her arms as wide as they'll go. "I care about what you think a whole, whole lot."

"You do?" I strip off her shoe and attack the other one. "Why?"

Her eyes fall closed. "'Cause you know me. And you, like, are deep in here—" she presses a hand over her heart "—where really important people live. So if you thought bad things about me, I'd be sad."

My next few heartbeats grow a little painful. Her unguarded expression, makeup-smeared face . . . They undo me. She never talks about this stuff. *Never.*

Shouldn't take advantage of her disinhibition, honestly,

but I'm *dying* to know why. Why did she allow me in this coveted place when she never lets people close?

Why is she scared to love?

Why does she sleep around, then vilify herself for it? Because a person who's 100 percent okay with their decisions doesn't worry if other people are judging those decisions unless *they're* judging those decisions, too.

What happened to make her wall herself off from everyone?

Shoeless, she curls up on her side, and I pull the covers over her.

"I don't think bad things about you," I say. "Ever."

Eyes closed, she smiles. "Good. You're the best friend I ever had."

"I'm going to my room to get you nausea meds, okay?"

Her smile grows. "See? This is why you're irreplaceable."

I pause at the end of her bed. Irreplaceable?

"Didn't realize until it was too late," she continues, half asleep. "Snuck inside. Got important. It's not fair. People are impossible to replace when lost."

"You won't lose me," I say so quietly I'm not sure she even heard it.

She releases a loud exhale. "Yes, I will. I lose everyone."

Jocelyn

Emotions aren't things you should crush
or try to change. They're communications
from deep within. Listen to them.
—My Therapist

OB call is the worst.

I'm already annoyed because my sister left today and I have no idea when I'll see her again, and now I'm stuck at the hospital until this woman delivers. She's been eight centimeters for ten hours, and she's adamantly refusing a Cesarean—despite that it was recommended four hours ago—*and* Pitocin—the only medication that could help her deliver vaginally.

It will give you adequate contractions.
It will progress your labor faster.
It will get a living, breathing baby in your arms.

But no. She's stuck on this idea that Pitocin is straight up devilry created by hospitals to disempower women or some shit. Somewhere, someone convinced her that *natural* is the only real way to have a baby, and women who do it differently are a weaker subset of the species. Her birth plan doesn't allow for any medications or pain relief, and it ends with an all capitals command:

DO NOT EVEN MENTION A C-SECTION TO ME. I WILL REFUSE.

The nurses say she fired her OB when he proposed it earlier. Now the hospitalist is caring for her.

Or attempting to, at least.

We should have a bucket of fortune cookies at the entrance to L&D, and all the fortunes say the same thing: You don't get points for doing it the hardest way imaginable.

If this woman broke her leg and her femur was sticking out of her body, would she want to heal naturally? If she contracted a flesh-eating bacteria and her skin melted off her body, would she decide to deal with that naturally?

It's natural to die. Does she realize that?

All of that only means one thing. At some point, her baby is going to crash and this will become an emergency, so I'm spending the night at the hospital tonight, and I want to stab knives into the walls. At least the cafeteria is open. I can drown my irritation in French fries and Tropical Vibe Celsius.

I'm halfway there, taking the shortcut through the busy emergency department, when a desperate voice shouts for help from one of the trauma rooms. An entire battalion of nurses and doctors darts inside, and I peek through the glass at a bloody mess of a man lying on the table. The monitors above him show his vital signs just fell to the floor.

A woman stands beside him, holding his limp hand

while screaming for answers—*"What happened? Why isn't he breathing?"*

Someone gently shoves her to the side to make room, and the professionals take control—doing chest compressions, shouting for meds. They run the code with cold perfection, because they've done it many, many times before this. Because this is the emergency department, and sometimes people don't make it out of here alive.

But I'm not watching the code. I've seen people die. I've performed those compressions myself. No, instead, my entire focus is zeroed in on the woman. Her tears. Her disbelieving cries of *"He was fine!"* I'm watching her hope dwindle with each minute that passes, as the odds of this man surviving grow dimmer. I'm beholding the exact moment she realizes she's lost something precious tonight. I'm witnessing her soul be shorn in half.

This is the picture of heartbreak.

And I can't watch anymore.

No longer hungry, I head blindly back upstairs. My skin tingles as memories rush beneath the surface despite my attempts to push them away.

Icy skin.

A fall beneath a roiling flood.

Laughter I'll never hear again.

A panicky gush of cold rises up, and I'm tempted to retreat to the hill in my mind, where I'm always safe and alone. Better to be alone than hurt. Why have I been forgetting this lately?

Proceeding gracefully—i.e. stomping—toward my call room, I smile at the night nurses before throwing myself onto the rickety, uncomfortable bed. At least these call room TVs have HGTV. I can continue my nighttime research on the mystery of how an elementary school teacher and a professional organizer can afford a 1.3-million-dollar home.

Lights off, I curl up under the thin blankets that keep my feet too warm and the rest of me too cold, and resign myself to misery. But as soon as I'm idle, my mind dredges up the memories of that photoshoot, just like it's done during every second of downtime since it happened.

Goddamn traitor, my mind is.

I *knew* that photoshoot was a bad idea. Before, how it feels to be held by Asher was a mystery to me. A faraway imagining. Now my stupid fantasies are on overdrive, flaunting the exact degree of warmth in his hands, the thin band of green that disappears when his eyes dilate, the absolute safety of his arms around me.

False safety, I have to remind myself, remembering the heartbreak I just witnessed downstairs.

This is Asher's fault for opening up to me. Deep down inside, I *am* female, and he plucked right at those very feminine instincts, the ones that urge me to nurture. I want to nurture the shit out of that man. And I sort of want to fuck him, too.

But I also want to toss him out of my safe space. He doesn't belong behind my walls. With him there, that mystery pain has taken up permanent residence in my chest, tugging, tugging, tugging. All the staring into his eyes and suffering the wonder of his skin against mine makes the pain worse.

I think Ali's right. I've caught feelings, and I need a cure. Fast. They aren't worth the risk.

I retreat to the lonely hill in my mind, searching for serenity. It doesn't work. My phone provides little distraction, but I try anyway. The hospital has sent *another* mass email to all physicians regarding optional Dragon training. This is, what? Email number forty-seven?

What *exactly* is the point of this?

"If I wanted it, I would have let you know by now," I mutter to the empty room. I start to delete it, then pause when a familiar name catches my eye. Asher has Reply All-ed to the email.

> Two very quick questions:
>
> #1 Will the dragons be provided by the hospital?
>
> #2 What kind of dragons will we be training?
>
> If they are provided, I would like to train the following kind—

A picture of Toothless from *How to Train Your Dragon* is attached in the body of the message. He closes the email with a professional, *Thanks, Asher Foley, MD.*

I am *dying*.

He sent this to the entire medical staff? I snap a screenshot and send it in a group text to Asher, Geoff and Yayoi.

> **Asher:** I know
>
> **Asher:** But listen
>
> **Asher:** I'm so sick of Dragon training emails
>
> **Asher:** I got desperate
>
> **Yayoi:** omg who all is CC'ed on that?
>
> **Geoff:** Basically the whole hospital
>
> **Yayoi:** Haha. You trying to get fired?
>
> **Asher:** I'm trying to improve my wellness.

I sigh at the last one. I don't know why my phone still does that, but at this point, my friends know it's a typo.

Asher: Titties? Where??

Very funny

Still giggling, I turn my attention to the TV. Halfway into a rerun of *House Hunters*, a red light on the ceiling distracts me.

I sit up and stare at it. The device is small. Round. Black. The red light gleams, pointing right at me.

Is that . . . a camera?

My mind blanks. How long has that been there? In my call room? Where I binge trash TV?

I scramble out of bed and hightail it down the hallway. The break room oozes the scent of hazelnut coffee, and a couple of nurses eat snacks at the large center table. They look up at my entrance, eyes going wide at my likely frazzled appearance. Luckily, I recognize them.

Charice and Preeti.

I brace my weight on the table. "Did they install cameras in the call rooms?"

Charice glances at Preeti. "I don't know. Isn't that illegal?"

"There's a camera in the anesthesia call room."

"What?" Preeti stands. "No way."

Both women follow me back to the room in question, where I point at the device on the ceiling.

Charice gasps. "I'm checking the locker room." She flees down the hall while Preeti whips out her hospital phone.

"Who are you calling?" I ask.

"Charge."

Right. The charge nurse always knows what to do. Charge nurses are like magicians, only their magic is real.

"Candi," Preeti says into the phone. "Can you meet me in the anesthesia call room? I have something you need to see." She hangs up and pockets the phone, then stares up at the camera, narrow-eyed.

Charice returns in short order. "No cameras in the locker room."

"This is . . . weird," Preeti says.

Candi's taken aback when she enters, pausing to eye each of us in turn. "What's going on?"

All three of us point at the camera, and Candi's eyes follow. When her gaze lands on the device, she scowls. "What the actual fuck?"

I throw both arms out toward her, palms up. "That's what I said!"

Candi pulls out her phone.

"Who are you calling?" Preeti asks.

"Security."

Yeah. That makes sense. Get 'em, Candi. Find out who the hell thinks they can spy on me while I'm lusting after TV homes? This is unconscionable.

The three of us dive deep into conspiracy theories while we wait for the security team, each of them more ridiculous than the last. The leading hypothesis is that it was placed by mistake.

Because, just . . . Why?

I glare at the offending red light.

This can't be real. Something is up.

Two pudgy men arrive after a full quarter hour, and I thank the Powers That Be that this wasn't a real emergency.

Pudgy Man Number One squares his shoulders. "What's the problem, ladies?"

Candi points up. "Is this a hospital camera?"

Pudgy Man Number Two squints at the device. "Uh—"

"That doesn't look like one of ours," says PMN1.

PMN2 looks around the space. "Isn't this a private sleeping area?"

I flap my hands about the room, pointing at the bed, the pillow, the piles of scrubs. "Yes!"

PMN1 stands tall, puffing his cheeks out. "It's illegal to place recording devices in places where there is a reasonable expectation of privacy."

Candi stares at the man, her mouth a flat line. "Thanks for the mansplaining. We are aware it's illegal. That's why we called you. Can you please remove it?"

PMN2 shakes his head. "Can't touch it. It's not hospital property."

Preeti choke-laughs. "You're kidding—"

"Nope." PMN1 rocks on his heels. "Not our jurisdiction. But we can call the police, and they'll take care of it."

By now, we've attracted a crowd, and the hallway behind the pudgy twins is clogged with curious nurses.

"Oh, for the love of—" I wave toward the nurses in the hallway. "Someone get me a chair." As an afterthought, I shout, "Please!"

A wonderful nurse named Sarai carries one of the break room chairs down the hall, and I climb atop it, Charice and Candi spotting me. Neither security guard moves to help.

Thanks for the help, fellas.

The plastic of the device is cold as I slide my fingers around it, searching for a button or a release. My fingernails hook behind the groove where it meets the wall, and . . . it loosens?

I yank. The device detaches and falls into my hands. Three two-way tape strips line the back of it.

It isn't wired in? What on earth? I shake it—isn't this too

light to be a camera? The base of it is plain black plastic with a covered battery compartment.

I turn it over. "What the—"

"What's wrong?" Candi asks.

A small square of paper is taped to the back. I peel it off to find a note on the other side.

Gotcha.
A.F.

My hand clenches around the plastic and I laugh. "That motherfucker."

Charice reaches for the note. "What is it?"

"It's a fake camera." I hand it to Candi. "From Foley."

Charice takes the note and a fit of giggles overtakes her. "Doctor Foley?"

Whispers spread down the hallway.

"Doctor Foley?" PMN1 straightens. "Do we need to report him?"

Candi glares at him. "Don't even think about it. We're no longer in need of your services. Thank you."

Preeti helps me from the chair while the security guards wind through the maze of nurses in the hall, seemingly glad to be rid of us.

"Doctor Foley did this?" one asks. "I just love him."

"He is so funny," says another.

"Yeah, so funny." I roll my eyes. "I'm cracking up."

Even no-nonsense Candi is laughing. "Oh, that man. If I wasn't married . . ."

Yeah, yeah. We're well aware of his fuckability. No need to remind us. I snatch the note back from Charice and grab my phone to take a picture. I send it to him even though it's the middle of the night and he's probably asleep.

> You.
>
> How dare you?

Surprisingly, the three dots appear almost at once.

Sounds like you probably deserved it.

For making people think they left instruments inside other people or something.

> I will pay you back for this.

I am still the reigning king. Pay homage at my throne.

> I had security up here and everything!

😌

> I hate you.

He sends a picture of his puppy-dog face, and I melt immediately. He's so frickin' cute.

Tug!

> Why are you even awake?

Masturbating

I snort, but that single word conjures up images of naked Asher—not something that will help this pain in my chest go away.

> Ew. Don't be extra.

Can't sleep.

> Probably a guilty conscience
> for doing evil things.

**Guilty conscience for
something, that's for sure.**

Hmm. Wonder what he means by that.
"Doctor Mattox," says a nurse at the end of the hall.
"Yeah?"
"Room nine has agreed to a section."
I chuckle. "But that's not natural!"
She shrugs. "I think she's decided modern medicine might benefit her."

> I have to go, but you watch
> yourself. I'm coming for you.

His last text of the night is the meme of Homer disappearing into the hedge. I release a soft laugh, then scroll up to his puppy-dog face, losing myself for a moment. The pain deep in my chest tugs a bit harder than normal, and I shove my phone into my pocket. Out of sight, out of mind.

But the softness of his voice floats back to me. My head resting on his heart, camera clicking, he spoke the words just for me, like he knew how overwhelmed I was standing in his arms. Like he understood my confusion in wanting to stay there.

I'm sorry it hurts.
Yeah.
I'm sorry, too.

Asher

When you don't know what to do, do nothing.
—My Therapist

In the dictation room in late July, I hide at the corner desktop, completing my morning charts while the nurses at the other computers chat. Vaguely registering some conversation regarding the bonuses offered to nurses who work an extra shift per week, I hunch my shoulders and power through labs and notes, checking my watch to be sure I'll make it to the OR on time.

Eight minutes until my C-section.

I got this.

"You ready to go back?" Jocelyn whispers near my ear. "The patient's good."

"Yeah, let's do it."

I follow her with my eyes trained on the back of her head.

Won't look elsewhere. The only way to rid myself of this ill-advised crush is to starve it. Friends don't admire other friends' asses, and they can't admire anything if they never look.

Joss equals friend. Nothing more. I've had to remind myself of that far too many times since the photoshoot. The one where posing with me in lovey-dovey pictures was so repulsive it caused her pain.

Won't think about that. Hurts a little too much.

The C-section goes well, and when the baby is shown to my patient, Malika, she coos, "Aw, honey. He has your nose!"

But about forty-five seconds later, she has a bit of a panic attack—a reasonable reaction to being tied to a bed and cut open—and Joss gives her some cocktail of drugs to calm her down so I can finish the operation.

As soon as I'm finished, I receive a page that my laboring patient is ready to push. Yenisley speaks English as if she was born to it, even though she wasn't. Only the slightest accent colors her fluent speech. Despite that, her nurse continues to communicate with her in extremely broken Spanish.

"Dolor mucho?" the nurse asks.

Jeez, Carol. Let's try indoor voices.

"No, it's okay," Yenisley answers with a strained smile.

With no epidural, she's likely in a shitload of pain, but she's stoic and endlessly sweet. Sweat dampens her brow. Her dark hair frizzes about her face. Between each contraction, she closes her eyes and focuses on controlled breathing.

She's a pro.

She whimpers the slightest bit when the next contraction builds. The father helps support one leg while Carol holds the other.

I grab a blue towel to prepare. "All right, Yenisley. You got this. Let's push."

The baby's head descends with each push, and the nurse pats Yenisley's knee in excitement. "That's it! *Puta! Puta!*"

My body stiffens. I don't speak Spanish, but I live in Texas. Even I know enough Spanish to know that *puta* does not mean *push*.

It means . . . bad things.

Yenisley's eyes widen at me, and the dad sputters, "What did she say?"

"She means *empuje*," I whisper.

From the back of the room, the patient's mother cackles in laughter. *"Gringa tonta!"*

Carol's face floods with red.

I shake my head and laugh while I encourage her, "Come on, Yenisley, push!"

A squealing baby slides out, squished and stunned, but cute despite that.

As I'm finishing up the repair, the dad slaps his hand on my shoulder. "Thanks, Doc. I have to say, I wasn't too sure when Yenisley picked you, but you've been awesome."

My gut reaction is to brush it off—after all, I did what any doctor would do under the same circumstances—but then I stop myself. Can't keep succumbing to these pathologic thought processes. I allow myself a moment to truly consider what he said.

You've been awesome.

And hang on. Is that—pride? In my chest?

I shoot him a smile. "It's my pleasure. Congratulations."

This is what Joss meant about mental snapshots. *Every good thing that happens to you—snapshot.*

The doting parents pay me no mind as I finish and clean up. With a quick congratulations, I slip out of the room to check on my C-section patient.

On the way, I pass Dr. Isaacs—a well-respected

urogynecologist—walking with Dr. White. I lift my chin in greeting. Isaacs either doesn't see me or he's an asshole because he walks by without even looking my way. *Dr. Dillhole.* Dr. White, however, slows to talk to me, and I inwardly cringe. This man should be my mentor, but instead he's a thing I have to endure. His wrinkled face always cracks into a smile like I'm his buddy, but he treats me like a naughty child.

"You hear that Murphy got herself knocked up?" he asks, referring to one of our female call partners.

I'd heard mutterings that Dr. Murphy and her husband were trying, but not that they were successful. "Really? That's great!"

He subtly rolls his eyes. "Yeah, great we'll be taking her call while she's on vacation."

I pause. Is maternity leave a vacation, though?

"She's the feely-good emotional type." He titters. "Her patients'll love you. Probably be flocking to you when she's out."

Because I'm also the feely-good emotional type? How am I supposed to take this? I settle on a laugh. "Yeah . . ."

"Lucky you, eh?" He claps me on the shoulder and walks away, chuckling.

The lead vest of inadequacy settles over me. Tums. Where did I leave them?

Wait, no. I force myself to channel Joss-energy. This doesn't matter. Let it roll off. No snapshot here.

In the post-anesthesia unit, Malika's just coming to. "Malika, can you hear me?" Jocelyn asks her.

"Stop yelling!" Malika shouts and thrashes in the bed.

"Okay," Joss says in a quieter voice. "You're in the hospital."

"I know that, bitch!" Malika's eyes open and she yanks at

the wires connecting her to the monitors before the nurses stop her. "Get your hands off me!"

Whoa. What the hell? Malika's combative while the dad stands off to the side, wide-eyed with a bundled baby in hand.

"Malika, it's Doctor Foley." I touch her ankle over the blanket. "You had a beautiful baby boy."

"Yeah, with a big fucking nose!" she snaps.

"Ha!" Jocelyn squawks before throwing a hand over her mouth. "I mean—" She gives a fake and halfhearted gasp.

I can't stop myself from snorting. She's a terrible actress. "What's going on?"

She leans closer and whispers, "Ketamine makes you mean. And honest."

The father looks half scared, half concerned. "Is she okay?"

Joss nods. "She's fine. It's the anesthesia. Give her a minute."

After a few more outbursts, Malika calms enough that she asks to hold her baby. A smile erases the angry lines on her forehead. "Such a sweet baby." She turns to me, still mostly drugged. "You are the best. Look what you gave me."

Did we all hear that? I'm the best. *The best.*

Another snapshot.

"Nah." I jiggle her shoulder. "You did all the work."

Feels good. Really good. Mood has moved solidly to the *terrific* range. As I leave Joss to finish up, I chuckle to myself. Two in one day. Who'd have thought? I'm halfway to the elevator when that resident, Gabriela, hurries up to me.

"Doctor Foley," she says. "Before you leave, one of your patients is in triage. Twenty-seven weeks, and . . . well, she has a bar of soap stuck in her vagina."

My steps falter, and I turn to look at her. No way did I hear that correctly. "What?"

Gabriela's apple cheeks bunch with her smile. "I know it's ludicrous, but I can't get it out. It keeps breaking apart."

I'll definitely be late, but this I have to see. I spin on my heel and follow her to the triage bay. When we enter the room, the patient hides her face behind her hands. "Oh, my god. I'm so embarrassed."

I sit in the chair at her bedside. "What happened, Leah?"

She peeks out from between her fingers. "It's getting so hard to clean down there! I couldn't see, and I guess I got too aggressive?"

"Too aggressive?"

She throws her hands in the air. "It just got sucked up there."

"What did?"

With a building giggle, she places one hand over her eyes. "A bar of Irish Spring."

A bar of Irish Spring. Sucked up into her vagina. What kind of turbo suction does she got on that thing? It takes everything—*everything*—in me not to laugh with her. "Okay. Let's see what we can do."

With Gabriela beside me, we try everything. Everything. All I manage to do is create a giant soapy mess between her legs. Eventually, the patient disintegrates into laughter so hard, it's silent. And that—full-on belly laughter—is what finally pushes everything out of her vagina.

"Hey, look!" I say as it plops into the bucket beneath the bed. "It's a girl."

Eyes glistening with elated tears, Leah meets my gaze. "I can't tell you how glad I am that you're my doctor right now. Can you imagine if that had been Doctor White?"

Dr. White. The guy Mrs. Mulaney trusted more than me to help her pee. The guy who refused to assist me with my difficult C-section. The guy who low-key gaslights me into thinking I'm a bad doctor.

Welp. Score's even, bucko. And *that's* another snapshot.

I am totally winning today.

"I didn't really do anything," I say. "Should I be cliché and say that laughter is clearly the best medicine?"

It's not even funny, but I think Leah is beyond that now. The laughter has invaded her entire person. Her continued apologies slur around giggles.

"You're fine," I say as I wash my hands, joining in her amusement. "That isn't even the weirdest thing I've pulled from a vagina."

"Oh, god. Don't tell me. I don't want to know."

She really doesn't.

"Well, that was an adventure," Gabriela says afterward.

I chuckle-nod while texting my temporary MA.

> Will be super late to office today
>
> Vagina emergency

> Thanks

Sigh. Miss Talia. Her replacement is boring.

Settling at a computer in the empty dictation room, I tap my badge to unlock LEGENDARY. Gabriela sits at the computer next to me. The hair on the back of my neck rises, and I glance over my shoulder. No one's there, but I do a double take at Gabriela, who's making eyes at me.

She gives me a tentative smile. "Your patients adore you."

They do. I've always known this. Just . . . forgot. So maybe it's okay that I bring a little more fun to the whole endeavor. The serious ones can find a different doctor.

Wish they didn't feel like they had to, though.

I shake my head at Gabriela because owning praise always feels weird. "Nah. She was just glad she didn't have to do that in front of any of my awkward partners."

"And humble, too." She rubs her teeth along her bottom lip. "You— Doctor Foley, would you like to go to dinner with me this weekend?"

Ah. Okay. Deflect.

"Yeah, girl." I give her my biggest grin. "Let's get some folks together."

"No." She turns to face me, hands clasped tight in her lap. "I meant just you and me."

My smile dims. "Oh. Um—"

"I thought— I thought maybe you had a girlfriend, but I heard you don't, and—" She takes a breath. "I know others have asked, and you always make it a group thing, but I'm interested in having dinner with you. Just you. I think we could be . . . good."

She really thinks that? Why? No, it doesn't matter why. I work with her, which means it's a no.

I lower my voice. "You're a resident."

"It's not against the rules, Doctor Foley."

I spin my chair and take her hand. "You aren't even comfortable enough with me to call me by my first name. You barely know me."

"Asher." She swallows. "I know you're kind. Funny. I know the way you are with your patients. I know you're generous with your friends. I know enough to know that I want to know more. If you're interested."

Her bravery finally fails, and her dark-eyed gaze drops to my knees. Lustrous black hair falls around her face.

She's quite pretty. I've tried not to notice this when we work together, but it's glaringly obvious right now, especially with the blooming rosiness in her cheeks. For a split second, the memory of Jocelyn gazing up at me in that field of flowers flashes before my eyes, ringing like a gong in my head. She was devastating in that white dress.

Just a friend, though. She doesn't matter.

Gabriela, on the other hand, is interested. So . . . now what? Say we go on a few dates. I find her charming and lovely and decide she's everything I've ever wanted. She likes me for a little bit, then decides I'm not serious boyfriend material and dumps me for Dr. Dillhole down the hall.

Then we have to see each other every single day. Ugh. Been there, done that. Won't do it again.

I squeeze Gabriela's hand. "It's not that I'm not interested. There's a reason I always make it a group thing. I have my own rules about dating coworkers, Gabriela."

Her gaze shoots up to mine. "Really?"

I nod. "I don't date at work."

"Right." She spins back to the computer, eyes bright. "Sorry I asked."

And I'm an asshole. She offers something real—exactly what I'm searching for—and I say no. Why? Because I work with her? Is that stupid?

I reach for her but stop short of touching her. "No—you don't—"

"Doctor Foley?" Jocelyn says from the doorway. "Can I talk to you about your patient?"

Huh?

She motions with her head, so I follow her toward the OR. "What's up?" I ask.

She says nothing until we're alone inside the double doors of the sub-sterile OR hallway, the antiseptic stench of chlorhexidine wafting around us. "You were about to make it worse."

Um. "You heard that?"

She nibbles her lip. "I—might have been eavesdropping a little bit."

"Ugh." I fall backward against a wall and scrub my face. Gnawing stomach pain returns. "Awkward. I'm such an asshole."

"You're not, but you were about to start qualifying, and that would've only made her feel worse."

"Is it a stupid rule?" I drop my hands. "She said all the right things. Is it dumb to say no just because we work together?"

"I—I don't know, Ash. Dating coworkers can be tricky . . ."

"But am I shooting myself in the foot?" I dig my hand into my hair and pull tight. "I'm *so tired* of being alone."

Funny how easy it is to say to her now. The first time, here in this same hallway a few weeks ago, it stung like ripping barbed wire out of my skin. Now it's freeing. Joss is the best sounding board ever.

But she's got her fingers on her angel wing earring, fidgeting. Have I upset her?

"I—I don't know if I'm the best person to answer that question," she says.

"Why?" I push off the wall. "You know me best. I want something real. Am I stupid to limit myself?"

Her gaze touches on me, then flits away. "I don't know. Maybe?"

"But not definitely?"

"I don't know how it will turn out, Ash." She paces away from me. "And it's hard for me to put it in perspective. Relationships terrify me. The potential pain outweighs any good. But you—you're not like me. You have to weigh the risk yourself."

It takes me a moment to decrypt those words, but I snag on a single part. "Potential pain?"

She grips her elbows, and in that moment she looks so small. So brittle. I've never met Brittle Joss. I didn't know she even existed.

"Yes, *pain*." Her voice wavers as she speaks, like the words are hard to say. "Okay. I'm going to tell you something about me that I don't ever talk about."

Curiosity rages to life. Is she about to tell me the deep, dark thing? Here in this sterile hallway?

"There is a reason I don't get close to people, Asher. The truth is, I'm terrified of loss. I've lost so many people, and I live in *constant* fear of someone else I love dying. To me, any human relationship just provides more opportunity for pain. It's why I try not to love people. Death is uncontrollable and it *tortures* the living."

Whoa. Torture?

"Joss—"

My voice echoes against the tile, but I'm unsure how to continue. I mean, I know she lost her parents and brother, but she's definitely not told me about every person she's buried. This is way more profound than I thought. Ali is likely the only one who knows the full story. But Joss never shows it. Never talks about it. Any quips she makes are succinct, the subject rapidly changed.

I'm damaged.

I had a nightmare.

I like to play chicken with my fears.

I lose everyone.

Life's short and everybody dies.

It makes sense that she'd have trouble strengthening ties out of fear of loss, but this . . . This has affected her deeply.

Intensely. The evasion from intimacy, the elusion of attachment, the habit of shifting the conversation if it ever drifts too deep. This is the reason, isn't it? Somewhere down in my gut, the realization hurts. Not acid this time. Ice.

"So I can't be the one to answer these questions for you," she says. "My perspective is too fucked up."

I almost laugh because *fucked up* is such a mild way to describe it. But I don't laugh because, right now, laughter would be cruel, and even I can rein it in when I need to. "So, you'll just never love anyone ever again because they might die?"

She covers up her wince with an absurd chuckle. "Pretty much. Sounds weird when you say it like that, though."

"Jocelyn—"

"The last guy I was in love with died." She hugs herself tighter. "So yeah. Relationships and I are— I think I'm cursed."

Her last boyfriend *died*? Jesus, no wonder she's so guarded. This is definitely the deep, dark thing. She practically shrinks on herself talking about it. Look how fragile she's become.

But just because something's fragile doesn't mean it will break. She's let fear drive her existence since her parents died. If she can force me to face my demons, then I can do the same for her.

Though I think this might take some finesse.

"You are definitely *not* cursed," I say. "And if you are, I'll break it. I'm a superb curse breaker. Best of the best."

She snorts and wipes her face, where a lone tear has fallen. I hate that tear. Want to do bad things to these beliefs of hers that caused it. I wonder if this is how she felt that night I spilled all my worst beliefs over FaceTime.

"You could probably charm a curse away," she says.

"Probably." I take a couple steps closer to her. "So . . . what you're saying is, on the off chance that Gabriela dies someday, I should definitely not go out with her."

With a small grimace, she shakes her head. "That's idiotic, isn't it?"

"A little, yeah. You should really think about that, Joss. For yourself." I dip my head, trying to catch her attention, but she won't look at me.

She stares around us—at the sterile white walls, the silver scrub sinks, the empty ORs. "We have got to stop having these serious conversations in here."

I smile. "What, the sterile ambiance doesn't do it for you?"

She lets out a small laugh, then sobers. "Sorry. I don't know how I made this about me."

"You didn't—"

But she interrupts before I can continue. "I think the only way to not be alone is to just . . . do it, Asher. So maybe you should take the opportunities presented to you and not worry so much about whether they come at work or somewhere else. If you don't want to be alone, then take the risk. If the risk outweighs the benefit, then don't do it. And if you choose not to try with her, then at least you have another snapshot for your collection—she is a girl who's taking you seriously. Either way, you're winning. And you're definitely braver than I am."

Aw.

For someone with such a cynical outlook, she's great at finding the silver lining. But her guarded stance . . . that single tear . . . the little hitch in her breath . . . Everything about her is screaming *Give me comfort!*

Adorable, nonsensical woman.

Despite my misgivings, the crush rears its head. I'll have

to smash it back down later, but I can't think about that right now. My problems disappear into the background. "I'll contemplate Gabriela's risk-reward ratio some other time. You—you need a hug, Joss." I open my arms. "Can I?"

She huffs and stamps her foot in a *What took you so long?* gesture. Her expression crumbles, and in a single instant, she's crying. "Duh. Yes, please."

Her tiny arms slide around my waist, and her face rests against my chest, mascara-laden tears soaking into my scrub top. My chin fits over the top of her head.

So tiny.

So sad.

Girl needs a day off and a bubble bath or something.

"I'm sorry I keep making you cry," I say.

"Why are you so mean?" she teases, but the jest loses its effect when her voice trembles around the words. More quietly, she adds, "It's not you. I just don't like talking about this."

"Hmm." I squeeze tight. "Subject change?"

"Yes, please."

I reach for something else—*anything* else—and come up with, "So was I super awkward when I turned her down?"

Her breathy laughter warms my chest. "No. You were sweet about it, as usual. But the qualifying . . . Bro, that's a bad look."

"Almost as bad as *any girl would be lucky to have you*, right?"

She smacks my back. "Shut up." Her pager dings, and she pulls away. "Sorry. I'm supposed to relieve Kevin for lunch."

"Lunch?" I check my phone. "It's only ten twenty-four."

She shrugs and wipes her face. "Rolling lunches. The OR stops for no man."

"You're still riding with me to Yayoi's birthday dinner, yeah?"

She nods.

I touch her soft, soft cheek. "You going to be okay?"

Her grin is forced, but at least it exists. "I always am."

•

YAYOI'S BIRTHDAY IS always the one we celebrate the quietest. She doesn't like big parties or large crowds or attention in general. Honestly, getting her out for an early four-person dinner is about as wild as she's willing to get.

After abandoning my scrubs for the less comfortable street clothes I brought to work, I head out to the parking lot. Jocelyn is already leaning on my truck, mint-colored dress sifting in the breeze. Wonder if she's moved past our little blip in the sterile hallway. Should I bring it up? Gloss over it? Let her lead the way?

Her attention is riveted to her phone. Probably planning another hookup. Don't love the way that feels like fishing hooks between my ribs. Ignore, ignore, ignore.

I parked by the pond. Always do—because ducks. And I'm not disappointed. Three of them are waddling by the shore, eyeing me as I pass.

"I don't have any snacks today, friends," I say.

Joss looks up from her phone and frowns at me, then catches sight of the ducks and chuckles, her mischief firmly back in place. "Have you married them yet?"

Ah. So we're glossing over it, I see. She swings around to the passenger side.

"Oh, yeah," I say. "It was a quiet ceremony. Family only." The truck unlocks automatically as I pull the handle.

She hops in. "And here I thought I'd be your best man."

"Ha ha." The engine roars to life and I slip my wallet from my back pocket—so annoying to sit on it—before doing a double take on her face. "Why are you staring at me?"

"No reason." She shrugs but doesn't look away.

Suspicious, I shift the vehicle to Reverse, and the backup camera view pops up on my center display.

A scream rips through my throat. Shrill. Embarrassingly feminine. My heart jumps clean out of my chest.

Amidst the multicolor guidelines, the horrifying image of Samara from *The Ring* emerging from her well glows on the screen.

Jocelyn howls in laughter so hard it's soundless, and joyous tears sparkle in her eyes. It takes me a few more seconds to verify the image is frozen on the screen and not, in fact, coming to murder me.

I turn on her. "You! What is this?"

Her shoulders shake and she covers her face, still lost to mirth. "I taped it to your backup camera," she gasps through the laughs.

"Truce!" I declare. "I call a truce. No more pranks, dear god, please."

Her expression lights up in pure venomous delight. "I win?"

"You win. Take the throne. Please get this off the screen."

My gaze lands on the image again and I squeeze my eyes shut. So manly. Dr. White would have a field day with this. She chuckles a little longer and swings herself out of the truck. Out of my peripheral vision, her fingers paw at the image, but I don't dare look.

Hate Samara.

Hate her well.

The whole premise of scary movies is that it's all fine. It's in the TV. No big deal. Then she comes out of the fucking TV.

My heart is still near jogging rate when Jocelyn returns to the truck, cackling. I shoot her puppy-dog face, and she wilts.

"I'm sorry." She scratches behind my ear like I'm a real dog. "Will you forgive me?"

"You're buying my dinner tonight."

She sighs. "Fine."

When I try to back up, the truck won't go, and she laughs again, releasing the emergency break. "Safety first, Asher. Duh. Couldn't have you slamming on the gas in sheer terror."

Frustrating, heart attack–inducing woman.

"I can't believe you caved," she says once we're on the road.

"You know all my weak spots, and you're willing to fight dirty. It isn't fair."

Her smile is pure devilry. "You wanted fair, you should have put down rules."

A fine point, really. Oh, well. You live, you learn, and I've internalized my lesson. Never engage Jocelyn Mattox in a battle of pranks. She's not above making me pee my pants.

•

ROOSEVELT'S IS A small gastropub, part hipster-industrial chic and part prohibition-era speakeasy. They locally source their menu and specialize in craft beer.

Yayoi loves it. She gets this thing called the Roosemelt that's basically a grilled cheese for DINKs.

When Jocelyn and I arrive, the place is slammed, but Yayoi and Geoff are already seated and have drinks. As I slide into the booth, Jocelyn beside me, I tilt my head at the three empty glasses in front of Geoff and the single cup of water before Yayoi.

She shoves a pee stick in our faces. "Happy birthday to me!"

The extremely faint positive pregnancy test is wrestled from her hands by Joss, who gasps. "Really?"

At Yayoi's nod, Jocelyn jumps from her seat and bear hugs Yayoi.

I raise my eyebrows at Geoff. "That was quick. Congrats, bro."

He chugs the rest of his fancy beer and jiggles it in the air toward a person I assume is our server. "Another, please?"

"You okay there?" I ask.

"I don't know how to be a dad," he whispers.

The server arrives at our table, and Jocelyn returns to her seat, asking about the beer selections.

"I told you, honey." Yayoi throws her arms around Geoff. "You're going to be the best daddy of all time."

"Who's your OB?" I point at a stout when it's my turn to order.

Geoff straightens. "Nuh-uhh! No way!"

Taken aback, I lay my menu on the table between us. "No way what?"

"No way are you delivering my baby."

The server takes that moment to slink away.

I blink at Geoff and laugh. "I didn't say—"

"No way are you allowed anywhere near her area, Foley."

I put my hands up. "I wasn't suggesting . . ."

Geoff takes a swig of water. "I don't care how clinical it is. It's still not happening."

Jocelyn folds her arms on the table, laughing. "You know, it would be nice to have an in with your own gynecologist. Can't ask a stranger to take a picture of the inside and show it to you."

I snort so loud, they all look at me. "You want a picture of your insides?"

She lifts her hands in defense. "It would be cool to know what my own cervix looks like. I *know* some of them are prettier than others. I want to know where mine ranks."

Her eyebrow rises.

My insides disappear.

I glance at the others. The table. Behind me. Does she mean . . . She can't really mean . . .

"I can't help you with that," I say. Why is my voice weird?

She frowns, perfect platinum waves shifting as her head cocks. "I'm not asking you to."

"Then why did you look at me?"

She moves her hand in a circle. Am I supposed to be making some connection here? Because literally nothing is linking up. I've gone utterly stupid.

"You're a gynecologist," she says. "You deal with lots of cervixes. Cervices?" She shakes her head. "More than one cervix."

I'm picturing it. Not clinically. Not gynecologically.

I'm picturing her naked. Spread open. The way a man pictures a woman he wants.

Stop picturing it!

Ears are ringing. Hum of the restaurant disappears. Darkness closes inward. Atmospheric Edison bulbs on the chandelier above us prove useless. What is happening right now?

My voice cracks. "I'm going to be real frank right now. I mean this in the friendliest way possible, but I *cannot* be your gynecologist."

Yayoi barely restrains her laughter.

Joss's frown turns into a full scowl. "What's *wrong* with you? I never asked you to be my gynecologist."

Geoff chortles around another gulp of water. "Yeah, when you finally let him put something inside you, I highly doubt it will be a speculum."

My entire body freezes. Joss's eyes go wide. Geoff slaps a hand over his mouth while Yayoi smacks his arm.

"I take it back," Geoff says behind his hand. "Can I take it back? Let's rewind."

Yayoi sneaks a quick glance at Joss and me. "Sorry," she whispers, then to Geoff, "How drunk are you, my love?"

"Well—" he picks up a glass "—these are eighteen percent and I've had five of them, so . . ."

"He was joking," I whisper to Joss.

She looks down at the table. "No, he wasn't." The waiter sets her beer before her. She slams it.

"I'm sorry," Geoff says. "Really. It was stupid."

"I have to go to the bathroom." Joss slides out of the booth and disappears. Yayoi smacks Geoff on the shoulder once more, then rushes after her.

I hurl a cardboard coaster at Geoff. "What the fuck?"

"I don't even know. It just . . . came out."

"Why the hell would that come out of your mouth?"

He lets out a drunken snort. "Come on, man. You're single. She's single. It's just a matter of time, isn't it?"

"We're *friends*. Just like I am with Yayoi."

He rolls his eyes and makes quote marks with his hands, then snatches up Yayoi's phone from the table. He *tap-tap-taps* before turning the phone to face me. "*That* is not friends."

On the screen is the edited version of one of our fake engagement photos. In true Yayoi fashion, she's glammed it up with a layer of enchantment, all golden and light filled. It's the one where we stood close, her hand clenched on my shirt. Half my face is hidden, nestled against hers. Only the curve of my mouth and chin is visible.

Her face, though. Hers is highlighted. The focus of the picture.

Eyes closed. Mouth slightly parted. Tipped toward me like she can't quite help it. It's a visual representation of longing.

I can *feel* it through the picture.

"See what I mean? Scroll to the next one," Geoff says.

So I do, my heart jolting at the photo of us nearly kissing, her bejeweled hand cupping my cheek. We're smiling, nose to nose, looking into each other's eyes like we want to erase that distance.

One by one, I scroll through them. With each one, more of my composure frays.

Gnawing ache is back.

Hurts.

This *hurts*.

So maybe it wasn't the posing with me that was so painful to her. Maybe she felt what I felt. The yearning. The confusion. The panic.

I slide the phone back to him in silence.

"Just friends?" he says. "If you're *friends* with Yayoi like that, then we need to have a conversation that ends in your death."

Force out a laugh. Feels wrong. "I get it, okay? But don't— You can't say things like that. Even if you're thinking them. Joss has a thing about people thinking she's slutty."

Geoff's face blanches. "That isn't how I meant it."

"You need to apologize to her."

He curses under his breath and nods.

When the girls return, Joss has pasted on her fake smile. She waves off Geoff's apology like it's no big deal and keeps an ample amount of space between us in the booth. The rest of the dinner is blissfully uneventful. Jocelyn, however, remains more subdued than normal, despite many attempts to draw her out.

"So, when are you guys leaving for the wedding?" Yayoi asks once the plates are cleared away.

I peek a glance at Joss. "Couple weeks. It's Labor Day weekend, so we'll get there the Friday before."

Yayoi smiles. "That'll be fun. It's on the beach, right?"

"Yeah. In Naples. A Ritz-Carlton."

Geoff whistles.

Joss leans into me and finally offers her full grin. "We can be fancy rich folks for the weekend. I'll get Rent the Runway and tell everyone they simply *must* come to the country house this spring."

"I'm sure it will be beautiful," says Yayoi. "Romantic spot for a wedding."

Joss raises a pert eyebrow. "I wouldn't call the beach romantic."

"Yeah, but you're the only one," Geoff says.

She toasts him, a silent *touché*. After a moment, she turns to me. "I'm tired. You mind if we go?"

Oh. Right. We rode together. "Sure."

As agreed, she pays, and we do the typical goodbyes. *Happy birthday. Congrats. Have a good night.*

Darkness has crept over the city by the time we make it to the main roads. The cab is silent, Jocelyn settling deep into her contemplative mood. It's only a matter of time before she sees those photos. What will she think of them? A hundred bucks says she outright panics.

I tap on my thigh. Radio might help this interminable quiet. I'm about to switch it on when she breaks the silence.

Her voice is dreamy, quiet. "Why do you think he said that?"

My hand flexes on the steering wheel. "I don't know, Jocelyn. He was drunk. Wasn't thinking."

Head resting on the seat back, she stares out the passenger window. "He made it seem like I'm stringing you along."

"That isn't what he meant."

"What other way could he have possibly meant?"

The blue glow in the truck cab casts her beauty in a sad light. She looks small again. Lost.

Fragile.

I've never really thought of her as fragile before, but I see it now. Could probably delineate all the delicate glass pieces that hold her together. Wish she'd let me closer. I could hold her together on those days she thinks she's coming apart.

Really shouldn't think things like that. Quite disastrous for my psyche.

Deep inhale. Slow exhale.

Disobedient organ in my chest doesn't care about the oxygen, though. Riotous heart-pounding refuses to calm.

I pull my truck to the side of the road and shift to Park. We're on a neighborhood street, so I turn off the headlights. A few houses have glowing front porch lights, but mostly the road is shrouded in darkness. Joss looks around, brow creased.

I grip both hands tight on the steering wheel. "He was being stupid, okay? Just forget about it."

She cocks her head. Blond curls frame her pretty face. "Does he think I eventually sleep with everyone, then? Or does he think I just hold out on you for fun?"

"That isn't—"

"Well, it's got to be something, Asher. Why else would his mind even go there?"

"Because he thinks it's inevitable that we'll end up sleeping together."

She jerks back. *"Why?"*

"Because we're both single and we spend a lot of time together. He was just drunk. He didn't think it through. It means nothing."

Her posture eases slightly, so I turn in my seat to face her.

Anxiety gathers at the core of my spine, branching outward. Hope this next part goes smoothly. Might be in for a lot of yelling. "You know how you said I need to focus on the good things that happen and not the bad ones?"

She nods, expression wary.

"I think you need to focus on what you have and not what you have the potential to lose."

Silence answers me, but her gaze is unwavering. Bright eyes. Motionless chest.

"Loss is a part of the human condition, Joss. It's natural to fear it, but this offense you take when you believe people are judging you . . . I think you know you're missing out on good things by pushing people away. I think you use your one-night stands as a replacement for the intimacy you're so afraid of. And I think you judge yourself because you know it isn't what you really want. And then you assume everyone else is judging you just as harshly as *you're* judging you."

She drops her head. "You sound like my therapist." Her tone is all grumpy. Way better than the offended shriek I was expecting. "Sounds more practical when you say it, though."

Ha. I thought the same thing when she told me to take snapshots. We make a good team, Joss and I. "See? You just needed a second opinion."

She directs a playful scowl my way. "No. This doesn't mean I'll listen to you and magically undo years of diseased thinking."

I laugh, soft and quiet. "You never told me you had a boyfriend who died."

Her face closes up. "I don't talk about that."

"I know, but you can . . . if you want."

She sighs. I reach across the console and take her hand. Her gaze falls on our joined hands and lingers there. "It was a car wreck."

"Did you love him?"

She nods once, choppily. "My first love."

First and last. "That must have been really hard."

"Yeah." Her hand tightens on mine. "I've been running from the loss ever since."

I brush a thumb over her soft knuckles. "You aren't running, Joss. You're hiding."

She blows out a slow breath, jaw clenching. "Maybe."

"Hey." I jiggle her hand, so she'll meet my gaze again. "I know it scares you to let people in, so . . . thank you for letting me be one of them."

She snorts. "I didn't *let* you. You Jedi mind-tricked your way in there with charm and pineapple White Claws."

"And ducks."

She throws my hand back at me, smiling. "Not the ducks!"

With a smirk, I turn to the steering wheel and shift to Drive. "You can keep denying it, but we all know the truth. The ducks are behind your walls."

She laughs—incandescent and tinkly. Love that. The most wonderful music, really, her laughter. Feels like helium in my chest.

"Don't be extra, Asher."

Ah. There it is. Perfect. Status quo achieved.

Jocelyn

Your love language is physical touch.
—My Therapist

Pool Party Saturday is terrible.

Cassie Hersl is here.

It's not Asher's fault. He tried everything to steer the conversation away yesterday in the OR physician lounge, but she was tenacious.

What are your plans this weekend? . . . Oh, that sounds fun. I'd love to come . . . Busy? No, I'm not busy at all . . . I'll bring beer.

She didn't even bring good beer.

Having her in my domain is like letting a porcupine into my bed. Suddenly, everything is far less comfortable. Any move I make might result in bodily harm. Dark hair perfectly slicked into a bun, sun-bronzed skin gleaming in the gold light, Cassie's like a goddess in a strappy one-piece that somehow shows off more skin than my bikini. The sheer white coverup I thought was so cute before feels frumpy now.

We've gathered at the porch table to eat, and Cassie's crowded into Asher's space. She keeps putting her hand on his arm.

Yes, it's technically Asher's house, but Asher is, like . . . mine. If she keeps hanging on him like that, I'll drown her in the pool.

Gah, when did I get so possessive?

I'm jerked out of my troubled thoughts when the entire table bursts into giggles, Cassie loudest of all. "You're kidding!" she says, beaming at Asher. "It splashed right in her eye?"

He shrugs. "I told her it isn't wise to do spec exams in triage without eyewear. The residents don't take me seriously. She laughed at me."

Evie, the OB hospitalist, throws a chip at Asher. "That's not even the funniest part. Tell her the rest."

The entire crowd leans in, waiting for the punchline.

Asher chuckles. "The swab came back positive for gonorrhea."

Ugh! Eyeball gonorrhea infection?

"Shit!" Cassie moves her hand to Asher's shoulder. "What did the poor girl have to do?"

I laser focus on that red-polished hand. Grazing that lean, tanned shoulder. I'm going to maim her.

"Eyedrops." Asher leans forward to grab his beer, effectively removing Cassie's hand from his person.

Thank you, universe.

Geoff shudders. "That's disgusting."

"Yeah." Yayoi holds a palm over her mouth, looking a tad green. "It didn't hit me this hard the last time you told me this story."

Geoff rubs her back.

She swallows and shakes herself. "Remind me why I wanted this baby?"

"Don't ask me." Geoff laughs. "I was just there for moral support."

"And charitable donations," Asher quips.

Everyone chuckles.

"Did you all hear what happened to Doctor Bender?" Cassie asks.

Eek. Not this.

I avert my gaze to the glass table between us. Bender voluntarily checked into a rehab program last week. Drug of choice was alcohol, but he'd progressed past the gateway to harder stuff. I had no idea he was suffering. The man always kept to himself, so the news came with a hefty dose of guilt.

I should have noticed. Anesthesiologists are particularly prone to substance abuse, and with my brother's history, this stuff hits harder.

The table discusses the gossip, but I'm busy remembering the three knocks that went unanswered on my brother's door. The chill of his stiff arms that proved I was far too late.

"Funny," Cassie cuts into my memories. "Of all of us, he's not the one I would've pegged as a partier."

Geoff laughs. "Yeah, I'd put my money on Aaron Beal any day."

That cuts through the cold memories, and I snort. Aaron Beal is as straitlaced as they come. His pious family is picture-perfect and lovely. Man won't even touch the spiked punch at our annual holiday party.

Cassie laughs along like it's one big joke. "I'd have bet on Joss." Then she winks at me. Like we're friends. Like she's teasing. Like she's allowed to make jokes like this.

I'm too shocked to reply. What the hell?

Yayoi lets out a single bark of laughter. "Joss? Yeah, right. I can't even get the girl to take a toke from my vape pen."

Asher's foot nudges mine under the table, and he adopts a playful tone. "But she'll go to town on a pineapple White Claw."

I meet his eyes and melt at the silent support there. The worrisome tug makes a painful pull at my chest, so I look away, forcing out a sarcastic, "Yes, I'm clearly an addict."

Geoff snatches the can sitting in front of me and finishes off the warm dregs. "You're not an addict. You're an enthusiast. You want another?"

He's been excessively nice, my friend Geoff. Maybe he should shoot his mouth more often. I'll suffer a few drunken insults if he's going to cater to me for days afterward. His stilted, sober apology the next morning was the most awkward thing we've ever been through together.

Just mouthing off . . . Didn't mean it . . . You're one of my best friends . . . So sorry . . .

"Nah, I'm good," I say, grinning his way.

Cassie, not to be outdone, knocks back her plain beer. "I've never been into those girly drinks, but hey, someone's gotta drink 'em."

It's hard to tell if I'm being insulted, but given it's Cassie, I'm leaning toward *yes*. I refuse to engage, though. Instead, I focus on the sunlight glinting on the pool water. Several of the MAs lounge on pool floats in the shape of burritos with arms because, according to Asher, *Mr. Burrito is hilarious!*

Asher stands. "You know what? All this talking about it makes me want one. Anyone else?"

Geoff, Evie and Yayoi all raise their hands in solidarity while Cassie frowns. I lift an eyebrow at Yayoi.

"I can sip it!" she says. "A sip an hour or something!" No way will she actually drink it while pregnant, but her loyalty here can't be questioned.

I love my friends, and these warm tinglies inside are really quite pleasant, but here's the deal: The pineapple White Claws are mine. Cassie's stupid antics are forcing my friends to steal *my* drinks. I will never forgive her for this. It might be worse than her hand on Asher's shoulder, or her gaze on his ass right now as he walks away.

When he returns, he doles out the alcohol and leans close to my ear. "I'll buy you more, I promise." Then he plops down in the empty seat beside me, leaving Cassie all by her lonesome across from us.

Tug, tug. Ouch, ouch.

I think you need to focus on what you have, not what you have the potential to lose.

My best friend is a smart, smart man. How did he cut so cleanly to the core of things? And then magically find a way to make me laugh afterward?

This tug is growing more insistent. I still don't know how to make it stop, or even if I can. I might suffer this pull toward him forever.

It's a tragic thought.

Meanwhile, Evie and Geoff chat about a combo case they scrubbed earlier this week, and Yayoi plays up her morning sickness with a pitiful moan, spurring Geoff to rub her back again.

Cassie leans her elbows on the table. "So, Joss. Are you dating anyone these days?"

Okay. Where are we going with this line of questioning? "Not really."

"Oh, that's right." She waves her hand toward me. "You're still into the online hookup thing, right?"

How does she even know that? "Actually, I haven't—"

Asher sets a hand on my arm. "What about you, Cassie? Getting serious with that one guy?"

Her smile fades a bit. "Ian and I broke up a couple weeks ago."

I might believe that sadness if she hadn't been hanging all over my best friend. "I'm sorry," I say, even though I'm not sorry at all.

"That's too bad, Cass." Asher's voice is so genuine. How does he manage it? "I was rooting for you guys."

"Yeah, well. He wasn't ready to get serious, and I decided I was, so . . ." The bitterness in her words is genuine, and I *almost* feel bad until she says, "But the casual hookup thing . . ." She motions toward me. "That works, too. For some people."

The offense is instantaneous. *Some people?*

AKA sluts.

"Awesome people, you mean?" Asher says, tone a little harder.

She ignores him in favor of drinking her nasty beer.

"Jeez, Cassie." Asher laughs once, humorlessly. "I wonder what drove Ian away."

The table goes silent.

My blood turns incandescent. Did— Did he just say that?

It takes Cassie a moment to register the insult, and she blinks three times before her face goes scarlet. "That's— I wasn't trying to offend."

"Right," he says, all disbelief.

Yayoi snickers behind her hand, while Geoff and Evie stare wide-eyed at the developing scene. Expression hovering near apologetic, Cassie reaches a hand toward Asher and me. She starts to stand, to say something, but it knocks the table, toppling his fresh can of White Claw right into his lap.

He springs up.

"Oh, shit." Cassie's eyes go wide. "I'm so sorry."

His trunks are soaked and—as usual—he laughs. "Guess I deserved that for being rude. Sorry I said anything."

"No, that's—" Cassie starts.

Ignoring her, he turns toward the back door. "I'm going to change."

He steals the center of my attention as he disappears through the sliders. In the background of my awareness, Cassie murmurs apologies and uses a towel on the mess beside me, Evie helping. Geoff mutters something and Yayoi answers. It hardly registers.

Cassie has spent years quietly jabbing me in my softest, most vulnerable parts, and Asher . . . He just defended my honor.

This isn't a tug. It's a hacksaw. And it's edging closer to my heart by the second. Back and forth, back and forth.

Dangerous and thrilling, like standing untethered at the edge of a cliff. Morbidly alluring, like a lethal dose of fentanyl.

I glance at Evie wiping down Asher's wet chair beside me. She meets my eyes and subtly nods toward the door.

Should I go after him?

I should go after him.

I stand. Step around Cassie and the mess. Head toward the sliders.

The house is chilly, the A/C on high like Asher likes. His sexy forest cologne lingers in the air. No one ever spends time indoors on Pool Party Saturdays, so the lights are off, everything still. My bare feet tread without sound over the cold wood floor, down the hall.

Conflicting desires war in my head. What am I doing

right now? What is this draw? And why—when I know it could be fatal—is it so hard to ignore?

I slip into his bedroom and close the door behind me. "Asher?"

He steps out of his closet, now changed into a dry set of trunks and a blue-striped tank. "Oh, hey. Crazy, right? She's so extra."

"Yeah." It's barely audible. Oxygen has abandoned me.

His brow creases and he points at his closet. "Did you need a T-shirt or something?"

"No." I approach slowly, tingles making my voice jittery. "I—um—"

"You okay?"

"I really liked that," I say because I don't know how to articulate this overwhelming gratitude and tantalizing heat growing in my chest. My hand gathers a handful of the flimsy coverup over my stomach, right where the nerves have concentrated.

"Which part? The part where she insulted you or the part where I got soaked?"

"The part where you defended me."

He chuffs. "That was the most boring part. What else was I supposed to do?"

What is happening in my chest right now? It's somehow expanding and imploding on itself. A supernova.

You aren't running, Joss. You're hiding.

I draw close enough to touch, and his thumb brushes my shoulder. "Joss?"

His hair is pool-messy. Sun-induced freckles dust the bridge of his nose. Chlorine taints the delicious scent of his skin.

He's perfect.

Something snaps clean in half—my restraint, probably—and I throw myself into his arms. His bewildered laugh prefaces the warmest hug I've ever experienced. I bury my face against his heartbeat, and his arms wrap tight around my shoulders.

"You got me a little worried here," he says.

I laugh into his stupidly hard chest and lift my head to look at him.

He isn't smiling. His dynamic eyes are troubled. Concerned. "What's the hug for, Jocelyn?"

My full name on his lips is obscene. Like dirty talk. It slinks over my skin with prickles and fire. His thoughtful gaze searches my face for answers, but I have none to give. He wants a reason, but I can't explain this. Something has cracked open inside me. I should be filled to the brim with panic. Instead, I'm weirdly calm.

Well.

Maybe not calm, exactly.

My heart is battering my rib cage, and a fine tremor has taken control of most of my muscles, but my mind is stable. Cemented on a single thought.

He is something vital.

Words won't form, but he must read the thoughts on my face anyway because his concern melts away to something less obvious, but far hotter. We're so close. Closer than we've ever been. Pressed chest to chest, arms wrapped tight, staring into each other's eyes.

He gives me a half-second warning in the form of dropping his gaze to my mouth before obliterating the remaining distance between us.

He doesn't ask. Doesn't hesitate. He just . . . kisses me.

Asher.

Kisses me.

His lips collide with mine, soft and hard all at once, and somewhere inside, a pressure valve releases. Tension breaks. Heat spirals around my spine, singeing my fears, burning any hesitation that might have surfaced to ash.

In his arms, I am safe, complete, and I suspect that I might have been wanting this—needing this—for a very long time.

He doesn't press for more, and within four, maybe five seconds, he pulls back, reestablishing space that I don't want. Space I can hardly stand.

Panic rises, and without even opening my eyes, I shamelessly fling my arms around his neck, connecting us once more. This time, the kiss is frenetic. Hard. Wild. A clash of lips and tongues.

My first taste of Asher Foley is heady, all thrill and temptation and pineapple White Claw. My fingers thread through his hair, and the subtle groan that reverberates deep in his chest settles in my stomach, low and heavy. I press my body against his, welding us together, and let myself memorize every detail of his hard planes against my softer curves.

He's in my arms. Lean muscle. Taut restraint. Confident hands grazing places he never has. Logic tells me it's a mistake, that I could be destroying something precious, but now that we're here, the locks on my outer walls are falling open. I should fear the breach, but in this moment, no panic surfaces.

No. This isn't scary. This feels like deliverance, like I might sacrifice my very soul to keep him here. Right here. In my arms.

As the revelation hits, an inner voice whispers to hide how much I want this, murmurs that he knows we shouldn't do this, that he's argued against it before, and if I reveal these dark desires to escalate—potentially obliterate—our friendship, he'll stop.

I don't want him to ever stop.

I barely recognize myself.

No longer gentle, his hands tighten convulsively on my waist, thumbs digging into the dips beside my hip bones. An aroused sigh climbs my throat, totally uncontrollable.

In a flash, he tears himself away, and my chest spasms with the need to pull him back. His eyes spark when he looks down at me, sending hot, wicked waves through my veins. We stare, breathing hard for several seconds before he takes my mouth again with an almost violent desperation.

I'm not sure who moves first, but locked together, we stumble toward his bed, landing atop the green duvet with a little bounce. His skin is fire against my hands when I delve under his shirt, each muscle rippling as my fingers pass over. One hand locks around my wrist, pinning it to the mattress while his mouth dips to my throat. He feathers a tingly sensation down the entire column, launching a wave of goose bumps across my body.

When he finds my free hand and pins that one, too, my legs open of their own accord. He takes every inch I give him, pressing closer until we are molded together. My veins turn to lightning when the hard length of him drives right where I want him. Sensitive nerves beg me to remove the slip of a bikini bottom that covers them.

While his mouth does sparkly things against my collarbone, I wrap my leg around him, trying to urge him closer, to make him *thrust*. A stupid, pathetic whimper escapes my throat when he won't, and he *laughs*, like he enjoys my suffering. He has me trapped beneath him, a prisoner salivating for her own cage, and my heart, still protected behind my innermost barriers, begins to beat his name.

Like he *owns* it.

That's when the fear rises, a great surge of it, dousing the blaze.

No, no, no. He can't have it.

I can't do this. I was wrong. There's nothing better outside these walls. There's only the potential for pain.

My eyes snap open.

He's too close. Dangerously close.

This desire is seductive, but deadly. Catastrophic to my protective walls. Fatal to our irreplaceable friendship. What am I doing, handing over parts of myself? I've already buried so many, I barely have any left, and I'm just . . . giving them away? Sacrificing the best friendship I've ever had in the process?

He can't have my heart. It's the only part that's still marginally human. If he takes it, and something happens to him, I won't survive it.

I can't lose another piece of myself.

"Wait."

He freezes at once, his quick breaths slicing against my tattooed collarbone. His weight is suddenly suffocating, and I push against his shoulder. He rolls away, landing on his back beside me, so we're both looking at the white ceiling.

Neither of us speaks.

My head turns, my attention landing on the ink on his shoulder—a smiling stick figure with legs akimbo above a trampoline.

"We can't do this," I whisper.

His eyes fall shut, and he raises both hands to rub his face. In lieu of answering, he takes a slow breath.

"Asher?"

"Yeah?" His hands still cover his mouth, so his raspy voice is smothered beneath them.

"Did you hear me?"

"Yeah."

I stare at the visible portion of his face, waiting for a more elaborate response, but it never comes. My heart slowly returns to a regular rhythm, safe behind its walls. Asher gives no indication how I should proceed, so I exist in the interminable, torturous silence, hoping I haven't decimated us.

"Why not?" he finally asks, turning to look at me as his hands drop to his sides.

I pause, studying the guarded light in his eyes. "Why not what?"

"Why can't we do this?" He says it like it's a test, like there's a right and wrong answer, and he's curious which I'll choose.

"You don't do casual." I slide my hand across the comforter, closer to his, but he lifts his away before we touch.

He rises to his elbows, studying me closely. "You—you think this would be casual?"

"Casual is just . . . all I'm capable of."

Silence follows, broken only by the gentle hum as the A/C kicks on.

"I don't believe you," Asher says eventually. "And I don't think you believe you, either."

I— What?

How—

That's not—

The words are a punch to the gut. I sit up, and when that doesn't make the ache go away, I stand, pacing away from him. Who is he to tell me what I do and don't believe about myself? Why does he think he has the right to push against my barriers?

"Yes, I do," I say. "This is how I've always lived my life, Asher. It's just easier—"

"Easier, but not healthy." He shifts forward, setting his elbows on his knees. His vacant stare lands on the hardwood, the same place I'd once shattered a glass of red wine. "I shouldn't have kissed you. That's not— We ... aren't ... like that, I guess. I'm sorry I did that. But you can't spend your life hiding from the deeper emotions, Joss. It's not me, sure, but it has to be someone."

Why does it have to be someone? If it was ever going to be anyone, wouldn't it be him? I'm just too broken to reach for the deeper emotions he wants. He doesn't understand— won't ever understand—so I ignore those words to focus on something else he said: *I shouldn't have kissed you.*

Best kiss of my life, and he regrets it. I'm not sure how to feel about that. I should probably regret it, too. I'll force myself to regret it at some point. Someday. But in the meantime, I have to know: "Why *did* you kiss me?"

He looks up at me through his lashes, expressionless. "You looked like you wanted me to."

Fair enough. I try to resurrect the bravery that the touch of his lips unleashed, the sense of freedom, like his arms could keep me safe from anything life might throw at me. But I'm too suffused with the familiar panic. The dread of potential loss. The fear of pain.

For an anesthesiologist, I have very little pain tolerance. Perhaps that's why I became one. There's a lesson in there somewhere.

"I did want you to," I say because I don't want him to think he did something wrong. "I just ... changed my mind."

He nods and drags his teeth over his bottom lip in a way that appears vaguely painful. The lack of a smile on his face jars something loose inside me, and another kind of apprehension wakes. "Are we okay, Asher?"

Ugh. The fake smile is almost worse than no smile. "Yeah,

sugarplum. Definitely." He doesn't meet my eyes. His gaze is trained somewhere above my left shoulder.

I glance in that direction, finding only an expanse of forest green wall.

No. No. No. We can't go out like this. I rack my brain, trying to find something that will fix it. Smooth it over. Stupidly, I settle on, "Are you going to be super awkward now that we've sucked face?"

He lets out one strained laugh. "Oh, yeah. Definitely. Awkwardness level is DEFCON 1."

My hands clench and unclench. "Well, why—why don't you show me a picture of the ducks, and we'll be back to normal."

His smile softens, as does his gaze when it lands on me. "We'll be okay, Joss."

I shoot him a skeptical look. Will we, though? Because he's acting super weird.

He shrugs. "It was just a kiss."

Right.

Just a kiss.

Asher

As long as you have hope, things will get better, and no one can take your hope but you.
–My Therapist

Sitting alone, cross-legged in the middle of my couch the next evening, I glare at my phone, hoping the woman on the other end of the line can sense my ire. "What do you mean there aren't two rooms available? The hotel says there are rooms reserved for wedding guests."

"There were rooms reserved, sir, but we have two weddings booked that weekend. Unfortunately, there's only one room left."

Eyes closed. Deep breath.

Charm. Must turn on the charm. "Come on, Lucy." I draw her name out like we're best friends. "There isn't anything? Not even a tiny room with a broken lock that's only ever been used by smokers?"

She laughs. "I'm sorry, sir. I know this is inconvenient."

Inconvenient doesn't begin to cover it. I can't share a hotel room with Joss. Not after yesterday. Not after that life-altering kiss. "Does the room at least have two beds?"

She clicks a few times, and says, "It looks like . . . this is a single king room."

The bitter laugh that rises in my throat tastes a bit like battery acid. Fused with the zest of desperation. Not a good combo. I drop my face into my hand. "Of course it is."

This is what I get for waiting so long to book the room. Procrastinators are always punished, but this penalty seems wildly out of proportion to the crime.

"Can I be real frank with you, Lucy?"

"Of course, Mr. Foley."

"I *need* two rooms. I'm going to the wedding of a girl I used to be in love with, and my date is my best friend, who I accidentally kissed yesterday. And I sort of think I might be falling for her, but she wants nothing to do with those sorts of shenanigans, and I cannot share a room with her, Lucy. I just can't."

Should have expected that pregnant pause. What else could the woman do? I'm a pussy, and we both know it.

Really need a better word for that.

Finally, she replies, "How do you accidentally kiss someone, Mr. Foley?"

"That is not the point, Lucy! Please help me. Please?"

More clicking. "Looks like there was a cancellation for a two-bedroom suite that weekend. Club level."

Club level at a Ritz-Carlton. This wedding is going to cost me my retirement. How rude would it be to cancel two weeks out?

My mother's voice shrieks through my thoughts. *You will do no such thing, Asher Ray!*

"Fine. I'll take the suite."

After I relinquish my credit card number and my firstborn child, Lucy chimes in with a chipper, "We look forward to your visit, Mr. Foley."

"I'm sure you do, Lucy. It'll be great."

Now I get to figure out how to tell Jocelyn we're sharing a hotel suite after I mauled her yesterday. Foresee a painfully awkward conversation in my future.

Hey, Joss. I know you're appalled that I kissed you, but hey! How'd you like to spend three days in very cramped quarters with minimal privacy? Oh, you despise that idea? Sure, I'll go fuck myself.

Just the teensiest bit scared how she'll react. Maybe I can sneak it in through text to minimize the fallout.

Can't believe I kissed her. What the hell was I thinking?

I had her under me. Her skin against my hands. Her mouth pressed to mine. Can't unfeel that. Untaste it.

Would have been better to never know. Ignorance is bliss.

Trust Jocelyn to serve up the best kiss of my life, then instantly follow it up with *I changed my mind. Can't take a chance on you. Sorry! You can't be weird about it though. BFFs?*

But that isn't the worst part.

The worst part is that I'm falling for her. Like the biggest idiot to ever idiot.

Before that kiss, I was so used to being out of sync. Didn't even realize my rhythm was off. Kissing her was like that feeling when your ear's been clogged for days, and it finally pops. It was that release of pressure when you extract that thing from between your teeth. It was the satisfying pop of a joint, one that restores full range of motion.

Somehow, Jocelyn Mattox has reset the rhythm of my

entire life. In her, I found harmony, and she won't even listen to the goddamn music.

Casual is just all I'm capable of.

Such lies.

She's capable of so much more. Just not with me, I guess. If she can't have me casually, she doesn't want me at all. Sounds about right. Did all the women in the world have a meeting or something? Reach some sort of consensus?

Periods suck.

Female beauty standards are unattainable.

Asher Foley equals casual.

Wish I could get a second opinion on that last one, but the universe seems pretty dead set on it.

My phone buzzes in my hand.

"Hey, Mom," I say after switching it to speakerphone.

"Did you forget to tell me something?"

I freeze. Shit. Did I forget a birthday? Mother's Day? Her anniversary? "Uh—"

"Why are there *engagement pictures* of you all over the internet?"

Oh.

Oh, no.

This is what my life has become. Timelapse destruction. A line of cascading dominoes heading straight for a cliff.

My mother has seen the photos.

Must force out a laugh for her sake. "*All over the internet* is extremely dramatic, even for you."

"When did you and Jocelyn get engaged?" she shrieks. "You never tell me anything."

"Mom, do you really think I'd get engaged and forget to tell you?"

Something that sounds a lot like a pot banging onto a

stove crashes through the speaker. "Sure looks like it. You seem pretty in love to me."

Ouch. That hurt more than I thought it might. "How did you even find them?"

"Mary Ann's girl is getting married in Galveston. She was looking at photographers in the area. You can imagine my surprise when I open the link she sent to find *you*."

I sigh. "We were just acting."

The faucet runs on her end. "What are these pictures, Asher Ray? And don't tell me they're nothing."

I dig my thumb and forefinger into my closed eyes. Sparks burst behind my lids. Doesn't help the gnawing in my diaphragm, though. "A friend of mine needed a couple to pose for engagement pictures so she could advertise her photography business. It isn't a big deal."

I can practically hear her deflate. "Oh."

"Yeah."

"Well, they look very convincing."

I know.

Her tone softens. "Tell Jocelyn she looks beautiful."

"Tell her yourself. You talk to her more than you talk to me."

"She hasn't answered my texts. Why do you think I came to you?" Something else bangs on her end.

"Jeez, Mom. What are you doing?"

"Making Sunday dinner. Your brothers want spaghetti. *Again*."

Something cold and lonely pulses deep in my chest. God, I miss Sunday dinners. Miss my parents and my brothers. Why did I ever think it was a good idea to move so far from my family?

Maybe I should move home.

What do I have here that's worth staying for?

"You okay, honey?" she asks, more quietly.

Hate that Mom thing. How do they always know when something's wrong? "I'm fine. Just been a weird few weeks. Work's been . . . work. And—"

"And what?"

I jerk to my feet. Need to do something with my hands. Also need Tums.

"Asher?"

"Yeah?"

"What's wrong?"

I wind up in the kitchen, wiping down counters that don't need it. "It's nothing, Mom. Really."

"Brandon!" she screams, and I wince. "Your brother needs to talk to you!"

"Ugh. Mom. Why?"

"Oh, hush."

A series of clicks and brushes precedes my big brother's booming voice. "What's doing, little bro?"

I sink my forehead onto my forearms right there on the kitchen island. "Hey, Brandon."

"Everything okay?"

I take two long breaths. How to extricate myself? Could pretend I'm on call. Would he believe me?

"Ah." His tone grows more serious, and the noise in the background dims to nothing. "Girl problems?"

"What?" Great. My spine has learned to absorb tension like a sponge. Not a fan of this development. "That's— No."

He laughs. "Okay."

"I mean . . . maybe? Are you alone?"

"Yeah. Is it the girl in the pictures?"

My hands clench, and I rise to my elbows, staring at the

blue veins in the granite beneath. Of course Mom would show my brothers. Discretion is not her forte. "Yeah. That's Joss."

"*That's* Joss? Christ, Ash. How have you been staring at that for three years and done nothing?"

Honestly? Now that I consider it, I'm not sure. Joss has always been on a different level than everyone else. Until recently, I was able to separate her from my baser desires. She stayed squarely in the Friend Zone despite her attractiveness.

Really fucked things up letting her in on my secrets. Never should have done it.

Now she's in a whole new zone. Totally out of bounds and impossible to reach.

"It was easy," I say. "Until it wasn't."

He sucks in a breath like *ouch*. "She mess you up?"

I slide my phone toward me, ignoring the repeat Dragon training email and idly clicking on things until I come across those forsaken photos. Worst mistake of my life, immortalizing these stupid feelings on the internet. How obvious is my face here?

I clearly want her.

Don't need to keep looking at it, honestly. Strange sort of torture. I flip my phone, so the screen faces the granite. The PopSocket on the back stares back at me—a rubber duck surrounded by the words "Dear Autocorrect, it's never DUCK."

Sometimes it is *duck*, though. Other times, it's most definitely *fuck*. Like right now.

"I think I want more," I say. Wow. The words actually came out. Can't take those back. They're in the universe forever.

"But she doesn't." It isn't a question, and for some reason, that stings. My brother thinks Joss is out of my league.

Joss *is* out of my league. But still.

"No." Hate that word, but it has to be said. It's the truth. "She doesn't. Found that out after I kissed her."

He grunts, all gruff like he's not sure what to say. I'm not sure what to say, either. Nice that he's here, though.

"Really sucks, little bro."

"Yeah. It sort of does."

"Well, come home, if you want. I'll take you to Jake's. We'll shoot some pool like the old days."

Sounds nice. Really nice. But impossible on such short notice.

"I gotta work, Brandon. On call this weekend and going to Florida for Labor Day."

His tone perks. "Oh, yeah? What's in Florida?"

"Friend's wedding."

"Oh. Then stop being a pussy and take a date, bro. Surely there's a lady down there willing to go to the beach with a fancy doctor."

Oh. No, no, no.

Don't want to tell him.

Can't not tell him.

"I'm going with Joss."

He's quiet for several seconds, and then: "Not smart, bro."

"I'm aware."

"Gonna get hurt."

My eyes fall shut. "I know."

He sighs. "What can I do? Anything?"

"Just don't tell Mom."

His booming laugh vibrates the phone against the granite. "Ash. Have you met Mom? She definitely already knows. Wouldn't be surprised if she knows the color of my future child's eyes."

He's right. Of course he's right.

Doesn't stop me from groaning. Last thing I need is my mother intuiting things like this. The woman has direct access to Jocelyn—and uses it frequently.

"Tell her it was a work thing bothering me," I say.

He's still laughing. "All right, little bro. Whatever you say."

Jocelyn

*Your walls don't have to come down all at once.
Maybe you could just add some doors and windows.*
—My Therapist

Two days after The Kiss, I'm almost certain Asher is avoiding me. I could have chalked yesterday up to chance—we don't see each other at work every day—but *today*? Today I witnessed him about-face and scamper off in the opposite direction as soon as I turned the corner onto L&D.

The little weasel.

I slink into the dictation room and plop into a chair.

> Are you avoiding me?

Maybe

> Why?

I am preserving my dignity.

> By running away like the chick who dies first in a horror movie?

Yes.

> Asher! Talk to me. This doesn't have to be weird.

To what are you referring?

> We kissed! It's not a big deal.

Can't talk. I'm training my dragon.

I laugh loud enough that the nurse beside me shoots me a weird look.

I hold up my phone. "Doctor Foley's making jokes."

She nods like *of course*, dawning a smile and a little twinkle in her eye.

See? Everyone loves the guy. But he will not distract me with humor. At my next break between cases, I march outside and snap a few pictures of the ducks on the pond, sending one his way.

> Let's see you avoid this, Foley.

Unfair

My kryptonite.

> I took more. I'll send them if you stop being awkward.

On a scale of 1–10, how cute are they?

> Ughhhhh
>
> Fine
>
> I kissed you. You rejected me.
> I'll forget it happened.
>
> Happy?

I send him the rest of the photos as a reward, but something about the word *rejected* leaves an acidic tang on the back of my tongue. Is that what he thinks I did?

Is that what I did?

By the simplest definition, yes, I did reject him, but . . . it's more complicated than that. He understands why I did it, right?

> I didn't reject you. I was
> trying to protect you.
>
> I don't need an explanation, Joss.
>
> It's over and done. Let's move on.
>
> Okay.
>
> Let's move on.

•

THAT NIGHT, CLOSE to 2:00 a.m., I wake in my bed from a nightmare about Asher. I was stuck in the attic of my childhood home, unable to do anything but watch as the rising gray water threatened to drown my family. But instead of my parents, it was Asher trying to save the couple across the street. And instead of elderly strangers, the couple was Geoff and Yayoi.

Miraculously, he saved them.
Then Cassie appeared. Asher reached for her.
They both disappeared.
I woke hating her more than I already do.
Wide awake, heart still throbbing in my chest, I snatch my phone from my nightstand, only to find a few texts from Asher.

> **So**
>
> **Funny story**
>
> **I waited a little too long to book the hotel rooms**
>
> **Had to get us a suite to share**
>
> **2 bedroom**
>
> **Hope that's okay?**

> Of course it is. It'll be just like Pool Party Saturday. Sleepover where we sleep in two rooms.

I imagine he'll be asleep and will reply in the morning, but the three dots pop up almost instantly.

> **You know**
>
> **When you didn't answer earlier, I had a minor freak out that I'd ducked up.**
>
> **So naturally I went into panic mode**
>
> **Then I had a fun time imagining you calling the hotel and going full**

> Karen to get us two rooms.
>
> But I should warn you that they are very stingy with their rooms at the Ritz

> > Titty
> >
> > Why are you awake?

> Can't sleep. Why are you?

> > Nightmare

> Oh. Who was it this time?

> > Yayoi and the baby

I'm not sure why I lie. Maybe the haunting reality that my nightmares now seem to deal exclusively with losing him has me a tad rattled. Who could say?

He takes a while to reply. Did he fall asleep? My finger taps on the side of my phone until the three dots finally appear.

> Must have been hard.
>
> Need anything?

You. I need you.

I can't say that, obviously, but the fact that the sentiment pops into my head at all is worrisome. I'm trying so hard not to need him. Why am I failing?

> > Just wish the nightmares would stop.
> >
> > Let's talk about something else.

> What are we going to do about
> this suite situation when you
> find a bridesmaid to bang?

Even typed out, I hate those words. Hate the sentiment. Hate what they could mean. Why did I even type them?

...

Are you joking?

> Yes. Obviously.

That wasn't obvious

In my defense, text lacks tone.

Can get confusing.

Just so we're clear, there will be no bridesmaids.

> Got it. How much do I owe
> you for the room?

What? It's on me. You're doing me a favor.

> Uh

Hate to break it to you, but you could get any girl to go with you on a free trip to Florida.

> You should be taking a real girl

It takes a couple of minutes before he answers. My stomach flutters with nerves I try to wash away with a huge gulp of water from the bottle at my bedside. Why am I nervous? This is Asher.

> **YOU'RE NOT A REAL GIRL?**
>
> **When did the robots take over?**
>
> **I haven't fully trained
> my dragon yet!**

>> You know what I mean.

> **I don't**
>
> **You're as real as they come.**

Prickles cascade over my skin. It's not even a compliment, but for some reason, it resonates.

You're as real as they come.

>> I meant a girl with potential
>>
>> A girlfriend

Another long pause follows my answer, and I pull the covers over my head. Why did I say that? I'm making things infinitely worse, but I can't seem to stop.

> **Jocelyn**
>
> **Please stop.**
>
> **I get it.**

My fingers freeze over my screen. He gets what?

> **If you don't want to go, it's
> really fine. I don't mind
> going alone.**

> Why wouldn't I want to go?
>
> I think we'll have fun

Ten minutes pass before he responds.

> **I won't kiss you again, okay?**
>
> **I'm really sorry**

A weight sinks low in my stomach, but I'm not sure why. Is it the unnecessary apology? The sadness I sense, even through the toneless text? The idea that he's assuming blame, like we did something wrong? The fact that he just declared, in no uncertain terms, that I'll never get another kiss like that again?

> Stop apologizing. You didn't do anything wrong.
>
> It was just a kiss.

> **Maybe for you**

My heart jolts with a sudden surge of adrenaline, tingling in the tips of my fingers.

> What does that mean?

> **Never mind.**
>
> **Good night, Joss.**

Before I can reply, the little blue crescent moon pops up.

Asher Foley has notifications silenced.

Argh! He ends the conversation with *that*? How rude is that? Leave a girl hanging, why don't you?

I think back to his weight on top of me, his desire pressing into my leg right before I pushed him off me. I don't really have room to complain here. We're both a couple of teases, in vastly different ways.

And maybe I don't want to know the answer anyway. If we're ever going to get back to normal, we need to reestablish boundaries.

Boundaries, like walls, are good. They're safe. They will keep us both sheltered from pain.

Sheltered from each other.

•

"WHAT ABOUT GOLD?" Yayoi holds up a satiny number with a low, square bodice. The warm track lighting of the department store shimmers over folds of gleaming fabric.

It's pretty.

Really pretty.

"Is it too much, though?" My hand curls around the whisper of silk.

Yayoi shrugs and sips her Tropical Tango smoothie from Orange Julius. "Didn't you say you wanted to one-up the bride?"

"I wasn't *serious*. It's still her wedding. I don't want to be a total bitch. Just, like . . . half bitch."

"Okay." Yayoi hangs up the gold dress and glances at the others around us, all different cuts, colors, fabrics. She takes another long draw on the smoothie, then stares at her cup. "This is the best thing I've ever tasted. The baby loves this."

I laugh. "What about pink?"

Her nose puckers. "Are you really a pink sort of girl?"

A teenager nearby snorts, then slinks off when we glare at her.

"No," I say, "but I'm also not a *wedding date* sort of girl."

She scoffs. "You are for the guy who asked you to go."

"He didn't ask." I yank out an electric purple thing—halter top, silver shimmer over the skirt. "I invited myself."

She hums, her hand drifting over green, blue and black options before she turns to me. "Did I tell you I put up the engagement photos? I've already gotten a couple calls to schedule sessions."

"Really?" I throw my hands in the air in celebration. "Yayoi! That's awesome. You didn't even tell me you finished editing them."

She smiles, the crests of her cheeks reddening. "You want to see them?"

"Sure." I weave through a rainbow of dresses to reach her side.

She pulls up her website and scrolls to the photos of me and Asher. "I haven't finished the ones of you and your sister yet, but I wanted to get these up as soon as possible. I'm really proud of them."

She hands me the phone, and my brain short-circuits. This isn't me, is it? This is *not* me. Definitely not Asher. Because I'm not looking at a photo of two friends acting. I'm looking at two people who have capital *F* Feelings. These people care for each other. *Deeply.*

That's . . . not us.

The first photo is the *Pride & Prejudice* one. His forehead rests on mine, and the sun behind us gilds every curve and line of our faces. His hand is grazing my chin, as if he wants to angle my face up for a kiss.

The next is the one in the grass, where we stare at each

other with blatant longing. Gah, do I always look at him like that? How embarrassing . . .

The one after, I stand with my face resting against his chest, gently smiling like no place on earth is better than his arms.

Photo after photo of joy and yearning and harmony. These people are so happy, so—my mind unhelpfully supplies the obvious—*in love*.

No. I hightail it in the opposite direction.

They're just pictures with really great editing.

"These look amazing," I say, my voice somehow faint and thick at the same time. I hand the phone back.

"I know." She stares at the last photo—the one of me on Asher's back, laughing. "You guys play off each other so well." She laughs. "You know, it's funny. Geoff said—"

Her abrupt stop has my eyebrow lifting. "Geoff said what?"

She waves her hand. "Never mind. It's nothing."

Well, now I desperately want to know what Geoff said, but Yayoi is already wandering off, pulling out dresses for consideration.

"Thanks again for doing that, by the way," she says, "even if you wouldn't kiss him for me."

Aaaand now I'm remembering The Kiss. Fuck, the man knows how to kiss. I've been so disciplined in not thinking about it, no matter where I am. Joking around at work this week, texting at night, accompanying him to the gym, lying alone and cold in bed—I've avoided thinking about it.

But I'm thinking about it now.

I pretend to scan the closest rack—an entire menagerie of white. Choosing white would definitely be evil. But it doesn't matter because I'm not seeing dresses. I'm seeing Asher.

Mouthwatering, tempting, dangerous Asher.

"Kiss him? Yucky," I say in a teasing tone. "No way."

"Ha. Right? You would destroy him anyway."

That catches my attention. I look over while she holds up a pale blue number I veto with a quick shake of my head. "Destroy him?"

"Yeah." She hangs up the dress and slurps more of her smoothie. "That boy is not fling material."

Confusion washes over me, alongside a fair bit of insult. "And I *am* fling material?"

Her head cocks, and a little line forms between the delicate wings of her eyebrows. "Isn't that what you prefer to be?" She moves quickly to my side. "I didn't mean that you're, like . . . worse in some way. I just meant that you only do flings, and he doesn't do them at all. So he'd end up getting hurt. You wouldn't *actually* destroy him."

My hackles lower. "Oh."

"Shit. I feel like I messed up." Her voice grows panicky. "It's all theoretical anyway. You guys are just friends. I shouldn't have said anything."

I laugh, though I think an invisible band has wrapped around my chest because it's getting harder to breathe. "It's okay, Yayoi. Chill."

"You're any kind of material you want to be, Joss. You're the best. You can be that fancy wool that's only made from sheep in the Andes or whatever."

"Yayoi." I grip her other arm to stop the spiral. "It's okay."

She takes a deep breath and sticks the straw in her mouth, sucking deep. "Sorry. I know you're a little sensitive about that stuff."

"About what stuff?"

She motions her cup toward my general person. "The anti-relationship stuff."

The tension releases completely from my shoulders. "Ah. Yes. That."

"It's okay to want to be single. You know I support you one hundred percent, right?"

"Yeah, I know." A smile tugs at my mouth. Affection, deep and true, dawns inside me.

Oh, no. Is this another wall crumbling to pieces? How much should I panic that they're falling at such an alarming rate? Because my gut instinct says *a lot*. All the panic. Infinity panic.

She returns the smile. "Good."

"I think I'll try on the gold dress." I step away from her to grab my size, ignoring the thick feeling in my throat like it wants to close and never reopen.

She gives me a thumbs-up. "Good choice."

In the dressing room, I twist back and forth before the mirror. The flattering overhead lamps play like fairy lights against the gold. In this dress, I'm magical. Ethereal.

My phone buzzes in my purse. An EverX notification lights up my screen—a message from a new match. I sigh and throw the device back into my purse, message unread.

It isn't fun anymore. I don't want these meaningless men, and that in itself is enough to raise the alarm. Because it only means I want something different. Something deeper. Deep enough to drown if I'm not careful.

I can't traverse these waters. Not safely. I've been wading in the shallows so long, I've forgotten how to swim, and there's no life raft in the ocean of life. It's sink or swim. I'm a little peeved that one kiss from Asher Foley has thrown all my long-held beliefs into disarray.

What do I have to do to reassemble them?

I stare at the dress. This perfect golden dress with its perfect golden shimmer that I'll wear for the perfect golden man.

Why am I going to this wedding? We need space to undo the damage of that kiss, not *more* time together. Since the night he sent that text—*Maybe for you*—everything in me is screaming this is a mistake, but I can't ghost him now. He's counting on me, and that matters more than my own psychological hang-ups.

I will go to this wedding with Asher, and I'll wear this lovely, stupid gold dress, but I refuse to allow it to blur the lines of our friendship any more than they already are.

I can maintain boundaries. I've been doing it for years. What harm could a single weekend do?

Asher

> Only you can determine your
> self-worth. It's not a contest.
> —My Therapist

Jocelyn spends the entire flight to southwestern Florida asleep on my shoulder. Said shoulder is still tingling when we exit the airport for the rental cars. Perky, well-rested Joss hops twice at the car pickup, all excited for vacation weekend.

I'm a little less thrilled. After examining the emotions surrounding this wedding a dozen times, I've finally landed on the reason for my dread:

Embarrassment.

Grace *knows* I was into her. Which means Julian probably does, too.

Why am I going to this wedding? And with a fake date? I'm like the guy who brings his cousin to prom.

Pathetic.

They *really* need a better word for *pussy*. I can't purge it from my vocabulary without a replacement.

I pat the front of my backpack. Isn't that where I stashed the Tums?

A silver RAV4 pulls in front of us, and I take Joss's carry-on from her hands. My shoulder sparks. Jeez. Must have pinched a nerve in there or something.

A half hour later, we're pulling into a drive-through portico. Valets rush to the car, shuffling us and our luggage into the lobby. I'm offered a claim ticket and a smile, and I hand the guy a twenty because I have nothing else in my wallet.

Joss charges through the marble lobby toward the check-in desk, and I follow at a more sedate pace. Potted palms and tall arched windows give the place an old Florida feel, with just a splash of Art Deco in the light fixtures and floor patterns. Bright and breezy.

At the counter, a dark-haired young woman smiles. "Welcome to the Ritz-Carlton. I'm Lucy. How can I help you today?"

My head cocks. "Lucy?"

A curious light flits through her brown eyes. "Yes?"

I shake my head. "Nothing. Um. We're checking in."

"Perfect." She focuses on her computer screen. "Can I have a name?"

"Asher Foley."

Her fingers stall on the keyboard, and her attention lifts to my face. "Mr. Foley?"

Heat. Too much heat. In my cheeks. "Yep. That's me."

She blinks twice, then her gaze slides to Joss, sizing her up. Zero subtlety. Not a single drop. When she looks back at me, her brows rise. "This is not what I was picturing, Mr. Foley."

Don't know what that means. Just want this to stop.

Joss glances between us. "Er—picturing?"

"Oh, I made his reservation over the phone." She clicks away on her keyboard. "By his voice, I pictured someone . . . shorter."

Joss's face lights up. "You guess people's heights based on their voices? That's fascinating. I'm going to start doing that."

Lucy makes some noncommittal noise. "Would you like to use the card on file?"

"Yes."

"The Visa?" The edge of her lip quivers with amusement. "You're sure you didn't give us this one by *accident*?"

Well, then. Lucy's a bit of a menace, isn't she? But she did me a solid in finding me a two-room suite, so I'll ignore the cheekiness. "I'm sure."

After she reviews the benefits of club level—will definitely be using the complimentary cocktail service—and we have our room keys, Lucy throws out an encouraging smile. "Good luck, Mr. Foley."

So awkward. "Er. Thanks, Lucy."

"That girl was super weird," Joss whispers as we walk toward the elevators. "Why do you need luck?" She mashes the up button. "And why would you give them an accidental credit card?"

Don't look at her. Might laugh. "For sure. So weird."

"Is she heightist, do you think?"

Laughter leaks out, and then I'm snickering as I board the elevator, pressing my palm over my eyes.

She cocks her head. "You have a nice voice. Maybe she's a huge Tolkien fan and was picturing you as a hobbit."

Or she's trying to figure out how I accidentally kissed you.
NBD.

"That's definitely it."

Our suite is on the ninth floor. The room is *excessive*.

Jocelyn's jaw drops at the sheer luxury. "Asher. Is this real life?"

She abandons her suitcase and explores the lavish surroundings while I roll our bags into our respective bedrooms, separated by a huge living space.

"I want to live in this bathroom!" Her voice echoes out from the room in question, all veined white marble and trendy gold fixtures.

When I peek inside, she's standing in the soaker tub, fully clothed, smiling. "This suite is bigger than my whole house."

"A shoebox is bigger than your house."

She laughs and stretches a hand for me to help her out of the tub, then immediately skips into the closest bedroom and leaps on the bed, arms and legs splayed. "If we didn't have these wedding activities, we could throw a hotel party."

I lean on the doorjamb, hesitant to come closer. Don't love the sight of her on that bed. Weird things are happening in my pants. Hot things. Hard things.

She rises to her elbows, mischief passing over her features. "Guess we still could. How would the bride feel about post-rehearsal dinner shenanigans?"

"Eh. Grace isn't really a shenanigans sort of girl."

Mock disgust wrinkles up Joss's brow. "What the hell did you see in her, then?"

I shrug. Can't even remember. Was so long ago.

Her expression softens, and she sits up. "It's her loss. You know that, right?"

"I'm *fine*, Jocelyn. It's all water under the bridge." I hold out a hand to pull her off the bed—for my own sanity—but she doesn't take it.

Instead, she stares into my eyes. Color leaches into her cheeks. So pretty. So, so pretty. "You don't say my name like other people do."

I scratch my neck. "I don't?"

"No." She stands, attention lingering on my face a few more seconds before she turns toward the balcony door. "There's something in it. Something different."

Probably the L word.

I don't say it, obviously. Would destroy this fragile peace we've created. But this feeling won't go away. It's scratching wildly at its cage, trying to get out, all heat mixed with tenderness and affection. I don't want to label it. Don't want to admit it. Don't want to let it out.

I can't fall in love with her.

But do I have a choice in the matter?

She slides the door open and steps onto the wraparound balcony. Humid, salty air rushes into the room, mingling with the sterile A/C of the suite. Outside, afternoon sun sparkles over the Caribbean-blue water. The wind is strong enough to whitecap the waves as they crash over the beach below us.

"It's beautiful, isn't it?" I say.

She hums. "Dangerous."

Right. Almost forgot. Joss and the ocean don't mix. Her hands white-knuckle the guardrail.

I've avoided touching her since our mishap in my bedroom, but she's turning into Brittle Joss again. In need of comfort. I'm somehow synced to her needs, so my hand rises of its own accord and presses against the middle of her back. Even through her shirt, her warmth seeps into my skin. Her body loosens ever so slightly.

Ugh. Someone's turning down the oxygen again.

"Do you ever wonder why the more beautiful something is, the more deadly it is?" she asks.

I tilt my head, keeping my gaze on the water.

"Think about it." She leans closer to the rail, peeking down. "The vibrant purple of nightshade. The sparkle of liquid mercury. The blinding brightness of lightning."

Guess we're going dark today. Which means I'm giving up on subtle. I drape my arm over her shoulders and pull her next to me. "There are beautiful things that aren't deadly, too."

She laughs, soft and humorless. "Like what?"

"Sunsets. Turning leaves. Rainbows."

Silent, she lifts her gaze to mine.

"Friendship." I brush her chin with my thumb and smile. "Family. Love."

Her head tilts. "Do you really think those things aren't dangerous, Asher?"

She looks so lost when she gets in this state, this *contemplating my mortality* mood.

Sweet, fragile woman.

I pull her into a hug. She fits snug against me, her arms a vise around my middle.

"Just being alive is dangerous, Jocelyn. It's not the circumstances of death that matter in the end. It's the life lived before it."

"Stop trying to logicize me off the ledge here. I want to wallow."

"Okay. Just wallow, then." I set my chin atop her head. "But *logicize* is a really dumb word and you shouldn't use it."

Chuckling, she squeezes me tighter. "I really like your hugs."

That's nice. But . . . Why is this familiar weight of inadequacy resting on my shoulders *now*? Is it the fact that she won't even consider the idea of us?

Casual is just all I'm capable of.

Casual might be all I ever get from *any* girl. Should have told Joss I was fine with it. Then maybe this itch would be out of my system.

Inadequate feelings definitely wouldn't be, but that's another problem.

"Hey, look," she says, smiling up at me. "We managed to have a serious conversation outside of a sterile hallway."

My chuff of laughter stirs the hair at her temple. "Look out, world. We're unstoppable."

•

THE REHEARSAL DINNER is located at a restaurant a couple miles inland and boasts a large gathering since many guests came from out of town. In a shimmery blue dress, Jocelyn practically glows among this crowd.

Why did the universe have to make her so beautiful? It's a little annoying at this point. She's like the dessert tray at a restaurant, all look but don't touch, smell but don't taste.

Fucking hellish.

Inside the restaurant entrance, someone shouts my name, stopping me dead in my tracks.

"Asher? Is that you?"

I turn toward the voice, the one belonging to the man of the hour, and paste on a smile.

"Holy shit." Julian beams and offers me a hand to shake. "I didn't think you'd come."

I laugh. "Why not? I RSVPed."

"I don't know, man. Been a long time."

He releases my hand, still grinning. He's wearing light gray chinos, a white button-up and an obnoxious amount of stubble. I know nothing about his life, but he looks rich and happy and very Italian, even though he was born right here in this cesspool of America. He doesn't quite smile but always *appears* to be smiling.

The guy is insufferably charming. It's unfair.

Julian's dark eyes travel to my companion, and I remember I'm supposed to introduce her.

"Oh. Julian, this is Jocelyn, my, um . . . my . . . friend?"

Wow. Smooth.

Joss's smile falters only a moment, and she shakes Julian's hand. "You're the groom? Congratulations!"

"Thanks. It's nice to meet you." He twists and searches through the people behind him—the room is quickly filling—then motions toward someone. "Grace! Look who I found."

She emerges from the crowd like a goddamn angel, looking *exactly* how I remember her. Wavy hair, flawlessly styled with silver glitter sparking along the brown strands. Golden freckles over her nose. Kind eyes gleaming with joy. She practically lights up at the sight of me.

I got nothing. Not even a spark. Teensy worry that feelings might return is thankfully laid to rest.

But no wonder I was so confused back then. Grace twinkles when she smiles. Happiness looks fantastic on her. *Good on you, Julian.*

Really drives home the fact that Jocelyn *doesn't* look like that around me. With Julian, Grace has come to life. With me, Jocelyn stands at balcony rails and laments over the danger of love.

My ironic laugh is mistaken for a real one, thank god, and Grace smiles.

"Asher!" She leaps into my arms, then backs away. She cups her hands around my face. "Look at you. You look good."

"Hey, Gracey-kins. Long time, no see. You're beautiful, as always."

She releases me. At once, a hand sneaks into mine, fingers lacing.

Is she—is Jocelyn holding my hand?

WTF?

Still beaming, Grace looks at Joss. "Who's this? Is this your girlfriend, Asher? She's pretty. You're pretty."

"They're just friends," Julian offers, but he has a weird glint in his eye that tells me he *knows*.

He always fucking knows. Too observant, this guy.

I meet his mirthful stare as Joss says, "Thanks. I'm Jocelyn." She puts on an Audrey Hepburn accent. "I'm madly in love with Asher, but he refuses to DTR."

I roll my eyes, and Julian snorts.

"Oh, really?" Grace's eyes widen in utter delight. She nudges Julian in a way that is probably supposed to be subtle, but is actually not subtle at all. Julian sets an arm around her shoulders to calm her matchmaking whims. She looks up at him, hearts in her eyes. "Remember when I refused to DTR?"

Julian smiles, but somehow doesn't smile. "Worst month of my life."

"I'm sensing a story," Joss says with an impish grin.

Grace pats Julian's chest and sighs. "Not a good one. Just me learning that everything is so much better when you finally . . . surrender."

Julian kisses her cheek, and they beam at each other in a vaguely sickening way. Jocelyn and I exchange a quick, awkward glance.

Still holding hands. Why are we holding hands again?

Grace shakes herself. "Anyway, thanks for coming. Have a great dinner."

She hugs Joss, who finally releases me to return the embrace. My hand feels weird where she touched it. All hot and prickly. Grace whispers something in Joss's ear, then moves on to the guests behind us. With a last nod at Julian, I take Joss's elbow and lead her farther into the dining room.

"Well, she was fucking lovely," Joss says, starkly sincere.

"Told you. Sweetest woman alive. What'd she say to you?" I check the names at the round tables, finding ours—Dr. Asher Foley and guest—at one in the corner, still empty. I pull out Joss's chair, and she slides in.

When I settle next to her, she leans close. "She said, 'I know it was a joke, but he's worth the wait.'"

Hmm. Is it, like . . . excessively hot in here?

Since entering this restaurant, my entire body has buzzed like a hive of bees lives under my skin. With those words, their stingers pierce my flesh. I reach for the ice water on the table and take a sip without looking at Joss. "She really took you at your word there."

She chuckles. "I see what you liked about her. And Julian is very charming."

"*I'm* charming," I mutter, annoyed that Joss noticed anything about Julian at all. Bro steals too much attention for himself. It's like he's the groom of this wedding or something.

Rude.

Her laughter grows. "Yes, but he's the refined sort of charming, whereas you're the goofy, lovable sort. The two aren't the same."

I gather the courage to look at her, flush be damned. "You make me sound like a puppy."

"Um. Puppies are straight fire, Ash. Just take the snapshot."

Smiling, I aim a fake camera at her and make a clicking noise while she sticks her tongue out.

"Foley!" booms a deep voice. Maxwell approaches our table, his arm around his wife, Cat.

Short for . . . Catherine? Caterina? Catwoman?

Don't know.

I stand and greet them both, introducing Jocelyn, even though they both met her two years ago. The couple settles at the table.

Maxwell graduated a year ahead of me and currently works as faculty at our residency program. Extracting gossip from him is something I've looked forward to this weekend—Is Dr. Chen still Chen-ing? Do the hospitalists still suck? Which residents shine? Who's sleeping with who?

Our table fills, but the four of us laugh and catch up, and before long, it's nearly over. When Julian stands to toast Grace, Maxwell makes his way over to give his own toast.

Speeches are made. Tears are shed. At the closing of the evening, Maxwell reminds me to meet them in the hotel lobby for bachelor party shenanigans.

"Are you sure you don't mind?" I ask Joss on the drive back to the hotel. "I don't have to go to the bachelor party."

She gives my shoulder a playful shove. "That's what we came for. Go! Enjoy your friends."

I smirk. "You going to party without me?"

"Nope. I'm going to lounge in that room like I'm a Kardashian. Someone has to enjoy all that luxury while you're getting drunk."

"I don't plan on getting drunk."

She lets out a dubious laugh. "We'll see."

In the hotel lobby, she pecks a kiss on my cheek and sashays away, blue dress sparkling as she walks.

Mesmerizing woman.

"She could hang with Cat if she wants."

I spin to find Maxwell behind me. "Hey, man. You mean Joss?"

"Yeah." He shrugs one buff shoulder. Is he bigger than the last time I saw him? He was already huge to begin with.

"I'll let her know. Are the girls doing anything?"

"I've been told it's not my business."

Ha. Dear Lord, help us all.

Jocelyn

You have to be scared before you can be brave.
—My Therapist

I'm not sure what I've gotten myself into.

Amid a gaggle of women—including the bride, the groom's sisters, Cat and a few of questionable relation—I've become quite tipsy. Grace's suite could rival ours, and I'm still drooling over the luxury. The alcohol makes everything glow, and I'm in love.

I want to live at the Ritz-Carlton.

"So, are you nervous?" Cat asks Grace, who's sitting cross-legged beside me, deep in the corner of the couch. She's wearing sweats and holding a tumbler of herbal tea because *I don't want any chance of a hangover.*

Right. Ten bucks says she's pregnant.

She looks at the ceiling like she's really considering the question. "Maybe a little? I don't like being the center of attention."

Julian's sister—Tori, I think?—bursts out laughing. "Then why didn't you pick the courthouse like I suggested?"

She huffs. "You know your mom would never let me do that."

One of the older sisters grins. "Our little BB is getting married. We have to do it right."

"BB?" I ask.

"Our baby." Another sister cackles. "Julian hates it."

Yeah, no grown man wants to be called *baby* by anyone he isn't sleeping with. I'm sure it drives him nuts. It would drive Asher batty, too. I must plot how to torture him with this.

Hmm. But maybe it would be weird if I started calling him *baby*.

Never mind. I gulp down a large swallow of wine.

"So, Jocelyn," Grace says, "you work with Asher?"

I startle out of my thoughts. "Oh. Uh-huh. Anesthesia."

The other women fall into a separate conversation, leaving Grace and me in our quiet corner.

She sips her tea. "Did he tell you he was my senior resident when I was an intern?"

No, but he told me he was in love with you.

I smile. "No, I didn't know that."

"He was the *best* senior. Do the residents at your hospital love him?"

Oh, yeah. Residents. Nurses. Certain catty anesthesiologists. "He's pretty popular."

She laughs into her tumbler. "No surprise there."

Her gaze is soft as she swirls a finger around the rim of

the plastic lid. The sparkly diamond on her left hand glitters in the ambient light. It occurs to me that this woman knew Asher at a time when I didn't. A younger Asher.

"Did you ever get the sense during training that he thought he was, like . . . not good enough?"

She lifts her gaze to me, brows drawn together. "Not at all. He seemed completely confident. BrOB-GYN to his core."

I snort. "BrOB-GYN?"

"Oh. He didn't tell you about that? His little group of guys. A little misogynistic, but I don't think he ever saw it that way. He's a little clueless sometimes."

Huh. So Grace *knows* Asher. I'm not certain how to feel about that. Pretty sure my heart thinks we should be jealous, though that makes zero sense. Grace is getting married tomorrow. To someone else. Oh, yeah, and *I don't want Asher Foley.*

If I believe it hard enough, it's bound to come true.

"Were you serious earlier?" she asks. "About being in love with him?"

"Ah." I snag a sip of wine to delay the answer. "No. We're just friends, actually."

She nods slowly, pondering. "That's too bad. He needs someone great." Her hazel eyes search mine. "You seem kind of great."

A tender flower blossoms in my heart for this girl. "Thanks. You seem sort of great, too."

The other women in the room erupt into laughter, drawing our attention, but Grace sets a hand on my arm. "I've got a bit of a soft spot for him. Just . . . look out for him for me, will you?"

I slide my hand atop hers. "I always have. Always will."

Her smile sparkles, and I remember how much Asher had been dreading coming here. How strange he's been since we set foot in this hotel, like a shadow of himself. I'm not sure what's got him so skittish, but it's not this woman. He'd been perfectly genial with her at dinner. Not a single sign that he'd once had deep feelings for her. His unease lies elsewhere, and I wish I knew where. How else am I supposed to fix it?

When I make it back to my suite around 11:00, it's still empty. The cold hotel air wraps around my limbs, and I decide to indulge in that soaker tub before bed. Bubble baths are what happiness is made of, and all the anxiety and tension drain away with the bathwater. Warm, content and drowsy from the alcohol, I curl up in bed and let sleep take me.

But dreams are cruel. Uncontrollable. Sometime later, the familiar nightmare of watching the water take Asher jolts me awake. I blink into unfamiliar darkness. The silence oppresses me. My skin is too tight, stretched across tense muscles and rigid bones. My traitorous, endangered heart slams hard against my ribs, robbing me of breath.

Just a dream.

It was just a dream.

I check my phone.

2:04 a.m.

Ugh. Why?

With zero hesitation, I slink out of my bed and tiptoe toward Asher's side of the suite on trembling legs. I just need to verify he's breathing, and I can go back to sleep. It will make the shivers stop. Simple.

But when I enter his room, I pause. The bed is suspiciously undisturbed. I pat it down in the dark. No Asher.

I flip the lights on. He isn't even here. Where on earth would he be at 2:00 a.m.?

Oh.

Oh.

Oh, no.

The obvious answer leaps to my brain, unwelcome and gross. He found a girl at the bachelor shenanigans, didn't he? He's probably in her room now. She's touching him. He's kissing her.

Well, damn. The heart that was pounding so hard before withers in my chest. I'm going to be sick. Why'd I drink so much wine?

I snap on the lights in the main room, flooding the luxurious space in a warm ambiance I can't feel, and sink onto the couch.

Would Asher do that, though?

He wouldn't. I don't think he would. He doesn't do one-night stands.

But why wouldn't he? He's entitled to fun. To making mistakes. He's probably drunk. Probably thought I'd be asleep, and assumed he'd be back before I woke. No harm done.

I'm not allowed to be jealous about this. I don't even want him. I just don't like thinking about him with someone else. Unfair, but true.

So yeah. That's it. That's all it is.

Calm down. Stop thinking about it. As soon as my heart returns to my chest, I'll go right back to sleep.

But it doesn't return. I am hollow, and I stay on that couch, staring sightlessly at the French doors to the darkened balcony, aching. I'm alone on my hill.

Not thirty minutes later, Asher stumbles into the suite, zigzagging through the hall toward the living room.

Something happens. Something invisible, but profound. The sight of him sets off a violent chain reaction inside me, causing enough pain to make me wince. I'm not sure what exactly happens to my body. It's like nothing I've ever felt before. Like falling, but also like standing on steady ground. Like something new with the comfort of home.

I've lost something, but gained something, too.

Large pieces of me are no longer mine. The hacksaw has removed them and dropped them right at his feet.

"Whoa," I say, shoving it all down below a locked hatch. "Are you a little drunk or totally wasted?"

He holds up a finger. "Julian eats shots."

"That . . . makes no sense."

He nods like *I know!* and falls onto the couch beside me.

I poke his shoulder. "Where were you?"

"Bar. Lots of pool. I lost. Even more alcohol. Lost there, too."

I raise an eyebrow, trying to tease. "Strippers?"

His eyes narrow. "Why're you awake?"

I sigh. "Nightmare."

"Shit." His expression falls, and he glances between his lighted room and my dark one before his inebriated gaze finds me. "You were looking for me, weren't you?"

The pattern of the sofa fabric draws my undivided attention.

"And I wasn't here." He slurs the words together, but his tone is clearly distraught.

I try to play it off with a laugh. "It's fine. I just wasn't ready to go back to sleep. I don't, like . . . *need* you."

His chuckle edges into bitter. "I'm aware, Jocelyn." His eyes close, and he rests his head on the back of the sofa, hands clasped over his abdomen.

Something lurches in my chest. The hacksaw, probably, trying its best to tear the remains of my heart open for him. What good are walls in the face of this?

"Who was it this time?" he asks, eyes still shut.

Breathing suddenly hurts. Each lungful of air burns with fear.

Scared to have him.

Scared to lose him.

Scared I'll wait too long and squander my chance.

Scared I already have.

You aren't running, Joss. You're hiding.

I draw my legs up and hug them, setting my chin on one knee. "It's always you, Ash."

My voice is quiet in the still room, but loud enough I know he heard it, even drunk. His head turns, and his bleary stare sharpens. It dances over my face, searching.

That feeling is returning, the one that's convinced he's vital to me. The one that would sacrifice immensely dear things to have him. The one that doesn't care about the potential pain.

Ahh.

How do I make it stop?

"You're very confusing," he says in the midst of my panic. "I'm too drunk to puzzle it out." He stands, presses a firm kiss to the top of my head and zigzags toward his bedroom. "If you have another nightmare, wake me up. We'll watch reruns of *The Bachelorette* until sunrise."

"I think you've forgotten I don't like *The Bachelorette*."

He stops in the doorway to look at me. "*The Bachelorette* is what's for me. My company is what's for you."

Asher

> This moment is not every moment. Whether the
> moment is good or bad, it will not last forever.
> —My Therapist

A wedding on the beach is cliché, right? Or is it pretty?

"Wow," Jocelyn whispers as we step onto the sand. "This is so pretty."

Okay, then.

White chairs stand in rows before a pink-flower-draped pergola. Beyond it, blue waves crash against gleaming sand.

I direct her toward a back row on Grace's side. Definitely the best place for us. "You don't strike me as someone who'd like a beach wedding."

A grin flashes as she sits. "No, but I appreciate a pretty thing when I see it."

My gaze touches on the shimmer in her makeup, highlighted by the sun. The platinum shine to her hair. The sheen of gold in her distracting dress. The peekaboo stars across her collarbone. "Me, too," I mutter under my breath.

"So." She crosses her legs and wiggles in her seat. "Has the ibuprofen kicked in?"

"Headache is a two out of ten now. Thanks, by the way."

"Anything for you, Ashie poo." She casts a wink at me.

It's always you, Ash.

Sort of wish I didn't remember her saying that. Rest of the night is a bit of a blur, but that? That I remember with crystal clarity. 4K Ultra HD.

Confusing, fickle woman.

I glance behind me at the guests filtering in. "Do you think the food will be as awesome as this setup?"

"I hope so. I'm starving. If there's not crab cakes, I'll punch Julian in the nuts."

As I burst into laughter, a couple in front of us turns to stare disapprovingly. Joss wiggles her fingers at them until they face forward again, muttering to each other.

"God, I'd love to see that," I say more quietly. "Highlight of the weekend."

We settle into a companionable silence. This weekend has really thrown into stark relief how I'm lagging on the road of life. Maxwell is a good enough doctor to be training new ones. Julian is marrying the love of his life today. Grace has blossomed into a confident and happy woman. And I . . . am stagnant.

Tolerating it all would have been infinitely harder without Joss. Her presence is like a security blanket. Feels a bit warm and fuzzy, truly. Sort of enjoyable. Comfortable.

I lean my shoulder into hers. "Thank you for doing this, Joss."

Her brow knits. "Doing what?"

"Just being here. With me. It's made everything a lot easier."

She smiles at her lap. "Well. It's not like it's hard. I really like you."

Ah. The mark of the Friend Zone. Perhaps the warm fuzzy is a bit too hot. Didn't know I was claustrophobic, but I'm definitely feeling trapped. Like I've entered an escape room with no real exit.

I breathe it away, using the sea air and the sun to refocus.

The ceremony is short and lovely. A little boring, honestly. Afterward, we shuffle into an elaborately decorated event space in the hotel.

Jocelyn whistles under her breath as we take in the tasteful decor. "This is the nicest party I've ever been to."

Well-dressed guests mingle and chat in groups. Some find their way to circle tables. Others stand at the windows to admire the views of the ocean. Outside, on the beach, the newlyweds pose for photos. In an unguarded moment, Julian touches Grace's face, then low on her stomach over the free-flowing gown. She presses her hand over his and smiles.

Ah. She's pregnant.

Isn't that . . . perfect?

I'm happy for her. For *them*. Truly.

Also unhappy for me, though. They have everything I want, and I'm annoyed that I'm envious. Fed up with my reality. Frustrated that such a future seems like a pipe dream.

"Yeah. Super nice." I steer Joss toward the open bar. "Let's drink."

She chuckles. "Didn't you have enough last night?"

"Yeah, but *you* didn't."

She stops and puts her hand on her hip. "Doctor Foley, are you trying to get me drunk?"

"I've heard it said that alcohol is the best lube."

She barks out a laugh and throws an open palm in my face. "Don't be extra." Sashaying away from me, her tiny, impeccable ass glimmers in gold satin.

Shit. Forgot not to look.

A couple beats pass before I pull myself together and meet her at the bar. She hands me a glass of champagne and shoots the evil eye at the bartender. "No hard liquor until later, apparently."

The man shrugs as if to say, *Not my decision*.

Over in the corner, a DJ fires up a playlist of dinner jazz and invites the guests to help themselves to hors d'oeuvres.

"Yes, please!" Joss grabs my hand and hauls me over to the food table. She loads a plate with bacon-wrapped dates, Caprese skewers, crab cakes, stuffed crescent rolls and about a dozen other things I don't recognize.

Smiling, she holds a mini quiche to my mouth. "Open."

And I obey. Even though I've lost my appetite. Because the acid has finally gnawed away my entire stomach.

"You're a professional grazer," I say once I swallow the food that tastes like rubber and salt.

She nods. "This is why it's here, Asher. To eat."

With an unsubtle nudge, I maneuver Joss and her overfull plate away. "Yes. For *everyone* to eat. Not just you."

At our assigned table, she scarfs down the food while we wait for the happy couple. A few strangers take the other chairs, nodding polite greetings. After a while, the DJ interrupts the music to announce the buffet opening. Grace and Julian enter with the wedding party, and a line forms to congratulate them.

Jocelyn slumps back in her chair, hand over her belly. "I might be too full for dinner right now. Should we go say hi to them before we drink more?"

"Sure." I stand and offer a hand, but halfway there, Joss stops me with a gentle tug. I glance at her, eyebrows lifted.

"Hey," she says, "you okay?"

"Yeah, I'm fine." How could she tell?

I'm not okay. I don't know why, but I'm really not okay.

"You sure?" She steps closer and lowers her voice so the strangers milling around us won't hear. "I know this weekend has been hard for you but remember what we talked about. You're awesome. Nothing about you is lacking."

Really wish she'd stop saying such nice things. Makes it hard to remember she doesn't want me. Should I hope for the black hole again? Just swallow me up. No more Asher.

It takes effort, but I shake my head. "I'm really fine."

"I hate seeing you like this," she whispers. "And I—I feel like I'm failing at being your best friend. Whatever you need, I'm there. You know I'd do anything for you."

And there it is.

The moment.

The line crossed.

The point of no return.

I'd do anything for you.

I am in love with her.

This woman who's afraid of love. The one who rejected me, point-blank. The one who's too afraid of pain to take a chance on me.

I love her.

Terrible thing, really. Can't foresee any good coming of this.

I'm really, truly, definitely not okay.

But I stretch my mouth into a smile because it's what she wants. Because it will make her happy. "I don't need anything, sugar cookie. I'm fine. Really."

That perturbed expression doesn't ease, but she nods and follows me toward the bridal party.

Brilliant yet fake smile plastered over my face, I envelop Grace in an embrace. "Congrats, Gracey-cakes."

"Thank you!" The sheer happiness in her glistens over her every curve and angle. "And thanks for coming. It's so good to see you."

I move on to her husband while she chats with Jocelyn, grasping his hand in mine. "Congratulations, man. Seriously."

He smiles. A *real* smile. One that is visible to the naked eye. "Thanks."

A tall, dark beauty at Julian's side elbows him, and he winces. A feline grin stretches across her face. "Introduce me?"

With a roll of his eyes, Julian gestures to me. "Asher, this is my sister, Tori. Tori, Asher. We did residency together."

Tori extends a hand to be shaken. "Hey, there."

Julian's eyebrows cinch as he stares at his sister, but the woman is still beaming at me.

Her hand is delicate but strong, and she doesn't release me. "You single?"

Oh.

Oh.

She's *interested*.

Julian's sister. Interested. In me.

An impulsive desire wakes, fueled by testosterone and cortisol and this looming emotional disaster on my horizon.

Julian got Grace.

I could take his sister.

In a strange, twisted world, I could act on her interest. I'm single. Available. The girl I brought has stressed, in no uncertain terms, just how much she doesn't want me.

And Julian would *know*. It would be in his mind for the rest of his life. He's winning at life, but I could have this.

Aaaaand I'm an asshole.

Why is this thought even in my head? Because Julian has everything I want?

It's not his fault my life falls short of his. Not his fault he's blissfully in love, with one on the way, while I'm secretly pining after my best friend.

"He's not single." Jocelyn's sharp voice beside me breaks through my reverie. The edge in it is new. Different.

I glance at her, only to find an uncharacteristic glare directed at Julian's sister.

Tori drops my hand and shrugs. "Too bad. He's pretty."

"Victoria." Julian squeezes the bridge of his nose. "Will you please stop hitting on all my friends? Look at them. They are clearly into each other."

The siblings continue to argue, but I'm distracted by the lingering scowl on Joss's face, the burnished red across her nose and cheeks. With one last nod at the newlyweds, I grasp Jocelyn's elbow and direct her toward an empty area near the windows. The guests mix and mingle. Laughter and music drift about us.

I seclude us best I can. "You okay?"

Expression schooled into nonchalance, she looks out the window, where the setting sun lights the sky on fire, and bright orange sparkles over the rolling ocean. "I'm— Yeah. I'm fine. I'm . . ." Her gaze swings to me. "What was that, Asher?"

Confused, I study her face but find no answers. "What was what?"

She waves an arm at the bridal party. "You actually considered it, didn't you? That girl?"

A deep furrow forms between her brows. Something's wrong. I've done something, but . . . what?

"No," I say. Why does it sound like a question? "She came on to me. I hesitated."

She swallows and glances back at Tori. "Do you want to go talk to her?"

"No." The gnawing in my gut returns at her suspicious expression. "You told her I'm not single. Hitting on her now . . . That's not a great look."

"Shit." Her hand hides her eyes. "I don't know why I said that."

Silence passes between us.

What . . . What's this tiny seed of hope sprouting inside? Stop it! Stahp.

Efffff. Why can't I stop it?

I pull her hand from her face. Her gaze is wary. Defensive. She's close enough that I can divide her into individual parts, a bevy of precious metals and gems. Rays of copper and gold in her irises. The onyx pen strokes of her lashes. The gleam of platinum in her hair. The shimmer of her ruby lips.

So beautiful. Right here in front of me, yet so distant. She's like a star. Glittering from afar, cold, but if she'd just let me closer, I know I'd burn. Something is mutating between us, despite her attempts to stop it. Surely, she senses it, too. Am I the only one falling?

"Jocelyn." I brush my finger beneath her chin. "Are you jealous?"

A false smile stretches her red lips but doesn't touch her eyes. A strained laugh flies from her mouth. "What— What are you even . . . What are you talking about? Of course not."

The longer I stare at her face, the more convinced I am. "You sure?"

"We're just friends, Asher."

"Yeah. You're right." Wanting free, the truth jackhammers against its cage. My blood spikes with a fresh shot of adrenaline as I give in to it. "But I kind of think you know I'd take more if you'd give it."

Her lips part, and she freezes. Doe eyes go impossibly wide as if a Mack truck heads straight for her.

Uh-oh.

No.

Shit.

Wait. I take it back.

She shakes her head. Takes one step away.

"Joss—"

Delicate, gold-tipped fingers press into the skin over her heart. She checks behind her.

"Joss, wait—"

Her hand rises in a sharp gesture to stop, and my voice dies. Time suspends. The room goes silent around us. Or maybe I'm about to pass out.

In one swirl of gold and glitter, the twinkling star falls, and she shoots toward the exit.

Away from me.

The tiny seedling of hope—that warm, happy, WALL-E quality leaf—curls up and withers in the face of another rejection.

Whatever is left in my chest follows suit.

Jocelyn

Being alone doesn't make you stronger.
—My Therapist

Why did Asher say that?

What is he doing?

I stumble through the crowded room, bumping wedding guests and murmuring apologies until I reach the hallway beyond. My feet don't stop. They take me out to the pool, glowing blue in the fading evening light. At this time of day, the lounge chairs are mostly empty, but a cabana on the opposite side boasts several patrons. The palm trees above are black against the clear azure sky, shadowed and distant.

Past all that, a gate opens toward the beach, and my rope sandals fill with sand as I trudge along the seashell-strewn pathway.

The scent of the ocean permeates everything. Sand and

salt and something elusive. Indescribable. It whips down the beach with the wind, curls over the sand with each wave.

I kind of think you know I'd take more if you'd give it.

My eyes close and I fight the sink of each footstep, drawing ever closer to the receding tide. Closer to my greatest fear.

Why would he say that? I'm not capable of more, even if I wanted to give it. I'm like the small shells on this beach—pretty on the outside, fun to play with, but ultimately a fading vestige of something whole and alive. These shells were living creatures once, just like I was, and they succumbed to the inevitable, just like I have.

Death is inescapable, and the fewer people I love, the less I hurt.

If love is dangerous, then Asher Foley is lethal, just like this deceptively calm water. I can't do it. I can't be more than his friend. If I submit to this roiling storm inside me, I'll drown. I'll agonize over every missed phone call. Every traffic jam that keeps him late. Every unanswered text.

The logical side of me knows this is stupid. Some things are impossible to control, and Asher—he's one of them. He already lives deep in my heart, behind the walls. He's a life raft, yes, but I need him to stop dragging me into the deep end just to prove it.

I can't—

I just can't.

So what do I say to him? How do I go back into that wedding and unwalk the path he paved for us?

Reliving the conversation, I cover my face with my hands. I'm such a bitch. I ran out of that room like it was on fire. He's probably sitting alone at our table while I try to convince myself I can't love him.

Nothing is more believable than the lie you tell yourself.

Heart pounding, skin tingling, my feet carry me closer to the water, right to the edge. The gentle evening waves lap at the sand inches from my toes. Deceptive tranquility.

I'm close. So close. But I can't take the last step. Fear has me frozen at the precipice, at the ocean's edge.

But it doesn't matter that I'm not brave. I won't let this ruin us. I'm just wish fulfillment for him. Easy and comfortable. This rift between us is nothing that can't be fixed with a little liquor and a frank conversation. We've talked through harder things than this. We'll come out stronger.

It'll be easy. A small slipup can't undo the steel bonds between us.

One step away. Then another. The last hints of daylight fade from the horizon, and the ocean dims to black. I turn my back on it and return to the hotel.

•

WHEN I REENTER the reception, Asher is on the dance floor, laughing with Maxwell, and the Gordian knot inside me releases. See? He's fine. He's too much of a glass-half-full person to let someone like me shake his foundation.

I edge the perimeter of the room so I can watch without him noticing. The two of them slip into some cheesy, practiced dance, like the choreography from a boy band music video. A crowd forms around them, cheering them on, but I stay silent, watching Asher.

He's a smooth dancer. I already knew that, of course, but the easy smile on his face now, the looseness of his limbs—they make me see how tense he'd been before.

Did I do that to him?

When they finish, the crowd explodes with applause, and Asher and Maxwell do that bro-hug thing. They make their way to Cat's table, chatting, and Asher pecks a kiss on Cat's cheek before sitting.

I watch a while longer, then decide I'm a creepy coward and head that way.

"I'm sorry," I whisper into his ear.

He startles and turns toward me, smile fading. "Oh. Hey." His gaze travels over my face. "Thought I'd lost you there."

"Nah." I slip into the empty chair at his side. "I'm here. Always."

I wave at Cat and admire her dress. She brushes it off humbly, but her cheeks pink up.

Asher rubs his neck before returning his attention to Maxwell. "Anyway, she—um . . . What was I saying?"

Maxwell glances at me, then back to Asher. "You said she was refusing meds?"

"Oh, right." Asher chuckles. "She was okay with being induced, but didn't want Pitocin, so she was asking me all the natural ways to induce."

Maxwell smirks and sips his beer, like he knows where this story is going. No way does he know. I nearly peed myself when Asher first told me.

"I give her the spiel—that nothing really works, but I mention nipple stimulation."

A little chuckle from Maxwell.

"In *passing*," Asher says. "I barely touched on it. Like, a single mention. But she latches on to that idea like it's her only chance. Her Hail Mary."

Maxwell's wife leans her elbows on the table. "I'm guessing it doesn't work?"

Asher has begun his *giggle*, the one where he's telling a story he thinks is hilarious, so he can't quite get the words out. "I tell her husband, 'All right, man. Go for it. Stimulate those nipples.' And I come back an hour later—" *giggle, giggle* "—and the guy has a sheet up, blocking his view of his wife, but his hands are under the sheet, clearly going to town—" *giggle, giggle* "—so I'm like, 'Why are you covering her up? You've never seen your wife's nipples?' And the patient shrieks, 'Ew! That's not my husband! That's my brother!'"

Asher drops his face into his hand and titters. Maxwell's eyes go wide, and his deep laugh fills the spaces between us all.

"Oh, my god," says Maxwell's wife. "What did you say?"

Asher's voice has risen in pitch with his laughter. "I just— I said I had to check on something and—and I left. I mean—" he looks up from his hand "—it was her brother! What the fuck? Just . . . why?"

Insides warm, I snicker. "That's some family dedication."

"Maxwell," a bridesmaid says as she approaches the table, "it's almost time for the speeches."

He nods and rises. "I'll see y'all after."

Cat follows him, leaving Asher and me alone. He turns my way and volunteers a rueful smile, wiping the gleeful tears from his eyes. "I made it awkward. Again. I can't seem to stop doing that. I'm sorry."

"No." I grip his forearm, thinly wrapped in soft, white cotton. "I'm the one who made it awkward. Can we start the night over?"

"Yeah." He takes a breath. "Weirdness never happened."

I grin. "Great. Yes. Exactly!"

His gaze drops to my mouth, then my neck, before bouncing back to my eyes. "So . . . how do we do that?"

"Um." How indeed? "Why don't we . . . dance?"

His eyes go utterly opaque. "Dance?"

I point at the DJ, currently spinning some high-energy pop tune. "Well, *you'll* dance, and I'll hop in place like usual."

That finally brings a smile to his mouth. "You aren't that bad."

"I can't even chicken dance." I grab his hand and drag him toward the dance floor, packed with swaying elderly couples, moms boogying with their adorable toddlers, and twentysomethings in a dance circle, drinks in hand.

Asher melts into the crowd like he belongs there. His moves are the same ones I've seen in bars back home, Oktoberfest tents, Vegas nightclubs. I like those moves. They're familiar. Easy to predict.

Mine, on the other hand, are erratic, and he immediately plunges into laughter at my expense. It's fine, though. His laughter is one of my favorite things in the world. Maybe I hurt him by walking away earlier, but I can fix it now by bringing him joy. With that thought in mind, I put a little extra zeal into my legs.

He grabs my wrist to keep me from toppling into a flower girl. "Easy there, wild thing."

I pat his shoulder. "We good?"

"We're always good, Joss."

We both slow after that, and he matches my smile with a soft one of his own. The pop music drifts into some smooth tune of Michael Bublé, and my stomach knots once more. Without hesitation, his warm hand engulfs mine. He takes me into his arms like I'm precious. His heated touch slides around my waist. "This okay?"

"Yeah." I wish it weren't, but it's so, *so* okay. I can't resist letting him closer. *Wanting* him closer.

"I didn't mean to put you on the spot earlier," he whispers. "It was impulsive. Can you forget it?"

I compel my face to smile. It feels awkward. "It's forgotten."

I'll never forget it, though.

I kind of think you know I'd take more if you'd give it.

He's opened a door, ripped it off its hinges, so I can't close it.

We dance slower than the surrounding couples. His hand brings mine close to his chest, and his other settles low on my back, heat bleeding through the thin satin, scalding my skin. My fingers slide up to rest on his shoulder and my temple nuzzles against the bristle of his cheek.

And everything is right.

But so, so, so, so wrong.

His arms are like home. Like safety. Like a life jacket in a heavy swell.

Why am I still swimming so hard against this riptide? My throat closes. Illogical tears burn behind my eyes. What is *wrong* with me?

The song ends, and he releases me. At the edge of the dance floor, he points at the food. "You hungry?"

I take in the buffet tables, silver chafers gleaming in the light. The food smells delicious, but I've lost my appetite, so I shake my head. Candles on each table lend the room a romantic glow, but the clinking of silverware on china, the gentle hum of conversation and laughter—it's suffocating.

The ding of silver on crystal alerts us to an impending toast, and I whirl toward Asher. "Let's go for a walk."

The room quiets, and an older gentleman takes the microphone stand near the DJ.

"Now?" Asher whispers.

"Do you care about the speeches?"

He looks around. Guests settle into their chairs. Catering staff pass out flutes of champagne. "No." He takes my elbow. "Let's go for a walk."

In the hallway beyond, the man's speech dims to the background, and Asher turns to me. "Where to?"

I set off toward the exit that leads to the beach, but outside the doors, I hang a right, and we walk along a path lined with tropical plants. The humid air wraps around us, and Asher rolls up the sleeves of his button-up.

"Already tired of the wedding festivities?" he asks.

"Starting to feel a bit crowded in there."

He glances at me, but says nothing, and we continue to walk the path that hugs the hotel. We pass the pool and the raucous cabana. He smiles over at the whoops and hollers from the bar. "Sounds like they're having fun. Should we join?"

Without looking over, I shake my head and keep walking, my sandals crunching along the sand-dusted path.

He falls behind and lets me lead, his voice dropping. "Something wrong, Joss?"

"No." I continue on, rounding the side of the hotel and traveling toward the entry road. A decorative pond takes up the center of the circle drive, complete with fountain and lovely tropical landscaping.

Asher grabs my hand to stop my march. "I said I was sorry." His gaze is penetrating, his smile absent. Highlighted by the gleam from the bustling entrance of the hotel, his face is etched with desperation. He drops my hand. "Can we please go back to how it was before? I— I didn't mean what I said. It was just . . . champagne. And this place. These people."

"Asher—"

"I'm serious." His tone goes sharp. "What do I need to do to fix this?"

"There's nothing to fix—"

He ignores me and steps closer. "I can tell you feel awkward. Please let me fix it."

I take a breath and try to hold his gaze, but my courage

has fled, leaked into a puddle at my feet. I stare at his throat, where his Adam's apple bobs, then at his hand, clenched into a fist at his side.

He's right. *Awkward* doesn't begin to describe the depths of my discomfort. But it isn't what he thinks. I'm not uncomfortable because he might care for me, might want me. I'm uncomfortable because I want him, too.

I've tried so hard to ignore this. To push it away. But I can't. Not without shutting him out entirely. And I can't— I *won't* do that. Losing him isn't an option. Having him isn't one either, though.

He turns from me with a swear and walks away, straight to the edge of the pond.

I stare at his back.

I kind of think you know I'd take more if you'd give it.

How much more does he want? What does *more* look like? Maybe I could have him, but still protect myself? What if we tried friends with benefits or casual dating or even just seeing how things progressed without trying to define everything?

What if I could give him more without giving him everything? Float in the deep end while holding a tether to the beach?

My feet move before I've fully considered it, bringing me closer to him. Everything in my life always leads me straight to him.

When I reach his side, he's smiling at the pond—a real, *sweet* smile.

I glance at the water, the fountain, then back at him. "Asher? You okay?"

He points at the row of waterfowl gliding along the surface of the pond. "Ducks. Can anything ever really be that bad when there are ducks?"

Later, I will probably look back on this moment and wonder why. Of all the things he's ever said, why is it the ducks that break my resolve? It disintegrates as he smiles at these birds. He's always so *happy*. Nothing gets him down for long, and I—I want to be a part of that.

With a sigh of relief, I allow myself to pay heed to the advice of Grace Santini. Because she's right. Everything will be so much better when I just . . . surrender.

My hands move. My body leans. He gives no resistance when I pull him down and kiss him.

The glass walls around my heart don't just open. They shatter.

His hands slide around me, lifting me closer. My arms encircle his neck. We squeeze together, his warmth invading my entire system.

In seconds, the kiss runs wild, a chaotic storm of released tension. There's no buildup. No tentative pecks. He was ready for this the moment I lowered my guard.

Lips and tongue and teeth scrape at my jaw, my throat. His fists tighten around the fabric at my back. The silk protests with a strained pop of threads, but he doesn't loosen his grip. Instead, his kiss grows harder, more insistent. One hand climbs up my spine and tangles tight in my hair. It shoots fire straight to my insides and buries deep.

Strengthening desire lays waste to my misgivings. Tonight will leave lasting marks, but I don't care. Cutting all the cords and diving in the deep end isn't nearly so scary when his arms are the ones dragging me under.

Drowning is inevitable.

At least it's going to feel good.

"Take me upstairs," I say against his mouth.

He doesn't hesitate. One hand snags mine, and he's leading me with purpose toward the hotel entrance. We ignore the knowing looks from the valets near the door. Asher tugs me so I'm in front of him. His hands land on my shoulders, and he pushes me through the automatic doors, his mouth at my ear. "You are so beautiful. Do you know that?"

The whisper tickles my neck, and goose bumps spread from the contact. I turn to look at him, and we're kissing again, stumbling into the lobby. Someone snickers behind me as I break the kiss, but Asher pays it no mind. He drags me toward the elevators, and as we pass the check-in desks, that weird girl from yesterday smirks.

"Have a good night, Mr. Foley."

He waves a hand at her without looking, then mashes the up button beside the elevator. The bell dings, and he pushes me into the empty car. My back hits the wall, and his mouth is against mine, pausing only to smash the nine button. His hands grow bolder when the door closes, sliding over my breasts on their way to my thighs. Silk bunches in his fist as he drags it up.

Maybe this is stupid. Maybe I should stop us. But I'm impatient now. On fire. My body has wanted this far longer than I've acknowledged, and it's unwilling to comply with my doubts.

"You're sure about this?" he asks against my throat.

No. I'm not sure about anything. The heat of his hands, the flames of desire—they're the only things keeping the icy floods of terror at bay. Nothing about this is safe. If I let him touch me, let him inside me, none of my hang-ups will dissolve, but everything between us will change irreversibly.

I want it anyway. I'm sitting in a roller coaster with no harness.

Wrestling with the buttons of his shirt, I nod. "I'm sure."

His bare hand climbs my thigh. "I've been thinking about this since that kiss. Before that, actually."

Air has forsaken me, but I manage to say, "Yeah? What did you think about?"

His fingers hook around the G-string beneath my dress and jerks it down. The garment lands at my feet as the elevator door opens. "Everything." He ducks to pick it up. From that position, he glances up and meets my eyes. Clothes half undone, hair in sexy disarray, he stares at me like he can't quite believe the proof of his own eyes. "Even though I tried not to."

My heart aches for him. Strains for him. Beats for him.

I want him. So much. It's overwhelmed my senses and plunged me deep into the most primitive of sensations: pain. This want hurts. It throbs and pounds and reverberates in my skin.

The elevator starts to close, but he jerks a hand out to stop it. He rises slowly, stuffing my underwear into his pocket. Strong fingers grip my waist, and he pulls me against him, spinning until I'm against the wall beside the elevator. I reach for him, but he grabs my wrists as he kisses me, then pins them to the wall.

His mouth travels to my ear. "The things I want to do to you . . ."

My entire body is one giant heartbeat, pounding hardest between my legs, and I don't care about the scene we're creating. If he dove under my dress in this hallway, I don't think I'd stop him.

He drapes my arms around his neck and lifts me from the floor.

I shriek-laugh. "You picked me up."

His low hum of agreement vibrates through my body as I hold tight to him. "You aren't getting away again," he says.

At the door to our suite, he sets me down to slide the key

card out of his pocket. Before he uses it, though, he cups my cheek. I think he might say something—or worse, second-guess this—but he just stares into my eyes. Memorizing, maybe? Or perhaps extracting my soul from my body since it sort of feels like I'm losing more of myself in his gaze with each second that passes.

What is this feeling?

Why is it consuming everything?

I kiss him again to smother it, and the taste of him—champagne with a whisper of sweetness—strikes a chord against my soul. He's deep in there. He's in my foundation.

"I want you," I say against his mouth. "Please."

Oh, he liked that *please*, didn't he? His eyes go all hungry, making my blood hum in my veins. With a quick tap, the lock clicks and allows us into the room. I can hardly move fast enough. Before the door has fully shut, I seize his clothes, wrestling them from his body while he walks me backward, tugging at the wide straps of my dress.

At the bedroom door, his slacks fall to his ankles, and he pauses to yank them from his body, along with his shoes. Insides tingling, I pull the side zipper of my dress. As it gapes, he loses focus. One sock is still in place, but he reaches for me anyway. Confident, insistent fingers peel the silk from my body. The bra that matches the G-string is sheer lace, and his gaze drops and lingers, luring heat to the surface of my skin wherever it touches.

He stretches around me to undo the back clasp. "I used to try so hard not to wonder what was under that black bikini."

He did? I can't catch my breath. My heart pounds in a painful, erratic rhythm. I splay my hands over the sharp planes of his chest and drag them down, pliant skin over toned muscle. "I used to wonder what it would feel like to do this."

"And?"

"And I want to touch more."

He grins. One slow finger trails down my sternum, between my breasts to my belly button. "You're so soft."

And he is so, *so* hard. It's straining against his boxer briefs. I'd almost forgotten that morning after Oktoberfest, the hint of his size. There's no hiding it now. When I realize I'm staring, I jerk my gaze toward his face instead. He cups my neck and kisses me again, nudging me back toward the bed.

My calves meet the soft cotton comforter, and Asher's hand glides from my neck, over my nipple, to my thigh. There is no hesitation or uncertainty. He may have confessed some insecurities to me once upon a time, but this man *knows* he's good at this. My body moves of its own accord, seeking friction, which draws a smile across his mouth.

It isn't his normal smile. No. This one's predatory. It unwinds the last of my sanity. "Say please again, Jocelyn," he says. "Beg me for it."

I'm no longer human. I'm a creature of want and heat and liquid pleasure.

He isn't just good at this. He's on another plane entirely.

"Please," I whisper.

With the faintest pressure, his hand slips between my legs, and I can't stop the sigh that flees my lungs. My head falls back, and he hums against my throat, but the touch is too soft, too gentle.

"Asher," I whine. "Come on. More."

"You want more?"

I nod, frantic.

His mouth touches mine, and finally, he grazes the exact right place. He needs no instruction, no hints. Confident fingers stroke the sparkly nerves like he's already memorized what my body wants.

My fingernails curl into his shoulders, gripping tight. He

moves faster, and bursts of pleasure spark through my abdomen, down my thighs. My knees threaten to buckle, so I cling to him, then gasp when he slides two digits deep inside.

He sucks in a breath. "Fuck, Jocelyn. You're—"

Wet as the ocean outside?

Yeah, I know.

I have no time to think of a reply because he retracts his hand, reaches behind my knees and lifts me again. I stare at him, face-to-face, barely coherent. One kiss to my lips, and he throws me on the bed. Hands grasp my ankles and tug until he has me positioned how he wants, then they slide to my knees.

He spreads them wide.

Kisses my ankle.

Calf.

Knee.

Up.

Up.

His mouth is sinful. Wicked. Perfect. And he knows how to use it, teasing and baiting until he has me begging exactly the way he wants. Fear doesn't exist in this space he's taken me. The world shrinks to smeared blues and greens, the scent of his cologne, the fever of his skin, the minutes upon minutes of unadulterated pleasure that builds and abates, swells and recedes, grows and fades.

His tongue. Edging me to paradise.

When it hits, I can't breathe. I can't see. I cease to exist in my current form and rise to something higher.

Coming down doesn't compute. Still tingling, the waves of pleasure crashing with each movement, I scramble out from beneath him and rip his boxers off. He rolls obediently to his back, and I climb on top of him.

And lose my Asher-virginity.

It is so much better than I imagined.

The slide. The fit. The rhythm.

We are made for each other.

And I'm still so sensitive that it takes only a minor provocation with his precise fingers to shatter me all over again. His cocky little chuckle at my second climax is the hottest fucking thing he's ever done. I'm uncoordinated and orgasm-drunk, so he takes over.

He rolls me to my back and nuzzles into my neck. "That feel good?"

"I'm dead." I throw my arms above me.

"Don't worry." His hands slide up my arms, fingers lacing with mine. "I'll revive you."

•

"SHIT," ASHER MUTTERS against my neck. I startle from my Lucy in the Sky level disorientation and turn my face toward him. He rises to his elbows, and I already miss the weight of him. "I didn't use a condom."

I instinct-panic for two seconds, my eyes going wide, before I remember—"I have an IUD."

"Oh." He collapses on top of me again. "Thank fuck."

"Wait. Did you bring condoms?"

His laugh rumbles against me. "No. This wasn't really on my radar."

I scratch my nails down his back, extracting a soft groan from him. "Bit of a surprise on my end, too." Though I definitely have condoms. I always have condoms. I've never forgotten to use a condom. I've never had sex without a condom. Not once. Even after I got my IUD. *That* is how responsible I am.

Asher is the first.

He has me so muddled that I'm forgetting basic tenets of

safety like a moron. Ignoring bright red, flashing warning signs all over the place.

Oh, god.

What have I done?

I can't— I can't undo this. Can't rewind. Can't erase. The familiar fear of drowning raises its head, growls and swipes vicious talons through the tentative, budding warmth in my unguarded heart, tearing it to shreds. Dread washes over the jagged remains in a great tidal wave. The washout leaves only frost, creeping a slow path through my veins.

What is *this* feeling? It's horrifying. Awful. Somehow beautiful and terrible all at once, like a rose in a graveyard. Innocence surrounded by destruction.

Then he kisses me.

Kisses my cheek.

My neck.

Down my chest to my breast.

The frost melts, and the sense of security returns. The night expands before us, infinite. Limitless possibilities.

If the first time was a frenzy of pleasure, the second is an ode to savoring, and the third is a playful exploration. The proof of our chemistry is the boneless heap in which he leaves me each time, waiting for my energy to restore so I can claw at him for more.

Things will probably look different in the morning, but I'll deal with that then. Right now, nothing could tear me away from him. Not the tidal wave. Not the fear. Not even these crumbling walls.

Asher

**Sometimes expectations can be the
most heartbreaking of all.
—My Therapist**

A warm body beside me shifts as I drag myself from sleep. Her soft skin brushes over mine. That velvety, alluring fragrance drifts across my dreamy awareness. It holds just the right amount of bite.

Perfect for Jocelyn.

Jocelyn.

My eyes fly open.

She's still naked next to me.

Holy shit.

Memories of last night filter through my drowsy thoughts. Every steamy, feverish moment. Didn't know sex could be that incredible. Probably should have guessed, though, given the simple thrill of the elusive Jocelyn Mattox pulling me in for a kiss by the pond last night was enough to nearly undo me.

I told her I wanted more, and she . . . agreed. That's what that was, right? It took a minute, but she finally lowered her barriers and let me in. She made the first move. Felt pretty spectacular, all things considered. Good enough that I didn't stop to wonder what changed her mind.

Probably should have wondered.

The sheets are tangled low on her waist, and my arm rests across her. Her chest rises and falls with each slow breath.

Briefly consider sliding my hand up to her exposed breast, but . . . that's rude. I kept her up late. I'll let her sleep.

Beautiful, sleepy woman.

I'd give her a medal for last night if I could. Hell, I'd probably give her a diamond ring if I thought she'd wear it, but I'm leaping miles ahead. I know where my head is—fully ensnared by a heart that belongs to her now—but hers? Hers could be any-fucking-where.

She's too easily spooked. Must tread carefully now that she's within my grasp. One wrong move, and she might run.

I slip out of bed to shower and dress, but it doesn't wake her, so I head downstairs to grab coffee and breakfast. Our flight home isn't until this afternoon. Plenty of time to linger. Lattes and egg sandwiches in hand—with a side of orange, of course—I reenter the suite to find her rubbing her face, still naked in bed. My shoulder braces my weight against the door frame as I enjoy the view.

And *what* a view.

When her gaze lands on me, she flushes a pretty shade of pink and pulls the blanket to cover her chest. The constellation on her collarbone stands out, stark on her fair skin.

"Morning, honey." I wink at her.

She laughs, still raspy from sleep. "Good morning."

I set her coffee and sandwich on her bedside table and toss her the fruit before pecking a kiss on her cheek.

She smiles and runs her nails over the orange rind. "You've been busy this morning."

"Thought I'd let you sleep in."

"Much appreciated." She scoots to the edge of the bed, still holding the sheet to her body, and places the orange beside her breakfast sandwich. "I'm pretty sore."

So much for careful. Unable to help myself, I pull her up for a hug. The sheet does nothing to hide the warm outline of her figure as it presses against me.

This is right.

She is right.

But . . . why isn't she smiling when she looks into my eyes?

"Asher . . . About last night . . ."

That's hesitation. In her tone. Why is she hesitating?

I release her like she burned me. Everything about her is guarded this morning—opaque brown eyes, tense shoulders. Oh, my god. This isn't hesitation, is it? She's bracing herself to deliver bad news.

Hurts like hell, this smile I throw on, but I do manage it. Kicks on the gnawing acid pump in my chest. Might throw up.

She's wearing the uneasy face. The it's-not-you-it's-me face. I've seen it before, on too many other women, but this can't be happening right now. Not with her. Not after last night. Not after she told me she was sure.

But it is. I can see it in her eyes, what she's about to say.

I ask anyway. "What— What about last night?"

She scratches her nose and looks away. "Do you think . . . maybe we . . . acted a little rashly?"

I back up and zero in on the tight angles of her jaw, the

tiny, telling twitches of her mouth. "Honestly? No. We've been heading this way all summer."

Expressionless, she cocks her head. "But we talked about this. We agreed that we want different things."

"No. *You* declared that you don't do relationships, so you didn't want me."

She lets out a short sigh. "It's not that I didn't want you, Asher. I just . . . I don't *do* this."

Glad I didn't drink that coffee. It'd be turning to lead in my gut right now. I stare at her, trying to find any hints of emotion, but she's a blank wall. She's raised her guard so high that even now, having been inside her body and watched her fall apart, I can't tell if last night meant anything to her. She's a fucking mystery in a shiny, tempting package. A Pandora's box set on tormenting me.

How can this be happening with her?

Please not with her.

Literally *anyone* but her.

"Then what was this?" I point at the bed.

"A mistake. You're my best friend. That's so much more important than just . . . casual sex."

Casual?

I freeze at that word. Must tamp down the frigid, zero-degree-Kelvin pain that word instills. Running a hand over the back of my neck doesn't help, but I try to collect myself. To speak calmly. "This . . . This wasn't casual for me. I'm confused why you thought it was."

She says nothing. Her gaze strays to the bathroom door like she's searching for an escape.

I lean that way, try to put myself in her sight line, but it's useless. She won't look at me.

"Just to be clear," I say, "I, um, I didn't think this was casual for you, either. Was I wrong?"

"Sorry." She shakes her head. "I just meant . . . You're more important to me than sex. And I think curiosity got the better of us last night. We weren't thinking."

I was thinking.

A lot.

About us. About love. About how good we could be if she'd let us.

Maybe she wasn't thinking, but I've never thought about something so much in my life. Stupid of me to assume she'd actually considered it and decided on me. No, she was *curious*. Something beneath the ice starts up a steady, aching throb. An axe splitting my insides into tiny pieces.

"So—" I slip my hands into my pockets "—you were just scratching an itch? Nothing more?"

She smiles, all *Yes! Puzzle solved!* "Exactly! It's like test-driving cars, you know? You try the Lambo because you're curious, even though you know it's only for fun. You're my Lamborghini."

Ha.

Oh, my god. Did she just say that? Out loud?

Should I be flattered? Because the extreme level of insult stings like a thousand fire ants poured over my flesh.

Only for fun?

I drag my teeth over my lip in an effort to say nothing. Can't stop the words from forming, though. "Just— Just so we're clear. *You* are not *only for fun* for me. You're more than that—"

"I know." The relief on her face makes no sense. "We are so much better than this. We can go back to how it was. This? It's nothing. A silly mistake. It's not serious."

My entire being cringes, though my face remains still. Calm.

Not serious.

There's that other word. She's two for two today. Must have downloaded a lingo app designed specifically to cut me. But like . . . Why am I surprised? She's only saying what every woman has said before her. I'm not serious. We all know it. Even Jocelyn thinks so.

Won't let this pain show. Hurts like a motherfucker, though. Not sure if I'll come back from it, but . . . problem for another day.

I paste on a smile. "Right. Of course. Yeah."

"Really?" The tension in her shoulders eases.

"Nothing that happens in Florida counts, baby doll. Didn't you know?" My voice is leaden, but her small, relieved laugh says she either doesn't notice or doesn't care.

How could I have misread her so completely? I asked her if she was sure, and she said yes. I thought she wanted *me*, wanted *us*, but really, she wanted to know what I'm like in bed. Is this barbed wire scraping through my insides or something? The pain is sharp enough that I should be bleeding.

I'm not, though.

I'm intact, and I can give her what she wants. I can move on. Pretend it doesn't matter. Ignore the resultant heartbreak.

At least one of us will walk out of this pain-free. We can stay friends, like she wants. Casual.

"It doesn't have to change a thing," she says.

But what if I want things to change? What if, for once, I want to be someone's endgame? *Her* endgame?

The words hover at the tip of my tongue—*I want to be more than friends*—but saying them might drive a wedge between us that will never disappear. I'd rather have her as a friend than nothing.

. . . Right?

Can I be in love with someone, see her every day and pretend I don't love her? Is maintaining our friendship worth the knife that will sink deeper into my heart with each smile, each hug, each grain of hope she hands me until she eventually finds someone else? Someone she's capable of letting inside?

She'll run to *his* arms. Sleep in *his* bed. Marry *him*.

And I'll be here again, in a hotel room at her wedding. Listening to a different woman tell me I'm not good enough.

Joss ducks into my line of sight. "Asher?"

I stare at the backlit white curtains, refusing to meet her gaze.

I've been in love before, but not like this. Jocelyn Mattox is my person. My always. It's a mere unfortunate—but predictable—set of circumstances that I'm not hers.

That's when it hits me.

I can't do this.

I *won't* do this.

My hands slowly clench. Blood drains from my head. Woozy, I take a breath and I— I decide to destroy it all. Fuck it. Fuck *this*.

"I'm in love with you."

She doesn't move. Doesn't breathe. Her brown eyes widen.

"I'm sorry to be so blunt," I say. "I just—I'm pretty sure you must not feel the same, but I think I need to hear you say it."

Her lips part. Nothing comes out. Not a great sign.

I rub my face and sigh. "Last night was— It meant a lot to me is all I'm saying, so . . . Can you see a future for us? Romantically?"

An interminable silence follows in which she remains frozen. Has she taken a single breath since I started talking? Maybe she's trying to induce a real seizure to get out of responding.

Because she's clearly not responding positively.

Her brown eyes cloud over, her shoulders rise and fall and then words finally form. Her voice trips over what I now know to be the two worst words in the English language. "I—can't."

Ah. Ouch. Thought the pain couldn't get worse. Universe needed to prove me wrong, I guess. Do people actually survive hurt like this? I drop my gaze to the floor. Looking at her makes it worse. Eyes are stinging.

Her breath hitches. "I . . . It isn't *you*. I'm— I can't—"

"You don't need to qualify it, Jocelyn." My voice is miraculously steady. "It only makes it worse."

Ten seconds of silence elapse.

"Take a shower," I say. "I'll pack up and we can head to the airport."

Another few awkward moments pass before the bathroom door clicks closed, and I'm alone in the bedroom, staring at a luxurious bed full of regret.

•

ONE GOOD THING about Joss not loving me: She bought a neck pillow. Shoulder is pain-free when we land.

Silver linings, am I right?

She makes a valiant effort at correcting the awkwardness between us, but I can't play along. Too worn down to pretend. By the time we're in my truck, she's mute. Given up on me, I suppose.

Can't blame her. I have to be the most pathetic man she's ever dealt with. Why would she even want to remain friends after this?

At her front door, I set down her suitcase. "Thanks again for coming with me."

She nods, arms crossed. "Yeah, of course."

I flee down the porch stairs, two at a time.

"Asher—"

I don't stop. "Yeah?"

Her gentle voice floats through the air between us. "Bye."

"See you around."

No answer follows, and I hop in my truck without looking at her again. There's no relief in being free of her. If anything, it's all the more bleak. Lonelier.

Back at my cold, empty house, I unpack the small suitcase I brought. When my fingers tangle in the G-string still wadded in my pants pocket, they clench involuntarily.

Can't believe that was last night. Less than twenty-four hours.

How can so much change in so little time? Feel hollow, like I'm coming home from a war where the battleground was my chest, and the fight left nothing but scorched, barren nothingness.

Jeez. I've gotten maudlin in my heartbreak. Need to snap out of this.

But like . . . she said she was sure. Why say it when she knew she didn't want more? She took advantage of my feelings for her. Used me to satisfy her own sick curiosity.

At the reality of that thought, a lightning bolt strikes the barrenness, bursting it into flames.

You're my Lamborghini.

Did she really fucking say that? I drop the lacy fabric in my hands to pull out my phone.

"Asher?" Geoff answers on the third ring. "You back? How was the wedding, man?"

"It was—" I trudge into my bedroom and collapse onto the bed. "I slept with Jocelyn."

A distant feminine voice shrieks over the line: "What?"

"Fuck, man," Geoff says, voice far clearer. "You're on speaker. Should have warned me."

Morose laughter is the only response I can muster. Because *of course* Yayoi was within hearing distance of that.

"Ask him how it happened," comes Yayoi's voice, to which Geoff hushes her.

I dig my index finger and thumb into my closed eyes until colors spark in my vision.

Geoff's tone softens. "I assume something is wrong by the way you said it."

I clear my throat. "No. I mean, it's not a big deal. She just . . . wants to stay friends. Easy enough."

"I take it you want more than that?"

"No, I'm fine."

He pauses a moment. "Then . . . why do you sound like a kicked puppy?"

I scowl at nothing and strengthen my voice. "Fuck you. I do not."

"You didn't call me to announce you slept with her, then hang up."

"Maybe I called to brag. I got laid last night. Did you?"

He laughs. "The constant throwing up kind of gets in the way of that."

"See?"

"Asher." His voice takes on a serious cast. "Come on, man. Why'd you really call?"

My ceiling fan needs dusting. Should take care of that.

"Asher?"

I sigh. "Sort of . . . hurt. I guess. Normally, I'd talk to her about it, but—"

"I get it," Geoff says. "Need anything?"

"Tranquilizer?"

He chuckles at the dumb joke, bless him.

"This is the best of both worlds, right?" I say. "She let

me have sex with her with zero accountability. Every man's dream."

"Sure. Good way to look at it. You put it out there. She said no. Now you move on."

"Yeah. Simple enough."

Sounds simple. Probably isn't. Suspect it will be quite hard, actually. Life altering. I haven't just lost the girl I'm in love with; I've lost my best friend, too. There's no way we're going back to normal after this.

"Want to grab a beer tomorrow?" Geoff asks.

"Abso-fuckin-lutely."

•

ON MY OR DAY, I arrive at the hospital an hour early to catch Cassie before she makes anesthesia room assignments. We're okay, Cassie and me. She apologized for her behavior at my house a couple weeks ago, and I'm incapable of staying mad at anyone for anything.

The woman isn't particularly nice, but she's excellent at organization. The entire department defers to her superior scheduling powers. I find her in the surgery office, head bent over some paperwork. A knock on the doorjamb announces my presence.

She looks up and smiles. "Asher. Good morning."

"Hey, girl. How was your holiday weekend?"

"Oh, fine." She waves a hand and returns to the paper before her. "I was on call for most of it."

In a move that isn't subtle, I swing the office door closed. The soft click draws her attention, and her questioning gaze bounces between the door and me.

I approach the desk and sit in the single chair facing it. "I was hoping to ask a favor."

"Oh?"

"The schedule today . . ." My fidgety hands are being super dumb. One of them knocks twice on the desk. Like . . . could my tension be any more obvious? "Do you think you could assign Kevin to my cases?"

She glances at the paper before her, then back to me. "Is something wrong?"

Luckily, I've prepared for this question. "Fantasy football starts today. I fucked up my draft. Trying to convince him to trade. Need every chance I can get." Not true, of course. My fantasy team is amazing. Cassie, however, hates football. I'll get away clean here. No suspicion. No follow-up questions.

"Oh." Her expression clears, then turns a little calculating. "That will put Joss with Van Camp. You okay with that?"

Van Camp is the skeezy colorectal surgeon constantly cheating on his wife with younger, blonder women. Joss hates him.

And yet . . .

I shrug. "She'll understand."

"All right, then. Will do." She scribbles something on the paper and looks up. "Does Pool Party Saturday continue past Labor Day?"

"Hell, yeah. We party all year."

She has a pretty smile when it's real. Makes her eyes crinkle. "Maybe I'll keep from spilling a drink on you next time."

My chuckle is forced. "Yeah, maybe."

Straightening, she gestures to the paper before her. "I'll take care of the schedule. Good luck with the fantasy stuff."

"Thanks."

Now there's ample time for a quick workout at the hospital gym before my first case. Need to release some of this pent-up energy. Because no matter how much I scheme to keep space between us, I *will* see Jocelyn today. I'll have to look her in the eye, remember I told her I love her, then watched her destroy all hope of a future for us.

Geoff finds me in pre-op. All around us, nurses hustle between patient bays, prepping them for surgery.

"Hey, man." I lift my gaze from my computer screen. "What you got today?"

He plops into the chair beside me as he ties his blue scrub cap. "Adult circumcision."

Oof. I whistle. "Dude's in for a rough week."

He huffs a breathy laugh. "We still on for tonight?"

"McNellie's, right? Yeah. I'll meet you around six."

"How you doing today?"

I lift an eyebrow at him. "I'm *fine*."

He raises his hands in submission. "All right. Just checking."

With a few more clicks, I wrap up my charting and head toward the OR. That's, of course, when Jocelyn appears. She's frowning at her phone but walking my way. Every molecule in my body contracts at the sight of her.

Should I run?

Play it cool?

Pretend like I don't see her?

Others traverse the halls between us—nurses and surgeons and scrub techs—so maybe she won't see me . . .

She slips the device into her pocket and looks up. Ahh! Haven't made up my mind. I panic like a kid out of bed after bedtime and dive through the closest door.

What is this? Is this . . . a closet?

Jesus.

Light's off, so I bang my knee on the edge of an electrosurgical tower.

"Damn it!"

I'm rubbing my knee when the door opens. Fluorescent

light pours through the gap, and Joss stands on the other side, the skin between her eyebrows deeply creased.

I jerk upright. "Oh. Hey, Joss. I—just—I—um—live in this closet now." I set my elbow on the electrosurgical equipment beside me and rest my head on my fist.

A bewildered chuckle answers me. "What are you doing?"

Hiding.

"Nothing."

She rests her back on the door frame and sighs. "Cassie assigned me somewhere else today. I fought her, but she wouldn't budge."

"Oh. Oh, that's—" Prickles wake along my nerves. "That's too bad."

Her head tilts. "We're okay, right? I think we need to talk."

The open door is *right there*. Escape is within my grasp. How rude would it be to push her out of the way?

"Can't talk now," I say. "Have surgery."

Her brown eyes stare without blinking, and her shoulders fall. "Okay. Maybe tonight?"

Desperate, I squeeze past her in the doorway. Refuse to breathe while I do it, of course. The hypnotic scent that clings to her skin is hardwired to pain receptors in mine. "Can't. Have plans."

She frowns. "Oh. What are you doing?"

I pause in the hallway and brave the storm of her eyes. "Sorry. I really can't talk right now. I have a case. Let's talk later."

Except we don't talk later. I finish my cases and head to the office for my afternoon clinic patients without seeing her once.

We don't text.

We don't talk at all.

It's what I wanted, so why do I feel ghosted?

How the hell did I end up here? My life is so pretty on the outside. On paper, I'm killing it. In truth, it's like someone threw a grenade, and I'm bleeding in the fragmented remains, ribbons of red marring my stellar résumé.

Broken hearts are asinine. What good can come from pain like this? It's useless. Meaningless.

At least Talia's returned from maternity leave. She steps into our shared office for afternoon clinic with a shriek that could rival a banshee. "Doctor F!"

"Oh, my god." I rise from my chair and engulf her in a bear hug tight enough to heave her feet from the floor. "My angel's back."

She hoots out a laugh. "I love that baby, but *man*, am I ready to talk to an adult. Got a quota of curse words I have to meet today."

"You have no idea how much I've missed you." I set her down and add in a whisper, "Your replacement was kind of dull."

"Ha! I'm irreplaceable. Give me a raise."

She deserves it.

"I'd give you all the things if I had that power," I say.

Her things topple into a pile on the desk before she settles in her chair. "Phew!"

I eye the mountain between us. "What is all this?"

"Purse. Breast pump. Cooler for breast milk. Lunch box."

"You need a lunch box? We're only here for two hours."

She sends me a flat, sassy stare. "Watch who you're talking to."

Chuckling, I raise my hands in surrender, then glance at my schedule to check my first patient.

Rosenberg, Heather. 47F. New patient problem: hormone imbalance.

Sighhhhhhhh.

If anyone has a hormone imbalance, it's me. I'm miserably in love with a girl who told me she doesn't want me, and the testosterone poisoning my head convinces me I still want to fuck her. Bad.

That's an imbalance.

FML.

Definitely don't have the patience today. Will manage, of course. I always do. But I refuse to be happy about it. Refuse to be happy about anything right now.

I grab my phone to text my brothers.

> What's up assholes?

Kyle: Having an existential crisis.

Kyle: What if when we die the light at the end of the tunnel is just us coming out of another vagina?

Ha. What an idiot. Love him.

> By that logic the human population would never increase.

Kyle: Oh.

Kyle: Right

Kyle: CRISIS AVERTED

Brandon: Ash has that doctor smarts.

> I have average smarts and understand the concept of recycling

Brandon: What's doing, little bro?

I see a few patients before I answer. What should I even say? A lie feels slimy, and the truth will make them bash Joss. Don't really want to weather insults against her, despite it all.

Milksop. Isn't that what they used to say instead of *pussy*? I should bring that back.

> Told a girl I loved her and
> she turned me down.

Kyle: F

Kyle: And you let me go on about vagina reincarnation?

Brandon: Sorry bro

Brandon: Don't believe what they say about getting under someone else

Brandon: Work through your shit first.

Brandon: Learned that the hard way.

Kyle: Fun while it's happening though.

Suspect sex with someone else won't really help. What could even compare to that night with Joss? The only balm for this is time.

Or maybe ketamine.

What truthful obscenities would I yell under the influence of ketamine?

I'm not a fucking Lamborghini!

> Thanks guys.

Kyle: Is the girl deaf dumb and blind?

> **Kyle:** I can't think of another reason she'd turn you down.

Lol. Sure.

> **Kyle:** She's definitely not of average smarts like you.
>
> **Kyle:** Not even good enough to smell your farts
>
> **Kyle:** Also mom said you need to vacuum the whole house so you better come home before she grounds you

Sounds like a dream, heading home. Abandoning everything. I'll work in Brandon's construction company and build houses all day.

Fuck vaginas.

Well. Not literally.

. . . Sometimes literally, though.

Back home, I wouldn't be inadequate. I wouldn't worry whether everyone thought I was incompetent. I'd relinquish the anxiety of call, of OB emergencies, of being in charge of people's lives. I'd escape the politics of the hospital. No Dragon training. No Dr. White. No Cassie Hersl.

No Joss.

My heart does some weird charley horse thing in mutiny.

Um. Ouch. Okay, I get it.

I can't leave. Need to face my demons like a . . . non-milksop.

You guys are all right, you know?

> **Brandon:** Just a phone call away. You know that.

Kyle: You're the pink Starburst.

Kyle: Don't let anyone tell you different.

Kyle: Also NASCAR rulez

Lol.

I *am* the pink Starburst. Lead with that confidence, and I can do anything.

Decide to pull up Gabriela's contact info before I second-guess myself. My last text from her was that day she sprayed a grandma with cord blood. She apologized via text approximately seven thousand times. I crack up all over again at the memory.

This is Chanel, child. I assure you, I am hurt.

Classic.

> You still interested in that dinner?

I set my phone down, but it dings before I return to my computer.

Absolutely.

Friday?

> Sounds good

> Send me your address. I'll pick you up at 7

Jocelyn

> You have an entire meadow in your heart you've watered with fear, but loneliness makes an ugly garden.
> **–My Therapist**

Several days after we return from Florida, profound worry has sunken its claws in me.

I think I've lost Asher. He won't talk to me, not like he used to. He still smiles—mostly. Still chats. But something's different. Colder.

And why wouldn't it be?

I'm in love with you.

My entire body breaks out in a cold sweat every time I remember the way his voice sounded when he said those words. Resonant and resigned. Dejected. Like he knew before I even spoke what my response would be.

But of course that was my response.

I can't.

I just . . . can't.

Dispirited in the OR physician lounge on Thursday, I stare between the vinyl blinds to the outdoor courtyard a floor below. It's noon, so nurses eating lunch have taken most of the tables. I have no appetite, but the cozy scent of brewing coffee on the other side of the room does draw my attention.

Cassie stands at the brew station. Because *of course* she does. My week couldn't get worse, so let's throw her in the mix, too. Her painted nails tap on the laminate countertop while the brown liquid fills the pot before her.

I turn back to the courtyard. It's a much prettier view.

You don't need to qualify it, Jocelyn.

But I want to *so* bad. He needs to know why. It isn't him. I'd give him everything if I had anything left to give, but I'm broken. Half-living. Sharing that night with him only confirmed I'm not brave enough, not strong enough, to raze my own vicious shortcomings. My emotional handicaps.

I can't have him every day, listen to his smooth voice whispering how much he loves me in my ear, then lose it. Far easier to never have it at all. It's such bullshit, the whole *better to have loved and lost* schtick. It's a lie we tout to widows to make them feel better about being halved by death.

I want to explain this to Asher. He knows my past. He'll understand if he lets me tell him. We can go back to how it was before.

Right?

"Trouble in paradise?" Cassie sits on the sofa across from me, blowing on a mug of fresh coffee.

I blink a few times and turn to her. "Huh?"

"Your boyfriend asked me to have someone else cover his cases the other day. Figured you guys were in a lover's spat."

He *asked* her to move me? That's—

Ow.

This is worse than I thought if he's actively removing me from his day-to-day life. God, I really am losing him, aren't I? The thought makes my eyes prickle, pushes fine-tipped needles straight into the most vulnerable places of my heart, but I refuse to cry in front of her.

With a sip of her coffee, she lifts an eyebrow. She's not gloating, which is . . . weird.

"He's not my boyfriend," I say.

Her lip quirks. "Then how do you know who I'm talking about?"

My stare transitions into a glare, and I face her. "What do you want, Cassie?"

"Nothing. Was just curious. Thought you guys would have kissed and made up by now."

I lean forward, resting my elbows on my knees. "Is it any of your business whether we've kissed and made up?"

"No." She sets her mug on the side table and sighs. "Listen. I'm, uh, sorry, or whatever, for, you know, that stuff I said at Asher's the other day. Or whatever."

Nonplussed, my glare does not abate. "Which part?"

The cat eyeliner somehow sharpens when her lids lower to stare at her nails. "Hmm?"

"Which part specifically are you apologizing for? The part where you implied I'm an alcoholic, or the part where you shamed me for using dating apps?"

She sighs. "All of it, I guess. It was a bad time for me. My ex had said some not nice things that morning, and I just— I'm sorry, okay?"

I let out a bitter laugh. "One grand, sweeping gesture, then?"

Her gaze snaps up, eyes blazing. "I don't like you." She

leans back and crosses her legs. "I won't lie and say I do. Every word you speak, everything you do . . . They feel like a front, like you're wearing a shield, and no one is important enough to lower it for, not even your friends. I tried in the beginning, but—"

"You *tried*? What do you mean you tried?"

"The girls and I invited you out several times when you started."

What? No, they didn't! "That's not how I remember it."

She curls her lip. "I'm not surprised. You barely even acknowledged I said anything. Always hiding behind that front. Posturing."

Is she calling me a poser?

"What the—"

In a cutting gesture, she raises a hand. Everything about her is razor-edged. "I'm not going to argue. I was only trying to say that I don't like you, but I'm not a cruel person, and what I said that day was mean. You didn't deserve it. I was . . . not in a good place. I apologize."

I want to tell her to piss off. My gut instinct is a raging bull of indignation and resentment. How dare she perceive the hostility between us as my fault? I've done nothing wrong.

Or . . . have I?

I try to recall my first days at the hospital. What had Cassie said?

The girls and I are heading to a wine bar.

The girls and I do an annual Christmas exchange.

The girls and I are attending the medical society dinner.

All in her haughty Cassie voice. Was I supposed to take those blunt statements as invitations? Where was the additional *Would you like to come?*

She thinks I hide behind a front? I don't. I hide behind fear.

Which is . . . a thinly veiled front, I guess. Shit. Is this what people think? That I'm fake because I won't engage below the surface? I'm just trying to protect myself.

I think you need to focus on what you have, not what you have the potential to lose.

You aren't running, Joss. You're hiding.

Argh! Why is his voice popping up now? Stupid Asher and his wise observations about my life. I swallow down the urge to spew hatred and try to smile instead. "Thanks."

"Wow. You look like you're in pain." Laughing, Cassie takes her mug and stands. "Good luck with your *non-boyfriend* thing. I heard he's taking a resident out this weekend, so I guess you're not lying."

Too shocked to respond, I only watch as she struts away, the boxy hospital scrubs somehow flattering her enviable figure. Asher asked someone else out? Some resident? Only days after claiming he's in love with me?

. . . And I rejected him.

He didn't even give me a chance to explain, and he's moving on?

Cassie's at the threshold of the lounge, one foot in the hallway beyond when my impulsive mouth betrays me. "Which resident?"

Pausing, she looks back at me, then laughs. "You don't even know which one? You must have really fucked up."

She walks away, shaking her head, and I'm left to question how my heart is pounding so hard when it has ceased to exist.

•

WHEN I ARRIVE HOME, I make a PB&J and open EverX. The app has been useless to me over the past couple months, but I need it now. If Asher's going to be seriously dating, I'll require distraction.

I scroll through my matches while my jaw fights with the overload of peanut butter in my mouth. My attention snags on a familiar picture.

Ashton.

Still labeled Sebastian on his profile.

Without stopping to consider, I open his message stream.

> You still dtf?

Aren't you the girl who said I look weird?

> I said you look like someone I know

> There's a difference

So I don't look like him anymore?

> No. You still do.

> But I no longer care.

Sounds like a win for me.

Tmrw?

After that's settled, I call my sister and spill everything: the words Asher said, his heart-stopping declarations, his artistry in bed.

"Do you love him back?" Ali asks after skiving off details of the sex the same way she'd take a peeler to a carrot.

"I don't . . . I don't know."

"You *do* know. Even I know." She sighs. "Why can't you admit it?"

Bent over my kitchen table, I drop my forehead to my arm. "How was it so easy for you to fall in love with Nic? Weren't you scared?"

"Of course I was scared, but I married him when I was

twenty. Before Leo. Just after you lost Aiden. For me, burying Aiden was a sign I needed to love Nic faster and harder because I didn't know how much time we had. For you, burying Aiden was proof love hurts. That isn't a lesson you unlearn. It's something you have to charge through and break apart."

My voice drops to a whisper. "I don't know how."

"Think about it like a math equation. Is losing him now worth it? Are you saving yourself pain in the long run?"

I tap my fingernails on the wood table. One, two, three, four.

"You're in for pain either way," Ali says in my silence. "You can pretend you don't know if you love him, but we both know you're lying. You're in love with that man from the bottom of your feet to the top of your fake platinum head. So, the question becomes . . . if I took him from you now, would the pain be any less today than it will be in five years? Twenty years? A lifetime?"

"I can't answer that question," I snap. "How do I know what it'll feel like in five years? I can only assume I'll continue to fall deeper and deeper in love with him every day. I'll continue to attach more and more of myself to him. Sounds like that will hurt a hell of a lot more."

"No, Leo! Don't touch that!" Ali's words drift away, then return. "Your nephew is a frickin' mess. Listen, Joss. Can you imagine pain worse than losing him today?"

I can't. I can't imagine it, but I'm still scared. It's fucking illogical. Why can't we go back to how we were? Why is that so hard?

The thick knot in my throat is difficult to speak past. "He has a date tomorrow with another girl."

"Then maybe you've already lost your chance. If he wants to move on, you have to let him. It isn't fair to hold him back when you don't want him."

I growl into the phone. "You have zero empathy."

"You don't need empathy. You need a kick in the ass."

Nic's voice filters through the speaker, as if from far away. "Jeez. Who are you talking to?"

"My sister," says Ali.

"Oh. Hey, Joss!" Nic says even though he can't hear me respond in kind. "Sorry my wife is kicking your ass."

I want to cry. I want to throw the phone. My eyes burn and my throat aches, but I manage a wobbly, "Me, too."

"Oh, crap." Ali softens. "I'm sorry, Joss. I— I can't tell you what to do. I can't heal your trauma or take away your fear. I would if I could. You know I would."

"I know," I whisper.

"I want you to be happy, but you have to be *willing* to be happy. Years of therapy, and you're just—you're still not there yet."

I sniffle, refusing to admit that I'm crying, that these tears exist at all. "I have to go."

"Okay. I love you, sister."

"Yeah."

I end the call and open EverX.

> Why not tonight?

> 11?

> See you then.

•

YAYOI CALLS WHILE I'm driving to Ashton's apartment. She's usually asleep by ten, so I paw at my Apple CarPlay to answer, convinced something bad has happened.

Is she miscarrying? Is Geoff okay? Is she dying in a ditch somewhere?

"Hello? Hello? Are you okay?"

"Whoa," Yayoi says. "Calm down. I'm fine."

"Jesus." I press a hand to my chest, willing my heart rate to slow. "Why are you calling me so late?"

"The baby thinks I should be vomiting at this time of night. You're the only person I know who stays awake past ten. Talk me out of my morning sickness."

I laugh, the flood of adrenaline shifting to giddy relief. "Okay. How do I do that?"

"Wait. Are you in your car?"

"Yeah." I stop at an intersection, tapping my fingers on the wheel.

"Where are you going this late?"

"To visit Grandma." I exchange an awkward glance with the guy in the SUV next to me. "Where do you think I'm going?"

A silence follows. "You're . . . meeting someone?"

"Yes, Yayoi. I'm meeting someone."

"Meeting . . . Asher?"

My stomach drops. "What? Why would you ask that?"

"Oh." Something rustles in the background. "No reason. Never mind."

Nuh-uhh. No way was that a coincidence. Super sus. "Do—do you *know*?"

"Know what?" Her voice is too chipper.

The distraction keeps my foot off the gas, and someone behind honks. "Shit." I speed through the intersection. "Did Asher tell you what happened?"

"He—um—no. He didn't tell me. He asked Geoff for advice."

"*Geoff* knows?" I rub my forehead. "He's going to hate me."

"No! No. He doesn't hate you." Yayoi's tone is sincere, but I can't believe her. Geoff is Asher's bro all the way. If

Asher pulls away from me, Geoff will side with him, and Yayoi will pick her husband, as she should.

Everything's falling apart around me. All the staples in my life, ripped out and warped.

"Right." The burning in my throat is back. "So, what was Geoff's sage guidance?"

Yayoi's sigh crackles in my car's speakers. "He told him to move on. That's all."

I turn onto the street leading to Ashton's condo. "Good advice. Is that why he's got a date with some other woman tomorrow?"

Yayoi remains quiet for a moment. "Aren't you heading to a date with some other man?"

I remain quiet because what can I say? I'm the monster who drove Asher away, the idiot who's destroying our entire group.

Her soft voice breaks my silence. "Do you want to talk about it? What happened?"

"I don't know." I park on the street. "We were having a good time, and then some girl came on to him, and I got jealous. I won't even pretend I wasn't jealous. And then he—he said some things. And then we were kissing. And then—"

Memories surge through me. The salty, woodsy taste of his skin. The graze of his night stubble against my thigh. The fire in his touch. The diamond-hard connection between us, linking my heart to his.

Beyond words. Beyond thought. Just . . . him.

"And then?" Yayoi prompts.

I shake myself. "And then a lot of stuff happened, and he told me he was in love with me, and I panicked."

Her tone sharpens. "He said that?"

"Yeah," I say, but it's more a breath of air than an actual word.

"Whoa. That's heavy."

"I didn't know what to say, so I didn't really say anything, and he just shut down."

She's silent a few moments, but then, "I mean . . . I did tell you he's not fling material."

"And that I'd destroy him." My tone has grown bitter, but I can't change it. I *am* bitter. *Did* I destroy him? I'm a monster.

"I didn't mean it like that, Joss. You know that. He's just more sentimental than you. That stuff means a lot more to him."

"Physical stuff?" I'm trying hard not to hear *slut* in what she's saying—I *know* she doesn't think that—but the self-consciousness is rising.

"Yeah." She laughs. "He's more like a girl that way, isn't he? And you're more like a guy."

I guess, in this world, being manly is better than being slutty. Though . . . men are sort of sluts, so it's kind of the same thing.

"I don't subscribe to gender norms," I say, injecting a false haughtiness into my voice.

We take a moment to laugh at the silly joke, or maybe at my idiocy, and settle into a peaceful quiet.

"Are you going to be okay?" she asks.

"I don't know. Do you . . . Do you think I put up a front?"

She hums. "I think you're guarded. It's hard to get to know you. But once you let someone in, you're *very* you. There's no front, and no apology."

So there's some truth to what Cassie said. People can see my walls. Maybe they aren't protecting me at all. Maybe they're trapping me.

She yawns. "I think the nausea has passed. I'm going to let you go, okay?"

"All right. Good night."

"Be safe tonight, okay?"

"I always am."

I exit my car, instantly awash in the scent of ocean. The waves on the other side of the building echo around me. I enter the lobby and give my name to the doorman like last time, studying the coastal-modern decor. When he allows me to board the elevator, I press the button for Ashton's floor.

An overwhelming thrash of wrongness whips across my spine.

I ignore it. Suppress it. Chalk it up to nerves.

In the hallway outside the elevator, I'm wowed again by the understated wealth. Glitzy seafoam accents play up the ocean theme. The plush carpet sinks beneath my feet as I walk. Soft lighting provides a calm ambiance. I knock on his door, and he answers after only a few moments. His brown hair is windswept, and he wears his black Henley like he's doing it a favor. His smile reveals cute dimples. This guy's looks are far too wholesome for a cheap fuck.

Beyond that, though, something else becomes starkly transparent.

He doesn't look like Asher.

He's missing the glimmer. The light. The indescribable *something* that makes Asher excruciatingly lovable. Exhaustingly irresistible.

"Welcome back," he says.

"Hello." I lift an eyebrow. "Ashton."

He chuckles and presses his back against the open door. "Good memory."

I take his silent invitation and enter his space. Soft alternative music plays from overhead speakers. The place is open-concept. Minimalist. Masculine. He has those kitchen cabinets with no handles and dim lighting to provide atmosphere.

The dude has money. A lot of it.

Once I reach the part of the space I'd consider the living room, I turn toward him. "What kind of doctor are you?"

"Interventional radiologist." He shuts the door.

"Oooh." I fan myself and perch on the back of the low sofa. "So fancy."

He chuckles as he approaches, slow and purposeful. "What about you?"

I shoot him a coy smile. "Take a guess."

"Hmm." His head cocks. "Dermatology?"

"Ha! No. I prefer my patients asleep."

"Ah. Anesthesia." He stops in front of me, close enough that I have to lift my chin to look him in the eye. His hands travel to the sofa back on either side of my hips. He doesn't touch me, but the warmth from his body radiates, speeding my heart. My skin beneath this thin, slinky dress prickles with discomfort.

I suppress the shudder.

His thumbs brush over my hips. A little crease forms between his brows. "Why are you here tonight?"

A laugh bursts from me. "What do you mean? Isn't it obvious?"

His eyes narrow thoughtfully. "Not really. You seem . . . conflicted."

"I'm not." The vehemence in my voice is excessive, and he backs away.

"Listen, if you're not—"

My hands grab for him and twist into his shirt, yanking him back. Our mouths meet in the middle, and I snake an arm around him. Our bodies converge, hard pressed to soft. His grip goes to my waist, and he lifts me to the sofa back.

Ignoring the furious and outraged voice in my head, I wrap my legs around him to deepen the kiss. He tastes like whiskey and wintergreen, and his cologne enters my lungs, potent enough to make me forget for three long seconds that I don't want this.

But I don't.

I don't want this.

Of all the times I've done this, all the instances I've worried what other people think, this is the first time I actually feel as if I'm doing something wrong. Most of me—*all* of me—is committed elsewhere. And this . . . This feels like cheating.

My heart revolts. It hugs a bomb to itself, lets it explode and pumps the shrapnel through my veins just for torture. I've made no promises to anyone, but this kiss is still a betrayal, and not just of this nascent, ineradicable emotion burning through my system for my best friend.

I'm betraying myself. Poisoning myself. I have more self-respect than this, and my body is screaming that I deserve the deep connection I experienced when Asher held me in his arms. I jerk back, releasing Ashton like he shocked me. Because he *did* shock me. I am shocked.

Strangely, he exhibits no surprise. Instead, he nods. "Kind of thought that would happen."

No amount of breath is enough to feed the panicked pounding of my heart, and I fear no quantity of soap will clean the ick from my skin.

Not that there's anything wrong with him. Or wrong with casual sex. Something has changed inside me. I'm the problem.

"Why?" I ask because I can think of nothing else to say.

"You're a beautiful woman." He puts some space between us. "You could have anyone, but you sought me out because I look like someone specific. You've clearly got some hang-ups."

"Maybe I have a type, and you fit it."

He shrugs. "Or maybe you're trying to fuck someone else out of your system."

I laugh without humor and slide off the sofa. My feet hit the floor with a thump. "How do you get someone out of your system when they've encoded themselves into your DNA?"

His eye twitches. "If you ever figure it out, I'd love if you could let me know."

My body sags. "You, too?"

A quick chin dip is my only answer.

I glance around the beautiful space, now seeing it in a different light. Empty. Lifeless. Lonely.

"I'm sorry I wasted your time," I whisper.

"You didn't. I don't sleep well anyway." He rubs the back of his neck and shrugs. "What the hell? You want to stay for a drink?"

I chuckle. "Sure. But only if I pour it."

He smiles, showing his dimples again. "Fair enough."

•

ASHTON UNKNOWNLASTNAME IS a fantastic drinking partner, but my aching head is mad at him the next morning and most of the day. He let me spill my problems all over his kitchen island, then disclosed some of his own.

The poor dude is heartbroken. I feel for him. Love obviously causes more pain than it prevents.

The only good part about Friday is that Asher has a noon case—a combo with Geoff. I manipulate my way into being their anesthesiologist, despite Cassie's—Asher's?—continued machinations, and smile as the two surgeons enter the OR. They're laughing when they push through the door, and both greet me with dude chin lifts and half smiles. For Asher, the move is essentially a firm tap of my on button. I blink a few times to clear the sparkles from my vision.

As usual, Asher holds his patient's hands as I put her out, then gets to work. He and Geoff shoot the shit through the entire case, leaving no room for me to interject. They banter with the entire OR.

Except me.

I am shunned.

Until about halfway through, when Geoff looks up. "You look tired, Joss. You get sleep last night?"

I startle at my name, jerking my gaze from the patient's vitals. "Oh. Um. A little, yeah."

"Yayoi said you were out late."

The scrub tech glances at me and singsongs a silly "Ooooh," but Asher ignores the conversation, concentrating on the surgery.

"Late? Everything is late to Yayoi." My voice is raspy. Why is my voice raspy when I want it to sound flippant?

Geoff chuckles. "True." He looks at Asher. "You know how I know I'm old? The thought of a date *starting* after nine makes me want to curl into a ball and go to sleep."

All the blood drains from my head.

No.

What is he saying? And *why*? It wasn't a date . . .

Damn it, Yayoi.

"You know how I know you're old?" Asher glances up at Geoff, only his eyes visible through the mask and scrub cap. "Even your nose hairs are gray."

The scrub tech titters.

Geoff shakes his head. "We're the same age, bro."

"Yeah, but I do it better," Asher says, eyes crinkling with the smile I can't see.

I stare hard at the unconcealed portion of Asher's face, searching for his reaction. I didn't want him to know about last night, and besides, nothing happened. But I can't blurt out *I didn't have sex last night* to the whole OR.

Or can I?

How long would it take to live that down?

Asher doesn't look at me. He says nothing at all. Not even at the end when he scrubs out, and I try to catch his eye. He pops the paper ties of his scrub gown with a smooth yank, ignoring me entirely. Geoff offers me a quick wave and a smile, then abandons me to my fate. After a chat with the circulator nurse, Asher moves to do the same.

"Doctor Foley," I say in a panic as his hand flattens on the push plate of the door.

His head turns. His expression is vacant. Lifeless. "Yeah?"

"Do, um . . . I didn't. That—wasn't—"

His forehead creases.

I swallow. "You okay with Toradol?"

"Yeah. Toradol's fine." He pushes open the door.

"Wait!"

He pauses again, and both the circulator and scrub tech turn to look at me, clearly suspicious.

"I—"

He waits for six seconds while I vacillate, then shakes his head. "Goodbye, Doctor Mattox."

Goodbye?

Goodbye?

What does he mean, *goodbye*?

I can't argue because I can't breathe—*goodbye* just crushed my lungs into some sort of torturous lemon press—but even if I could breathe, what would I say? How do I fix it? He has a date tonight, but maybe I can catch him before it. Maybe he'll listen. Maybe he'll understand.

I wait for the text. The call. Anything.
Nothing comes.

I finish my shift and make it to my silent home without so much as a duck pic. The agitation stirs. Ants crawl beneath my skin, and my nerves vibrate like struck piano wires inside my body. Eventually, I can take it no longer, and I pull out my phone to text him.

> How are the ducks today?

I didn't see them today sadly

> How did you survive??

There's always tomorrow.

> Titty

Sigh. Not the vibe I was going for. And he doesn't respond, which isn't promising.

> Asher. Do you have a sec? Can we talk?

Can't. I'm not alone.

> Oh? Who you with?

He doesn't answer, but I know.

It's Gabriela Acevedo.

Some minor sleuthing in the L&D dictation room after Cassie dropped the bomb earned me the information. Gabriela spread it everywhere, and she was *excited*.

Rightfully so. She has no idea the gift the universe has thrown her way.

What if he sleeps with her tonight? What if he melts her mind like he did mine? It isn't fair of me to be jealous, but the thought of his mouth on another woman is like drawing my finger down the sharpened blade of a knife—a cut so fine and deep, it's both invisible and excessively bloody.

I fall backward on my sofa and throw my phone to the coffee table. With my eyes shut, I retreat to the hill in my mind and lay my hand on the familiar trunk of my oak tree. My glass walls are secure about me, dulling this pain.

Asher can do whatever he wants with this girl. Maybe he needs it. Maybe if he falls in love with someone else, our friendship will reforge. The awkwardness will fade.

This is a *good* thing. Gabriela can be his girlfriend, and I'll be—

The girl who sleeps in the next room?

A growl rumbles in my chest, and I jerk away from the couch, stomping toward my bathroom. With a violent twist of the hot water lever, my shower sprays to life. I strip off my clothes and step in before it has a chance to warm.

The icy jet brings goose bumps to the surface of my skin, but I ignore the discomfort.

A girlfriend won't let me stay in his house. She won't let me text him at all hours of the day. She won't appreciate my evolving relationship with his mother. And if he loves this girl, he won't want me there, either. His time, his attention . . . They'll belong to her.

It's as if someone pushed me off a cliff, and my body has broken over serrated glass at the bottom. No matter what happens with him and Gabriela, I'm going to lose him. Someday, he will find a girl who says yes. He'll fall in love with someone else. He'll leave me behind.

What we had is gone. It was over the moment I said, *I can't*.

Suddenly, it's all too much. These walls are killing my every happiness. They're barricading me from potential joy.

They're ruining relationships and giving strangers the impression I'm a poser.

It all collides on top of me, brutal and inevitable.

My knees fall to the hard fiberglass floor of my shower, the water now hot enough to scald my naked skin. Tears claw through everything. Raw, ugly tears. Sobs so deep, they hurt.

I'm standing in a glass box on my lonely hill, staring at the world as it goes by me. I'm screaming. Crying. But no one can hear me. I thought the walls would save me, that they would protect me, but it's more torturous hiding in here alone, watching the things I want drift away, the things I could have if I'd only break the glass. This is a lovely, deceptive prison.

I'm isolated. Shredded to pieces.

Worse, a waterspout appears in this prison beside me, and my respite, my safe space, my entire world . . .

They begin to fill with water.

Asher

> Happiness isn't a goal one reaches, like
> climbing the peak of a summit. It's the tide.
> Inevitably, the lows rise and the highs fall.
> **—My Therapist**

Surgeries like the one I just performed with Geoff are the reason I became an OB-GYN. The woman was suffering, and I fixed it. The operation was pristine. No complications. The anatomy was textbook, with tissue that melted away like butter. Estimated blood loss was about two red blood cells.

Perfect case.

But I can't quite glory in it, this proof that I'm a fine surgeon despite what Dr. White might think. Too keyed up.

Jocelyn's mere proximity is enough to set me on edge, so her sitting at the head of the bed was a tad unsettling. She rips my emotions open—a cat's claw across a bag of birdseed.

Feelings are dumb, and they're spilling out of me in torrents. Rage. Jealousy. Misery. Disbelief. Hurt.

What's missing? Hope. All hope is extinguished.

She slept with someone else last night.

I enter the men's locker room with a violent yank on the door, ripping the paper scrub cap off my head at the same time.

Geoff's sitting on a bench near the lockers, legs outstretched before him, ankles crossed. "I told you she was with someone else. You didn't believe me."

Without a word, I storm past him and arrive at the sinks, washing the latex scent of surgical gloves from my hands. No, I didn't believe him. Didn't think she'd actually do that. Is she *trying* to kill me?

Geoff stands. "See? Now you know. You really can move on."

I pull paper towels from the dispenser, then meet his eyes. He says that like it's easy. Like *moving on* is as simple as stepping on an auto walk at the airport. A man doesn't simply *move on* from a woman like Jocelyn Mattox. I'll have to untangle her, one thread at a time, and each thread is barbed with the fractured hopes of the relationship we'll never have. It's all entwined hopelessly together, making extraction both time-consuming and painful.

I'm an idiot for letting her dig this deep, this selfish girl who's incapable of love.

Geoff's brown eyes hold mine for no more than four seconds before he glances away and rubs his face. "We still doing the pool tomorrow?"

I toss the wet paper into the trash. "Why wouldn't we?"

"Do you think she'll show?"

"Yes."

I know Jocelyn. Based on that interaction in the OR

just now, she has something on her mind, but whatever it is, however much it bothers her, she'll never say it. Instead, she'll come to my house tomorrow and pretend nothing's wrong. She'll hide like she always does.

I can't believe she slept with someone else last night. The gnawing acidy feeling kicks up a frenzy in my stomach, and I yank the bottle of Tums from my locker. Chalky raspberry this time. Appetizing . . .

There aren't enough Tums in the world to make this pain go away.

She used me. Compared me to a luxury sports car. Practically ignored my confession of love. Then let another man screw her. All in the space of five days. That's how little she respects me?

Someone else was inside her body last night. Did she think about me while she did it?

Ha. Wow. I've gone full Alanis Morissette. That's fun.

But I hate how much it hurts, how jealous I am. I want to break things. I want to go on this date tonight and fuck this girl so thoroughly that I can't remember my own name, let alone what Jocelyn's doing with her body.

But I won't do that.

Because I'm not an asshole.

Stupid to choose a girl I work with as my first date when she's so obviously serving as a rebound.

Geoff sighs. "If you get lucky tonight, maybe you won't care so much."

"I'm not getting lucky tonight." I stride toward the exit.

Geoff follows. "You never know."

"Yes, I do."

I hate everything. Every. Fucking. Thing.

Before I reach the door, a nurse barges through it. Whoa. "Uh," I say. "This is the men's room—"

"I know." She pauses to catch her breath. "You weren't answering your pages. Doctor White needs you in the OB OR. *Now.*"

Hold the phone. Dr. White needs *me*? What the fuck? Someone's dying. It's the only explanation. And now I'm about to have a heart attack.

We rush for the OR, and she fills me in on details along the way. Emergency C-section for non-reassuring fetal heart tones. Large baby. Difficult delivery. Bleeding, bleeding, bleeding.

"She's already lost a liter of blood," she says. "The one thing she said before they put her to sleep was 'Don't take my uterus!' But Doctor White is already talking about a hysterectomy."

Fuck.

When I scrub in, Dr. White is barely able to keep up with the bleeding. The anesthesiologist is emergently hanging blood products. The patient is intubated and under general.

"Thanks," White says, voice calm despite the pool of blood he's operating in. "Needed a second pair of competent hands for this one, I think."

Competent?

I shouldn't pause on that, given the emergency occurring before my eyes, but this guy doesn't give compliments. At least, not to me. Has the world gone wonky?

"What's happening?" I ask.

"Thought placental abruption at first. Then I got in here and saw she ruptured her uterus." He chuckles darkly. "So much blood I thought I must have somehow gotten into the goddamn aorta, but nope."

"We're at fifteen hundred cc blood loss, Doctors," a nurse says behind White.

Now that I'm helping, the surgical field is clear enough to

visualize the multiple fountains of blood that pour from this flayed uterus. Christ.

"I'm going to take her uterus," he announces to the entire OR.

Against her consent?

"Hang on," I say. "We haven't tried everything yet." Cesarean hysterectomies aren't simple surgeries under the best of circumstances. There's true risk of morbidity. Mortality.

Plus, the patient *wants* her uterus.

"Organ is bleeding," White replies, returning to his usual *are-you-an-idiot?* voice. "Cure is removal."

I hold a hand over the field. "Let's try to get it under control first. Even if we can't save her uterus, it'll make the hyst easier."

White nods, and we get to work. We try to sew the organ back together with brisk, efficient throws of suture. Both of us attack it at different angles, tying knots tight enough to make the muscle turn white. It still bleeds, but the fountains slow to trickles. I snag a particularly helpful bit that closes off one gushing artery.

"Nice move, kid," White says.

"Two liters, Doctors."

"Is the hysterectomy kit open?" White demands.

No, it's working! Can't he see that? If we take her uterus, we steal her fertility. She'll wake up to a world of devastation.

I work faster. Clamp, clamp. Knot, knot.

"Just wait." I start a baseball stitch along the torn pieces. Inside to outside, inside to outside.

"Two point five liters."

Gradually, it comes back together, and the bleeding diminishes to nothing. White lets me work, proving to be a phenomenal first assist. When the uterus looks like a uterus again—well, a Halloween-y version of one, anyway—White raises his blue eyes to take me in. Is that a twinkle I detect behind his eyewear? "Impressive work, Doctor."

Impressive?

"I didn't think we'd get it." He holds his hand out for the needle drivers, throwing a few more sutures so we'll both sleep better tonight.

I chuckle, cutting the thread for him. "She wanted to keep her uterus, right? Where there's a will, there's a way. Or some shit like that."

He barks out a laugh. "Had a case like this before. Long time ago. I took her uterus." He leans in closer. "She cried to me for weeks. It was such a headache."

I nod, unsurprised. Stories like that are why we have terrible reputations now. Look at me, tearing down the system, one patient at a time.

"I like your style, son," he says. "Heard you were good in the OR. Nice to see it's actually true."

He— He'd heard . . . what now?

"So much is changing around here, but looks like they're still training doctors the right way."

Well, perhaps a little more humanely than the old days, but yes. My training was excellent.

"Did you know they're removing the transcription service?"

I didn't even know we had a transcription service. Such an antiquated way to chart—dictate over the phone, so someone can type it out for you? Why would anyone do that? Faster just to type it myself, especially with templates.

I retract tissue so he can close the fascia. His technique is flawless, but I suppose that's what thirty years of experience will get you. "I didn't know," I say. "Don't really use it."

He hums. "Us old guys never learned to type like you young'uns, you know. Why do you think I pushed so hard for them to pay for that Dragon software?"

Omg.

OMG.

Ha.

Of course.

All the puzzle pieces fall together in my mind. This old man with connections and clout doesn't want to type, so he persuades some upper-management guy that the hospital needs a speech-driven charting tool. Because he's old AF. Stuck in his ways. Stubborn.

His eyes glint playfully. "Convinced them they'll save money this way."

"Will they?"

He chuckles. "Probably not. But if they make me type my operative notes, I'm retiring, and I know several of the old guard will do the same. Told them if they want to prevent a mass exodus, they'll help a fellow out."

A laugh is all I can manage. Of course admin's pushing it on us—they want to justify their investment. Here I thought this Dragon crap was being foisted upon us for nothing, when really, the hospital is begging us to appease those who can't keep up with the times. I thought this man believed I was a child-doctor-idiot, but he's just used to medical hazing.

He would have taken her uterus. I saved it.

Well, hell. I'm not inadequate after all, am I? I'm just young. I'm innovative. I can type seventy words per minute. I save uteruses.

I do things differently. Nothing wrong with that. Why did it take me so long to understand that? It's . . . freeing.

Will probably still need the Tums, though. These aren't beliefs that reverse overnight, and my job isn't exactly a vacation. But hey, this is a fantastic start. Thanks, Dr. White, you decrepit bastard. Asher 2.0 will be the best one yet.

•

GABRIELA ACEVEDO IS ENCHANTING. Outside the hospital, dressed in something other than scrubs, she's so refreshing, she makes me feel like I can breathe again. We sit at a bistro table on the outdoor patio of a beachside grill, the surface littered with half-eaten appetizers. Our dinner plates lie before us, untouched since we can't stop talking.

She works that black dress like she knows how to use it, and her laugh is infectious.

"I'm serious," she says with a chuckle as I call bullshit on her story of delivering a vaginal breech baby in triage the other day. "The nurse screamed for help, and I came running, and the butt was crowning—wait, butts can't crown. Is there a name for a ring placed around the ass?"

"Uh. Toilet seat?"

She snorts. "Okay. The baby was toilet seating, and I just . . . did it. My attending showed up about three minutes later."

I high-five her. "Badass."

The patrons at the table behind her leave, and she scoots her chair closer to me. A half hour past sunset, and the sky still glows orange. Beside us, the wooden railing gives way to a short drop to the beach. The gulf beyond is calm, the waves lapping at the shore in a peaceful rhythm.

Love this. The ambiance. The company. I *needed* this.

Her eyes brighten. "Badass, huh? You really think so?"

"Hell yeah, girl. But I'll admit I'm still skeptical, since I didn't hear about it. The nurses tell me everything."

She picks up a fry from her plate. "That's because they love you."

I lean toward her. "You want to know a secret?"

Chewing her fry, she nods.

"I love them, too."

She chuckles. "I know. It shows."

"It does?"

Gabriela throws a fry at me. "You're nice to everyone."

I glance down at my plate. "There's a reason for that, you know."

"Oh, yeah?" She rests her elbows on the table. "Tell me."

I search her face. "You really want to know?"

Her nod is thoughtful. Slow. Like she knows I'm about to share a part of myself.

I cast my gaze toward the waves. "A few years ago, I was at a party. There was this pretty girl I was interested in, and I'd recently heard a rumor about her that she was—um, like, easy, or whatever."

"Oh, no."

I smile ruefully. "Yeah. Here's where Asher learns not to listen to rumors. I was saying some . . . not nice things about her, and she overheard me."

Dark eyes go wide. "No. What did she say?"

"She totally called me out. Pretty glorious on her part. Then it turned out that none of the rumors were true, and I felt bad for—I don't know—a year? The girl was super sweet. It's one of those scenes my brain still throws at me right when I'm about to fall asleep, so I can wallow in the embarrassment all over again."

"I have a few of those myself," she says with a laugh.

"So, now, I don't say shit like that. Never know who's listening. Lesson learned."

Her pink lips curve in a smile. "That's sweet."

"No." I toss a grin back at her. "It's just proof that I'm a recovering asshole."

"You're nice because you don't want to hurt people's feelings. That's—" She shakes her head and sighs. "Can I ask you a question?"

I finally take a bite of my fish. Pretty decent. A little too lemony. "Sure."

"Why are you still single?"

Oh. Okay. So we're just going there, I guess. Cold tendrils creep over my shoulders at once. I slowly finish chewing and sip my drink.

She straightens. "Sorry. That was forward. You don't have to answer that. It's . . . You—you're so . . ."

An invisible fork has lodged between my ribs. Breathing is *not* comfortable. "I'm so what?"

"You're *nice*. Funny. Successful. Super hot." She ticks them off on her fingers like a grocery list, and I lose the ability to look her in the eye. "How has some girl not snatched you up?"

Ignoring the sudden heat in my face, I drop my hands beneath the table, so she doesn't see them clench. "I don't really date."

"Right." She sips her cocktail. "So, can I ask you another question since you didn't answer the first?"

"I didn't answer because I don't know the answer, but sure."

The outdoor lighting twinkles in her eyes when she stares directly into mine. "Why'd you change your mind about me?"

I blink twice, then return my attention to the darkening beach, the black waves beyond. "It seemed like the right thing to do at the time."

Her voice softens. "But it doesn't anymore?"

The jittery crushed sensation reappears. I raise my hand to lay it atop hers on the table. "I—um . . . The truth is, I don't think I'm ready for this."

Her smooth forehead creases.

I clear my throat. "You're funny and smart. So beautiful. You deserve someone who's fully present. Fully available."

With a tilt of her head, she pulls her hand back. "Available? Are you seeing someone else?"

"No. But I would be, if she'd say yes."

She stares at me, silent, brown eyes sparkling. Then she smiles. "No offense, but whoever that girl is sounds like an idiot."

The statement is so blunt, I can't help but laugh.

Gabriela snickers. "Wait, seriously. She said *no*? Did she have a stroke? Was she hit upside the head? Is she secretly a princess from a distant land and isn't permitted to fraternize with commoners?"

Still laughing, I shake my head. "Um, no. At least, I don't think so."

"Maybe she's a robot. You can do better than a robot, Asher." Her teasing wink sparks something deep inside—proof that my body still knows how to respond to a woman who isn't Jocelyn. It fizzles quickly, but still. A spark is promising.

I lean closer to her. "Maybe she's a spy, and being with me would compromise her mission."

Gabriela eats another fry. "The mission! Of course. It's life or death."

This woman truly is enchanting.

She sips her drink and gives me a frank stare. "Or maybe she isn't good enough for you."

My chest tightens. "Maybe not."

"Just something to consider." She pushes away from the table. "Excuse me. I'm going to use the restroom."

I can't help but watch her walk away. Gleaming black hair rests in ringlets down her back, and her hips sway as she makes her way through the other tables. I'm not the only one staring. The woman draws the eye.

She might be good. Great, even. She might be the one. Perhaps Jocelyn is the hurdle I must leap to reach the ultimate goal, but I doubt it. Even the thought of her—the potential of her—it grates on my conscience. This isn't fair to her. Or to me.

I pull out my phone while I wait, surprised to find a text from Joss.

> **How are the ducks today?**

Seriously? Classic Jocelyn, ignoring it all.

> I didn't see them today sadly

> **How did you survive??**

> There's always tomorrow.

> **Titty**

Ha. At least that's still capable of making me smile. But I don't know what to say, so I set the phone down and stare at the text stream. The three dots pop up and disappear six times before she says anything else.

> **Asher. Do you have a sec? Can we talk?**

With a twist of my stomach, my appetite disappears. I shove my plate away. Part of me wants to shut her down. The other is aching to know what she'd say. How does she possibly expect to fix the broken pieces?

Never should have admitted to loving her. Silent suffering would've been better than this excruciating awkwardness. I don't know how to be around her anymore.

> Can't. I'm not alone.

Oh? Who you with?

My thumb hovers over the screen. Should I admit the truth? She didn't tell me about her date last night. Clearly didn't want me to know about it. Indecision has me swiping out of the messaging app altogether. Instead, I slide down my notifications and scroll through useless information from Starbucks and Amazon and Google, clearing it from my screen. A MyRadar notification from yesterday pauses me.

Tropical Storm Franklin forms in Caribbean.

I tap on it and read through the article. The storm is east of the Yucatan Peninsula, but we're at the extreme edge of the cone of uncertainty.

Meh.

Gabriela returns to her seat, so I pocket the phone. "You want to get out of here?" she asks.

"Absolutely."

We flag down the server, and when he hands the check to me, Gabriela extends her hand, palm up. "I'm the one who asked you out. Give me that."

A laugh bursts from me. "What? No. I'm paying for your dinner, Gabriela."

"Give it to me! You're adhering to antiquated gender norms that don't—"

"You're a resident. You make like two cents an hour. Let me pay for your damn French fries."

She tries to subdue that cute smile—pinches her lips, scrunches her nose—but it breaks out anyway. "I ate ramen for dinner six days in a row."

"Exactly." I hand off the check with my credit card and shake my head at her. "Gender norms? Really?"

With a contrite smile, she raises her fists and gives them a weak shake. "Down with the patriarchy."

I rest my head on my fist and give way to laughter. "I like you."

"Yeah." She glances down at the table between us. "As a friend, right?"

I pull in a deep breath and nod. "Yeah. Probably. For now."

With a click of her tongue, she downs the half-full cocktail sitting on the table.

My eyes widen. "Whoa."

A quick swipe of her mouth, and she shrugs. "I just went on a date with a man who's pining after another woman. Give me a break."

I'm not pining. Much.

No, the pining comes much later, when I'm in my cold bed alone, dithering over a text I'm not sure I should answer.

> I had a date.

There. Now she knows. I'm not hiding.

> Oh.
>
> Did you have fun?
>
> I mean . . . you're already home texting me
>
> So maybe not?

Heat floods my face, my hands.

What the hell? That's what she leads with?

The impulsive, reckless answer that would hum like magic in the moment but burn with self-loathing for the rest of time jolts to my fingertips.

Not all of us fuck on the first date.

I suppress that urge, but it takes a minute. In the interim, she continues . . .

> That was a joke
>
> Asher it was a joke.
>
> You could be with her right now. What do I know?
>
> I shouldn't have said that

Her clear panic softens me. Jocelyn has some sorcery in her blood. It weakens even the firmest resolve.

> It's fine.
>
> I'm tired though. Going to sleep.

> Asher.

I anticipate another text, but nothing comes, so I prod her.

> What?

Pre-sleep wonderland steals my awareness for several minutes while waiting for her to answer. The light from my phone jolts me awake.

> Are we going to be okay?

Her text holds me enthralled. Can't pinpoint why exactly. Perhaps it's the *we*. That word is a tether. Verification that

I'm not in this alone. That I'm not the only one experiencing pain. Jocelyn cares about me, too, even if it's not the way I want. It's a balm, but it's also a dreary reminder of the truth. We might not be okay.

> I don't know.

•

THE NEXT DAY, pool waves lap at my waist while I pretend to watch the water-volleyball match before me. Can't help but monitor the conversation happening behind me. Skeezy bit of eavesdropping, if I'm honest. Hopeful for information I probably don't want.

"How you holding up?" Yayoi asks.

"I'm fine," Joss whispers. "You know me."

"Yeah, which is how I know you're not fine."

Exactly. Score one, Yayoi.

Joss snorts. "What do you mean?"

"Well, for starters, your smile looks like Willem Dafoe when he played the bad guy in *Spiderman*."

Ha. Don't laugh! I rub my mouth, hoping that will stifle the snicker.

"What does that even mean?" Joss asks, all offended.

Yayoi's tone turns thoughtful. "Sort of . . . deranged."

Joss huffs. "There's nothing wrong with my smile."

"Smile like a normal person is all I'm saying."

Luckily, Talia swims over to me before I burst into laughter. "You hear about this hurricane, Doctor F?"

"Franklin? Category one now, right? When are they saying it'll hit?"

"Landfall Tuesday morning." Her mouth spreads in that impish grin. "You know what that means?"

She wins a chuckle from me. "Office will be closed?"

"Office will be closed," she says with a wild hoot of a laugh and a shimmy in the water.

"We aren't even in the cone."

She sighs. "I know. Anyway, I got to get home. Been three hours, so my boobs are about to explode."

I jiggle her shoulder. "Your oversupply is out of control. You have to stop pumping after you breastfeed, dollface."

She brandishes her hands at me, shooing me away. "Quit doctoring me."

I shoot her a look. "I'm your doctor."

"Mind your business."

She struts away through the water as I boo her. The conversation behind me has turned from interesting topics to hair products, which . . . No, thanks. Not interested. Instead, I hop out of the pool and head to the porch, where a lively argument over hospital hurricane policies takes place.

"It isn't fair," Kevin says. "The Team A people have to stay in-house until the all-clear. That could be forty-eight hours or more if the storm is bad."

Cassie splays her palms over the table, full on serious mode. "We can't expect people to drive in for their assigned shifts in the middle of a hurricane. That's ridiculous."

I slip into the only empty chair, the one beside Geoff, who leans onto the table. "That's not what he's saying."

Cassie crosses her arms. "Then, please, enlighten me."

"Team A and Team B should both be in-house," Geoff says, "and they can switch on and off until the all-clear."

She throws her hands up. "That's preposterous! We'd have to pay both teams disaster pay the entire time. That's double the amount of salary."

Defeated, Kevin slumps in his chair. "It's not fair."

Cassie rolls her eyes. "You're only mad because you were Team A last time."

"It sucked." Kevin takes a sip of his beer. "So boring, and the food was shit."

"I put everyone's name in a hat. It's luck of the draw."

Hmm. Pretty fair.

Kevin perks up. "Can you leave my name out, since I had to do it last time?"

She cocks her head, silky black hair flowing over her shoulder. An ebony river. "I'd have to do it for everyone on Team A, though. Not feasible."

"So how was last night?" Geoff asks under his breath, referring to my date.

I shrug. "Fine."

"Did it help?"

"No."

He sucks air through his teeth. "Have another drink, then." He glances over as his wife approaches with Jocelyn. "And, hey, go cook my cheeseburger."

Right. I can take a hint. I rise from my chair. "Okay, okay."

"You need help?" Cassie half stands, eyes hopeful.

"Nah, sugar. I got it."

Jocelyn's gaze snaps to me, but I won't look. Refuse to look. Must make myself busy with food. The grill was pre-warmed, so I pull the tray of meat from the outdoor fridge. The sizzle is a comforting cadence for my frazzled nerves. Grilling is simple. Easy. Soothing. And the aroma is unbeatable.

Well . . .

In a contest, the fragrance of Jocelyn's skin would probably win. It thoroughly distracts. Enraptures. Both seductive and edible.

Ugh. The girl has taken over my mind.

I still bought her pineapple White Claws. I was at the store, and they were there and . . . habit. Sort of hate myself for it. When she appears at my side fifteen minutes later and thanks me, gazing at the can like it's a diamond tennis bracelet, the regret is overwhelming. Don't want her thanks. Don't want her praising my favors. Don't want her near me, looking like that.

She's in the black bikini.

Beautiful. Glistening. Torturing me.

Maybe the tantalizing expanses of skin wouldn't bother me if I didn't know how they tasted. Did she wear the black bikini on purpose? Maybe not. Maybe she doesn't care and isn't even trying. Maybe I'm a milksop.

"It was really nice," she murmurs, so no one else hears, "to buy these for me."

"Sure." I swallow against a knot in my throat. A bit painful, that. Do emotions clog there like hair in a shower drain? "Why wouldn't I?"

Her stare pelts my face. "Maybe because you can't even look at me right now."

Behind us, the others laugh and screech as they jump in the pool. The group at the table is now in the midst of a rowdy discussion regarding the merits—and vast degrees of evil—of social media.

I set down the spatula and face Joss full on, giving her a fake, bright grin. "I'm looking. What do you want?"

Her hair is messy, her eyes hollow. She wears no smile, no expression at all. "I just . . . I hate this, Asher. This isn't us. You're drifting away from me, and I want you back."

Back? I'm not the one who turned her down. My voice lowers. "You rejected me, remember?"

She drops her gaze to the ground and says nothing.

"Jocelyn, that's not how things work. You can't have it both ways. If you want me, you have to be mine, too. You can't turn me down, then expect things to go back to how they were. You can't sleep with other men and expect me to be waiting for you with open arms. It isn't fair, and it's selfish."

She flinches. "I'm not sleeping with other men."

I go still. What? She . . . Did she just say . . .

"I didn't do it," she says. "I went there, but I didn't sleep with him."

Uhhhh. What is this new tingly sensation, sprouting up through the pain? Is this *more* hope? I thought it had been murdered irrevocably. Maybe hope is a vampire. Immortal. Dangerous.

"Why not?" I ask.

She rubs her nose and looks away. "You know why."

The dying organ in my chest thumps hard against my ribs. "I don't. Say it. Be specific."

Warm brown eyes turn toward me. "Did you sleep with Gabriela?"

Oh, no. She isn't getting out of this so easily. "Would it bother you if I did?"

Her mouth opens to answer, but Geoff yells, "Yo, Foley! You burning my burger?"

Shit. I grab the spatula to scoop up the smoking burgers. Meanwhile, Jocelyn tries to slip away. My hand darts out and grasps her wrist before she leaves.

"Would it?" I ask.

A beat passes, the cinnamon in her eyes turning glassy. When she speaks, her voice is barely more than a whisper. "Yes."

The desperate, scared look on her face has me pulling her closer. "Where is your head, Joss?"

A tear splashes over her cheek. "I'm drowning, and I can't find my way to the surface. Let me go."

Does she think I'm an anchor?

"Foley!" Geoff rises from his chair. "What the fuck are you doing?"

I glance down at the smoking mess on the grill, and Jocelyn's wrist slides from my grip. By the time I've trashed the food and turned off the grill, I've been subjected to another annoying lecture from Geoff—*"That girl's going to kill you"*—and Joss is nowhere to be found.

When I peek out front, her car is gone. She doesn't call, doesn't text. She chooses the path of least resistance, just like I knew she would. She ignores it all. For the first time in over two years, she doesn't spend Saturday night at my house.

•

BY MONDAY AFTERNOON, the weather has turned gray and windy. Rain spits just enough to make everything cold and moist. Franklin was upgraded to a Category 2 hurricane an hour ago, but we're hovering at the edge of the cone. Still, Jocelyn's probably freaking out.

At least she's texting me back now—unlike yesterday, when she ignored me until late at night, pretending like she'd forgotten to charge her phone.

Yeah, right. The girl never forgets her phone. It's her lifeline. She just didn't want to deal with me. Deal with any of it, more like. Kind of annoyed with her. Hot-and-cold thing isn't my favorite. Wish she'd make up her mind.

You team a or b?

B again.

I'm sorry.

> You're welcome to come to my house.

It's okay. I'll be fine.

> You sure? It's supposed to get bad overnight.

I'm sure.

Sitting in my truck in the parking lot of the hospital, I glare at my phone. This is getting tiresome. Jocelyn hates these storms. Is Operation Avoid Asher really more important than that? She'd rather be alone and terrified than be subjected to my company?

> You're staying at your house then?

Yeah. We aren't even in the cone.

> Did you buy water and food?

I spent a large portion of Sunday performing hurricane chores—purchasing water and non-perishables, filling gas cans, topping off the propane tank, pulling all my loose outdoor furniture inside. Jocelyn isn't a planner. Did she even remember to buy bottled water?

I'll be fine.

"Why won't you talk to me?" I scream at my phone and throw it to the passenger seat.

Irritating woman.

For someone so concerned about me drifting away from her, she's certainly doing her best to run full tilt in the opposite direction. Guess she didn't like that little admission I pulled from her.

Whoops.

Sorry not sorry.

Still don't know what to make of it, though. She's jealous at the idea of me with other women, yes, but whatever other emotions she's harboring in there make her feel like she's drowning. The dichotomy is somehow promising and also exceedingly bleak. Jealousy isn't enough to build a relationship on. It's a disease that spawns on itself. A cancer that makes people behave in strange, pathologic ways.

But hey. At least it's proof she cares a little.

A small airborne branch smacks against the windshield, startling me. All right, then. Time to get home. All outpatient offices closed at 1:00 p.m. Talia's enthusiasm for a day off had dimmed substantially in the face of the reality heading toward us. Franklin is slowing and strengthening, and even if he doesn't hit us, there will be damage. But unlike Talia, who has a type-A husband, Jocelyn has no one to look out for her. Her decision to remain alone in a house that hasn't been updated since the 1960s during a Category 2 hurricane could hurt her.

The very male portion of me has a strong inclination to kidnap her. She can kick and scream all she wants, but she'll be safe doing it. Can't freak her out, though. Just barely have her speaking to me again.

And there my mind goes, right back to Saturday.

I went there, but I didn't sleep with him.

That's just . . . fan-fucking-tastic, even if I don't know why she couldn't go through with it.

You know why.

Wish I did. God, I really want to know why. This hope is hazardous to my health. Potentially lethal. Can't believe

I let it blossom amidst the scorched earth she left behind. Fully aware this makes me weak. Keep committing the same mistakes, like an insane person. Can't seem to stop myself, though. The optimist in me is hard to kill.

I'm certain if I push my luck now, she'll flee again.

But she's being stupid AF.

I'll be fine.

How does she know?

I drive home through congested roads strewn with debris. The wind whips the palm trees lining the streets, their fronds dragging the trunks sideways. Lines of cars clog the gas stations, most of which are now empty of fuel. With the truck housed safely in my garage, I enter the house and settle in. By evening, the storm tracker on my app is far more optimistic than the doomsday weathermen on the local news. The cone has shifted south a bit, but the storm is still Category 2.

To distract myself, I start a match on Fortnite. If the storm turns out as bad as they say, I'll lose internet at some point. May as well enjoy it while I have it. Before the match begins, I make one last pass at Jocelyn.

> Storm is getting closer.
>
> I don't care what's going on between us. I'll always be here if you need me.

It's gonna be okay

> Promise me you'll call if you need anything

I will. I promise.

Jocelyn

Of all the ways to die, heartbreak is
the only one you can live through.
—My Therapist

After promising Asher I'll tell him if I need him, I set down my phone and sink onto my couch. This is the smart thing. I can't continue to rely on him for everything. I can brave this—my greatest fear—by myself. I'm strong. This hurricane is predicted to be mild, and I prepared for it. Water. Food. Easy peasy.

First, survive the hurricane. Second, repair the fissure between me and Asher. What that repair involves is still a bit foggy. Is it releasing him to go fall in love with someone else? Is it leaping onto him with both arms and legs and never letting go?

Who could say?

Not me, and definitely not while 90 percent of my headspace is wondering if I'll be dead in the next twenty-four hours. Storm tracking while I distract myself with my latest novel, I make it through most of the evening without losing my cool. Regular updates to Ali help me relax, though she's vocally irritated at my decision to remain in my *death trap of a house* instead of shacking up with the boy who owns a brand-new Cat-5-proof home.

The news is obnoxious. The idiot anchors keep cutting to onsite reporters out in the thick of it, standing in abandoned streets while sheets of sideways rain pelt them. Even a few hours ago, the wind was strong enough to knock them off their feet.

Morons, the lot of them.

After nine, I give up on the novel and call Ali, but it doesn't fully ease my nerves. We chat about everything except the weather while I try desperately to forget the potential destruction heading my way. Why did I do this to myself? Am I secretly a masochist? That's the only logical explanation, right?

The jitters have me nauseated, and the thought of food makes me gag. Someone has taken a hand mixer to my insides and scrambled everything out of place. My heart is in my throat. My stomach in my feet. The horrendous assault of the wind outside makes me cringe, and I do the toddler thing where I press my palms over my ears to make it stop.

I am the world's biggest dumbass.

The storm worsens close to midnight, so I take to my bed with earplugs. Block it out and it doesn't exist, right? Trying to sleep during a hurricane in a wood-framed house with no shutters is perhaps the hardest—and stupidest—thing I've ever done. Each gust of hundred-plus mile per hour wind slams against my home like a freight train, rattling the vulnerable single-pane windows. Debris peppers the siding every so often, making me flinch despite the earplugs.

Category 2 sounds so weak. Two out of five? This hurricane would get a D in math class. But around 1:00 a.m., I finally admit to myself I should have stayed with Asher. My house rocks with each wind gust, and the minced ends of my overstimulated nerves recoil at every thump. Lying in my bed in the wee hours of the morning, staring at my ceiling, I own up to my mistakes. I shouldn't have listened when they said it wouldn't hit us. That's exactly what my parents did.

It's what the majority of people do. Ignore the warnings. Play with fire.

Hours pass while I suppress the rising panic.

I'll be fine. This is fine.

A bang crashes above the roar of the storm, and my ceiling fan stills. The dim night-light from the bathroom disappears. The cool air from the vent in the floor stops.

Power's out.

Night has barely given way to an approaching stormy sunrise, so the sudden darkness envelops me. I sit up in bed. The covers pool around my waist. Fingers and toes cold, face hot, I swing out of bed. My phone at my bedside table lights up when I grab it.

A series of emergency alerts glow over my screen.

National Weather Service: A HURRICANE WARNING is in effect for this area for dangerous and damaging winds. Urgently complete efforts to protect life and property. Have food, water, cash, fuel, and medications for 3+ days.

National Weather Service: A STORM SURGE WARNING is in effect for this area for the danger of life-threatening flooding.

> Urgently complete efforts to protect life and property. Follow evacuation orders if given for this area to avoid drowning or being cut off from emergency services.
>
> EMERGENCY ALERT: Your county has issued a mandatory evacuation for flood zones A, B, C. Emergency services have been suspended. Please leave the area immediately.

What the hell? What happened in the few hours I've been trying to sleep? And why didn't my phone make a sound?

With a single bar of signal, I open the local news website. The storm has grown and slowed. Now upgraded to a Category 5, Franklin's turned his course dramatically. The bastard is close and heading straight for me. The storm surge has already started.

Fuck. I scurry from my bed.

Another loud crack rocks my house while I scramble to put on clothes and sturdy shoes. Above me, the ceiling creaks. My gaze lifts right as the plaster splinters apart and the giant oak from my front yard rips through my bedroom.

With a scream, I leap for the doorway. Branches claw scratches into my skin while I crawl to safety. With the house torn open, the howl of the storm is deafening. Lying on my belly in the hallway, I try to catch my breath. The pounding in my chest makes it impossible.

Fuck, fuck, fuck.

I'm going to die here, aren't I? Rain showers my bedroom, and I spy my phone screen glowing on the floor between the leaves of the tree.

"Shit!"

That phone is my only source of communication. I army crawl through the destruction, pushing aside branches until I reach the main trunk. The phone lies barely out of my grasp. The useless foliage does zero to protect me from the storm above. Stinging rain pelts my body as I stretch my arm beneath the wood. My fingertips grazing the plastic case.

Bark digs deep into my shoulder, and something pinches in the joint, but my hand closes over the wet device. I slide it toward me and clamber out of the bedroom. In the hallway, I lurch to my feet, wiping at the water on my scraped skin. My shoes skid over wood floors, and I trip in my haste to reach the front entryway, where I keep my car keys. As my hand clenches around the keychain, the street outside the front window grabs my attention.

The life-sustaining organ in my chest abruptly slows, skipping too many beats at once. My vision goes fuzzy. Black closes about the edges. Weak gray daylight illuminates a horror scene. The street is flooded. My front yard is flooded.

I can't drive in this. I'm trapped.

With a clang, the keys fall to the floor. My knees give out and I sink to the wood beneath me. At the bite of pain in my joints, I come to and lift my phone. My fingers find Asher's name and hit the call button. At my ear, no rings come through, so I pull away to look at the screen. When did I lose signal?

The call fails.

I open our message stream. The last text he sent glares at me. Judging.

Promise me you'll call if you need anything.

I waited too long. I let fear cloud my judgment, and now terror has me frozen, reverting back into that frightened fifteen-year-old who didn't know what to do. Who dove into rising floodwaters to save a mother she'd never see again.

> Asher I need you

The bubble is green instead of blue, and I stare at the bar at the top for two full minutes while it tries to send. A little red exclamation point pops up beside it.

Not delivered.

A sob catches in my throat. My gaze strays again to the gray, eddying water outside, now lapping at the cement stairs of my front porch.

I'm going to drown. I'm going to die today. Alone. I could have been alive. With him.

My brain struggles to organize itself. Survival mode switches on and I stare around me. The highest point in my house is the bar in my kitchen. It can be my last resort.

I hop to my feet and run toward the attached garage. It sits a foot lower than the rest of my house. An inch of water already covers the floor. I pause for only a moment to stare at the proof of danger, then snatch a push broom from its spot against the wall.

I try to shoot out another text.

> Asher please I need help

Not delivered.

In a quarter hour, the surge has reached my porch. Skin slicked in sweat, I stand far back from the window, letting my heart pound out its last beats.

The water rises.

Memories flash through my mind.

. . . my parents dancing in our kitchen . . .

. . . Leo pulling me from the storm surge . . .
. . . Grandma helping with my history homework . . .
. . . Aiden telling me he loves me . . .
. . . Ali in her wedding dress, hugging me close . . .
. . . her children laughing at their first birthdays . . .
. . . Yayoi's giddiness from her positive pregnancy test . . .
. . . Geoff claiming I'm one of his best friends . . .
. . . Asher . . .
. . . his smile . . .

Water spills over the porch, seeps toward my front door.

. . . his teasing laugh . . .

The wood groans when water trickles through the cracks. I clutch my broom tighter.

. . . the sparkle in his eyes when he looks at me . . .

Water builds against the windows on either side of the door.

. . . I want something real . . .

The glass creaks against the slap of the rising tide.

. . . I'm in love with you . . .

The waves crash against the door. Water inches inside.

. . . Can you see a future for us? . . .

Why couldn't I give in? Give him what he wants? I've been so terrified of everyone else's death, I never paused to consider my own mortality. I'm going to die, but does it count as death if I've never really been alive to begin with? I've hidden in shadows. In excuses. In a glass box nearly full of floodwaters.

With a great crack, the thin glass windows shatter, and water spills into my home. My face is wet, breath short, but I square my shoulders. Broom in hand, I stomp to the door and turn the knob. One sweep at the inches of water spilling inside is ineffectual, but I keep trying.

Sweep.

Flood.
Sweep.
Flood.

I poke my head out the door. My face and hair are whipped by wind powerful enough to kill. It's not easing up in the slightest. If I had cell service, I could check the radar, figure out where the eye is, determine how much longer this storm will brew with such violence.

Sweep.
Flood.
Sweep.
Flood.

Behind me, the tide rages against my back doors—glass sliders. It's only a matter of time before they break against the weight of the water. I stop sweeping and peer down at my feet, now ankle deep.

The broom drops out of my hands. Splashes beside me.

My tears are soundless, but numerous. Hundreds of them. Thousands.

Tears for myself. For what I'll never have. For every person I've lost. Every person I'm about to lose.

Eyes locked on the rising surge, I splash through the water to my kitchen. I slowly lift myself to the countertop, feet dangling. I pull out my phone once more.

I need you.

Not delivered.

I love you.

Not delivered.

I'm sorry I never told you.

Not delivered.

> Just know you were the last thing I thought about.

Not delivered.

> I'll love you until the end of time.

Not delivered.

Asher

> Disaster is simply a mediation
> between damage and growth.
> —My Therapist

Something hard hits my house minutes before sunrise, jolting me awake. My hand grasps clumsily for my phone, hoping to find an update from Jocelyn. Instead, a series of emergency alerts litters my lock screen, and my mom has texted sixteen times, asking if I'm okay. Even with only a single bar of service, my answering text of reassurance goes through. Thanks, Verizon.

No such luck with my attempt to call Joss. It rings once, then disconnects.

With a sigh and a quick face rub, I rise from the bed and head to the window.

Holy shit.

The world on the other side of the curtain is a hellish landscape of wind, rain and debris. The sky is a churning mess of terror. I run through the house to my front door and step out onto the porch. The street is still visible, but the ditches are overflowing. Neighbors' houses are dark. Power must be out.

With my minimal service, I prowl the internet for information. News sites won't load, but Twitter or whatever it's called now is going strong. #HurricaneFranklin helps tremendously.

My stomach clenches into knots. Snips of roofs collapsing. Pictures of boats crashing into homes. Video feed of the storm surge drowning the beaches. Maps of the expected wreckage.

The cone shifted while I was sleeping. It's making landfall on top of me right now.

Category 5. Wind speed 155 mph. Storm surge twenty feet. Catastrophic damage.

How was the forecast so wrong? Thirty-six hours ago, we weren't even in the cone. When I fell asleep, a Category 2 storm was heading two hundred miles east of me.

Woke up to hell on earth.

Each video is worse than the last, but I search for clues about the flooding. Where is it? How far has it spread? Another attempt to call Joss fails. Send her a text instead.

> Are you okay?

No answer.

My dark house is suddenly too dark, so I dive for the wall switches. Light floods the room. Thank god. At some point, the backup generator must have kicked on.

Jocelyn sneaks back into my thoughts.

At best, she's terrified. At worst . . .

More videos. More updates. More chilling photos. A search for her cross streets, her neighborhood, anything that might clue me in yields nothing. No platforms or outlets have the information I need.

Until I open Snap Map.

A single video from the street next to hers was uploaded nearly an hour ago—a panoramic shot of the flooding road, the water creeping up to old houses that stand mere feet above sea level.

No, no, no.

Call her again. No answer.

> Please text me back.

No answer.

My attention travels to the sliders looking out to my backyard. Deathly winds send roof shingles and plant detritus flying through the air. Would be suicide to go out in this. Truck could wash away. Debris could kill me. Current from the rising waters could steal my balance and drag me under.

And yet—

One more call. It rings three times before it disconnects, and I hurl the device to the other side of the couch. Bracing my elbows on my knees, I hide my face in my palms. She's probably fine. A flooded street isn't life-threatening if she stays indoors. She said she'd call if she needed me.

But there's no service, whispers a fiendish, logical voice in my mind.

What if she needs me and I'm not there? What if I do nothing, and something happens to her?

Beyond the window, devastation reigns. I'm a fool for even contemplating going outside, but I head back to my bedroom with reckless desires. Will lightweight clothes and thick-soled tennis shoes work as rescue gear? She probably doesn't even need rescuing.

But what if she does?

With no idea what I'll need, I tear through drawers in my kitchen and laundry room. There isn't much in the way of Useful Gear to Survive Outside in a Hurricane, but what would such a list even include?

Utility knife and a flashlight.

All right, then. Good enough. We'll MacGyver this shit. I yank my keys from the holder in the kitchen and head to my truck in the garage, ignoring the overbearing sense of idiocy. I'm going to die trying to save her, the girl who doesn't even want me.

Fuck. I forgot the Tums.

Can't go back now.

The garage door opens a portal to Hades.

Ignore, ignore, ignore.

The truck roars to life, and I back it into the stupidest decision I've ever made. Battered in the wind, I'm imagining one giant Ty-Foo from *Super Mario* following my every move. Asshole makes driving a hectic battle for control while the remains of plants, houses, street signs assail me like missiles.

Under normal circumstances, Joss's house is a ten-minute drive. Due to flooded roads and downed trees, it takes me half an hour to reach the road leading into her neighborhood.

Ha. This is madness. The street descends into the floods. It's practically a boat ramp at this point. I need a fucking pontoon. I stare at that turbulent water. Am I really doing this?

I'm really fucking doing this.

My hand reaches for the truck's door handle of its own volition. The gale nearly rips the door off its hinges, but with

Herculean effort, I get it shut. Violent gusts of rainy wind assault every part of my body, and I throw an arm up to protect my eyes.

Forget the flashlight. Goggles would have been convenient.

I jog best I can into the flood, then slow once it reaches my thighs.

Whoa. Hell! Don't fall.

This current is stronger than I imagined. My muscles fight against the more powerful force of nature beneath me. I'm soaked through. My skin freezes and burns all at once. The rubber soles of my shoes provide a decent grip, but I'm careful not to slip. One wrong move, and this could carry me away.

In the minutes it takes to wade closer to her house, the water rises, splashing against my stomach. Something gives way beneath my feet. Before I can stop it, I submerge to my neck. The water carries me several yards downstream before I snag the pole of a stop sign. Gritty saltwater splashes into my mouth and the metal digs into my arm, opening a gash.

Drawing first blood, Franklin? I see how it is. He's literally pouring salt into my wounds.

Asshole.

My feet slip again.

Christ! I can't do this. She's probably fine! What am I doing out here? Trying to die? They're going to engrave my headstone with my supreme foolishness.

He died in a hurricane because he was stupid.

After righting myself, I take stock of my surroundings. Down the street, I get a glimpse of her house—the one with the tree lying on top of it. Panic claws through my system, lighting it on fire. She could be trapped in there. Drowning.

I could be too late.

A surge of adrenaline helps me battle my way to the house. The door is wide-open. I could swim into her living room.

"Jocelyn!" I yell.

No answer.

I knock aside floating furniture and head toward her bedroom where the tree fell. She's not here. The relief is tiny, but it does exist. Means I haven't lost hope, I suppose. Yay for optimism.

"Jocelyn, are you here?"

Maybe she evacuated when the flood started. Something cold wraps around my bones as I consider that. She evacuated and didn't come to me? Didn't even tell me?

I wade toward the garage to check if her car's still here, pushing through the hall and living room to reach the kitchen. The garage door is already open. Her Benz is flooded to the windows.

"Jocelyn?" I call again.

A weak voice behind me answers. "Asher?"

Yes. *Yes.* She's here. She's alive. Coiled fear loosens and I choke out a breath. I spin toward her voice. My gaze darts around and lands on the hunched body curled on the far edge of the bar top. She's on her side, shivering, blinking at me.

"Fuck. Jocelyn!" I flounder through the water to reach her, splashing wildly. She tries to sit up, but her shaking arms buckle and she falls back to the laminate.

Stupid, stupid woman!

My hands clamp onto her clammy fingers, and I pull her toward me. "Are you okay?"

Shallow scratches mar her fair skin. Tear tracks paint her face. But she appears otherwise unharmed. Miracles *do* happen. Her entire body trembles as I draw her closer to me. Her blank expression doesn't change. "Am I dead?"

"What? No." I try to haul her off the counter, but she's

immobile, legs dangling. "Come on, Joss. We have to get out of here."

"You're here." She touches my cheek, head tilting dreamily. "Heaven must be real."

Is she in some sub-space of terror? Dilated eyes gaze deep into mine. Her quivering body lists toward me. I grip her chin hard and sharpen my voice. "Jocelyn. Listen to me. We have to get out of here."

She blinks once, twice, and her spine straightens. "Asher?"

"Yes, it's me, but we have to go."

One moment, she's lethargic and hallucinating. The next, she's clawing at my neck, gripping so hard that pain shoots through my muscles. She cuts off my windpipe.

Hnghhh. I'm suffocating. I yank at her arm and suck in a breath.

"You came for me?" she asks.

She's attached to me—painfully, yes, but attached—so I make my way toward the front door. Every second we stay here, the water only rises higher. "Of course I came for you. Did you think I wouldn't?"

She pulls back to look at me. "Did you get my texts?"

"No. Service is down. You're going to have to walk, Joss, okay?"

She nods and allows me to set her on her feet. At her front porch, I pause.

Hmm. Right. Quite dire, this is. Not sure what to do, honestly. Rushing gray waters. Floating debris.

"This is insanity," she says.

I can barely hear it above the wind.

Her hand snakes into mine. "We can't go out in this. People drown in smaller floods than this."

"My truck is at the entrance to your neighborhood. I made it here. We can make it back."

"I'm a lot shorter than you." Her bottom lip pulls between her teeth. "This is how my parents died."

I turn back to the house, considering our options. A twenty-foot surge will submerge this home. I didn't come all the way over here just to drown with her.

"Get on my back." I step down onto her porch stairs.

"What?"

"I'll carry you to higher ground, and we can run to the truck."

"Asher—"

"*Now*, Jocelyn."

A fun fact I wish I hadn't learned the hard way—trying to beat rising floods is like racing a cheetah. The water is at my ribs by the time I make it to the street. Joss's arms around me hold tight, her limbs trembling. It's approximately seventeen times harder to walk with her weight on me, but these waters would take her shaking body for their own.

Won't let her go. Not sure I'll ever be able to let her go again.

Once the road starts to rise, she says she can walk, but I wait until I'm in a mere foot of water. She slides down my back to unsteady legs, and we race toward the mouth of her neighborhood. My truck still sits at the entrance, though it slid several feet backward. Again, the wind tries its best to tear the door away, but I get both of us settled in our seats without injuring anything.

And then I breathe. My heart slams painfully in my throat, clogging my airway, but I suck in oxygen and stare unseeingly through the windshield. It's only in this moment—the moment *after*—that I realize I didn't think I'd make it. Such an absurd thing to do. Life-threatening. Suicidal, even. I could have died. *She* could have died.

But I did it. I saved her.

Holy shit.

With shaking hands, I peel off my sopping, freezing, bloody-armed shirt and throw it in the back. "Put your seat belt on, please."

She obeys, still shivering, her stare riveted to my face.

I start the engine. "I can't believe you stayed there. You don't even have hurricane shutters."

"I can't believe you came for me," she whispers.

I keep a towel somewhere . . . Oh. I grab it from the back floorboard and hand it to her, then blast the heat. As I start onto the street, grip tight on the steering wheel, she dries herself. The center console keeps us separated, but when she finishes with the towel, her body leans as far toward me as possible. Cold hands slide over my shoulder and stomach.

Not suggestive. Giving reassurance. Taking comfort.

I spare a moment to squeeze her arm. "We're almost done."

She touches the gash in my arm. "You're hurt."

"I'm fine. It's not even bleeding."

The streets are worse now. Streetlights and power lines clutter the roadway, far more dangerous than before. Wind slides the vehicle all over the road, but we arrive at my house alive and unharmed. My neighborhood roads aren't even flooded.

At the click of a button, the garage door shuts behind us, muting the violent winds outside.

And it's over.

The steering wheel is a good object to clench, apparently. Don't think I can remove my hands. They're glued here forever, I guess, so I take a moment to simply sit in the silence.

This was both the smartest and most foolish thing I've ever done. I leapt into a hurricane and *survived*. I'm fucking Superman.

She's alive and so am I.

My hands tremble when they finally release. Adrenaline and cortisol for the win. My gaze drifts to Jocelyn, but she's already staring at me, expression dazed, almost awestruck. She doesn't blink. Doesn't speak.

She just . . . stares.

Okay, then. She's gone catatonic.

With my phone and keys secure in my pocket, I jog to her side and slide her trembling form from the truck. She clings to me like a child, arms and legs wrapped tight around me. I carry her through the laundry room and into the kitchen. Outside, wind whips debris and rain through the air, but the impact windows will protect us. With the elevation of my house, it's unlikely—not *impossible* per se, but unlikely—that the floods will reach us.

"You're safe," I whisper as I set her on the closest piece of furniture—the kitchen table. Her legs remain clamped around me, but her arms loosen.

"You're freezing." I rub her shoulders. "Let me get you some dry clothes."

But when I try to move away, her legs hold firm, locking me in place. Her skin is ashen, her eyes dilated. Wild. Ravaged. She stares at me like I'm a wonder. An impossible miracle she's privileged to witness.

That's not doing great things to my heart. Has it ever beat this loud? Can't keep looking at her. Might kiss her or do something equally stupid. When I avert my gaze, she grabs my face and turns it back, forcing me to confront the storm head-on.

Five seconds pass. Ten volatile heartbeats.

Then her cold lips crush mine in a hungry, savage kiss.

Skrrrrrt. What?

What is happening? Is this some culmination of realized

fear and pent-up energy? Her fingernails dig into the skin of my neck, and her legs squeeze tighter around me, wringing water from her sweatpants that drips down my calves.

"Joss—" I say against her mouth, trying to pull away.

"Please don't stop." Her voice wobbles over the words. Hands sink into my wet hair. Her tongue brushes my lower lip.

Easy to give in, really. Probably too easy. She can erase her anxiety in my kiss if she wants. It's bad for me, sure, but what's one more kiss? I grip her neck and surrender. Just . . . sink deep into it. She tastes of ocean salt and the bare hint of some cherry lip gloss she must have applied hours ago. Every luxurious, inflammatory second poisons my willpower further. Or maybe the near-death experience has me forgetting about consequences. It's sort of . . . intoxicating.

I should stop. This will only end in pain. But her hands slide down my bare chest, over the sopping elastic of my shorts, and I can't find the will. Long, excruciating moments when I feared she might have died tortured me today. I might have lost her.

She's here. Alive. Kissing me. Why overthink it?

But . . .

She isn't in a good headspace right now. She's overloaded and drunk on adrenaline. Keep going now, and we'll both regret it. I turn my face away, but she only peppers kisses down my cheek and throat. Words weave between them.

"Thank you . . . God . . . Thank you . . . I want you."

Don't know what to do. Can't keep going in good conscience. Can't stop, either. Stuck in the in-between.

"Please . . . I need you . . . Love you . . ."

Love you?

Did . . . Did that word just come out of her mouth? The *L* word. From Jocelyn's lips?

Love you.

Sounds like music. Feels like silk. Tastes like candy.

Can't be real.

"You *what*?" I ask, trying hard to extract myself from her death grip. Don't get far. She's a ball and chain, holding me in place, but she finally detaches her face from my neck and looks up with entranced eyes.

"What did you just say, Jocelyn?"

She blinks twice. "I'm an idiot."

Yeah. To that, I can agree. But that isn't what she said, and a profound disappointment descends on my shoulders. Should never take declarations of love made in the heat of the moment seriously. What am I? Some sort of n00b? This is Relationships 101.

"I tried to pretend it wasn't happening," she says. Her voice is trembling. *Actually* trembling. "You—you just, like . . . spilled yourself out for me that night over FaceTime, and it totally unlocked me. Before that, I knew you were attractive. Objectively. After that, I could *feel* it—your pretty face and your beautiful soul."

I almost laugh. "Oh, no. Not *feelings*."

She scoffs, still all trembly. Should I get her out of these soaked clothes? She has to be freezing. But I don't want her to stop talking. Need her to keep talking until she says *the* words. The ones that matter.

"And then we had that stupid photoshoot." Her scowl is quite ferocious. Must still be really pissed at that photoshoot.

I get it. That day was eye-opening in the worst of ways. "Yeah, that was rough," I say.

Her expression softens. "I knew what was happening. I tried to convince myself I could make it stop."

"Make what stop?"

Her icy fingers rise to rest gently on my cheek. "Falling in love with you."

Someone's turning down the oxygen again. Or maybe I've just forgotten how to breathe. I can't move. Can't look away. Can't speak. I just . . . stare.

"That night, after the wedding, you dismantled all my walls. But then the next morning—I panicked."

"I remember." Don't particularly want to think about that. Makes the lack of oxygen a touch painful. Must breathe at some point, though. Requirement for ongoing life.

Her eyes flutter shut. "I'm an idiot. I thought we could just ignore it. That I could rebuild my walls, and things would go back to normal, but it just—"

"Doesn't work like that." Air finally enters my lungs as I realize what's happening. I'm getting a romantic speech. This is Jocelyn Mattox's version of a loving confession. She's *Pride & Prejudice*-ing me, and her hands *are* cold.

This is fantastic. Like . . . truly phenomenal. Today has been a terrible shit show of a day, but *this*. This is some sort of miracle. Akin to facing down a hurricane and surviving. I should play the lottery or something. The odds are ever in my favor.

She shakes her head. "I kept thinking I couldn't love you because if I loved you and lost you, I wouldn't survive it. But my heart didn't really care about that dumbass logic. It just sort of tiptoed into your hand while I wasn't looking. Flipped me the bird on its way out, too."

I move a couple fingers to her chin, lifting it so she'll open her eyes.

She exhales and matches my gaze. "It's yours now. So . . . maybe, like . . . don't break it, or whatever."

Endearing woman. Look at her, being all vulnerable.

Then her eyes harden. "And don't you dare fucking die."

A snort makes the salt still coating my sinuses burn all the way into my brain.

"I mean it, Asher." She grabs my face with both hands. "You are now immortal."

That's a lot of pressure. Won't be able to go diving into hurricanes all willy-nilly anymore—isn't great for longevity. Hesitant to make unkeepable promises, I settle on, "I'll try my best."

That makes her happy enough. Her grip on my cheeks loosens. "I love you." She shakes herself. "I mean . . . I've always loved you, but now I'm also *in* love with you."

There it is.

The real declaration.

Finally.

Feels better than I thought it would. Like a drug. Think my heart just did a line of coke. Can't stop the smile, but I mold it into the crooked one she seems to like best. "You luuuuuurve me?"

With a roll of her eyes, she tries to push me away. "Don't be extra, Asher."

I grab her before she puts any distance between us and steal another kiss. "I love you, too."

She melts at once, her arms slipping around me again while she lays her ear against my heart. "I can't believe you braved a hurricane for me."

I glance at the destruction outside the windows. Thirty seconds in her embrace, and I totally forgot about that . . .

"I thought I was going to drown," she says. "That I'd die today."

I sort of did, too. Don't mention that, though. Isn't good for morale.

Her voice drops to a whisper. "I've been so busy fearing other people's deaths, I didn't even think about my own until it was staring me in the face."

As she sniffles, I hold her close. "You're safe."

When she looks up, tears glisten on her cheeks. "I'm always safe with you. I feel like a moron. I fought and pretended and lied, but it all seems so stupid in the face of *this*."

That's because it was, but if therapy has taught me anything, it's that fears can't be conquered until you're ready. Glad she came to her senses, though. The whole bit was rather torturous on my end. All those words tangle in my head, in my throat, and I can only brush my fingers over her wet cheek. Her gaze is open. Loving.

She kisses my chin. "Can you forgive me for taking so long to realize that?"

"Nope. You'll have to find some way to make it up to me."

Playful light sparkles in her eyes. "Yeah? How?"

A grin breaks through, yanked from deep within. Is this happening? To *me*? Such a small thing, in the grand scheme. People declare their love across the world every day. It's a normal part of life—from the outside.

I understand now why authors and poets spend their lives trying to capture this feeling on paper. Why songwriters make millions celebrating love or lamenting the loss of it. Why filmmakers immortalize love stories with perfectly delivered lines.

This feeling . . . It's everything.

She is everything.

I slide my hands under her thighs and lift her into my arms. "Let's take a shower."

Her smile dawns, and she obediently slides her arms around my shoulders, holding fast. "I still can't believe you did that. You could have killed yourself trying to save me."

In my bathroom, I set her on the floor and turn on the water. "You weren't picking up your phone. I was terrified."

"I tried to call you. I didn't have any signal."

I pull my phone from my pocket. I now have enough service that notifications are coming through—messages from my brothers and parents, from Geoff, from the National Weather Service. And seven texts from Joss.

"Did you bring your phone with you?" I ask.

She pats down her body, pulling out a waterlogged phone from her pocket. "I doubt it still works."

Oh, it does. Staring at my screen, I will my rioting heart to calm.

> Asher I need you
>
> Asher please I need help
>
> I need you.
>
> I love you.
>
> I'm sorry I never told you.
>
> Just know you were the last thing I thought about.
>
> I'll love you until the end of time.

She really thought she was going to die, didn't she?
Poor girl.

I turn the phone to show her.

Her face grows scarlet, and tears spring to her eyes once more. "I didn't think I'd ever see you again."

My arm sneaks around her waist, and I kiss her until I can't breathe. She thought she was dying, and with her last words, she told me she loved me. That's a fucking story for the grandkids.

Steam from the hot water crowds us together, but I can't get close enough. I drag her toward the shower. Our bodies mix and mesh and fight for purchase. Talking portion is over. Need her closer. Wetter. Wrapped around me. Will never stop needing it. Her. This woman who loves me enough to go to war with her own inner demons and win.

Perfectly imperfect and difficult as hell, but mine.

"Isn't this a little cliché?" she asks after I have her pinned against the shower wall, my fingers digging into her thighs wrapped tight around me. I can't believe I tried to forget what it feels like to be inside her. This is paradise. I'm going to have trouble ever wanting to do anything else.

Must focus on something else or I'm going to climax before she does. "Cliché?"

"At the very least, it's unoriginal."

"You're about to come," I say. "Probably multiple times. Why are you complaining?"

"I'm just saying." She flaps her arms against the tile. "I have nothing to grab onto."

"Me. You grab onto me." I shift her higher on the wall, hitting a spot that makes her bite her lip and suck in a pleasured breath.

She pretends it didn't happen. "Meh. Shower sex seems sexy, but it's more work than it's worth."

"I'm the one doing all the work. Do you think this is easy?"

She grins, bold and cheeky. "Maybe I want to do something for you for once."

"Yeah? Like what?"

She licks water from my neck. "Put me down, and I'll show you."

My hands clench on her thighs as her eyes glint with

challenge. Droplets coalesce and collect in her dark eyelashes, but she doesn't blink. Our lips find each other while I do as she asks, releasing her legs until she's on her own feet.

With one wicked smile, she drops to her knees, and I have officially arrived in heaven.

Jocelyn

> You either evolve, or you make the same
> mistake again and again. Growth is a
> painful but necessary progression.
> **—My Therapist**

Was this inevitable? Was it predetermined? Did some force lead me to him, deep in that hotel basement three years ago? Because this feels like fate. I can't believe it took me so long to see it. And why did I fight it, thinking it would hurt? A vast ocean of endless sparks has erupted between us, and for the first time, I want to drown.

The man saved my life. Shattered my glass walls. Pulled me from the literal floods. Even after I hurt him, rejected him, turned away from him, he still took me back.

I'm in awe. And so immutably in love with him.

After a luxurious, mind-melting shower, I crash into his

fluffy pillows to catch up on the sleep I missed the night before. The worst of the storm moves inland after about eight hours, but warm and clean in Asher's bed, I barely notice. I don't worry about my house, my things—decades worth of books, irreplaceable photos and furniture likely all destroyed by the flood. None of that matters.

I'm alive, and I stir in the arms of the man I love when he shifts away from me. With weak, sleepy limbs, I reach for him. "Wait."

A soft kiss lands on my temple. "I'm starving. I'm going to make us something."

Groaning, I blink my eyes open. "What time is it?"

"Six. You slept all day."

What? Wow. "Damn. How's the storm?"

The bed jostles as he leaves it. "Eye has moved inland. Flooding's pretty bad, though. Beaches are destroyed. They think some bridges collapsed."

I sit up and rub my face. "Really?" I glance out the window. Still windy, but less violent. The yard is flood-free. "Have you heard from anyone?"

He slides on a pair of sweats. "Geoff said they didn't flood. They're okay. He's the only one who responded. I think the cell towers were knocked out. Service is in and out." He throws his phone on the bed. "Check that."

A time-lapse beach-cam video shows the incoming surge destroying the beachside restaurants and shops, washing away hotels. The pier withstands the wind and water for a while, but eventually, it's taken by the storm, leaving only a series of pilings in the thrashing waves.

My wide eyes lift to his when it ends.

He takes his phone back. "I know. I think the storm surge is receding now, but . . . a lot of damage. Your sister has been updated, by the way."

"Thanks." When he pulls on a T-shirt, I become starkly aware of my nakedness. I yank the blankets up to cover myself. "Can I have some clothes?"

He smirks. "No. I like you better without them."

"Asher!" I throw a pillow at him.

Laughing, he points at the closet. "You know where my stuff is. I'm going to make some food."

He leaves, and I raid his closet for the coziest, most Asher-scented items. In the kitchen, the bacon somehow overpowers the sexy forest smell. I traipse up to him, sliding my hands around his middle while he cooks.

"Can I ask you a question?" he says.

"Shoot."

He removes cooked slices from the grease and adds raw strips. "That night in Florida. Were you really only curious about me, or did that mean something to you?"

Oh. He's just going there, isn't he? Has it been bugging him, thinking I didn't feel that deep connection we had? Articulating what I felt that night might be difficult, but he deserves the truth. With a single deep breath, I try to get the words out. "I didn't—I didn't *want* it to mean anything, but . . . it did. I think . . . It was like . . . It was like you rearranged my DNA that night."

His muscles shift beneath me as he flips the bacon. "That good, huh?"

"No, that's not— Well, yes, it was that good, but I meant it was . . . life-changing. I saw what we could be, then convinced myself I didn't want it. I got scared. I lied to myself. To you."

"You compared me to a Lamborghini."

Heat rises to my face, and even though he can't see it, I hide my wince in his back. "Yeah, that sucked. To be fair, you're like the Lamborghini of humans, though."

The skillet sizzles as he lays more bacon in the grease. How much bacon is he expecting us to eat?

He sets his tongs down and spins, arms settling around me. "I am?"

My lips press together, but the chuckle rises anyway. "Best ride I've ever had."

A second passes before he gives way to laughter. His forehead drops to mine as it fades away. His voice lowers. "You nearly killed me, Joss."

My heart squeezes, and I hug him tight. "I'm so sorry. I'd take it back if I could."

A gentle hand runs over the back of my head. "You went through a lot today. A lot of emotions."

I let out a slow breath. "Yeah."

"So . . . are you *sure*, Jocelyn?"

Confused, I look up at him to find a guarded expression. "Sure?"

"I'm all in on this, but if you're not sure, if you have doubts—" he caresses my cheek "—I don't know if I'll survive another rejection like that."

Ugh. I really hate myself right now. His uncertainty, his fear— I did that. I can't believe I hurt him, this beloved unicorn of a man, so I don't give him another second to doubt me. "I'm all in. All yours. As long as you want. As long as you love me."

A tiny smile flickers on his face. His eyes gleam with humor, and he busts into the Backstreet Boys song.

As long as you love me.

I press a hand to his mouth. "Don't be extra. Shh."

Beneath my hand, his song morphs into the Justin Bieber tune, growing stronger by the second.

My giggle breaks loose. "I can't take you seriously when you sing."

"Oh, I'm serious." The words are still smothered under my hand, but the look in his eyes is solemn. "Deadly serious. You're all in with me?"

I nod. "All in. Submerged completely. One hundred percent."

In one smooth move, he yanks my hand away and kisses me soundly. "I believe you, but break my heart again, Mattox, and we're going to have a problem."

•

NOW THAT I'M HOMELESS, I decide to skive off Team B relief efforts the following day. In fact, I let Cassie know I'll likely need an extended leave of absence given I have no transportation or worldly possessions for the time being.

Asher, however, covers his shift like a good little doctor while I lounge in his clothes at his house, eating his food. Once he connects to the hospital Wi-Fi, he sends me distressing updates on my phone—somehow still functioning despite being submerged in floodwaters. Thanks, Apple. You da best.

I can't make calls, but I can receive texts, and Asher's are by far the funniest.

> **Traffic is insane**
>
> **No streetlights**
>
> **Hospital is still on generators**
>
> **Legendary is down**
>
> **Joss the sewers are backed up**
>
> **Can't flush.**
>
> **People are shitting in bags**

Save me.

Is it cruel that I'm snorting at his plight? After his shift, he arrives home with a harried glint in his eye. I try hard not to laugh.

He merely shakes his head. "No power. No gas. Water is undrinkable. Half the roads are un-drivable. There are boats in the streets. People are starting to loot."

I ring my arms around him. "Have you heard from anyone else?"

"Yeah." He kisses my cheek. "Everyone's okay. I called your sister. She was freaking the fuck out."

"I've been texting her all day. Did she think I was lying about being fine?"

"The pictures on the news are pretty bad. She said you can stay with her if you need."

I smile. "Did you tell her I have somewhere to stay?"

"I told her I got you covered." His lips move to my jaw, then my neck. "She had a lot of questions."

"I'll bet."

When his tongue touches my pulse point, I lose focus on the conversation and speak with my hands instead.

A few days later, we drive to my house even though I already know nothing is salvageable. My landlord went by the day before, and according to him, "The place is trashed."

Standing in my entryway is a surreal experience. A layer of sand coats the wood floors, and my furniture is thrown haphazardly around like a tornado blew through. The car in my garage is destroyed. The oak tree still rests in my bedroom, and my closet isn't even accessible—not that I could wear any of the ruined clothes inside.

Asher leans on the jamb of the front door while I slowly peruse the destruction of my material assets. Good thing I'm not sentimental, or I'd be in tears. I have nothing left.

In the living room, I flop my hands out, dejected. "I need to find a new place."

"Stay with me."

I glance at where he's still perched in the doorway. Always leaning. "Yeah. But I mean . . . I need to find a permanent solution."

He nods and throws on an earnest expression. "Stay with me," he says again.

The meaning behind his words trickles through my brain, lighting it on fire. I move closer to him, close enough to read the hope in his eyes. He wants me to live with him? "Don't you think that's too fast?"

He flashes a smile at the floor like I've said something funny, then looks at me through his lashes. "I'm going to be totally frank here, and I hope this doesn't scare you off, but dear Lord, girl. *Fast?* It took three years of foreplay just for us to kiss. We are the slowest humans on the planet."

"That's . . . That's not true."

"True? You want something true?" He puts one finger beneath my chin, tilting my face up. "The truth is, I would have married you yesterday if I thought you'd let me."

My stomach falls. Married?

"So, no," he says. "I don't think it's too fast."

"Wh-what?"

He chuckles and drops his hand. "Jocelyn. Is living together really such a stretch? We already know the worst parts about each other."

I toss out a playful scowl. "There are no worst parts of me."

"Right," he says, choosing that moment to ignore me in favor of the destruction in my living room. "Because the obsession with HGTV and your deathly fear of attachment are absolute joys to deal with."

"Hey! At least I don't get a boner for ducks."

He gives me the godforsaken puppy-dog face. So cute.

"No fair," I mutter.

"You love the ducks." He says it with such assurance, like there is no other option.

With a laugh, I yank him closer, and his arms encircle me at once. "This is the real deal, though," I say. "We'll be cleaning up each other's messes. Fighting over the remote. Making indelicate use of the bathrooms."

He snorts. "Such a pessimist."

"I hog covers."

"I already know this."

With a frown, I snake my arms around his shoulders. "I leave the lights on."

His shrug accompanies a quick kiss. "That's what switches are for."

"I never replace the toilet paper."

"Heathen!" The next kiss is longer, more persuasive.

"I always use all the hot water."

He pauses. "Well, there's the dealbreaker."

I sneak my hand beneath his shirt to pinch his side, and he laughs.

"It's no pressure," he says. "If you aren't ready, it's okay. You can stay with me until you find a place."

My gaze snags on his, and his smile fades into something softer, more serious. I press myself into him. "Did you mean what you said? About marrying me?"

His smile is slow to dawn, but it's bright. Coruscated. "Didn't I tell you I was going to marry you the first day I met you?"

I roll my eyes. "You were joking."

"Was I? Can't recall." He cups my face. "Come live with me, Joss. Be with me. I'm showing you my hand. It's your turn. Call, raise or fold."

All at once, the ruination behind me doesn't sting so bad. Instead, a dawning excitement bubbles to the surface, lighting my blood neon. I've tossed the old, scared, guarded Jocelyn in with the detritus of my former life, and from the destruction, someone healthier has risen.

A fresh start.

I give him my biggest, truest grin. "All right. Fine. Let's go home."

EPILOGUE

Jocelyn

10 MONTHS LATER, POOL PARTY SATURDAY

He's holding a baby.

My Asher. Holding a baby.

I never thought such a thing would affect me, but here I am. Confounded.

Yayoi and Geoff's genetics produced an especially cute specimen of human, and Asher's in love. This isn't the first time he's held baby Isley. It *is* the first time the sight has made me want to tear his clothes off.

He took her to the rocker on the other side of the porch while Yayoi, Geoff and I eat at the table. Most everyone is still in the pool, shouting about who's cheating at volleyball.

I can't take my eyes off Asher. Maybe it's that goofy smile

on his face. Or that he keeps calling her Isley Sugar Pops in his baby voice. Or maybe it's just him. I'm still not sure I want kids, but maybe I'm forming a second opinion. Besides, I don't particularly mind practicing for it, and my body kind of thinks we should practice *right now*.

"I know that look," Yayoi whispers near my ear.

I don't deny it. "What is it about men holding babies?"

She shrugs. "Biological instinct. Your cavewoman brain is telling you he'd be fantastic at protecting your offspring."

I try to hum, but even to my own ears it's more like an aroused and telling purr. "He'd be good at making them, too."

"Ew." Geoff shoots me a disgusted face. "I'm eating."

I ignore him in favor of staring Asher down—predator watching prey—and like I called out to him, he looks up. Our eyes meet, and happiness blossoms in his addictive smile.

I love you, I mouth.

I love you, too.

I am his. He is mine.

And this love between us is stronger than death.

★ ★ ★ ★ ★

Acknowledgments

Asher's love story was not one I was originally intending to write, but the bro was such a fan favorite that I couldn't let you all down. I hope you enjoyed his journey to happy-ever-after! He's flattered you wanted him to have it.

As always, I'd like to thank my readers for their love and support. Without you, none of this would be possible. Getting my books into the world has been a lifelong dream, and as long as you continue to want them, I'll continue to write them.

Thank you to Tess, who helped refine this story into what it is today. If not for you, Asher would still be a clueless prankster with a debilitating case of imposter syndrome. You are the absolute best.

Thanks to my original beta readers, as well as my queens and harlots—Kat, Christie, Shaylin, Maggie, Melissa, Noreen, Emily, Sasa, Lauren. I owe you all a drink for the many roles you play in my life, the least of which being the receptacle into which I put all of my anxiety. I'm glad I'm navigating this maze with you bitches at my side.

To my cheerleaders—SG, Ashlin, Rachael—I love you all. Remember that time we all lived in the same city? Let's do that again.

To my family, thank you for your love and support. Gemma and Ethan, I love you beyond measure. Olen and Ali, I'm taking a page out of Jocelyn's book—you are everything, so please don't die. No excuses.

About the Author

Deidra Duncan spends her days (and some nights) living the dream as a board-certified OB/GYN, where every minute is either routine monotony or sheer terror. She lives in Florida with two human tornadoes and the wonderful man who helped make them. She's usually dressed in either scrubs or glitter, and would love for someone to magically combine them. She devotes every rare moment of free time to writing or reading.

**Discover Grace and Julian's swoonworthy
enemies-to-lovers romance in . . .**

Love Sick

The first year of residency is hard, so when a rumour
starts that intern Grace Rose slept her way into the
program, she's determined to set the record straight.
But after confronting fellow first year Julian,
the situation goes from bad to worse.

Julian Santini worked hard to get onto this program,
and he can't afford to get distracted. Especially by
his beautiful colleague, who seems to hate
everything about him . . .

But with the pressure mounting, they'll need to work
together to survive. Can Grace and Julian put aside their
rivalry to save their jobs? Or will the sizzling tension
between them spell the end for them both?

Available now in paperback, ebook and audio

RAISING READERS
Books Build Bright Futures

Dear Reader,

We'd love your attention for one more page to tell you about the crisis in children's reading, and what we can all do.

Studies have shown that reading for fun is the **single biggest predictor of a child's future life chances** – more than family circumstance, parents' educational background or income. It improves academic results, mental health, wealth, communication skills, ambition and happiness.[1]

The number of children reading for fun is in rapid decline. Young people have a lot of competition for their time. In 2024, 1 in 10 children and young people in the UK aged 5 to 18 did not own a single book at home.[2]

Hachette works extensively with schools, libraries and literacy charities, but here are some ways we can all raise more readers:

- Reading to children for just 10 minutes a day makes a difference
- Don't give up if children aren't regular readers – there will be books for them!
- Visit bookshops and libraries to get recommendations
- Encourage them to listen to audiobooks
- Support school libraries
- Give books as gifts

There's a lot more information about how to encourage children to read on our website: **www.RaisingReaders.co.uk**

Thank you for reading.

---

[1] OECD, '21st-Century Readers: Developing Literacy Skills in a Digital World', 2021, https://www.oecd.org/en/publications/21st-century-readers_a83d84cb-en.html

[2] National Literacy Trust, 'Book Ownership in 2024', November 2024, https://literacytrust.org.uk/research-services/research-reports/book-ownership-in-2024